W9-AAX-854

FALSE FLAG

JOHN ALTMAN

FALSE FLAG

BLACKSTONE
PUBLISHING

Published in 2017 by Blackstone Publishing
Cover and book design by Kathryn Galloway English

Printed in the United States of America

First edition: 2017
ISBN 978-1-5047-9772-6

1 3 5 7 9 10 8 6 4 2

CIP data for this book is available
from the Library of Congress

Blackstone Publishing
31 Mistletoe Rd.
Ashland, OR 97520

www.BlackstonePublishing.com

FALSE FLAG: the technique of posing as an enemy to execute a covert operation and provide casus belli, "a case for war."

PROLOGUE

MOUNT HOOD, OR

She feigned sleep.

At last, silently, she slipped from the bed. Navigating by moonlight, she crept to the doorway and out into the front room. Here she paused, listening. From the bedroom, his breathing maintained its slow, even rhythm. From outside came only the sounds of the mountain: owls and rustling field mice and cold October wind whispering darkly through cedar and fir.

Her purse sat on the couch, beside his oil-stained Levi's. Brushing a strand of hair from her face, she took a penlight from the handbag. The narrow beam swept around the room, illuminating empty forty-ounce beer bottles on the coffee table, a woodstove, an old Frigidaire in the attached kitchenette, a large Confederate flag hanging on one wall.

She opened the stove and stirred embers and ashes with a heavy iron poker. She looked inside the refrigerator, behind the flag, beneath the sink. She rifled through cupboards and drawers. In the small bathroom, she explored the medicine cabinet and the toilet tank. She returned to the front room and circled the perimeter, softly thumping the molding and the low ceiling, searching for drop panels or loose baseboards.

She went back into the bedroom. The penlight's beam found swastikas, Celtic crosses, SS insignia, and Tyr runes tattooed across the sleeping man's bare chest.

She looked beneath the bed frame. She opened dresser drawers. She pulled the nightstand away from the wall, gently, gently … and found nothing but dust bunnies and an unused electrical socket.

She slipped into her shirt and moved back through the front room, to the cabin's single door. Outside, shivering in the cold wind, she walked around the cabin, bare feet crunching softly on dead leaves. Hiking trails wound off into the dense forest. Wind sighed through moonlit trees. The air smelled of pine sap and fresh rain.

On the west-facing side of the cabin, she found a woodpile covered with a frosty tarp. Out back, a padlocked toolshed. Near the shed, a hatch trapdoor leading to a sunken cellar. The trapdoor's wood was splintered and mossy, but its Uline padlock was gleaming, brand spanking new. The toolshed, by contrast, was secured with only a rusty old Grainger. She hammered the shed open with a strike of one palm. The penlight swept across an air compressor, a gas can, bungee cords, a chain saw, a pole tree pruner … bolt cutters.

The bolt cutters made short work of the Uline. Lying facedown on half-frozen ground, she played the penlight over the dark crawl space. She saw crenellated concrete and moist, worm-cast earth, a rotting support beam, an ossified dead rat, a patch of green, almost phosphorescent moss. And there, tucked far back in shadow, unlabeled wooden crates, carefully stacked.

As the wind rose to a growling moan behind her, she clamped the flashlight between her teeth and slid nimbly through the hatch.

She picked her way carefully forward, over crumbling concrete and frigid mud, through a mysterious subterranean breeze. Using the bolt cutters as a crowbar, she set to work on the first crate. Spiders and centipedes scurried frantically away. With an effort, she got the top off. Inside, she discovered neatly rolled rags smelling faintly of oil. Inside the rags were M16 lower receiver parts.

In the next crate were AR15 rifles, to which the M16 parts could be attached to create fully automatic weapons.

She kept going. Ka-bar knives, modified practice hand grenades, fuses and detonators, stacks of white-power literature: *The Protocols of the Learned Elders of Zion*, *Traitors Beware: A History of Robert Depugh's Minutemen*, *Fighting for the American Dream*, *The Turner Diaries*, *Ambush at Ruby Ridge: How Government Agents Set Randy Weaver Up and Took His Family Down*. Taking a pamphlet from one stack, she opened to a random page: "The issue with Jews is not their blood, but their identity. If we could somehow destroy the Jewish identity, then they wouldn't cause much problem. The problem is that Jews look White, and in many cases are White, yet they see themselves as minorities. Just like niggers, most Jews are always thinking about …" She let the pamphlet fall to the ground.

On the sixth crate, she knew even before removing the lid that she had hit pay dirt. Odors are the most powerful triggers of memory—the olfactory nerve lies adjacent to both the amygdala and the hippocampus—and as she winkled a nail out of crumbling plywood, her brain made a sudden and vivid cross-connection.

She had been manning a checkpoint in Haifa with Asher. Much scowling, no smiling, hands never leaving the stocks of their Glilon assault rifles. Asher had waved forward a boy wearing a checkered kaffiyeh. Approaching, the youth had reached beneath his loose-fitting robe. And Jana had caught a vague but unforgettable whiff of Composition-C RDX: sour and chemical and faintly toxic, like a child's plastic toy left too long in the sun. And then her world had turned to fire and blood and agony.

She pulled out another nail, set aside the lid, and lifted free a brick of plastic explosive: bluish-white, soft to the touch, and surprisingly heavy.

The crate was filled with it.

The last crate was unlabeled, and lighter than the rest. Prying off the lid, she removed a faded black briefcase with a combination lock. Holding the latch in the open position, she set the leftmost number to zero and tested the other two wheels. Loose. Still holding the latch, she reset the leftmost wheel to one. Two … At three, the middle wheel gave resistance. She repeated the procedure. The combination that opened the case was, perhaps unsurprisingly, 3-1-1—code for a triple repetition of the eleventh letter of the English alphabet: KKK.

Inside, the penlight beam illumined eight wallet-size plastic packets, labeled in Cyrillic, German, and English: *Handhabung siehe Anleitung.* SOMAN, SARIN, V-GASES.

Inside each wallet she found ten glass ampoules, tipped blood-red.

Light splashed from the open trapdoor behind her. Her heart vaulted into her throat. Dousing the penlight, holding her breath, she backed up against one wall.

"Th'fuck?" His voice was thick, blurred with sleep, weed, and Mickey's malt liquor. "You down here, you bitch?"

She sank as far as possible back into shadow. He descended clumsily through the hatch—a slab of tattooed muscle, backlit by pale moonlight and brandishing a lantern flashlight in one hand.

"Th'fuck?" he said again, wonderingly, as his light found the opened crates.

She stepped up behind him, raising the bolt cutters with both hands.

She swung hard. He staggered; the lantern seesawed crazily. She swung again. A sickening crunch, and he went down.

The lantern rolled and fetched up glaring directly into his face. Ice-blue eyes shocked and staring, lips slightly parted. A pulped wound in his right temple pulsing out blood.

She retreated from the spreading pool of gore. She had never killed before. For a few moments, she swallowed against her hitching gorge. Then she made a small "*uh*" and put her hands on her knees, breathed, and counted down. *Five, four, three, two …*

Better.

She straightened again. For a few moments more she stood

motionless, looking at the dead man, the still-widening pool of blood, the open crates of plastic explosive and white-power literature and red-tipped ampoules, as the soft wind whickered through the trees outside.

An owl hooted somewhere nearby, breaking the spell, and she moved again.

PART ONE

CHAPTER ONE

PRINCETON, NJ

A soft breeze ruffled the gold and crimson leaves.

Dalia Artzi sighed and rearranged her hands in her lap. Her gaze moved restlessly away from the mullioned window, back to the study where she sat. Mellow late-afternoon sunshine fell across dark wood, pearled wall sconces, shelves jammed with leather-bound classics, a heavy marble hearth sheltering a single ash-encrusted log.

Her eyes drifted shut. Behind closed lids, she saw the lecture hall where she had spent most of her afternoon. Wrenching the attention of fidgety undergrads away from smartphones, MacBooks, and the bright Indian summer day outside had required her most commanding tone. By the time she had reached her conclusion, her throat was dry, yet she had dug deep, found an untapped reserve, and restated her thesis with the same vigor she displayed at the start.

"*On the battlefield*," she had declared, "*no single quality is more decisive than maneuverability*."

She had moved out from behind the lectern: a broad-shouldered woman pushing seventy, wearing a button-down tweed suit and purple d'Orsay pumps, with dark hair shining silver near the roots. "*Not that all of my esteemed colleagues, I should mention, will agree.*" Her English formed too low in the throat, yet it was precise. Her carriage was sturdy and flat-footed even in heels, suggesting hardy peasant forebears.

"*Richardson at Yale, for instance, continues to value the conventional model of attrition warfare: two armies square off, and the more powerful in terms of resources, firepower, manpower, and matériel eventually achieves victory. In his model, maneuverability is of secondary concern. And, of course, he is entitled to his opinion. But I can think of no lack of brilliant generals—from Khalid ibn al-Walid, military counsel to the Prophet Muhammad during the seventh century, to George Washington, striking a vital surprise blow across the Delaware River on Christmas night of 1776, to Trần Văn Trà, architect of the Tet Offensive in 1968—who might beg to differ.*"

A man in a gloomy blue suit had slipped quietly into the rear of the hall. Dalia's gaze flicked momentarily in his direction. Gaunt and high-cheeked, he possessed the look of someone hailing from outside academia—the corporate world, perhaps, or inside the Beltway.

"*When you read Keegan's depiction of Agincourt over the weekend,*" she had continued after a brief pause, "*put yourselves in the place of the French: better equipped than your enemy, better rested, better fed, better armored, better reinforced, far more numerous, fighting on your home terrain. And yet, mired in mud, fatigued by sixty pounds of heavy plate mail before you ever joined combat, crushed and crowded against your fellow soldier, outflanked and outmaneuvered at every turn by Henry's lighter, more mobile longbowmen. And then convey this feeling to me, if you would be so kind, in an essay of approximately thirty-five hundred words. Quail not, my friends. As Henry himself might say, 'Stiffen the sinews, summon up the blood.'*"

As the students filed from the amphitheater, the stranger in the blue suit had approached the lectern. And now, forty-five minutes later, Dalia Artzi found herself here, in a stone cottage tucked into a forgotten far corner of Princeton's ivy-draped campus, with the hour reserved for her afternoon nap ticking steadily away.

Her eyes opened again. A family of deer had appeared outside the window. Two spotted fawns nosed through the waving bluestem. The doe sniffed the wind, one ear twitching.

Again Dalia rearranged her hands in her lap. Her eyes moved past the browsing deer, to the crooked fence at the meadow's far end. The sprawling woods beyond concealed the Institute for Advanced Study, where Einstein had spent the last years of his life in vain pursuit of his elusive unified field theory. "*A quaint and ceremonious village* ..." he had called Princeton, before adding, "... *of puny demigods on stilts.*"

And beyond the forest rambled the hilly field where, on an icy morning in 1777, George Washington had given the Great American Experiment a crucial early boost. Upon being offered her visiting professorship to Princeton, Dalia had immediately anticipated witnessing firsthand the battle's annual reenactment. But it had turned out to be a travesty: the positions of the armies reversed, the date wrong, General Mercer's crucial martyrdom altogether absent, and hot dog vendors where the redcoats' heavy cannon should have been.

A man entered the study. He was chubby, sixtyish, wearing a starched white dress shirt. Dark circles underscored his intelligent green eyes. In his left hand, he held a half-empty Styrofoam cup of oily black liquid as his right reached for a handshake. "They found you," he said. "An honor, madam. Jim McConnell's the name."

Dalia shook the hand firmly. She followed McConnell from the study, past mounted heads of elk, moose, and antelope, and into a second room strikingly similar to the first. A picture window gave a slightly different angle on the foraging deer. A bird feeder, lighted by the low-hanging sun, hosted a robin. Or a cardinal, maybe? She was not good at American birds.

"Coffee?" McConnell closed the door gently behind him. "Tea? Aperitif?"

"No." As an afterthought: "*Toda.*" Thank you.

"Please, sit." He waved at a burgundy club chair, then took a seat opposite. For a few moments, he concentrated on a dark vein of wood in his armrest, choosing his next words carefully. Somewhere on campus, not far away, a young woman laughed.

Abruptly, he smiled. "It really is an honor. I've enjoyed your books immensely."

She dipped her chin modestly.

"Thank you for making the time. I appreciate how busy you must be. How are you enjoying Princeton?"

For the space of several heartbeats, she regarded him coolly. "Too much bureaucracy," she finally said. "People try to be polite instead of saying what they mean."

He blinked. "Er, yes." Clearing his throat, he shifted in his chair. He raised his Styrofoam cup, looked inside with distaste, and set it aside. "Well. So I'll get right to it. You must be wondering why I've asked to see you today."

She said nothing.

"Let this meeting remain between us, Professor, if you don't mind. I'm affiliated with a subsection of the Joint Chiefs of Staff. I serve as liaison with several universities. My particular office is TS/SCI—Top Secret, Sensitive Compartmented Information—only."

He paused, leaving another space that invited filling. Dalia waited him out.

"Some of the country's best and brightest work for us. And many of them consider you an inspiration. I'm told you're the greatest strategic thinker since John Boyd."

She gave a bored shrug.

"Myself, I'm a humble middle manager. Not equipped to judge. But when these people say that in the field of maneuver warfare you're the woman to beat, I listen." His eyebrows lifted suggestively. "Of course, I'm acquainted with your feelings about … How did you put it? 'America's ill-fated macho posturing in Iraq, driven by an archaic empire-building urge'?"

She gave an arid smile.

"As I said, I've read your books. Clearly, you're nobody's fool." Leaning away, he stroked his sagging dewlaps thoughtfully. "A political naïf, perhaps—forgive me—but a tactical genius. I flatter myself, madam, that I can talk some sense into you. There's too much at stake for me not to try."

Very slightly, but with a distinct note of challenge, she lifted her chin.

"You must recognize," he continued after a few moments, "that we face a common enemy. If Arabs put down their guns, the fighting stops. If Jews put down *their* guns, Israel is destroyed. You can't make peace with an enemy that wants to obliterate you."

"A friend of Israel, are you, Mr. McConnell?"

"Anyone who values democracy—freedom—is a friend of Israel."

"Until things get messy. At which point you withdraw your troops and leave others to fight your battles."

"Don't make the mistake of—"

"I've made no mistake." Her dark eyes blazed. "And as you say, I'm 'nobody's fool.' Once, perhaps, during my kibbutznik days. But those were a long time ago."

Again he paused. He laced fingers together carefully in his lap. "At the risk of overstepping, I have a son myself, Professor. And if *he* had been subjected to … God knows what, paraded as a war prize, kept from public view for half a decade, I promise you, you would not be able to hold me back if someone offered me the opportunity I'm offering you now. You of all people should value Israel's right to defend itself."

"I value," she said icily, "the right of *all* people to defend themselves." She stood up. "I wish I could say, sir, that it has been a pleasure."

She turned neatly on one d'Orsay heel and left him looking after her.

NORTH OF TEL AVIV, ISRAEL

Inside a house of pale limestone, atop a hill near the Trans-Samaria Highway, cold moonlight angled through two large picture windows.

Seated behind a piano, a man picked out chords—melancholy minors, tense augmented triads, to match his restless mood. He eased into E-flat major, the key of kings, triumphant and regal. Then into a snatch of Wagner, with its schizophrenic shifting tonal centers. A terrible anti-Semite, Wagner, but only a fool would deny his talent.

The man's fingers came to a rest. He glanced at the Roman-numeral clock hanging on one wall. Getting late. Too much wine. Tomorrow he must visit the office, weekend notwithstanding. Too many important projects under way. No rest for the wicked.

Yet he ran a hand across his bald pate, took another sip of Cabernet Sauvignon, and returned to the piano. He attempted Beethoven's Sonata no. 14 in C-sharp Minor—appropriate, considering the pale maiden floating beyond the picture windows. But he was weary and had perhaps imbibed too freely. He butchered the piece, losing every subtlety.

Giving up, he closed the lid above the keys and sat for a moment, lost in dark thought. Then he gave his head a little shake and pushed back from the piano. He was short, wiry, his trim physique maintained by an ascetic lifestyle—occasional overindulgence with claret wines excepted—since his long-ago days as a commando in the finest of all Special Forces units, the Sayeret Matkal.

Before he could rise from the bench, his wife appeared in the arched stone doorway. "Yoni is here," she said. "Shall I bring wine to the garden?"

The *ramsad*—head of the Mossad—covered his surprise with the ease of a professional liar. He nodded casually, as if this after-dinner visit at home, on the Sabbath, were the most natural thing in the world. "Thank you, *ahuvi.*"

Seated in the courtyard of Jerusalem stone, surrounded by

desert flowers, his clothes ruffling in the warm wind, Yoni Yariv looked much like the young man the ramsad himself had once been: wavy black hair, intense blue eyes, powerful chest beneath the loose open-collared shirt. Yoni had also served in the Sayeret Matkal. And he, too, had graduated from the elite commando unit directly into the HaMossad leModi'in uleTafkidim Meyuḥadim, the Institute for Intelligence and Special Operations—Mossad.

At the older man's entrance, Yoni half-stood and accepted a clumsy embrace. Naomi brought two glasses and a fresh bottle on a porcelain tray.

Yoni waited until she was gone before sitting again, and then said beneath his breath, "Better here, now, I thought, than at the office tomorrow."

Taking his seat carefully so as not to weave, the ramsad made a nonchalant gesture.

"I don't want to burden you with details." Translation: I understand that it's my job to keep you insulated. "But you should be aware …" Translation: I'm covering my ass; you can't say I didn't warn you.

The ramsad slowly poured two glasses, listening.

"It's Jana," said Yoni solemnly.

Jana ... Jana. The director had to grapple to place the name. Yoni's wife? Daughter? No. He remembered. An undercover operative who had infiltrated the white-power movement in America as part of the initiative called Di Yerushe—inheritance. The operation extended the tactics of Mista'avrim and Duvdevan, undercover units posing as Arabs within the occupied territories, onto the global stage—an unfortunate necessity when local governments had proved unable to deal satisfactorily with terrorist threats. The program had taken shape after a series of missteps shook Mossad's faith in the Americans and Europeans. First, the German BfV lost track of a Hezbollah agent trying to buy seventy tons of yellowcake on Germany's black market. (A Mossad assassin corrected their mistake.) Then the Belgians fumbled the removal of a Canadian engineer working inside their borders to procure parts for Saddam Hussein's Project Babylon supergun. Then the final straw: the CIA ignored Israel's warning of a "major assault on a large-scale target," deeming the intelligence "not credible"—one month before the attacks of 9/11. Now Di Yerushe routinely infiltrated extremist organizations around the world, watching closely the traffic in weapons of terror, trusting no one but themselves.

Yoni gave his wine a small exploratory sip. "She's ended up in Portland, Oregon. Last week a shipment came in by sea, from Boulogne-sur-Mer. She seduced the man who received the cargo, and then found it in his cellar. Unfortunately, the man interfered … and is no more."

The ramsad used thumb and forefinger to pick invisible flecks from his eyes. Against his better instincts, he allowed himself a gulp of wine. Then he leaned back and asked, "When?"

"Just hours ago." Yoni leaned away too, unconsciously mirroring his commander's body language. "She contacted me immediately, seeking further instruction. This man lives—um, *lived*—in a remote cabin, held no real job. By the time he's found, she'll be long gone. The question is less about the man than about the intercepted shipment." Something gleamed in the young man's eyes—excitement, thought the director, perhaps ambition. "Several kilos of *plastique*. And eighty ampoules of liquid sarin."

The ramsad blinked.

Yoni nodded, obviously pleased with himself. A half smile flickered across his full lips.

The ramsad closed his eyes, processing. Eighty ampoules of toxic nerve agent … Maniacs. Savages. A terrible tragedy had been narrowly averted. Yoni and his operative, Jana, should be well rewarded.

His mind ticked ahead. Only by leveraging every crisis into an opportunity had Israel survived as long as it had. What else, now, did it stand to gain? They might backtrack the shipment, roll up whatever militant group in France had provided it.

Of course, the political possibilities dwarfed the tactical. World opinion teetered on a seesaw, tilting in Israel's favor after the latest terrorist action on Western soil, only to reverse again after the nation's latest effort to defend itself. The UN's criticism grew ever harsher. Israel's greatest ally, the United States, blew hot and cold. Something like this, dramatically revealed in the court of public opinion, would prove conclusively who the true barbarians were. But one must tread lightly, of course. A Mossad operative working undercover inside America's borders; a murder—for so they might consider it—of one of their citizens ...

A shame, in a way, that the maniac had not seen his mission through. A tragedy on US soil was worth a million equivalent tragedies in Israel. As the record showed, the sleeping giant embraced moral relativism and was truly roused only by the shedding of its own blood. A successful attack of this magnitude might change the course of history. And there was a rapidly shrinking window of opportunity in which to make such a change. Iran's assertion to the International Atomic Energy Agency that its nuclear program would remain exclusively peaceful was rubbish, of course. Inspectors would be duped. The same processes that led to nuclear energy also led inevitably to nuclear weapons. Israel itself had played that same game, back in the years before the Six-Day War, back when America still treated Israel like a rogue state—and came within a hair of throwing the burgeoning Jewish homeland to the wolves ...

And then the idea came, all at once, beautiful and terrible in equal measures.

His eyes opened again.

A balmy wind blew through the *korizia* trees surrounding the courtyard. The moon glowed coolly overhead. The ramsad could almost sense his younger self, regarding him as if across a great divide, wondering how they had reached this place.

But most of his mind was racing ahead, parsing details. He had worked with explosives in the Sayeret, but for this he would need a real expert, a munitions specialist acquainted with the state of the art. And where? The closer to the bone they could strike, the greater the impact. Of course, a convincing backdrop would be necessary for whoever actually pulled the trigger. A path would be laid, leading directly to Iran's door. Then the juggernaut that was the United States would finally drop the leash and let Israel handle its business. The Dimona reactor had become active in 1962. Mass production of atomic warheads had begun in 1967. Now Israel bristled with an arsenal of over two hundred Jericho nuclear missiles, ready to be released from underground bunkers, Sufa jet fighters, Dolphin-class submarines.

The war would be brief but decisive. America might wring its hands in public, but in private thank Israel for doing its dirty work, as usual. Other Arab nations would fall into line once they saw which way the wind was blowing. The short-term cost would be high. But the long-term benefit—a solution, finally, to the Gordian knot; an end to fighting, once and for all—would be priceless. He would take the burden onto himself, dirtying his hands and his conscience for the sake of future generations.

But right now the priority was the sarin, the *plastique*, the operative with blood on her hands, whose capture could ruin everything.

"Jana," he said aloud.

Yoni nodded.

"You have faith in her?" the ramsad asked.

"Absolute faith," the young man answered without hesitating. "She's the best I've ever trained."

"She must bring this matériel far from the scene of the … incident. To the safest of safe houses."

Yoni nodded. "Already arranged."

"Immediately," said the ramsad. "Then wait for further orders."

Yoni nodded again. He stood and gave a slight ceremonial bow. The half smile flickered again, and he saw himself out.

For a few moments more, the ramsad sat alone in the moonlit courtyard, looking abstractedly at the wind-tossed *korizia* trees, his head cocked as if listening to some melody that only he could hear. Then he got up, listing only slightly from all the wine, and went inside to make a call.

MOUNT HOOD, OR

In the gravel driveway to the cabin, Jana folded her slender frame behind the Ford's steering wheel.

Using keys she had found in the dead man's jeans, she fired the ignition. The engine purred. The gas gauge's red needle rose—three-quarters full.

She spent a last moment trying to remember anything she may have forgotten. Then she shifted into reverse. Backing out of the driveway, she checked the truck's bed in the rearview mirror. The bungee cords held tight; nothing beneath the tarp shifted.

During the half-hour drive into Portland, her right eyelid kept twitching. She counted back from five, again and again. Yoni's trick for handling anxiety. *Five, four, three, two, one. Five, four, three, two, one. Shvoye*—patience. When he had taught her the technique, they were sitting on a Herzliya balcony at dusk, holding glasses of sweet plum wine. The air rich with smells of the nearby beach and their just-finished lovemaking. After showing her the trick, he had given a half smile, the most smile he was capable of. That night, she had realized for the first time that from then on, any separation between her personal and professional life was gone. The lovemaking had been part of the training. Everything would be part of the training now.

Five, four, three, two, one.

But now the speedometer's needle was creeping up. Moistening her lips, she eased off the gas. There might be speed traps, heading into the city. Haste would work against her.

She passed through a West Hills neighborhood of glazed terra-cotta roofs, then descended into the modest working-class area that she had called home for almost three years. Turning onto a tree-lined street of duplexes and fourplexes—kids chalking sidewalks, laughing and catcalling, gliding on skateboards beneath streetlamps—she ran a quick cost-benefit analysis. She would be occupied inside her apartment for perhaps ten minutes. Better to park by the curb, where she could keep an eye on the payload beneath the tarp? Or a few blocks away, so nobody would connect her to the vehicle?

She had already been seen in the bar. When the man's body was discovered—and it was definitely a matter of *when*, not *if*—they would start looking for her. By then she would have changed vehicles anyway.

She parked by the curb. Locking the truck's doors, she went swiftly up the front walk, toward the porch. Switching the stolen keys for her own, she let herself into the vestibule. Just as she entered, the door across the way opened. Her superintendent poked his graying head out. "*Wondering* when you'd get back," he said.

She could feel his gaze crawling over her rumpled black blouse and skintight jeans—the same outfit she'd worn out last night—making calculations and judgments, noting details that would be repeated with salacious relish to the police whenever they came knocking. But she managed a bright, disarming smile. "You caught me," she said lightly. "Here I am."

The old man sniffed disapprovingly. He had reptilian eyes and a drinker's veined nose. "I worry," he said.

"No need." Jana opened her own door. "I can take care of myself. G'night, Mr. Camber." Before he could answer, she was in the apartment and closing the door behind her.

She put down her purse, moved to the window, and hooked aside the curtain. The red Ford pickup remained parked by the curb. Enough toxic nerve agent sat beneath that frosty tarp to send God knew how many people to a horrible, convulsing death. And rowdy teenagers skateboarded right past, hooting and yelling, oblivious. But strangely, she felt less nervous now. She was entering perhaps the time of greatest peril—she must, for a few minutes, leave the truck unobserved, its contents unsecured, while she made preparations. But the eyelid had stopped twitching.

She turned from the window and went to pack. After filling a suitcase, she found a lockbox hidden beneath a loose floorboard. Keying in the combination (5-8-4-8, Israel's independence day), she withdrew a rubber-banded deck comprised of a passport, driver's license, Social Security card, Visa card, and MasterCard, and a smartphone containing snapshots, numbers, and addresses to back up her new identity: Charity Leeds, from Poughkeepsie, New York. *Just on my way back home, Officer, after visiting some friends out west. Nothing to see here.*

In the bathroom, she found beneath the sink a cosmetics bag containing a wig and contact lenses to match the face on the license and passport. She packed toiletries on top, then zipped it. She would wait to actually change until she had gone some distance from here, in case the nosy superintendent was watching out a window.

She spent a few moments studying her reflection in the bathroom mirror. Beneath the fading makeup, her face looked disturbingly slack—a defensive reaction, she supposed, to having taken a human life. But they were at war. He had been the enemy. He would have done the same to her. Indeed, he had been planning as much, and worse. She made herself smile. It looked ghastly.

In the living room, she checked the truck through the window again. Then she walked around the house, making a final pass. Her DNA and fingerprints were everywhere. No time to bleach it all. But there was nothing that might shed light on her true identity. She had not allowed herself to keep even a single photograph of Yoni, although the sight of his message on her phone this morning had reawakened him in her mind's eye with startling clarity.

She put him from her mind. *Later.*

From a hollowed-out King James Bible in the living room, she took a thick roll of small-denomination bills and put it in her purse. She soaked her old phone in tap water, then used the haft of a kitchen knife to smash it into pieces, which went down the garbage disposal. Then she slung the purse over her shoulder, picked up a bag in each hand, and went to the doorway.

For an instant more, she paused. She had not expected to feel any sentiment about leaving this apartment. It had never truly been *home*, of course. Everyone here knew her as Tiffany Watson, originally from Maine (she had traded one Portland for another, ha-ha)—a twenty-four-year-old cashier at Rite Aid, with a deep-seated lode of racism and a penchant for muscly guys with tattoos. Nevertheless, standing now on the threshold for the last time, she felt a surprising pang of … *ergah* was the Hebrew—bittersweetness. Three years of her life, charade or not, had played out here.

The feeling passed. She moved forward, locked the door behind her, and marched purposefully down the front walk to the waiting pickup.

She climbed behind the wheel again, started the engine, and pulled away.

The road from Oregon to Vermont was essentially a straight shot, forty-odd hours mostly on I-80, bringing her through Cheyenne, Omaha, Chicago, and Cleveland. Follow the signs, keep pressing east, and she wouldn't go wrong. En route, she would change cars, drive through the night, grab a few hours' sleep if absolutely necessary, and reach the safe house by Sunday.

Merging onto Route 84, she turned southeast and quickly left the city behind. The ghostly pale silhouette of Mount Hood soon followed. Empty black land rolled out endlessly on either side. The full moon was a floating saucer of milk. She switched on the heater, dialed it low. Keeping the speedometer at sixty-five, she put her hands at ten and two on the wheel.

Her eyelid twitched again. The anxiety was back. With it came a headache, thudding a steady counterpoint to the broken yellow line vanishing evenly beneath the left front tire.

HOPEWELL, NJ

With no light pollution, the night sky glimmered brilliantly.

Dalia left behind the tiny main street—one bakery, one coffee shop, one gas station, one dentist—and hit open countryside. Her Prius rocked along unpaved roads, past red barns and rickety silos. Wooded hillocks rolled into the moonlit distance. The full moon hung low above a black tree line.

She turned again. Soon a dirt driveway branched off, ramping slightly upward. She parked beside a silver Nissan Altima, before a cozy stone Cape Cod with old-fashioned gables and dormer windows. The remote cottage was surrounded on three sides by forest, on the fourth by a broad, rolling field. One curtained window glowed softly. Nearby, a peaked wooden roof sheltered a hand-dug well. The front door was unlocked. The cool, dim interior smelled of men living without women: fry grease, stale tobacco, lingering hints of body odor, and dog.

Sitting on a love seat opposite a mantle, a sleeping gray German shepherd at his feet, Gavril Meir held a miniature cup of Turkish coffee. When Dalia entered, he bestirred himself slowly. He looked several pounds heavier than he had just six weeks ago. His handshake was too strong, bordering on painful. But this was how the man went through life: crushing things before they could crush him. One glass eye—the result of a grenade on the wrong side of the Suez Canal more than a quarter-century ago—peered disconcertingly off into shadows.

After the handshake, he sat down again, heavily. "You've earned me fifty shekels." His teeth, when he showed them in a grin, were crooked. "Feigenbaum already gave up on you."

David Feigenbaum came out of a back room, rubbing sleep from his eyes. "*Yom asal, yom basal*," he said philosophically—a day of honey, a day of onion. He shook her hand and then settled, with nary a creak, into a rocking chair across from the couch. He was as light on his feet as Meir was heavy.

Both men faced her expectantly. Dalia lowered herself onto the love seat. "And I quote: 'A particular subsection of the Joint Chiefs of Staff, serving as liaison with several universities. Top Secret, Sensitive Compartmented Information only.'"

Meir's brow rose approvingly. Feigenbaum stroked his wispy gray intellectual's beard and grunted.

"Of course, I played hard to get. But in a day or two I'll go back, tail between my legs. After having thought it over, how could I do otherwise?"

The men exchanged an almost imperceptible nod. Dalia had expected more praise for a job well done. Of course, Feigenbaum, the old *yekke*, was naturally undemonstrative. Tell him he had inherited a fortune from a lost uncle, and he would just keep stroking his gray goatee in contemplative silence. But Gavril Meir, a fire-breathing Russian Jew like herself, a Galicianer, took his morning piss with his *shmekel* in one hand and his Uzi in the other. He was a bellower, a brawler, a taker of bulls by the horns. Apparently, two months in the quiet New Jersey countryside, far from the fig trees and blossoming wild mustard of Israel, had damped his inner flame somewhat.

Meir lit a Noblesse cigarette and exhaled a short, hard gust of smoke as his glass eye looked just over her shoulder. "Are we ready for this, Dalia?"

She smiled tightly. "Meir," she said, "we were born ready."

* * *

On the drive back to Princeton, she turned that one over in her mind.

Her ancestors had been marched into gas chambers at Auschwitz, burned to death in their farmhouses by the czar's secret police, scattered during the Diaspora, carried off from Jerusalem by Nebuchadnezzar. They had been so persecuted across the millennia that entire new vocabularies, of pogroms and blood libels and Zyklon-B, had developed to describe it. The suffering of Jews was part of Dalia Artzi's DNA. And as a Sabra, part of the first generation to be born in the modern state of Israel, she, along with others like her, had been inculcated with a single overwhelming priority: *Never again.* Indeed, she had literally been born ready.

And yet …

Bouncing along the raw country road, she gripped the steering wheel too tightly.

And yet, until they took Zvi, she had remained a sincere pacifist. Never blindly—she was, as she and McConnell had agreed, nobody's fool—but earnestly. For Islam was not the real enemy. Extremism, be it Muslim, Christian, Jewish, or something else, was the real enemy. The supreme goal of Judaism was not to deliver a crushing deathblow to their enemies, but to gain real peace, to practice *tikkun olam* and repair the world. Cooperation, moderation, sympathy for the disadvantaged—these were the core values, too easily forgotten. During the millennia of persecution, Jews had always been the underdogs. Now it was not quite so simple.

But she had lost her son. Show her the mother who, under such circumstances, would not strain at the leash when offered the chance that Meir and Feigenbaum had offered during their visit to her office at Tel Aviv University.

They had shown up just an hour after she accepted by email the visiting professorship at Princeton. (How long had they been watching, listening, waiting?) After offering obligatory *nachas*, Gavril Meir had delivered the pitch leaning forward in his chair, immobilizing her with his off-kilter gaze, as Feigenbaum wandered about the office, quietly inspecting the military relics on her shelves.

"*We find ourselves,*" the heavier man had said, "*faced with a unique opportunity to penetrate the defense department of the world's greatest superpower. This once-staunch ally, I am sorry to say, has recently wavered in its devotion to us. Bending over backwards to make deals with the Persians, kowtowing to the United Nations Security Council, leaving us standing alone against the Arabush hordes ... They claim to be on our side. But when their back is to the wall ... ?*" A sad twitch of the shoulders. "*The blood-wind is blowing again. We have never been more isolated than now. And Israel's next mistake might be her last.*"

Dalia had shaken her head because she had known such rhetoric and resented it when she heard it. And because, although her son had already been lost, her daughter's children were rapidly approaching the age of military service. And Dalia Artzi knew better than anyone, both as a historian and as a bereaved mother, that an occupying army could never truly be safe. Her grandchildren deserved better than to find themselves manning checkpoints, presenting targets for car bombs and explosive vests. They deserved real, lasting, stable peace. They deserved to be neither oppressed nor oppressor.

Meir, taker of bulls by the horns, had sensed her resistance but continued undaunted. "*Your expertise in your field is beyond question. Your well-established affiliation with Meretz works in our favor; the Americans will not consider you a threat. And the tragic abduction of your son, of course, offers them a fulcrum to lean on. Take it all together, and you make the ideal lure. The chances of an approach by their Department of Defense during your stay in Princeton have been calculated at nearly eighty-five percent.*" He had straightened in his chair, communicating with his posture the triad of Israeli hardliner attitudes: haughtiness, pride, and disdain. "*They can't pretend any more that Vietnam was an exception. They can't deny, after Iraq and Afghanistan, that asymmetric warfare trumps brute strength, that your theories reflect reality more accurately than theirs. Their mission has indeed not been accomplished. And their morale cannot withstand the loss of another major engagement. They need a win.*" A significant pause. "*They need you, Professor.*"

Still she had shaken her head. For an entire long career, she had encountered men in her field who assumed they understood Dalia Artzi better than she understood herself. They could not fathom that she devoted her life to the study of war only to better enable herself to prevent it.

"*Of course,*" Feigenbaum had put in mildly from the bookcase where he stood, inspecting a fragment of a Minié bullet, "*your contribution will be remembered. We make no promises. But if, perhaps, a prisoner exchange becomes feasible ...*"

He had trailed off artfully, seeing from her sudden stiffening that he had said exactly enough.

"*But,*" Meir had added gently, "*you must do your part.*"

Part of her had seemed at that moment to watch herself from the outside, from somewhere near the office doorway. She had seen a woman in her late sixties, too thick around the middle, too frugal to spring for the salon dye job that would hide her silver roots more convincingly; a woman some might have called a hypocrite, who had studied battles, taught battles, theorized about battles, walked battlefields long after the fact, bent creakily to take souvenirs from old battlefields to save on shelves in this office from which she earned a healthy living by teaching and studying and theorizing about those battles; a woman who had grown elderly, or nearly so, ensconced in various ivory towers, never actually taking part in the battles that she profited from, protected by younger and braver men and women who ran the risks she herself had never run. Instead, she had wielded a hoe, and an unyielding philosophy, at a now long-defunct kibbutz. In the years since, unlike many of her academic contemporaries, she had managed to avoid ever consulting for a military, ever moving beyond the classroom. (John Boyd, for one, had not only lent his services to the Pentagon—the devastating "left hook" of Operation Desert Storm had been his—but had lived to see his theories warmly embraced within the realms of business, litigation, and professional sports.) But now, suddenly, on the other side of the scale was Zvi, rotting in some filthy Arab prison, five years older than the last time she had seen him, his last trace of boyhood innocence blown away; malnourished, blindfolded or hooded, manacled, bloodied, and bruised—if in fact he still lived at all. In the face of that image, the youthful ideals she had still stubbornly clung to seemed as rusty as the old hoes she had swung on the kibbutz.

And although she had suspected, in some secret, true, preconscious place, that she was making a mistake, she had slowly nodded.

For Zvi.

Those who play with the devil's toys, Fuller had written, *will be brought by degrees to wield his sword.*

She gripped the steering wheel even tighter.

As she neared Princeton, the houses grew thicker. Beyond the houses, a warm red glow spread across the horizon—another new day, ready or not.

CHAPTER TWO

PRINCETON, NJ

McConnell seemed unsurprised to see her.

After offering refreshments, he placed a call and then led her out through a rear exit, to a waiting black Land Rover. The gaunt man who had escorted her from the lecture hall yesterday was driving. They turned north under a lowering sun. As soon as the wheels found smooth tarmac, Dalia, exhausted from a sleepless night, was out.

A plaintive voice cut through darkness. *Mommy?* Beside her in the dream, her husband drowsed. He could sleep through anything. But Dalia was the opposite, forever teetering on the edge of wakefulness. In the dream, she clambered out of bed and padded through the gloom to her son's room. She knelt and, in the glow of the night-light, found Zvi's small hand. *Mommy, I'm scared. It was dark and there was a monster hiding in the shadows. I couldn't see him, but I knew he was there. He was coming to get me.* Dalia leaned forward. *Just a dream*, she murmured within the dream. She planted a kiss, a single delicate blossom, on his beautifully smooth forehead. *Over now. Go back to sleep.*

The Land Rover thumped across a pothole. Her eyes snapped open. McConnell was looking at her sideways while pretending not to. Dalia did not let herself sleep again.

They left the highway near Newark Liberty International. Getting out of the car, she wrinkled her nose. Back home, the fresh sea air carried undertones of olive groves and flowering eucalyptus. Here the evening wind felt turgid, swampy, bearing hints of sewage, exhaust, and offal from the rendering plant. In Israel, they had been forced to get creative, ingeniously using the Jordan River to turn barren desert into a flowering Eden. Here in America, with so much arable land, they let toxic runoff turn their good soil to a poisoned waste.

McConnell got out after her, and they entered a compound of institutional white brick set behind spike strips and polycarbonate guard booths. Inside the foyer, he found a key card and took Dalia through double doors of smoked pebbled glass, conspicuously bare of any agency logo. They moved down threadbare carpet without passing through any metal detector. She was allowed to keep her phone. It was a far cry from her expectations: a windowless, lead-lined subterranean room in Langley, where she would consult with military intelligence advisors wearing sober thousand-dollar suits, and chiefs of staff in spangled and beribboned full dress uniform.

With fraying furniture, drooping houseplants, and recessed lighting turned low, the conference room they came to moments later might have belonged to a cut-rate lawyer. On the other side of a wide window, factory smokestacks and an old Budweiser billboard rose in silhouette. Seated around a table, four men and one woman watched Dalia intently as she took a seat. The men's clothing was seedy like the office—not actual business suits, but sport coats with similar-colored slacks. The woman was better dressed, wearing a charcoal jacket and rimless spectacles, with an Afro elegantly graying at the temples. All wore name tags and sat a little straighter in turn as McConnell introduced them: Bharadwaj, Wingfield, Gangjeon, Reed, and Ms. Stember.

McConnell took the chair at one end of the table—symbolic *pater*. Dalia took the only other available seat, opposite his—

symbolic *mater*—and waited. With a gesture, McConnell ceded control to Bharadwaj.

"First," said the man officiously, "let me assure you, Ms. Artzi, that this is a genuine honor. We are all your devotees here, if only through your books."

She offered a perfunctory smile.

"The question on the table at the moment," he continued, giving his comb-over a reassuring touch, "is how to get the most out of our communications budget during future overseas engagements ..."

The disagreement was laid out in bold strokes. One camp, led by the pudgy yet formidable Mr. Wingfield, strongly supported digitizing battlefield communications. The other, led by Ms. Stember, maintained that digital networks were overly susceptible to both failure and sabotage, which was why 90 percent of exploitable intelligence in Iraq had come the old-fashioned way: from PRC-119 combat radios. The first faction called the second "Luddites"; the second called the first "technofetishists." McConnell gestured again, quieting the room. "Thoughts?" he said.

Dalia tapped one lacquered fingernail reflectively against the tabletop. She steadied herself. Four decades of ideals, out the window.

Her own damned fault. "*It's not as if they took him from nowhere*," she had blurted following her son's capture. Microphones shoved in her face, dazzling lights burning from every side—she had given in to resentment, impulsiveness, determination not to be browbeaten into mongering war ... and stubbornness, her fatal flaw. "*They took him from a tank shelling women and children.*" With that single ill-considered statement, she had demolished any reasonable chance of a future prisoner exchange. Despite the deep-rooted Israeli principle of "leave no soldier behind," the trade of a thousand Palestinian prisoners for a single man was a contentious proposition, requiring public opinion to be firmly behind the soldier in question. For the son of a traitor—for so she was quickly branded by the hawkish old-boys' network that had lately become Israel's ruling class—there were too many complications. Or *had been*, until Meir and Feigenbaum had come to visit her office in Tel Aviv.

She tucked a silvering strand of hair behind one ear. "Halfway methodology," she said, "quickly turns counterproductive."

Stember glared ice at her, but McConnell nodded encouragingly. "America's problem," Dalia continued, "is that it clings to the perceived advantages of superior firepower. Perhaps it's just human nature. Perhaps the playground bully always wants to believe—"

"Israel's problem," interrupted Stember, "is arrogance: willful, inexhaustible arrogance. Without this 'playground bully,' as you call us, your country would have long since—"

McConnell silenced her with an upraised hand and beckoned Dalia to continue.

"Your Marine Corps, your Special Forces, your SEAL teams, have some of the best soldiers in the world. But you keep them on a short leash." She shrugged, not meeting Stember's glare. "*Too* short. You're frustrated that your enemy disappears into mountain caves and ruined cities, that the killing blow never gets delivered. But you don't use their own tactics against them. Instead, you go halfway. You implement Boyd's left hook, then draw up short. Because you remain at heart a Christian nation, with all the hypocrisy that implies."

She was watching herself from the doorway again. Now she saw a jaded, selfish old woman who stood by her ideals as long as they suited her. A woman applying her knowledge for the first time to the real world, in a real way that would have real consequences—and cost real lives.

"You know the answer to your own question. But you need me to say it." She nodded. "*Far vos nisht*?" Why not? "You require decentralized command down to the regimental level, over distances that cannot be predicted. The range of PRCs is strictly limited. Therefore, you must embrace digital connectivity, and accept as unavoidable any losses that come. As radio replaced telephone wires between the World Wars, now satellite replaces radio. One cannot implement isolated aspects of the maneuver warfare doctrine and expect success. Guderian didn't achieve victory over the French, after all, simply by adding Panzers to his infantry. He also took his enemy off guard, penetrated deep behind its lines more quickly than anyone thought possible, split the Allied army in two, let his tank commanders press their advantage once they'd found it. Like Hannibal at Cannae, he orchestrated a magnificent concerto, in which all the parts worked together. Combined arms, order of battle, flexibility, knowledge of terrain, decentralized command, the element of surprise."

Stember stared fiercely. McConnell stroked his jowls.

"Commit yourselves," Dalia finished. "Release the leash. Let slip the dogs of war."

Bharadwaj nodded slowly. "Of course," he said, "this raises its own set of practical questions. Does every dismounted rifleman carry a device with battery pack? Or do we, at least during a transitional period, limit small-unit initiative and instead focus on battalion- or even division-level communication paths?

ELLICOTT STREET NW, WASHINGTON, DC

After a few moments, Stacy stood and went into the kitchen.

The tap ran. The stove clicked and caught. Listening, Michael Fletcher scratched the cat's ruff. The big Maine coon stretched lazily, flicking one ear, turning onto her back, tail gently switching.

From three blocks away came the faint sound of traffic, both vehicular and pedestrian, on Wisconsin Avenue. The Saturday evening crowd just gearing up: laughing, drinking, having fun. Later they would come home, happily tipsy—stumbling, hugging, touching, kissing, making love.

The teakettle whistled. His wife returned, stirring a Grumpy Cat mug, giving the impression of a woman tightly controlling herself. She sat down again, a few symbolic inches farther away on the couch.

"I guess," she said, "on some level, this feels … overdue."

Her intense self-control made him think of a kid named Ashenmiller, one night in Kirkuk: manning a turret gun on a Humvee, swiveling constantly but never actually firing, so ruthlessly self-contained that his face, in the endless muzzle flashes provided by other, less inhibited soldiers, remained perfectly set and expressionless.

"I didn't picture it like this." She spoke slowly, with utmost care. "And I'm sorry. I really am. But I think it's for the best … right?"

She looked at him hopefully. Humiliation tried to curdle into anger. He forbade it. "Stace," he said, and then had nothing to follow it with.

"You said it yourself: things haven't been good for a long time." She put her hand on his and patted softly—a sister's gesture, not a wife's. "It won't be easy." Her eyes were dry, her tone flat. She seemed like an actress, and not a very good one, reciting scripted lines. "I'll miss you. I'll miss *us*. But it's time, Michael. It's past due. It's for the best. You know?"

"Stace." And again he had nothing to follow it with.

She made a sad face. Leaned forward and gave him a brisk, efficient hug. She stood, hesitated, seemed about to add something else … and then went to pack a bag.

* * *

They went together to tell their son.

Silas piled into the Hyundai, spilling the contents of a goody bag across the backseat as he worked the seat belt. "Benjamin hurt himself," he said breathlessly. "He fell down and he wouldn't stop crying. Oscar's mommy got scared. But actually Benjamin was okay, he started bouncing again before we had pizza."

Michael, behind the wheel, looked at Stacy, who looked away.

"After pizza we had cake and Rachel dropped hers but then she ate it off the floor. Oscar's mommy told her not to but she did anyway. And Julia was being mean to me; she didn't want to bounce next to me. I told Oscar's mommy but she said it was up to

Julia who she bounced with, so I don't like Julia anymore."

Michael waited for a break in traffic, saw his chance, and pulled away from the curb too abruptly, making Stacy's head rock.

"So I said okay, then I don't want to play with her anyway." Silas was gathering up scattered candy, colored pencils, and plastic toys from the upholstery as he spoke. "When it's my birthday, I don't want to invite Julia and I don't want to invite Brian, but I want to invite Rachel and Victor and Oscar and Isabel. I want to have pizza and cake and then give away goody bags with Star Wars Pez …" He noticed the direction they were heading. "Are we going to Grandma's?"

"Honey," Stacy said. "I'm going to Grandma's. Daddy's going back home. It's up to you where *you* want to go."

"Grandma's," the boy said promptly.

"Buddy," Michael said. Hands steady on the wheel. "Mommy's going to stay with Grandma for a while. But if you decide you want to come back home, tomorrow or whenever, you just let me know and I'll come get you."

A long minute passed. Michael stole glances at his son's face in the rearview mirror. Wheels were grinding inside that five-year-old skull. God only knew what would come out of the mouth next. Sometimes, the boy's perceptiveness could be downright frightening.

"Are you getting a divorce?" Silas asked at last.

Stacy stiffened. "Where did you learn that word?"

"At school. *Are* you?"

"Mommy and Daddy still love each other," Stacy said, "very much. And we always will. But we've grown apart, honey. It's not your fault. It won't be easy, but—"

"Yes," Michael said. "We're getting a divorce."

* * *

He ran.

North on Forty-First Street, where wind stirred the scarlet

oaks like helicopter rotor wash. Left on Garrison. Right on Forty-Second, heading toward Wisconsin Avenue, heart thudding, breath raking, sweat dripping.

He ran through a Saturday night crowd—families going to dinner, couples getting drinks before an evening out—and at the same time he ran up the Hill of Woe outside the eastern gate of Eglin Air Force Base in Valparaiso, Florida, sliding back half a step in the sand for every step he gained. He passed through a blast of hot exhaust from a bus pulling away on Wisconsin Avenue, and at the same time he passed through a gust of heat radiating from a smoking ruin in Kirkuk: Ashenmiller scanning the night with the turret gun, choosing who he would kill and in what order, but awesomely, terribly self-controlled, never actually firing.

His right knee throbbed. Ironically, only the right leg gave him pain. The left flexed regularly and easily. A marvel of engineering. The first year of rehab had been hell, but now he was better than ever. *We can rebuild him. We have the technology. We can make him better, stronger, faster.*

He passed T.J. Maxx, J.Crew, H&M, their lights burning holes in the gloaming; and he passed recruits who had washed out halfway up the Hill of Woe, sprawled in the sand massaging their charley horses. He had started Explosive Ordnance Disposal in a class of thirty and would graduate in a class of eight.

"*It's time. It's past due. It's for the best. You know?*"

On one level, he supposed, she was right. Twenty-eight months had passed since they last made love. Something had to give.

He ran past newsstands and bus stops and Qdobas, and packs of teenagers posing for selfies with studied duckfaces; and he ran past men wearing Kevlar and two-inch-thick visors and bizarrely protruding air snorkels, yelling, *"Stack up! Breacher to the door! Fire in the hole in three, two, one, go, go, go, go, go! You there, hold the fuck still! Don't fucking move or I swear to motherfucking God I'll blow your brains all over the ..."*

He had been pretending things would get better. But he had

been kidding himself. And Stacy had done it right, following the unwritten law of the military wife: stick it out all through deployment, drop the bomb after he had readjusted to life back home. She had actually hung in longer than most, all through rehab and beyond. No one could say she hadn't tried.

He returned home dripping, light-headed, knee throbbing, shin aflame. He leaned against the doorjamb for a long minute before letting himself in. As the door opened, Licorice, lying in wait, came whipping out. He scooped her smoothly up, ignoring her protesting meow.

For an instant, stepping over the threshold, he saw the front room as he might have seen it back in college: a moment caught in time, worthy of a pretentious black-and-white photographic portrait. This was the day Stacy had left.

He moved past the staircase, past wall-mounted photos of happier times. Taken together, the pictures told a story. Here was young Michael Fletcher, a mere cub, playing with his older brother Seth: building snowmen in the backyard, swimming at the neighborhood pool, licking ice cream from his fingers at Baskin-Robbins. And a slightly older Michael, gawky, yarmulked, with brown hair and brown eyes and long, lanky limbs he had yet to grow into, standing over the Torah before the bimah with old Rabbi Gluck. Here was Michael graduating from Full Sail nine years later: filled out, handsome, cocky, having earned his associate's in video production; Mom matching his impish grin, Dad stoical, Seth mugging for the camera. Less than a year later, Seth had made aliyah to Israel. Three days after arriving, Michael Fletcher's only brother had been killed, along with eleven other innocents, by a Hamas bomber on a Jerusalem bus.

Here were artsy shots Michael had snapped with his vintage Pentax 67 back in those first days after losing his brother, back when he had still believed he would become a real photographer someday instead of just a cameraman. Rain on windowpanes, trash-strewn vacant lots, picturesque urban decay. Suffering,

suffering, suffering. Then a portrait of Stacy, looking painfully young, taken at the National Cathedral during their courtship. A stiff posed wedding photo; a snapshot of the newly minted couple, arm in arm during their Niagara Falls honeymoon. But Michael looked somber, distracted, at least half of him somewhere else.

Then Michael Fletcher, now a young man, striking a pose in uniform before a sand dune. When he decided to join up, he had gone back to Florida, to Eglin. Partly because the state was familiar from college; partly because Explosive Ordnance Disposal seemed a natural choice to a man who had always loved tinkering with cameras. The remaining pictures were, tellingly, only of their son: swaddled like a burrito inside his Isolette at the hospital; frolicking at playgrounds, Chuck E. Cheeses, birthday parties, before the Cocoa Cruiser at Hershey Park.

In the kitchen, Michael drew a glass of water, drank it, and set the glass gently in the sink. That dredged up a memory of sliding a fuse gently from a two-thousand-pound bomb on the streets of Hawija: the strange sharpening of the senses, the metallic taste of fear at the base of the tongue. But he had put the fear neatly from his mind, put all of it neatly from his mind, because with a two-thousand-pound bomb you couldn't afford to be distracted. You had to set up your leads and pulleys and rebar stakes just so. You had to pull out your fuse perfectly straight on the first try so it didn't hang up, or the bomb would detonate and puncture your soft, compliant flesh with ball bearings and nails and nuts and bolts and chunks of older bombs, all moving at a speed of what those in EOD called "Mach Oh, My God," which could turn a man into pulp of about the same consistency you might find at your local ShopRite, back here in civilization, floating inside a bottle of Tropicana.

He moved around the house, feeling as if he were looking at a museum exhibit of someone else's home. Stacy's toothbrush was gone. So, too, her favorite sweater, her bathrobe, her Kindle, her lotions, her perfume, her travel bag, her purse.

But Silas' room was still cluttered to overflowing with toys, stuffed animals, maps, globes, dinosaurs, action figures, and two solar system mobiles. The sight made something inside Michael Fletcher loosen a notch. Silas would not abandon him. Silas would be back.

In the master bedroom, the sweat helped him slip the wedding band from his left hand. He put the ring inside a drawer. Then he sat on the edge of the bed and took off his left leg, the pin clicking nine times. He stared blankly at the carpet as Licorice wound around his right ankle. He thought he might cry, or maybe laugh. He thought he might go take a shower. He thought he might have a drink, or maybe half a dozen. Instead, he just sat, breathing evenly, staring blankly at the carpet: whorls, paisleys, baroque interlocking circles, looping forever back into each other, each ending a new beginning.

NORTH OF ANDOVER, VT

After killing the ignition, Jana approached the house obliquely, picking her way over fallen branches and dried leaves.

Ancient forest towered high on every side: spruce, oak, elm and aspen, hemlock and maple. She made a cautious circle around the house—an echo of the circle she had walked around the cabin back on Mount Hood. A blue Mazda hatchback was parked before a closed garage with three garbage cans against one wall. A bag of Kingsford charcoal briquettes leaned against a grill. The trim needed paint, the roof some new shingles. She saw no evidence of cameras, sensors, trip wires, or an alarm system. Not even a dog. The lack of security was astounding—and concerning, given what was at stake.

She crept toward a first-floor window, taking care to avoid stepping on a branch, which might snap and betray her. A bird called from the darkening forest, a clear liquid trill: *trr-iiii-lip-lip-lip-lip-loooo!*

She peered over the sill. On the sofa, concentrating on a laptop computer balanced atop his generous gut, sprawled her contact.

He was older than she had expected, perhaps fifty. And fat—well over 250 pounds. He wore a dirty blue T-shirt and faded chinos, and a salt-and-pepper beard. He looked relaxed, as if he had spent the past three years waiting fatly on this couch with his computer, stuffing himself with American junk food. As, meanwhile, Jana had risked her life, given herself to men who revolted her, surrounded herself with fanatics. *Shonda*, she thought—disgrace.

She caught herself. The fat man could not be as careless as his slovenly appearance suggested. Otherwise, she would not have been sent here. Yoni knew what he was doing.

After a moment, she retreated from the window and deliberated briefly. She might still err on the side of caution—return to her car and watch the house for a few hours. But fatigue was an expanding black sphere pressing against the backs of her eyes. She needed rest, sooner rather than later.

Before ringing the bell, however, she took a few moments to note escape routes winding into the shadowed forest. Then she leaned briefly against the button. (There was, of course, no mezuzah.) Inside, chimes sounded a descending arpeggio. Waiting, she steadied herself by counting down. *Five, four, three ...*

A lock worked. She was pleasantly surprised: by his speed and stealth in reaching her, despite his bulk, and by the way his T-shirt pinched slightly near the small of the back when he swung the door open, suggesting a concealed weapon. Not such a fool, perhaps, after all.

"Are you a friend of Abby's?" *Sign.*

She smiled cheerfully. "No, I think I'm lost. I was just going to meet an old friend." *Countersign.*

He stepped aside. "*Yalla.*"

* * *

The bedroom window gave a view of wooded dark mountains crowding close above the horizon.

After looking outside for a few moments, she turned, pried off the black wig, and set it on the dresser top. She took out the contacts, then released a breath she hadn't realized she was holding. Now a hot shower, and then she would get rid of the car.

But she was too exhausted to do anything at the moment, except spill down across the bed. She had driven two thousand miles with hardly a pause. Five minutes, she thought. Then she would get moving again.

Next thing she knew, she was waking to accumulating purple twilight, barbed wire tangling across a highway, hovering helicopters. A police jeep blocked off two lanes, channeling traffic into a third. A boy in a checkered kaffiyeh threaded nimbly on foot between vehicles, reaching beneath his loose-fitting robe. She caught the oily whiff of RDX. Then the world blinked and slanted sideways. Her ears rang, a high, quavering note. She saw daggers of fire, puddles of blood rippling in the heat. A severed leg, bits of bone. A disembodied hand holding a Glilon assault rifle. The same hand that had explored her body tenderly, in secret humid darkness, just the night before. And then came the pain, searing her from scalp to toes, and she sank gratefully down into a thick, anesthetizing broth of catalepsy.

She sat up.

On the other side of the window, the moon was fat, the color of old bone.

She left the bedroom. The house was quiet, moonlight falling heavily across furniture. No sign of her contact, who must be sleeping. Initial appearances notwithstanding, his professionalism had impressed her. He had asked for no name, nor supplied any. He had given no indication that he knew anything about her cargo, and didn't waste her time with senseless chatter. Instead, he had fed her, offered the room and keys and a Wi-Fi password, and discreetly removed himself. He would play his part and keep out of her way.

She went back to the bedroom. She wanted to collapse again and sleep for a full day. Instead, she plugged in the smartphone, ran through half a dozen encrypted proxies, and connected to Yoni's server. She checked in vain for a new message containing further orders. Then she brought up Google Maps, switched to a topographical skin, zoomed in, and considered the layout of nearby roads and lakes and ponds.

From her suitcase she took a flashlight, a dark Gore-Tex parka, and blue jeans. Three minutes later, she was letting herself into the attached garage. Her light picked out clutter leaning against walls. Jumbles of rakes and fishing poles and lawn equipment, bags of grass seed and mulch. Her eyes were drawn to an old lever-action .30-30 carbine, then to a broad-bladed Razorback shovel.

Before approaching the car, she walked in expanding circles through sweet-smelling forest, looking for a good place to dig. Rags of mist hung in the branches like wisps of burial shroud. Insects buzzed. A distant loon called. She found a suitable spot beside a gnarled yellow elm: accessible but secluded, bare of roots or stumps. The shovel bit into frosty soil. Two minutes of labor left her exhausted. She leaned against the handle, chest burning, trying to catch her breath. Her training was a distant memory. Finally, she hefted the shovel again and plunged the blade back down with a grunt.

The car was parked in a wooded thicket well off the driveway. She unlocked the trunk and transferred her cargo one armload at a time, covering it with freshly turned earth, then loose branches and leaves and pine needles.

Before returning the shovel to the garage, she wiped the blade clean against dewy grass. She arranged the jumble of tools just as she had found it. Her gaze lingered again on the .30-.30. Might be wolves out there. Coyotes, maybe bears. She picked up the carbine and worked the lever. Empty.

Leaving the gun in the garage, she slid behind the wheel of the Grand Marquis. The access panel was still loose. She had stripped the ignition wires back in Salt Lake. Now she bridged the slots, and the engine coughed reluctantly to life.

Using her phone as a GPS, she struck out. At the end of the

unpaved driveway, she turned right. Headlights pushed back the darkness but not the chill. Shivering, she twisted the heater on. She dialed it higher, angling the vents, warning herself not to empty the gas tank prematurely.

Reaching the fire road, she turned the heater down and consulted the GPS again. No service out here. She was on her own.

She bumped ahead, craning her neck to see through the gloom. The road followed the contours of the land, rising and falling. She drove ever more slowly across ever rougher terrain, looking for a place she might turn, push through a clearing, and gain access to the lake.

The first possibility was blocked by a fallen tree. The second seemed promising, then tapered abruptly as evergreens crowded in. The third went all the way up to the water's edge, the small lake opening before her like a smooth black mirror. But it lacked a slope to roll the vehicle down. She tried parking, leaving the car in neutral, throwing her entire weight against the rear fender. But she couldn't budge the heavy Mercury even a centimeter. For a full minute she pushed, gritting her teeth, feet slipping and sliding. Then she gave up, climbed inside again, and thunked it into reverse.

She was considering other options—the next significant body of water was thirty miles away, and the gas tank dangerously low—when another clearing opened to her left. Twisting the wheel, she bounced, rocked, and jounced across rocky terrain. The field steepened sharply near the bank. *Perfect.*

She parked again and left the car. The grass was long and wet, not easy to walk through. She snapped a branch from a tree and tested the depth of the water by the shore, moving along the edge, prodding, seeking. Grass whisked against her parka. Algae dripped from the tip of the stick. She nearly lost her footing and, with a shudder, scaled higher up the bank, proceeding with greater caution.

She was leaving footprints in the cold mud, but there was nothing for it. By the time she finally found a spot that met all her requirements, she had come nearly a hundred yards from the Grand Marquis. She marked the site by plunging the stick into the ground.

Lining up the car wheels, she put it in neutral and pulled the parking brake. Then she slipped out, leaned back in, and let the brake go.

The Grand Marquis rolled, gaining speed, the open door flapping. It hit the water with a splash that sent up a flurry of startled birds from a lakeside tree. The car vanished beneath the boiling black surface … and then, with an antic bob, floated just as quickly back up.

For the next three minutes, waiting on tenterhooks, she watched the big sedan drift. It rotated clockwise, coasting slowly farther from shore. After describing an eccentric U, it listed suddenly, hard to the right. The left fender rose; the right dropped. And all at once the Grand Marquis was gone, leaving behind only a sigh of bubbles.

She watched, making sure the car did not magically bob back up again.

At last she turned, moving back across the field, retracing her route to the fire road.

She liked hiking. Wear out the body, quiet the mind. Trails covered Israel from northern Galilee to southern Eilat, winding through deserts and forests and along cliffs and riverbeds. Israelis grew up wandering their land, working it, feeling it, knowing it, treasuring it.

Of course, it was one thing to hike through a balmy Mediterranean paradise with a loved one, as she and Asher had marched endlessly outside Batar Zikim during *tironut*—basic training. It was quite another to press through this oppressive ancient forest in midautumn, through smells of resin and turpentine and leaf mold, tripping over roots and vines, with gigantic trees towering high on every side. A girl's imagination could run away with her in a forest like this. She wished she had brought the rifle just in case, even if only for use as a club.

But if there were bears out, they kept to themselves. She

plodded doggedly on. Reaching the fire road, she followed it. The route was longer but safer. Get lost in these woods and she might never find her way out again.

Cold wind sliced through the parka. She took deep breaths as she moved. Flood the blood with oxygen, and the body generated extra heat. Something hidden in the forest—bats?—squeaked and squealed as she passed. Something else lowed, long and deep. She pressed on, wearing out the body, quieting the mind.

Mud squished underfoot, making every step slide. Should have brought boots. Despite the discomfort, she was glad to be here. She had been Tiffany Watson for too long. She had lost touch with her true self. She remembered the tick of hesitation she had felt before crossing the threshold of the apartment back in Portland: a kind of Stockholm syndrome.

It took longer than expected to reach the crossroads—so long that she became convinced she had taken a wrong turn. Still no bars on her phone. She kept going. Finally, she encountered gravel. Then asphalt. She turned right.

At last, with the first rind of pinkish radiance showing behind the planet's rim, she reached the house again. She let herself in through the garage's side door, drank a glass of water in the kitchen, used the bathroom. In her new bedroom, she stripped down to underwear, then collapsed back across the mattress.

She rolled over, punching the pillow, and exhaled. Outside, a morning breeze replied. Thorny shrubs scratched against the windowpane. The mountains rustled beneath vanishing stars. She felt tired but satisfied.

Soon she slept again, this time deeply, without dreams.

NORTH OF TEL AVIV, ISRAEL

The ramsad helped himself to the dog-eared pack of Gauloises and accepted a light, cupping his hands against the courtyard's teasing wind. Exhaling a curl of smoke, he raised a questioning eyebrow.

Before Yoni Yariv could speak, Naomi came out of the house, bearing a platter and a cardigan. She set down the tray and then tried to drape the sweater across her husband's shoulders. He shrugged her off.

"You'll catch cold," she scolded.

"I'm fine."

"He complains." She gave Yoni a wink. "But he likes to be babied." She draped the sweater again and made a final finicky adjustment before leaving them alone again.

When she was gone, the ramsad poured two glasses and then gave Yoni his undivided attention. The younger man had acquired a light suntan, the director noticed, during his brief visit to France. But the fatigue showed in his drooping, red-rimmed eyes.

Yoni lit a Gauloise for himself. "The cell," he began. "As it turns out, already on our radar. But we underestimated them. Didn't consider them worthy of Di Yerushe." His thick lips narrowed. "*I* underestimated them. I accept full responsibility."

The director said nothing.

"Their leader is named Maranville. Affiliated, in the past, with National Front and Generation Identitaire. But never accomplished much beyond making a fool of himself. Full of sound and fury, signifying nothing. Or so I thought." His eyes, lit with a strange fire, hung without focusing on the middle distance. "The gendarmerie agreed. They missed the shipment, just as we did. It won't happen again. I've got an operative already worming his way into Maranville's confidence. Now that we know what the fool is capable of, let's see what else he might lead us to."

The director sampled his wine and gave a small nod.

"Evidently, the sarin came from Russia. An ex–Red Army elite, looking to make a few extra rubles. Smuggled out through Pankisi Gorge; then through Molenbeek in Brussels, into the southern suburbs of Paris, where Maranville took possession. He knew he had something hot. But with Vigipirate on heightened alert, he decided to look abroad for opportunities. And so contact was made with an American associate: Posse Comitatus. Also on our radar, of course. Delivery was arranged via CMA CGM."

The ramsad snorted. French and American neo-Nazis working together—still, one had to admire the spirit of cooperation. Of course, the shipping corporation's involvement was hardly a surprise. With four hundred ports internationally, CMA CGM, the world's third largest container transport company, had been caught repeatedly—by Israel, South Africa, Nigeria, the United Arab Emirates—shipping weapons under false cover to Iran. Anything for a buck.

"In Portland, Jana caught the scent." Yoni moved his shoulders. "And the rest you know."

The ramsad smoked pensively. "She is at the safe house?"

"Awaiting instruction." Yoni took a small sip of wine, then reached into his leather messenger bag and handed over a file. "For your information."

The director found himself regarding the familiar Mossad seal, a seven-lamp menorah encircled by the verse Proverbs 11:14, *Where there is no guidance, a nation fails, but in an abundance of counselors there is safety.*

The dossier began with a standard IDF personnel file: a young woman, in stark black-and-white, staring insolently into the camera. Cool gray eyes flecked with harlequin sparkles. A pretty girl, and interesting looking. Something of the fox in her hungry, slender face, but also something of the rabbit.

Jana Dahan had received her Tzav Rishon, or First Notice, in Jerusalem six years before. She had scored highly enough on her matriculation exam to qualify for an elite unit but had opted instead to join the ordinary Military Police Corps. Eager to get her service done, no doubt, with a minimum of fuss and danger. Just another young girl pressed into compulsory service, far enough removed from the Shoah to take the existence of Israel for granted.

She had trained at Bahad 4, commonly known as Batar Zikim. For ten months, she had performed her duties, diligently but unexceptionally, at a Haifa checkpoint. Then—turning the page—she had been wounded in a suicide bombing sponsored by al-Aqsa Martyrs' Brigades. The attack had claimed the lives of two of her fellows. Jana had suffered burns all down her right side: face/head, neck/shoulder, chest/abdomen. A second photograph, taken in a hospital bed, showed the pretty face now welted in scars, and considerably less insolent.

Full-thickness skin grafts had followed. After six months' recovery, she had transferred to Haman, the intelligence corps, where she had distinguished herself as a fast, precise, and intuitive translator of Arabic and English. An administrative remark upon discharge cited exceptional intellect, ingenuity, and commitment to the cause. The nameless administrator then submitted a recommendation for possible continuing fieldwork.

One could fill in the spaces between the lines easily enough. Just another compulsory conscription—until she became the victim of an act of violence. Then, having lost friends, having had her beauty marred, having felt firsthand the fragility of her own mortal coil, she had become a patriot at last. Finding herself for the first time in a position to supply more than mere cannon fodder, she had excelled. Upon discharge, she was recommended for "continuing"—read *clandestine*—fieldwork. Now Jana Dahan found herself centrally entangled in the most important operation of the director's career.

He turned another page. The IDF file ended, and the dossier picked up with Yoni Yariv's own notes. Jana was an only child, whose mother still lived in Ramat Denya. Her father, a longtime editor at *Yedioth Ahronoth*, Israel's largest newspaper, had died of a heart attack eighteen years before. The mother had never remarried. Jana had spent childhood summers with an aunt in New York City. This intimate acquaintance with America, coupled with her newfound patriotism, had made her an ideal candidate for Di Yerushe.

Here was another photograph: a more mature Jana, scars mostly but not entirely gone; face leaner, foxier, than ever. The insolence was back, but tempered now with a curious hint of dark mirth.

Further training had followed, in tradecraft, cryptography, and Krav Maga, the hand-to-hand combat taught to Israeli Special Forces. Under Yoni's supervision, she had assembled multiple alternate identities in America. Then she had gone deep undercover, severing communications with her handlers. Bringing the war to their enemies before their enemies brought it to them—the kind of able young woman, thought the ramsad with a flash of pride, that the ultimate fate of the Jews depended on.

Lighting another cigarette, Yoni said, "I've given some thought to what comes next."

The ramsad closed the file and tilted his head.

"Pull our punches and we risk wasting this chance. They will hem and haw but stop short of sanctioning a truly decisive response. But if we seize the opportunity—if we have the balls—we might accomplish something genuinely historic." A pause. "*Keef zoobuk?*" How's your cock?

A suspended moment, as the director marveled at the youth's impudence. Then he murmured the expected response: "*Zie Hadeed.*" Like steel.

"So." The youngster nodded with satisfaction. "I've considered, and rejected, some less challenging targets. Ground Zero, for one. Killing a handful of tourists does not make the most emphatic of points. Besides, too much depends on the wind."

The director shot a restless glance back toward the house. Naomi was nowhere to be seen.

"More challenging," Yoni continued. "And more rewarding: Times Square on New Year's Eve. To get near the best targets, of course, one must pass through stringent security. But it's possible. Vacuum-seal the chemicals against sensors, trick the dogs with false scents. Again, however, there's the question of wind. Also ..." Listlessly flicking his cigarette ash onto the courtyard's clay pavers. "Dramatic, yes. The point is made. But does it really *surprise* anyone? Does it *maximize* the psychological impact? We might achieve an even more profound effect. The greater the risk, the greater the reward."

The director waited. From inside the house, he heard the faint rumble of Naomi starting the dishwasher.

"Washington." Yoni affected a modest tone, but his self-regard shone through. "Of course, we have potential accomplices everywhere. Thank our enemies for that. Any Jew with half a brain finds, in any day's news, reason to extend himself on our behalf. He knows that soon it will not be SCUDs and suicide vests killing our innocent women and children, but ballistic missiles, chemical plagues, nuclear fire. Soon, one side or the other will strike the critical blow at last—and history will be written by the victors."

The boy was enjoying this too much. He was orating without appreciating the intrinsic pathos of their subject.

But that did not mean he was wrong.

"One of our allies might deliver a package to a press conference. Onto the White House lawn, inside the briefing room in the West Wing. Perhaps even into the Situation Room, or the Oval Office itself. Which started me thinking: dream big, and who knows what we might accomplish."

Yoni paused, letting the wind move and shift insinuatingly through the courtyard. When he spoke again, his voice was hushed, almost reverent.

"Which brings me to my recommendation."

CHAPTER THREE

ELLICOTT STREET NW, WASHINGTON, DC

Michael Fletcher strapped on his leg. First the skintight liner, hugging the stump beneath his left knee. Then the limb itself: molded plastic casing, carbon fiber outer shell. With nine distinct clicks, the liner's pin ratcheted into its housing mechanism. When he put his full weight down, the aluminum ankle flexed naturally, accepting his two hundred pounds with ease.

He did fifty push-ups and then leaned against a wall, breathing hard. He dropped and did fifty more, then leaned against the wall again, panting, chest and arms burning, veins on his biceps standing out blue and engorged.

He dressed in his usual white shirt and dark slacks. Cotton stretched taut across shoulders that were heavier, broader, stronger now than they had been in Iraq, thanks to the incessant exercise. Phil Eggleston, his care coordinator at the DC VA, encouraged the exercise. Eggleston urged him to take it even further, to take up boxing or a martial art, push himself to the limit. But of course Eggleston would not give Michael the top-of-the-line prosthesis, the one that used biosensors to read the muscles' intentions, that would make such activities truly feasible. Electromyographics, Eggleston had explained, were given only to those cases the VA deemed most in need. Transtibial amputees qualified only for good old-fashioned affordable modular prostheses, with all the attendant joys of worn stumps, contracture formation, and degraded skin.

In his son's room, a motionless lump hulked beneath blankets. Michael sat down on the edge of the bed. "Hey, buddy." He nudged the lump. "Up and at 'em."

A thick moan.

"Get on up, kiddo. You know what day it is?"

Sleepy blinks.

"It's Halloween! Get up, get dressed. Brush your teeth. Breakfast."

Heading downstairs, he detoured to turn the thermostat up a few degrees. In the three weeks since Stacy left, Indian summer had retreated, winter advancing impatiently to claim the territory. Rolling his shoulders beneath the clinging shirt, he went into the kitchen and started coffee. He freshened Licorice's food and changed her water. He unhooked his phone from its charger and double-checked the time for the day's first hearing: 10:00 a.m.

He scrambled eggs and poured orange juice. Silas wandered down a few minutes later, toothpaste smudged around his mouth, blankie trailing from one hand. He was wearing his Batman costume, shirt backward, sans mask, and carrying a board book, *Good Night, Darth Vader.* Climbing into his chair, the boy positioned the book and the blanket carefully on either side of his plate, like sentries.

As Michael forked out eggs, Silas asked, "What does 'growing apart' mean?"

The fork paused. The kid had a hell of a memory. Sometimes things percolated inside that mysterious little brain for days, even weeks, before suddenly popping out, seemingly apropos of nothing.

After a moment, the fork moved again. "It means growing up, bud. But growing up in different directions."

"But you and Mommy are already grown up."

"Even grown-ups keep growing up." Michael pulled out his chair. "Everybody keeps growing up, for as long as they're alive."

"Sheila's parents are divorced, and so are Eric's. And they get more candy now because their mommy and daddy both give it to them all the time."

"They must get lots of tummy aches."

"Why did Mommy say it's not my fault?"

"Because sometimes, when mommies and daddies split up, kids think it's their fault."

"Why?"

"I don't know. They just do, sometimes."

"But *is* it my fault?"

"Absolutely not, buddy. Don't ever think that."

They ate in silence for a few moments. Then Silas asked, "Will you marry someone else?"

"Not anytime soon."

"Will Mommy?"

"Not anytime soon."

"But after a while?"

"I don't know, buddy."

"Will you have more babies?"

"Not anytime soon, that's for sure." Michael pushed back his chair, picked up his barely touched plate. "Hurry. We're late. And turn your shirt around. It's backwards."

He drove to preschool in Brookland, double-parked, and walked his son inside. Hallways decorated with stick-figure families and capital-lowercase letter pairs, and aswarm with pint-size superheroes, ninjas, aliens, and Jedi. Kneeling, he administered a goodbye hug and kiss. Clinging for a moment too long; sinking into the warmth, the clean fresh scent of the boy's neck. At last he let go.

He walked back to his car, nodding hellos to teachers and parents he recognized. Rowdy kid voices drifted over from the playground: "I got you!" "No, I was safe!" "Tag, you're it!" "No. I was safe. I'm *safe*!"

* * *

The rap of a gavel began the day's official business.

"The House will be in order," said the Speaker. "Our chaplain, Father Conroy, will give the prayer."

The chaplain found his place between the U-shaped desks fronting the Federal-style lectern. "Let us pray. We give you thanks, merciful God, for giving us another day …"

Michael pulled the camera onto the chaplain's face, blurring the Ionic marble columns of the frontispiece. He nudged the focus wheel, bringing the lectern's carved wreaths, laurel branches, and inscribed words—UNION, JUSTICE, TOLERANCE, LIBERTY, PEACE: IN GOD WE TRUST—into sharp relief. Another nudge, catching both face and frontispiece without losing the letters. A final adjustment, and he also had the banner-size American flag in the background. Perfect. And just in time—from her control room, Allie was calling the crossfade, from the slow zoom to Michael's close-up.

"… may these days be filled with hopeful anticipation. May the power of your truth and our faith in your providence give us the confidence we must have to do the work required for service to our nation. Give all members the strength of purpose and clarity of mind to do those things that bring justice and mercy to people, and maintain freedom and liberty for our land. May all that is done this day be for your greater honor and glory."

Allie called a master shot. Michael tipped his camera back onto the Speaker and tweaked the focus again. "The chair examines the journal of the last day's proceedings and announces to the House his approval thereof. Pursuant to Clause One of Rule One, the journal stands approved. The gentleman from North Carolina will lead us in the Pledge of Allegiance …"

Soon they were onto HR 1610, the Biennial Budgeting and Enhanced Oversight Act. The representative from Wisconsin's eighth congressional district approached the microphone and cleared his throat. "This bill amends the Congressional Budget Act of 1974, the Congressional Budget Impoundment and Control Act of 1974, and the Rules of the House of Representatives to change the process for the president's budget submission, congressional budget resolutions, appropriations bills, and government strategic and performance plans …"

Michael leaned away from the viewfinder. Only two of gallery eleven's ten camera positions were occupied today, reflecting the degree to which HR 1610 was setting Washington ablaze. His partner was Steve Kokemuller, a towering cameraman who managed, even in jacket and tie, to look like a member of the ironworkers' local. As the gentleman from Wisconsin droned on, Steve caught Michael's eye and simulated putting a gun muzzle to his temple and pulling the trigger. Michael nodded, pantomiming with his hand a slow-motion explosion of brains from his skull.

"… creates a point of order in the House and Senate against authorizations of appropriations that do not include specific authorizations covering at least each fiscal year in one or more bienniums …"

Michael's gaze kept wandering: down from the overhead gallery, past sparsely populated armchairs arranged in a semicircle on tiered platforms. Weak turnout today. The air was dry; the scant audience coughed, shuffled, sniffed.

He closed his eyes. For a moment, he simultaneously occupied both this chamber and a dry, dusty marketplace in Hawija: booths and stalls covered by rainbow tents, a hostile crowd pressing close on every side, yelling and brandishing rocks; John Hicks waving his 30 mm chain gun from atop the Bradley, yelling at the crowd to get the fuck back, disperse the fuck immediately, or he would fucking shoot; a frisson crackling through air redolent of rotting garbage and diesel fumes and burning trash and dead dogs.

Then Mitri, the Shiite translator with a sixth sense for trouble, had caught Michael's eye, nodded toward a woman in a hijab near the front of the crowd. Michael's rifle had snapped up, sending two warning shots over her head. This had earned him some derision back at FOB—one shot, the Marines insisted, should equal one dead haji—but it had done the trick. The woman had ducked back into the throng. The Bradley had turned a corner. Disaster averted.

"… subtotals of new budget authority and outlays for nondefense discretionary spending, defense discretionary spending, Medicare, Medicaid, and other health-related spending …"

His eyes opened. He pressed down a cough, adjusted his headphones, sneaked a glance at his watch. Ten past ten.

The beginning of a long day.

* * *

Lunch was two hot dogs on the stone steps by the reflecting pool.

Joggers circled. A mallard drifted by with three ducklings in tow. Flags atop the Capitol dome ruffled in a brisk breeze. A pickup crew from WJLA was shooting man-on-the-street interviews before the fluttering backdrop of red, white, and blue. A young reporter wearing a meaningless smile shanghaied costumed tourists: cowboys, pirates, sexy witches, and pretty French maids.

Michael crumpled a hot dog wrapper, pitched it at a wastebasket, missed. He bent to retrieve it, being careful of his balance. He was just killing his Diet Coke when a voice called his name. His head turned, pulling his starched collar tight—his neck had grown two sizes since he bought the shirt.

Matt Gutierrez was trotting over from the mall. They had met ten years ago, when Michael, fresh out of Full Sail, had toiled in the storeroom of a DC facilities house, and Gutierrez had been a runner for a production company. It was back when networks still sprang for assistants to lug the kit, back when Michael Fletcher still carried his Pentax everywhere just in case inspiration suddenly struck.

"Your ears must have been burning last night." Gutierrez came to a stop, breathing hard though it was only the short jog.

He was fifty pounds overweight; the closest he came to exercise was marathon *Call of Duty* sessions with his teenage son. "Your name"—*huff, huff*—"came up at my dinner table."

"Uh-oh."

"Linda's friend does Pilates with"—*huff, huff*—"a friend of Stacy's. Trouble in paradise?"

Michael sighed, hesitated, then nodded.

Gutierrez pulled a face. "What happened?"

"What ever happens?"

"How bad?"

"Bad. Gone to her mother's."

"Fuck," Gutierrez said with his characteristic eloquence.

"Yeah. But maybe it's for the best. At least, that's what I keep telling myself."

"So you okay, man?"

"Yeah, I think so." But was he? "Yeah. I'm okay."

"What happens next?"

"Six months living apart, and we can file uncontested. We agreed: Keep the lawyers out of it. Everything straight down the middle. Split custody."

"Fuck," Gutierrez said again.

"Yeah."

"How's Silas holding up?"

"Rolling with the punches—at least, far as I can tell."

"I'm sure goddamn sorry, Mikey."

"Thanks, man. I appreciate it."

"Shit happens. You flush it and move on. What else can you do?"

Michael nodded again.

"Well, look; Linda's got some good-looking friends. We'll get you back into rotation. Come on over for—"

"Thanks, but too soon."

Gutierrez frowned deeper. "I don't like the thought of you sitting alone in that house."

A gallows grin. "Got my cat."

"Don't gotta gut it out alone, Mikey. You got friends. We're here for you."

"Next time."

Gutierrez put up both hands in a gesture of surrender. "Grab a beer soon?"

"Definitely."

Michael's old friend started back across the mall, dodging a cluster of Japanese tourists. For an instant, Michael felt tempted to call him back. Accept the invitation. Get "back into rotation," as Gutierrez called it, and rejoin the flow of regular life.

The temptation quickly passed. His last chance at regular life had disappeared along with Stacy, almost a month ago. To get back into the dating scene, to climb back aboard the merry-go-round as if he were still the man he once had been … The prospect made his nads shrink self-protectively up into his body.

But maybe laying it all on Stacy wasn't fair. Maybe she had been a victim just as much as he had. Maybe they both had lost their chance at happily-ever-after at the instant, four years back, when Michael Fletcher had driven past a ruined bridgehead in Kirkuk and seen a hand lying in a bed of smoking rubble. Just the hand: skin and fat and bones and blood. Funny how you could tell it belonged to a child, even without anything around it to give it scale. At that instant, he had felt something slip loose inside him, falling out of place. The machine still ran, but something rattled around now, floating free, gumming up the other works.

Or maybe it had been the day his brother climbed aboard that bus in Jerusalem. Seth Fletcher had been on his way to a football match: Beitar Jerusalem versus Hapoel Tel Aviv—right versus left. Michael pictured him laughing with his friends, joshing and joking. And then into their midst had stepped a young Palestinian wearing a loose thawb and, beneath it, a belt of explosives. And in the span of a single heartbeat, the bus had transformed from a party into a funeral pyre, a gaudy cauldron of blazing hopes and dreams.

Or the day Michael had been sitting outside a Humvee in

Hawija, working the F6A bomb robot, concentrating hard on the array of dials and joysticks and toggles, and a motorcycle had pulled up alongside and dropped something into the road, then put-putted away. Michael had glanced over at the water bottle and wondered what was inside. Not water, that was for sure—too dark and oily. And when he woke up, his left leg was missing below the knee, and he was, then and forevermore, less than a complete man.

Or the evening when, four months after coming home from Iraq, he had walked into the Israeli embassy on International Drive after strolling past three times. Telling himself that he was just stretching his leg, so to speak, that he couldn't stand being cooped up for another night with Stacy and the baby. That Cleveland Park, with its nineteenth-century homes and its smattering of Art Deco, was a lovely neighborhood, a perfect place to walk and brood. It beat getting stinking drunk by himself in some miserable hole of a bar. A knot forming in his stomach, ripening into a lump of dread as he had reached for the intercom. Ringing that bell had felt like a spur-of-the-moment decision—an impulse acted on without reflection. In retrospect, he guessed it had probably been brewing for years.

He had never been to Israel. But he recognized from the shitty-smoky-sweaty streets of Iraq the Middle Eastern vibe in the lobby: earth tones, beige brick, arched windows; loose fabrics, a general lack of deodorant, the sweet scents of *knafe* and olivewood. Soldiers had searched him, and not gently. Then they escorted him to a small room, furnished with a table and two chairs, walled with Lucite to frustrate parabolic microphones. For five minutes, he had sat alone. Then a pretty young woman came in. Brunette, sultry. Twenty-five at the most. Wearing a pencil skirt and a brusque manner. She had asked in crisp, rapid-fire English what, exactly, he was doing here.

He had just been offered, he replied, a job as a cameraman inside the House Gallery. Compensation for his loss in the line of duty. Throw a three-legged dog a bone. He would start in less than a week. Then he would have access … to use as Israel saw fit.

Her mouth had tightened. And what did he expect in return?

He had tried to explain. He was Jewish; he had lost family in the Holocaust; he had served in Iraq, been turned into less than a man, and, upon coming home, been shortchanged by America's VA system. His brother had made aliyah to Israel and been killed by an Arab bomb on his way to a soccer game. His grandfather had changed his name upon immigrating from Europe. Nate Fleischer, a good name, a proud name, a workingman's name—literally *flesh*-er, butcher—had become inoffensive and goyish Nate Fletcher, because even in America there had been signs outside stores that read No Irish, Jews, or dogs. His grandfather had been ashamed and frightened. But Michael was not ashamed. Michael was not frightened.

She had looked at him, frowning. So he had clarified: he wanted nothing. Service would be its own reward.

She had not softened. What did he have to offer as bona fides?

Nothing yet, he had said. But after he started the job inside the House … well, try him and see.

She had considered him at length, a speculative light flaring and dying inside her dark eyes. Then she had told him to leave immediately—counterintelligence watchdogs may already have seen him enter. But his claims would be assessed. There was a bar called Fiddler's, on Irving Street NW: casement windows, a famous cheeseburger, a bus stop out front. He knew it? On the third Wednesday of every month, at 7:00 p.m. sharp, he should check the graffito above the rightmost urinal in the men's room:

FOR A GOOD PRIME CALL 555-793-7319

If he found a cross etched into the wall after the last digit, he should leave the bar, wait for the next bus out front, and sit as close to the back as possible.

He had nodded. Of course they thought he was a dangle, a

countermove to Pollard, too good to be true. But they would test him. And they would see.

And so they had. Three times in as many years, he had found a new cross scraped into the wall of the bathroom, and boarded the next bus. A different person had sat beside him each time. First, a tall young redheaded woman, who had given him a package and an address in Foxhall. He had driven there the next day, parked in plain view on the street, rung the doorbell, handed the package to a housekeeper. And that had been that. Seven months had passed before he found another cross. This time a swarthy middle-aged man had led Michael off the bus a few blocks from Fiddler's. They had walked up to a second-story apartment, and for two hours Michael had drawn detailed diagrams of security leading into the House Chamber: guards, metal detectors, dogs. And that, too, had been that. The following week, he had walked past the same second-story apartment. Through the window, he could see that it had been cleared of furniture.

He had not heard from them again for fourteen months. Then, one Wednesday, he had found another cross beside the graffito. Again he had boarded a bus. A courtly older gentleman in a pin-striped suit—the kind of man who had no business riding a bus at all—had come and sat beside him. The man had asked, softly, if Michael had ever taken a life. Michael remembered the careful phrasing of the question, the gentle tone of voice. He had answered honestly: "*not to my knowledge.*" In the fog of war, of course, these things had not always been clear.

Then the man had asked what he would be willing to do for Israel. Michael had again answered honestly: "*anything.*" The man had looked into his eyes and announced that they would be in touch again. That was nine months ago.

Soon, he thought, he would find another cross on the bathroom wall.

Just a feeling.

He nodded to himself, once. Then he upended the Diet Coke,

searching for a final drop that wasn't there, pitched the bottle, and turned toward the first checkpoint separating him from his afternoon labors.

NORTH OF ANDOVER, VT

Four hundred fifty miles north, Jana listened to the thorn branches scrabbling against the windowpane as she read. Reaching the end of Yoni's message, she took a deep breath and read the orders again. This time, she managed to cultivate a clinical distance. Amazing—and a little sad—how quickly one adjusted. Humanity was nothing if not adaptable.

Then her eye twitched. Her mouth pulled involuntarily. She quickly recovered her composure and smeared a hand down, wiping her face clean of emotion.

Plastique, sarin, and now a honeypot operation in Washington, DC. But of course, the implications were not her concern. She was merely the tool, to be used as Yoni saw fit. No sane person chose to be the pivot upon which destiny turned. Rather, the choice was thrust on them. The pilot of the *Enola Gay* had not requested his mission, but he had nevertheless completed it.

She read the message one last time. Then, having committed the salient points to memory, she closed it. The encrypted communication deleted automatically.

She started packing at once. The same intuition that had told her to check her phone told her now to get on her way as soon as possible.

It promised to be a full day.

* * *

By the time her contact wandered out from his bedroom rubbing sleep from his eyes, the sun slanted all the way across the kitchen floor. As he opened a can of sardines, she said, "I'm leaving."

If he felt surprise, he covered it well.

"I'm taking the car," she added. "I'll be back. Don't know when."

He nodded mildly, forking fish onto a plate.

"I'm told to ask you for some equipment. Laptop, pinhole camera …"

"After I eat," he grunted.

* * *

She was on the road by one. Autumn foliage flaming yellow, simmering orange. But already half the trees were bare. "Stick season," they called it—the long purgatory, in the American north, between autumn and winter.

She passed looming scarecrows, rolling brown cornfields. Farmers saving money by letting the corn die and dry on the vine. But at a cost: fire hazard, mycotoxin contamination of next year's crop. America, land of plenty, land of waste. *Goldene medina*—the golden country.

In midafternoon, she caught her first glimpse of the nation's most populous city. She had not seen the skyline since the completion of the Freedom Tower. The mirrored obelisk plugged the hole left by the country's all-too-brief taste of reality. The sight struck her as poignant but ostentatious—an inviting target.

The familiar jagged horizon brought back summers with Aunt Becca, and the room Jana had shared with Cousin Miriam. Stuffed animals lining the bunk beds. A poster on the wall picturing a kitten climbing out of a toilet bowl. ONE OF THOSE DAYS, the caption had read. In that bedroom, they had asked a Ouija board to reveal their futures. (Tall, dark, handsome strangers awaited them both.) They had danced on the bed, breaking the box spring. They had fallen asleep listening to Alicia Keys. She had smoked her first cigarette, leaning halfway out a window six stories above Madison Avenue.

Those had been good summers, full of firsts: not only first cigarettes, but also first beers, first parties, first kisses—the last two on the same night, on a rooftop on Sixty-Eighth Street. "*My dad is kind of a big deal,*" the kid hosting the party had told her solemnly. The boy's name had been Robert Thorpe Jr. III, which Jana had never understood—wasn't that redundant or something? His tongue had explored her mouth like a dentist searching for cavities, hitting every corner.

Miriam, only one year older but vastly more experienced—a year meant a lot at that age—had laid out the facts of life before the party. "*Guys like girls who wait. Let him offer you a beer. If there's a joint, wait for him to pass it; never reach for it. Let him make the first move. Hang back. Be cool.*" Not the most feminist advice, perhaps, but it had worked. When Jana had tried a similar tack with Asher years later, however, he had been too shy. Finally, fed up, she had made the first move herself.

Where was Miriam now? Had she ever met her tall, dark, handsome stranger? Jana had found hers, only to lose him to a terrorist bomb. The Ouija board had not mentioned that part.

Dusk—shadows quickening, temperature dropping. She reached Beltway traffic an hour past nightfall. Eye twitching, she alternated between a snail's pace and a standstill.

Her second time in DC. But she had never before visited the Columbia Heights neighborhood of the safe house: lower income but gentrifying, with a tapestry of ethnicities that she might easily blend in with. As she parked, she heard from the next block a sound that might have been either a backfire or a gunshot. And Americans thought Israel was dangerous.

Jack-o'-lanterns leered from stoops and windowsills. Trick-or-treaters moved in unruly groups down the sidewalk: princesses, vampires, skeletons, ghouls. Teenage girls revealing the maximum possible acreage of bare skin. Strange holiday, thought Jana. In Israel they also wore costumes, on Purim, but for a purpose: to commemorate salvation from the Persians.

The address she sought was squeezed in between a liquor store and a check-cashing place. No trick-or-treaters inside, no hint of the festive vibe on the street. She climbed four flights of stairs, receiving hints of lives behind closed doors: an audibly aspirating dog, a squalling infant, frying onions, disinfectant.

She found the key taped to the bottom of the welcome mat. Inside, two rooms offered a view of a church across the street. Dirty white marble Virgin Mary out front. Exposed radiator on the wall, exposed pipes on the ceiling. Water damage. Cockroaches. It reminded her of the shabby old Jewish Agency house she had grown up in.

She explored. Sheets folded neatly on bare mattress. Bureau with peeling veneer. No soap in the bathroom. Kitchen cupboards stocked only with flour, sugar, rice. In the Vermont house, her contact had often cooked food from back home. Israeli breakfasts of eggs and smoked fish, challah on Shabbat, and soup with *kneidlach*, and tahini with everything. Here she would be on her own.

She went back to the Mazda and brought her luggage upstairs, then fell across the bare mattress, eyelid twitching. An incipient headache probed. She hadn't eaten since morning. She would make some rice. Better yet, go shopping. Buy some soap and real food. Some hair dye—according to Yoni, her target liked blondes. Change the license plates, move the Mazda to long-term parking at the airport. But for now she just lay still. Gathering her energy. Preparing herself.

She listened against the mattress to her own faint but steady heartbeat. She had chosen this path, she reminded herself. She could have been just another mindless Hasid cow, getting knocked up, handing away her selfhood in service to husband and children. She could have stayed in the intelligence corps, collecting hemorrhoids and backaches. She might even have moved to America, gone to prep school with Miriam, perhaps sired Robert Thorpe Jr. IV. But she had wanted more. She still wanted more.

Of course, this was what she had signed up for. She had given herself willingly, as a tool to be used.

Head throbbing, eye twitching, she lay on the mattress, looking at the swirling patterns of frost on the grimy window, trying to make herself get up, get moving, get started.

NORTH OF TEL AVIV, ISRAEL

Yoni's Subaru was parked in the driveway again.

After her driver helped carry her parcels inside, Naomi stood alone in the kitchen, listening. Her husband and Yoni Yariv sat in the courtyard, talking in furtive voices. Straining to hear the words, she registered only the low creak of the front gate closing behind the departing limo, the night wind rustling through the *korizia* trees.

She loaded spices and pastries into cupboards and refrigerator, then considered making herself a bit of supper. But her stomach felt sour, uneasy. She settled for a glass of juice. Then she carried a bag of jewelry and hand-embroidered scarves up to the bedroom, switching on lights as she went.

After making space in the closet and jewelry box, she wandered over to the window and looked down into the courtyard. Her husband's bald pate glinted in the moonlight. A bottle of wine and two glasses sat on the small table, alongside a small stack of file folders. The two men leaned in toward each other, intimate as lovers. Three times a week lately, Yoni came over and they talked softly and intently … about what?

No food, she noticed. She might bring them a platter. And she might conceal her iPhone beneath the linen. Then she could find out what they were talking about.

She gave her head a small shake. Things had gotten bad, yes. But not so bad that she was going to start spying on her husband. She was not ready to become that woman.

She moved into the bathroom, shucking off clothes as she went. She ran water, and as the tub filled, she looked dispassionately at her own naked body. Skin ever more translucent, as if the veins were forcing their way to the surface. Belly flesh sagging like a deflated football. Perhaps her husband was hooking up with one of Yoni's young girlfriends. Some slut with a taut stomach, flexible enough to hook her ankles behind her ears, easily impressed by an older man's achievements. Perhaps the file folders were filled with potential candidates, eager volunteers …

Naomi sank into the almost too-hot water, submerging her head briefly, then surfacing and letting her wet hair fall heavily around her shoulders. She sank down again, resurfaced. After soaking for a few minutes, she left the bath, toweled off, and ran a comb through her hair. She wiped away condensation and considered her reflection in the glass. She would be scowling but for the browful of Botox that prevented it.

She dressed beside a marriage bed that had not known the rumpled disarray of lovemaking for longer than she cared to remember. She had broached this subject, gently, a month ago. Her husband had responded with a joke about conjugal obligations varying by profession, according to the Talmud, and donkey drivers being largely exempt. His point being that he spent his days since the promotion wrangling with politicians and bureaucracy, and she should therefore expect less of his attention. She wondered if that was really all there was to it.

No harm, she thought as she buttoned her blouse, in learning what they were talking about out in the courtyard—just to set her mind at ease.

She took her phone from the nightstand. In the kitchen, she assembled a platter of pita with *sayadiya* and *besarah*. Beneath the small plates went a paper doily. Beneath the doily, a sheet of linen. Beneath the linen, her iPhone.

When she carried the platter into the courtyard, her husband stopped talking, glowering at the interruption. But Yoni Yariv found a winning half-smile, versions of which had doubtless tumbled no end of young ladies—and perhaps a few more mature specimens—into countless beds over the years. As she set down the tray, Yoni said: "*Shookran*, Naomi."

She returned the smile warmly, with a half-ironic curtsy.

She went inside again, fear fluttering like a hummingbird in the hollow of her chest. What would happen if they found the phone? God have mercy on her soul.

She would not even listen to the recording. After Yoni left, she would count her blessings that she had not been caught, and delete the file.

She dallied in the kitchen, aching to reverse her mistake as soon as possible. Then made herself stop. If she loitered too long down here, they might grow suspicious.

Upstairs, she changed into a nightgown, brushed her teeth, flossed. She reached for the book on her nightstand. But she couldn't concentrate. She closed the book, held it in her lap, frowning. Lost track of time. At last she heard a door downstairs open and close. A lock turned, clicked soundly home. The alarm system chirped.

Her husband climbed the stairs. He came into the bedroom without brushing his teeth, changed into pajamas without saying a word, and slipped beneath the covers and switched off his lamp.

A few seconds later, Naomi put down her book and followed suit.

She waited, the hummingbird now a great crow flapping in her chest.

Shadows slid across the ceiling. His breathing slowed, coarsened. Otherwise, the silence was absolute.

At last, she put her legs over the side of the bed and padded back downstairs. Darkness pooled in corners and behind furniture. She moved quietly past the piano, into the courtyard. Two wine bottles stood empty. The platter of food was untouched. She retrieved the iPhone from beneath the linen. The app was still recording. She brought the phone inside, locked herself in the bathroom off the kitchen. The device had captured nearly thirty-five minutes of sound. The file was named by date and time. She started playback. Wincing, she reduced the volume and held the speaker to her ear.

As she listened, cold fingers closed around her heart; pinprick hackles rose along the nape of her neck.

A soft footstep outside the bathroom door sent a gust of alarm tingling through her solar plexus. She stopped playback. Making a split-second decision, she found SHARE and scrolled through the contacts. A name leaped out. No time to look further. She selected Gavril Meir's number, pressed SEND, and watched the recording drift out across the digital ether.

She deleted the message thread. Hiding the phone in a pocket of her nightgown, she worked the lock, turned the knob. Her husband stood very close to the bathroom door, his eyes two heavy-lidded crescents.

With an effort, she affected a light tone: "You're up."

"What are you doing?"

She touched her stomach. "I had some bad fish in the souk." Reproachfully: "I was hoping for some privacy."

She started to step past him. He seized her wrist. She snatched her hand away, clutching it defensively to her chest, tight against her thudding heart.

He grabbed her wrist again, twisting sharply, bearing down, forcing her to her knees. She lashed toward his groin with her free hand. He dodged without releasing her wrist. Then he was atop her, trying to slam her head against the floor. The phone skittered from her pocket. They were grappling, her thumbs fumbling for his eyes. He twisted like a dervish, whipping his head back and forth. Grunting, straining, muscles cording in his neck. She raked her nails across his cheek, digging up bloody furrows.

"*Kus ima shelkha*," he snarled. Fuck your mother.

A sound rose in her throat—a howl of pain and fear. Suddenly, he released her, changed position, grabbed her windpipe with both hands.

Her screams choked off. She kicked, hit air. Kicked again and hit air.

Her mouth opened soundlessly. She felt her eyes rolling back. *Let me go.* Had she said it out loud, or only thought it? *Let me go.*

A terrible pressure filled her breast. The phone gone, lost. Her husband panting, his breath in her face like a sink backing up, like effluvia belched up from the sewer. He was talking, but she could not make out the words.

Rocking her hips, she tried again to dislodge him. Again, more weakly.

She gave up. There was warmth and comfort in giving up. Something in the perfect center of her skull gave a short, hard *snap.* Then embroidered darkness folded in. She collected it, wrapped it around her, and let go.

PART TWO

CHAPTER FOUR

HOPEWELL, NJ

As the recording played, Gavril Meir watched Dalia closely.

When the voices had finished, the speakers conveyed a few moments of scratching wind, like the runoff groove of an old record. Then Meir stopped playback and there was only silence, broken at last by the snap of Feigenbaum's lighter.

"You and I," said Meir, "have more in common, my dear, than you might recognize."

Dalia said nothing. She was still trying to get her head around what she had just heard. A murky, amateurish recording, but clear enough. She had listened with dark, sick wonder, but not with surprise—in fact, with whatever was the opposite of surprise.

"Of course, you are the more naïve. Teaching an entire generation to stretch out their throats for the Arab's *jambiya*." He shot Feigenbaum a quick, indecipherable glance. Before the fireplace, the German shepherd twitched its tail in a dream. "But these hawks, with their fairy tales of boot heels crushing the enemy once and for all—*these* are our common enemy." He reached for a cigarette and flicked open the lighter. "Not true Israelis, if you ask me. More like Brownshirts."

She gave a distant nod. Her scalp was crawling.

"So …" A pause to exhale smoke. "Connect the dots. I'll wager we are hearing the plans for a false-flag operation. A high-value target in Washington, DC. To strengthen America's resolve against our enemies."

"Not without precedent," Feigenbaum put in dryly.

Another dazed nod. In 1959, Israeli military intelligence, faced with the UK's decision to withdraw from Egypt, had concluded that the British would stay if faced with a crisis. A series of bombings, dressed up to seem the work of restive Arabs, had targeted Western interests across the region. The plot was exposed only because a makeshift bomb had exploded inside the pocket of a young Zionist in Alexandria, who had proceeded, under duress, to confess everything.

Meir examined the ember of his cigarette. "Did you recognize the voice on the recording—the older one?"

Feeling numb, she nodded again. She traveled in similar circles as the *rosh hamossad*, who had once been a senior advisor to the Israeli General Staff. She had met him in person more than once at lectures and fund-raisers.

"So you understand why we cannot, in devising our response, turn to the Mossad." He smoked. "What remains? We might try the CIA, the FBI. But a whiff of this caught by the wrong nose, twisted to suit someone's political ambitions, could do serious harm."

"*Lashom harah*," said Feigenbaum. The halachic term—literally, "evil tongue"—for derogatory speech that, although true, becomes destructive when known to the public. "We cannot lose our most important ally because of one rogue intelligence leader."

She opened her mouth to say something, then closed it.

"We might do nothing," Feigenbaum continued rhetorically. "Let the cards fall as they may."

"Or perhaps, if we extend ourselves, we might find some back channel that pays dividends. You have some personal acquaintance with Lee Chazan?"

She started. How had they …? But of course, before

approaching her they would have investigated every past romance and ill-considered dalliance.

"He has risen"—Feigenbaum jetted smoke from his flaring nostrils—"to a position of some authority. Yes? Executive director of Israel's largest lobby. Undoubtedly, he has the ear of the prime minister."

"He might solve our problem," Meir suggested. "At its source."

She shook her head. *He drank the Kool-Aid*, she almost said. Made appearances on Fox News, hitting every talking point, defending policies of evangelical Christians who believed that the Bible was the literal word of God, who wanted Jews in the holy land so that the end-times could come as prophesied. But deep down, of course, Lee Chazan was smarter than that. Deep down, his real crime was opportunism.

"I saw him interviewed recently," said Meir. "He struck me as reasonable."

Feigenbaum gave one cuff a fussy tweak. "He wouldn't throw you under the bus … right?"

Both men strained invisibly toward her. She could feel the palpable grasp of their need. Smoke from two cigarettes collected beneath the low ceiling. The dreaming dog kicked restlessly. Outside, the wind gusted. Her heart sped up, leaving almost no space between beats.

Lifting her chin slightly, addressing the smoky air halfway between the two men, she said, "Get me my son."

"Dalia." Meir paused to shave the sharp edge off his voice. "It takes time—"

"Get my son. Then we'll talk."

"Listen to reas—"

"Fuck your reason."

Feigenbaum was shaking his head. But Meir's heavy brow was lifting, and to her surprise, she caught the Galicianer smiling at her chutzpah: a quick approving flicker, then gone.

* * *

She drove too fast between serried legions of rustling corn stalks, back to Princeton.

She parked two blocks from her faculty housing. Inside the tiny kitchen, she splashed a finger of Remy Martin into a glass and downed it, the burn fading to a glow.

She followed the narrow hallway connecting the tiny kitchen with the tiny bedroom. Sitting on the edge of the unmade bed, she kicked off her shoes—*thump, thump*—and lay back, closing her eyes. Too tired, too wired, to sleep. But she could drift. And if a jaded, selfish old woman such as she could feel guilt, so would she feel.

But nothing would change. She had rebuked McConnell, after all, for embracing half measures. She would not repeat his mistake. She would commit fully to whatever had to be done. She would save her only boy, whatever the cost.

Waiting in darkness, she conjured up the last time she had seen Zvi in person. She had driven him back to his base in the Golan Heights. The radio was tuned to Galei Tzahal, the army station. At the perimeter, Dalia had pulled over, and her son gave her a manful, back-thumping embrace. Then he left the car, humping his canvas duffel over one shoulder, and plodded up the hill toward the gate.

In the twilight of consciousness, the memory played again, on a distorted loop. This time, as Zvi plodded toward the gate, he turned to look entreatingly back at her.

Awake.

Cold dawn nosed through the window. For a moment, the interplay between light and shadow suggested, to Dalia's tired eyes, shuffling refugees. Mothers and children bundled in faded rags. Syrians, she thought. Or Jews, escaping annihilation by the skin of their teeth. Or Palestinians, driven from their homes by air strikes and ever-expanding settlements.

Outside, a first-delivery truck prowled down the block, pausing every half minute to unload something. She found the glowing digits of the clock. In one hour, she would return to Hopewell to hear the verdict.

She rose. Her weight had lain oddly on her left leg, and the foot was asleep. She hobbled around, bringing it back to life. Rubbed coconut-scented lotion onto dry elbows, stepped into her shoes, slung on her coat, and walked to Starbucks. She carried the steaming cup to the Fountain of Freedom, where ten-foot bronze statues depicted the Chinese zodiac: snake, horse, goat, monkey, rooster, dog, pig, rat, ox, tiger, rabbit, and dragon. At this hour, the plaza was deserted. She sank onto a stone bench, sipping her latte. The campus stirred, slowly coming awake. Students moved past: joggers, go-getters, walkers of shame sneaking back after an ill-advised sleepover. Her stomach growled. Her breath steamed beside the hot coffee.

She remembered the last time she had seen Lee Chazan. Over dinner in a Ramat Gan restaurant, they'd had a loud and public argument. The subject had been David Grossman, one of Israel's most popular writers. Grossman had lost his son in the Second Lebanon War. Yet his commitment to peace had only redoubled. "*We cannot afford the luxury of despair*," he said. "*We risk becoming a suit of armor with no knight inside*." Lee Chazan had called Grossman self-loathing. Dalia had called Lee, "*shtick fleisch mit oigen*"—Yiddish for "lump of meat with eyes."

Eventually she got up from the bench and walked back to her rooms, where she ate an apple and quickly washed up. The fire-hose American water pressure made her think of Liyana, her housekeeper back home. An IR, illegal resident, who had once claimed with a straight face that it was a pleasure to clean Dalia's dirty dishes—the water pressure in Tel Aviv was that much better than on the other side of the Green Line. Dalia had gone to bed that night thinking of Voltaire: *There is no God ... but don't tell my servant, lest he murder me in the night.*

She drove west over Cherry Hill and into Montgomery, houses thinning, forest thickening. Through a crossroads—technically, the town of Blawenburg—and past Brick Farm. Into Hopewell. Past the bakery, coffee shop, gas station, and dentist. Barns and silos. Woods heavy now, civilization left ever farther behind.

She parked beside the silver Nissan Altima. Inside the cottage, Feigenbaum looked surprisingly rested. But Meir seemed not to have slept. Darkness puddled beneath his eyes, and he spoke in blunt, impatient bursts of Hebrew, like automatic-weapon fire.

"Dalia," he said as she settled onto the love seat. "You have my word. We're doing everything we can. But you must listen. You must understand."

Feigenbaum calmly sipped his coffee.

"I tried," Meir said. "I've *been* trying. But it will take. More. Time." He ran a hand through his thinning hair. "Full disclosure: we've had a report. Only a rumor, and vague at that, so take it with a grain of salt. From Khan Yunis. A prisoner passed through. Two years ago. Fitting Zvi's description." Pause. "Overly aggressive inquiries will work against us. Tact, finesse. Patience, patience."

"We need more time," said Feigenbaum. "But this ..." Indicating a USB drive sitting on the table, he did his artful trailing-off thing.

"This." Meir picked up the drive and shook it. "Can't. Wait."

In her mind's eye, a flashing strobe: Zvi plodding again up the hill to the gate. Turning to look imploringly back at her.

Meir waggled the drive, inviting her to take it.

Family came first. A mother could be only as happy as her unhappiest child.

But Zvi was not her only family. Soon, her grandchildren would be taking up arms, taking their own turn in the crosshairs. Risking everything for a nation that had, in recent years, started banning books; labeling any dissenter a traitor, an "Arab-lover"; singing the anthem "Hatikva" even as they denied one-quarter of their citizens equal education, social services, infrastructure, employment, legal rights. The great democratic Jewish state had become, in practice, democratic toward Jews and Jewish toward Arabs. The calamity of the Holocaust, the Shoah, was being answered with the tragedy of the Palestinian Nakba—the catastrophe. *We risk becoming a suit of armor with no knight inside.*

One last tic of hesitation.

Zvi, forgive me.

She nodded shortly, and took the thumb drive from Meir.

NORTH OF TEL AVIV, ISRAEL

The ramsad's eyes kept trying to slide back through the study's open door, back to the living room, where Naomi now lay rolled up in an Oushak carpet. The drama played out yet again on the old man's forehead, the great, furry brows crinkling together, almost touching before pulling apart again, like caterpillars meeting on a branch. The same drama that had been playing, with subtle variations, ever since Yoni's arrival.

"Drink," the younger man urged gently.

The chief of Mossad blinked, then seemed to remember the glass of wine in his hand. He drank slowly.

Yoni returned his attention to the phone. He had reloaded deleted messages from the server. Now he scanned them briefly, lips pursing. He shut the email program, opened SMS messages, scrolled through threads.

He turned to the computer on the desk. Beside it, pictures of Naomi were encased in a plastic cube: swim-suited with her husband on the beach, making a face after taking a sip of some exotic drink in a café, agitating for women's rights with Nashot HaKotel at the Wailing Wall. (And in the process, if Yoni remembered correctly, causing her husband no end of tsuris with the Orthodox.) He found a USB cable and plugged the phone into the computer. After entering the serial number, he selected the operating system, disabled the autolock, and started data extraction. They watched the program count off seconds.

He created a folder to receive the data, then skimmed through the cache: every email and SMS message ever to have crossed the phone. His eyes were drawn immediately to a massive audio file sent out twelve hours ago …

… to Gavril Meir.

His hands clenched into fists on either side of the laptop.

Surrounded by enemies, barbarians at every gate, fighting for survival itself—and yet, the bitch indulged this. In-fighting. Spying. Betraying.

He disconnected the phone and closed the laptop. Beside him, the ramsad was looking again into the living room, at the rolled-up carpet.

Cold wrath burned in Yoni's chest. How much damage had she done?

However much, it would be contained.

His lips pressed into a grim line. He would handle it personally.

FORTY-SIXTH STREET AND LEXINGTON AVENUE, MANHATTAN, NY

Reaching the awning, Dalia checked the address against her phone.

The numbers matched. Yet there was no club name on the door. She found a mirrored surface and spent a few seconds trying to primp. Every trial of a long life seemed to have been carved deep in the grooves of her face. *Those who live on vanity must reasonably expect to die of mortification.*

She was searching for the bell when a buzzer sounded. She entered a foyer of mahogany and polished oak. A uniformed man took her coat. Another lingered discreetly. When she turned toward him, he said, "Mr. Chazan is waiting in the game room."

As indeed he was: the only occupant, on this sunny weekday afternoon, of a high-ceilinged chamber with vaulted windows. Billiards table, chess and backgammon boards, glimmering gold and silver accents. He stood to meet her—trim, expensively turned out, hair a sophisticated gray. She wished she had put on some lipstick, at least.

An indecisive moment turned into an awkward embrace. He squeezed hard. "So good to see you."

"It's been a while."

"So glad you called. So glad it worked out."

"Thank you for making the time. I know how busy you must be."

"*Feh.* If I'd known you were in Princeton, I'd have called long ago."

He was drinking seltzer with lime. Dalia asked for Moroccan chamomile. Then she and Lee Chazan were left alone. They sat, just looking at each other for a few moments, smiling.

Their affair had happened—God have mercy—a full half century before. Lee Chazan had come to spend a summer on the kibbutz. He had fascinated Dalia, questioning loudly every aspect of communal life, saying aloud what she had hardly dared think. Why were women so often relegated to service jobs, despite all the lip service paid to gender equality? And was it really right for children to be separated from their parents, raised in the Beit Yeladim? And the lack of emphasis on higher education. Yes, Jews must learn to work the land, to shed the image of pale moneylenders hunched over dusty ledgers in dark basements. But Lee, like Dalia, loved books and learning and had resented making himself stupid just to confound the stereotypes of others. They had first kissed during a hike among terebinth groves in the Galilee. They had first made love in the kibbutz's dairy barn—a literal roll in the hay. Old milk cow lowing, chickens chattering. Chaff and straw in the air and up the back of her shirt. Lee's fingers fumbling with her buttons, his erection a hard chisel poking into her belly …

Her tea arrived. He waved the menus away. "Sorry," he said, "but I've got to be at the UN in forty-five minutes."

Nodding, she considered and rejected several opening salvos.

Looking around, Dalia then took out her laptop, plugged in flash drive and headphones, and beckoned him to lean closer.

She could hear the reedy voices coming through the tinny speakers. As Lee listened, thunderclouds gathered on his brow. When the recording had finished, he gestured for her to play it again. After it had run its course a second time, he took off the headphones and leaned back, tenting his fingers. He did not look particularly surprised.

"Is that …?"

She nodded.

His face was difficult to read. Some distress, perhaps. But also some cold satisfaction. Outside, a siren wailed in the distance. "And what," he asked at last, "do you expect me to do with this?"

She paused. "You've got the PM's ear."

"And if I bring him this, what happens? You and I both …" He snapped his fingers.

"Don't be dramatic."

"Don't be naïve. A recording of one of his oldest friends, making a move many would consider not only justifiable but inevitable—what do *you* think happens?"

"It's madness," she said.

"But not without a method. You can't deny."

"Oh, yes. One hell of a pinpoint operation."

He stiffened, recognizing, of course, the reference to the then secretary of state John Kerry's exasperated comment, caught on mike during an interview before cameras had started rolling, about the 2014 Gaza operation that had taken thousands of civilian Palestinian lives.

"It's reality," he said after a moment. "Push hard enough, eventually we push back."

"*A nahr bleibt a nahr.*" A fool remains a fool. "I gave you more credit, Lee."

"Clear the shit out of your ears, Dalia, and hear what I'm trying to tell you. I bring this to the PM now, like this, mark my words: he gauges which way the wind is blowing, then chooses the path of least resistance."

"So we threaten to leak it."

"He'll recognize an empty threat. God knows he hears enough of them."

"I won't just stand by."

"Give me something solid, then. A fait accompli. There was a plot, but it's failed. Now it'll be exposed with or without or his blessing, so he'd best get on the right side of it."

He pushed back from the table and stood, then took a moment to smooth down his jacket. "A fait accompli," he repeated. "Until you've got that, you've got nothing."

He left her staring after him.

E STREET NW, WASHINGTON, DC

The woman was sitting three stools away. She was visibly bored, apparently alone, and pretty in a middle-aged sort of way: slightly broad-shouldered, with classical bone structure and lovely dark hair flowing past her shoulders. She was checking out Jana from the corner of her eye. When Jana caught her looking, the woman smiled.

Jana smiled back. She ordered another drink and then nursed it. In the mirror behind the bar, she saw the woman's chardonnay gradually become empty. Then her target sidled two stools closer, dropped down beside her, and signaled the bartender for another round.

Jana crossed her legs. The motion was both protective—closing off her personal space—and provocative; the black mini she was wearing rode high up one lean thigh.

The woman smiled. "Meeting someone?"

Jana shrugged. "Are you?"

"Yeah. I'm meeting you."

Jana laughed. "Ouch."

"I'm Bev." Christina Thompson offered her hand. Jana looked

at it, considered, and then shook it lightly.

"Sophia," Jana said.

"Haven't seen you here before, Sophia."

"Haven't been here before."

The bartender brought another round. Christina motioned to have it added to her tab. A new song came on the jukebox—something with lots of jangly guitar. In the next room, a live band was setting up, lugging amplifiers.

The woman leaned closer. Jana caught a hint of expensive perfume mixed with an adolescent cherry scent—lip gloss or bubblegum. "That's a beautiful name: Sophia."

"Listen, you seem like a nice person and all, but I'm not interested. All right?"

"You wouldn't be here if you weren't interested."

From the back room came a whine of feedback, an amplified tapping. Jana said nothing.

"Let's get a room."

"Oh, my."

"I'm direct. It's one of my charms."

"Oh, my."

"That's not no."

Cue the twinkle in the eye. "No," Jana allowed. "I guess it's not."

* * *

The room was elegant but simple: desk, dresser, quilted bedspread. A peek-a-boo view of the Capitol dome between buildings. The air smelled of bloomy potpourri, emanating from a bowl atop the dresser.

Christina came into the room behind Jana. The door had barely closed before she was reaching forward. Gently but firmly tilting back Jana's head. Kissing her, lightly at first, then more insistently. Jana felt the woman's tongue in her mouth. She pulled away. "Hold that thought," she whispered.

Into the bathroom.

She slipped off blouse, black mini, bra, panties, socks. Folded them neatly, hiding the camera—a TT520PW wireless pinhole, broadcasting a high-resolution image directly to the memory card inside her purse—between layers. She took a moment, holding the eyes of the blonde stranger in the mirror, bracing herself. The white-power goons had been far more repulsive than Christina Thompson, and she had done that. She could do this.

Five, four, three, two ...

She flushed the toilet and left the bathroom, casually setting clothes with camera on a rolltop desk facing the bed.

Christina had not undressed, seemed not to have moved. Now Jana took the initiative. "*Let him make the first move*," Miriam said in the back of her mind. "*Hang back. Be cool.*" She unbuttoned the woman's blouse and slipped free surprisingly ample breasts. Leaning down, she took one into her mouth, rolling her tongue until the nipple turned hard. Maneuvering slightly so the camera would have a better view, she lowered the woman onto the bed and worked her way down.

The belly was still relatively taut. She reached a C-section scar, unfastened a zipper. *Do the alphabet*, she had heard somewhere, so she did, flicking her tongue. *Aleph, bet, gimel.* Christina's pelvis began to buck. A few instants later, the legs clamped hard together, then relaxed.

The woman was touching her shoulder, urging her to trade places. Jana complied. But from this angle, Christina's face would not be visible to the camera, so Jana, under the guise of getting more comfortable, repositioned them both. She lay with eyes half-lidded, looking at the visible sliver of the Capitol dome. Eyes on the prize.

She moaned, stirred, counted back from five again and again, and kept her gaze steady on the Capitol.

HOPEWELL, NJ

When Dalia finished speaking, the men did not immediately react.

Meir examined an unlit cigarette. Feigenbaum looked blankly through a window, following the course of a blipping red dot across the night sky. Something man-made, thought Dalia. A plane, a drone, a satellite.

"*Er toig nit*," said Meir at last. He's worthless.

"Not necessarily." Dalia rubbed one eye wearily. "In fact, he may have a point. But he needs his fait accompli."

"And how in hell do we give him that?"

Feigenbaum seemed unperturbed. "You and McConnell enjoy good *chevra*"—comradeship—"eh?"

She blinked. "I suppose so."

"You might offer your new friend a deal. A counteroperation must be mounted. On American soil. Outside the usual channels. No involvement of the White House. We supply the intelligence. He supplies the manpower. And with our combined efforts, we uncover the operative mentioned in the recording. Chazan brings her to the prime minister, who takes it up personally with the ramsad."

"You're asking me," Dalia said slowly, "to enlist the US Department of Defense … to assist a Mossad plot … to stop *another* Mossad plot?"

Feigenbaum shrugged, nodded.

Meir watched her without blinking.

Dalia hesitated. McConnell was a realist. He understood that the futures of their countries were entwined. He appreciated the danger of *lashom harah*—evil tongues. He might agree to help. But Dalia would be surrendering her only leverage: exposing herself to the Americans as an Israeli spy, leaving herself nothing to offer the Mossad except feeble reminders of an earlier promise. While Zvi, if he even lived, rotted in some Arab prison.

If he even lived.

"We're meeting tonight," she said. "If it feels right, I'll ask."

* * *

An airplane whined overhead, bumped down against cold tarmac a quarter mile away.

McConnell sat with eyes closed, apparently lost in thought. Dalia watched, waiting. In the next room, the coterie from the Joint Chiefs—joined tonight by a cadre of analysts from CENTCOM—would be finishing their bathroom break and finding their seats again around the conference table. In another minute, they would start looking at their watches, wondering why they weren't yet back to the subject of foreshortening OODA loops and the limits of air power.

She was about to poke McConnell's shoulder when his eyes suddenly opened. He looked at her directly. Her cheeks burned at the implications of that stare, but she managed to return it without flinching.

He paused to let the slow thunder roll of an approaching jetliner build, crest, and fade. "I have a friend," he then said, "with the State Department. Discreet. And sympathetic to Israel. He happens to be currently attached to the Trenton HSAP field office."

Her mind raced to unpack the words. HSAP: Homeland Security and Preparedness. "State Department" might be code for NSA, or perhaps CIA.

"I suggest we go back in there, you and I." Gesturing with his jowls toward the next room. "We proceed as if this conversation never took place. And then we go see my friend."

She nodded.

"But for future reference, Dalia, I don't like being lied to. And I don't like being used. Unless, of course, you're going to try to tell me that the Mossad contacted you just today, out of the blue."

Her lips formed a tight line.

"I'll give you credit there, at least. You know better than to double down."

"Jim ..."

"Let's ... just don't." McConnell seemed about to add something else, but the moment passed. Somewhere down the hall, a toilet flushed, pipes hissed. He took out his phone and sent a text. The reply came almost instantly. He read it, then nodded. “This is the last time we’ll be meeting with the Joint Chiefs, by the way. Do me a favor: don’t embarrass me by being invaluable or anything.”

They went back to the meeting.

Afterward, they rode in the black Land Rover back to campus, said their good-nights for the benefit of the cadaverous chauffeur, then regrouped five minutes later before the Fountain of Freedom. They took her Prius down Route 1 South, effectively reversing the path George Washington had followed on January 2, 1777, after the Battle of the Assunpink Creek. Washington’s ragtag army would have crossed black woodland and icy brooks. Now they passed strip malls, Whole Foods and Babies“R”Us, Staples and Home Depot and Walmart. Applebee’s advertised half-price appetizers. ShopRite offered a free Thanksgiving turkey or ham with your Price Plus Club Card, limit one per family.

Leaving the highway after twenty minutes, they hit Trenton: churches and small houses, boarded-up windows, sneakers dangling from power lines. They wound into a residential neighborhood: factories converted to lofts and apartments, garbage cans and recycling containers overturned at the curbs.

They parked in a shallow driveway behind a navy blue Lincoln Navigator. Dalia followed McConnell up a concrete walk to a front porch. The white-framed Victorian was noticeably better tended than the other houses on the block. Manicured box hedges lined the facade. An unseen dog yipped from a neighbor’s fenced-in backyard.

McConnell banged a wrought-iron knocker down three times. The door opened to a crying baby, a TV blasting *SpongeBob SquarePants*, and a harried-looking man of about forty, with black curling hair and graying five o’clock shadow. Dry orange crust—strained carrots, Dalia guessed, or maybe squash—stained the V-neck of his green sweater vest.

“Dalia Artzi,” said McConnell, “Jacob Horowitz.”

The man shook Dalia’s hand while openly taking her measure.

He turned and led them down a dim hallway strewn with Legos, pieces from board games, and headless plastic action figures. Waving them into a study, he closed the door gently but firmly and gestured to the two chairs before an old Steelcase desk. Dalia stood for a moment, her gaze ticking around the study, gathering information. Framed diplomas behind glass: Williams, Notre Dame. Awards from the Director of National Intelligence and the previous New Jersey Governor's Office for, respectively, leadership and professional achievement. Horowitz followed Dalia's gaze and gave a crooked smile. "Those are what they gave me instead of a bonus." He was so soft-spoken that she had to concentrate to catch the words.

On the olive-drab desk sat a mug crusted with old coffee, and another filled with pencils and pens, bearing an inscription from the Talmud: "If you are planting a tree and you hear that the Messiah has come, you finish planting the tree before going to greet the Messiah." On a high shelf, a small golden Buddha smiled alongside candles, incense, and a brass singing bowl. On the next shelf down, a plaque reading *THIMK!* On the shelf below that, a faded Kodak print of a gangly grinning boy—perhaps young Jacob Horowitz himself—standing splay-legged over a seventies-era purple banana seat.

A toddler in the next room screamed, then dissolved into tears. Horowitz shrugged with weary embarrassment. "Jim said to keep this off the record. That means staying away from Homeland offices."

Dalia nodded.

"So." He leaned against the desk, arms folded. "He made it sound as if you had something to share with me."

Dalia hesitated for a few seconds more. Then she reached into her purse, fished past the sugar-free gum and Kleenex travel packs, and came up with the USB drive.

Horowitz took the drive, frowning. He turned around a laptop on the desk. The computer woke up, displaying on-screen a happy baby, all cheeks, buckled into a playground swing. When the operating system found the plug-in, a media player opened automatically. He switched on the attached speakers. Then the amateurish recording was emanating into the study: muffled clattering, wind stirring through digital hiss. "*Shookran, Naomi.*" The voice echoing as if down a long hall of stone.

Dalia translated in murmurs as each sentence was spoken:

> "Where were we?"
>
> "He will see it through, I was saying—at least, according to the psychologists. Textbook PTSD, misdiagnosed by his own government as mere combat stress. Now the added trauma of a failed marriage—they estimate ninety-six percent certainty. There is also a young son to be used as leverage if necessary."
>
> "And he can get how close?"
>
> "Close enough to whisper a secret. And within an arm's length of countless secondary targets. We'll reach dozens. Maybe more."

Horowitz clicked pause. "What are we listening to?"

"Do you recognize the voice?"

He rubbed the bridge of his nose, then traded a glance with McConnell.

"It's the *rosh hamossad.* The director of the Mossad."

A moment of silence, broken by another squall from the next room.

Horowitz, stone-faced, resumed the playback; Dalia resumed her murmuring translation.

> The younger voice: "The woman in charge of the event itself …"
>
> An anticipatory pause. The flick of a match, followed by a short exhalation. Then the voice continued: "She's completely *farmisht.*" The nearest English translation was "dysfunctional." "A married mother of four, a churchgoer,

a trusted pillar of her Washington community. Yet in private …" A clunk as something, perhaps the pack of cigarettes, was set down on the microphone, obscuring the next few words. Then: "She has worked hard to keep her secret. But people who make it their business to know such things have long since become aware."

Horowitz clicked pause again and stared into space, parsing, meditating. A fly landed on the coffee-rimed cup, prayed briskly, and took flight again. The Buddha watched from his high shelf.

Horowitz started the recording again.

"Promising."

"I've taken the liberty of moving Jana into position. She awaits only the final order to proceed."

Another pause. And then, probably, a nod or gesture, to which the younger voice replied: "Very good."

Digitized wind echoed off stone. The older man murmured something unintelligible. Chairs scraped, and muffled thumping was followed by more wind.

Horowitz stopped the sound file. He stroked his unshaven chin, and Dalia noticed for the first time a pronounced cleft. "This is genuine?"

"It is."

"How do you know?"

"I trust my source. A friend in the Mossad. One with a different idea of what's best for Israel, it goes without saying, than the *rosh hamossad.*"

"Who else has heard this?"

"No one."

"If it is what it sounds like …" Horowitz picked up a pen from the blotter and turned it over broodingly. "I agree, prudence would be advisable. And, in the long run, beneficial for Israel. But …" He looked to Dalia, then to McConnell. "What, exactly, are you asking me to do?"

"You hear one name: Jana. 'I've taken the liberty of moving Jana into position.' Find this operative. We'll take it from there."

"When was this recorded?"

"Three days ago."

"It raises more questions than it answers. This 'event.' This 'primary target.' This 'woman in charge' …" He drummed a brief tattoo with the pen against the desk. "Hebrew school was a long time ago. I'll need a written translation."

"You'll have it."

"You're one hundred percent."

"One hundred percent."

"I'm not a miracle worker." *Tap-tap-tap* went the pen. "Tell your 'friend' I need something more to work with." *Tap-tap-tap.* "A full name. A face. A license plate. Something."

Another moment of silence stretched out, broken at last by a child's piping laughter, high and sweet and pure, from the next room.

CHAPTER FIVE

BEN GURION INTERNATIONAL AIRPORT, TEL AVIV, ISRAEL

The boy who took Yoni aside was about nineteen, nervous but trying to hide it, with hair shorn so close that every tiny bump and mole in his scalp was visible. He wore crisp Border Police fatigues and stood painfully straight, as if striving to avoid any suggestion of a child playing dress-up. He looked from ticket to passport and asked gruffly, "What is the reason for your trip?"

"Visiting my sister," Yoni said.

"Where, exactly?"

"Montparnasse."

"Her occupation?"

"She works in a food truck, owned by her boyfriend."

"Her name?"

"Levana Harel."

"Israeli?"

"Yes."

"Her boyfriend is French?"

"Yes."

"And Jewish?"

"Yes."

"Why visit her now?"

"I haven't seen her for a year. The timing worked out. I'm between jobs."

The boy looked up sharply. Yoni pushed down his frustration. This exhaustive intrusion, he reminded himself, was why Ben Gurion had never lost a plane to hijackers. "I quit," he elaborated. "I wanted more in life than selling tickets."

"Where did you sell tickets?"

"At the Museum of Art."

"How long did you work there?"

"Nearly three years."

The boy looked down again. "How long will you be away?"

"Ten days."

The boy handed back the ticket and ID. "Bon voyage," he said dryly.

Fifty minutes later, the runway fell away beneath the El-Al Boeing 737-800. Yoni held his armrest as they turned, arcing out across the Mediterranean coast, wheeling slowly into blinding sun.

He accepted a plastic cup of orange juice from a flight attendant. His seatmate, a middle-aged Parisian businesswoman—nobody in the world put themselves together more neatly than middle-aged Parisian businesswomen—tried to engage him in conversation about the difference between Israeli and French orange juice. Every kind of fruit, she opined suggestively, tasted better in Israel. Yoni gave a noncommittal smile and opened his in-flight copy of *Atmosfera.*

Ten minutes later, he leaned back, closing his eyes. The funeral would be getting under way about now. Then would come the *levayah* procession to the graveside—joining, bonding, escorting the deceased back to the souls of her ancestors. Mourners reciting Psalm 91 seven times, with a pause following each recitation. The corpse would be interred, shovelfuls of earth thrown atop the coffin. The grief-stricken ramsad would watch it all.

His seatmate jostled him as if by mistake. He didn't take the bait. The hostess offered dinner. He ignored her. Someone a few aisles up blew her nose honkingly. Yoni kept his eyes shut tight.

When they touched down at last, passengers who had behaved respectfully all across the Mediterranean and Italy became suddenly rude, all elbows. He waited, still and silent, for his turn to deplane. Filing into terminal 2A of Charles de Gaulle Airport, he rode automatic walkways into the central terminal's main chamber. His second visit in as many weeks to his new home away from home. A tangle of suspended escalators rose and fell beneath a tremendous skylight. One hour earlier than Tel Aviv. The evening light was an uncanny amber. The French had a particularly evocative term for twilight: *entre chien et loup*—between dog and wolf.

He passed through customs as Amin Harel, the same identity under which he had left Tel Aviv. Harried men and women staffing the checkpoint asked no questions, barely raising their eyes.

In long-term parking, he found a waiting Fiat. He drove into Paris aggressively, dodging Opels and Peugeots with centimeters to spare. The safe house occupied a trendy block in the center of Marais. The apartment was furnished well enough to pass a cursory inspection. A locked antique desk in the bedroom opened with Yoni's key to yield a passport featuring a biometric chip and his own photograph.

At Gare du Nord, he bought a ticket and filled out a border agency landing card. By 8:00 p.m. GMT, he was settling into a comfy maroon seat aboard the Eurostar. In the central waiting area of terminal 5 at Heathrow, he would find his next set of papers. From there, America.

As monotonous dusky landscape whisked by the windows, he drifted into a dark reverie. Of course, the series of hoops, although an irritant, was a reasonable precaution. Still, he envied the simpler days enjoyed by the older generations. Running in beneath coastal radar, taking men from their beds in the steamy Amazonian night, checking by touch for the small scar beneath the left armpit—a relic of the tattoo bearing an SS officer's blood type in case of severe wounding. Making an escape in the same small airplane, or perhaps switching to a boat and becoming a fisherman for a day or a week. For every Adolf Eichmann held publicly accountable for his crimes, countless other verdicts and sentences had been rendered secretly and, hence, far more efficiently.

But never unjustly. If he ever doubted that, Yoni need only remember the tales told by his great-grandfather. Ghettos surrounded by barbed wire. Starvation diets, filth and lice and rampant disease. Shuls burned to the ground, select handfuls of community leaders taken …

"*Don't let that crazy* alteh kocker *fill your head*," his mother had warned.

"*Your mother doesn't want you hearing my stories, nuh?*" the old man had said. Flashing his dentures, pushing a plastic chessman across the board. "*Too much for you, she thinks. But* I *think, my boy, that you can handle it.*" And beneath his breath, he had continued. Community leaders taken out and shot …

"*Why?*" Yoni had interrupted in a whisper. "*Why let themselves be shot?*"

"*It wasn't a matter of let, my boy. When ten Gestapo*"—pronounced with the Yiddish "sh"—"*with machine guns break down a man's door in the middle of the night, drag that man from his bed, put him against the wall …*" A shrug. "*Any resistance he puts up is doomed to fail, and the consequences to be borne by his family. There is nothing he can do. It was not a matter of* let."

The inside of Elter-Zayde's upper left forearm bore a six-digit number, tattooed in faded blue. Of ten brothers and sisters, he had been the one survivor.

"So. It started with the Einsatzgruppen, the Special Action Groups. They came into a ghetto or a village or a town and ordered the prominent Jews to gather the rest together. They announced that we were to be transferred to a new location. They shot the

leaders, burned the temples. Then came the 'resettlement.' These were the words they used. 'Resettlement,' 'transfer,' 'special action.' That is a good one, nuh? 'Special Action.'" An off-kilter grin. "*It all came down to the same thing: first slave labor, then extermination.*"

From the next room had come the sound of Yoni's mother vacuuming, his brothers and sisters—he was the youngest of six—playing unconcerned.

"*We handed over our valuables and jewelry. We boarded the slave transports, the railway cars. Packed tightly together. No food or water. No room to sit, let alone lie down. No hygiene, no toilets, not even straw; the sick along with the well—who, of course soon became sick themselves. To the Germans we were subhuman,* Untermenschen. *We deserved no better. Standing at first in urine, then in feces and corpses. A woman once told me, through tears, that she had birthed a baby in one of these cars and had no choice but to throw the newborn out the window during the journey. And in this horror before God, she was far from alone.*

"*And then, upon arriving at the camps, came the Vernichtungslager, the selection. Men from women, old from young, healthy from infirm. Bullets were not to be wasted, you understand, if it could be avoided. Instead, we were starved to death, worked to death. A man from Mauthausen told me of a favorite method there. Men, women, and children were led barefoot in the morning to a quarry. At the bottom of the steps, guards loaded rocks onto their shoulders and made the prisoners carry them to the top. Raining blows upon their bowed backs the entire way. Then the prisoners came back down, accepted a still heavier load, and climbed again, beneath an even thicker storm of blows, accompanied now by strikes from a bludgeon. By nighttime, bodies were strewn all along the staircase. And not a bullet had been 'wasted.'*"

Yoni blinking back tears; his great-grandfather leaning forward, speaking ever more intently, but softly so Mother would not hear.

"*But sometimes, out in the field, 'liquidation' did require the expenditure of valuable ammunition. There was a time in the Ukraine. In the grand scheme, a relatively minor mass execution, but one that was reported at Nuremberg and so became a matter of record. And did it bring a hush of horror over the courtroom? It did, my boy. It did. A sworn affidavit given by an engineer of a branch office of a German construction firm. On October the fifth of 1942, he witnessed the murder of five thousand Jews.*

"*Men and women, children of all ages. Ordered to undress by an SS man who carried a riding crop. Forced to sort their clothes by shoes, top clothing, and underclothing. Herr Graebe, the engineer who gave the report in Nuremberg, said that there were great piles of clothing, thousands of pairs of shoes. Then the men and women and children moved, naked, to line up by a mound of earth. There was no crying, said Herr Graebe; no pleading for mercy, no weeping or wailing. But were there tears standing in eyes? There were, my boy. There were. He described one family: a silver-haired grandmother cooing to a year-old girl, making the baby laugh with delight, as the young father stood with his ten-year-old son, holding the boy's hand, talking to him in a low voice, pointing at the sky, seeming to explain something to him.*

"*Then the SS man with the whip began counting off groups of twenty, who moved around the mound to the edge of a pit. Another SS man sat there, feet dangling over the edge, cigarette dangling from his mouth, holding a tommy gun. And the pit was filled with bodies, nude and covered in blood and excrement, men and women and children and babies, some still alive, writhing, twitching. And the newest batch was ordered to climb in among the sea of previous victims.*

"*Nineteen forty-two. They had not yet perfected their techniques with their cursed German efficiency. Not yet realized that the pesticide Zyklon-B could, in extreme doses, liquidate six thousand Jews per day without 'wasting' a single bullet. In Auschwitz, we had four great gas chambers. Two doctors—doctors!*" Here Elter-Zayde had paused, turning his eyes beseechingly heavenward. "... *two doctors on duty at the gates would separate incoming prisoners. Anyone deemed incapable of heavy work was earmarked for what they were told was delousing. Of course, that included the children of tender years, too young for hard labor. Women would sense something—the stench from the crematoriums could not be entirely concealed—and try to hide the children beneath their clothes. But they were always found out. Those selected were marched away from the others, over well-kept lawns and pretty beds of flowers, all to the accompaniment of sweet and soothing music, an orchestra of pretty young German girls playing merry selections from Viennese and Parisian operettas—nothing heavy or foreboding like Beethoven. Then they were locked inside hermetically sealed chambers. If they had not realized from the nauseating stench on the air that something was amiss, surely they did now, seeing that these so-called delousing showers had no drains, and that they were packed in like sardines. But, of course, it was too late. Men, women, and children. Men, women, and children.*

"*Mushroom-shaped lids in the ceiling were lifted. Amethyst-blue crystals of hydrogen cyanide, Zyklon-B, rained down. Those in charge knew when everyone was dead, because the screaming stopped. Still, they routinely waited another half hour, to be certain, before opening the doors and hosing off the shit and the blood, for Jews in extremis would not only befoul themselves but would pile against the door, clawing at each other in their desperation to escape. Only then, after half an hour of silence, would the Nazis twist out the gold from the mouths of the dead.*

"*And did the world know? Of course it knew. Something like this is not concealable. Six million men, women, and children. Of course the world knew. And it turned a blind eye.*

"*So! Your mother wants to spare you these tales, my boy. She is a tender sort. And your brothers and sisters: soft. But you, my boy, are hard. I see that in you, Yoni. And I urge you most vehemently: never forget. Those who forget history must live through it again. Nobody looks out for Jews except Jews. We must never again let down our guard. Even now, looking around, one sees an ill wind blowing.*"

That had been fifteen years ago. Now Elter-Zayde was dead. And the ill wind had picked up.

Yoni had not forgotten.

You, my boy, are hard.

His head rocked gently with the motion of the train. *Never again.*

PRINCETON, NJ

"And so, despite the multitude of cavalry, despite the vast advances in ballistic warfare during the six centuries since Agincourt—and the battlefield at Waterloo was doubtless, thanks to heavy black-powder artillery, a tremendously noisy and smoky affair—the crucial element, the *crisis* of the battle, remained the clash of infantry versus infantry." As Dalia spoke, her eye wandered across the front rows of the amphitheater. "Even in today's era of remote-control warfare, infantry remains the single most crucial element of any army. Air power can effectively degrade an enemy but cannot, alone, destroy one. A bomber or drone cannot hit a small contingent of soldiers under cover without a friendly land force offering guidance. And terrain, once seized, cannot be held without infantry to hold it."

Students bowed over laptops, typing notes, checking Instagrams, playing solitaire. One girl wore bright red ribbons in her hair. A boy with hooded eyes looked still drunk from the night before.

"As you bend to this weekend's essay, picture in your minds the rich, harrowing tapestry of wounds suffered at Waterloo. Injuries from grapeshot and musket and blade and lance. Heads and limbs taken off by cannonball. Envision a battlefield covered with moaning, feverish casualties. Dying horses whimpering among the men. Shock, sepsis, peritonitis, dehydration, loss of blood. Men missing hands, arms, jaws. Legs, feet, ears, tongues. Germs festering. Imagine the sounds, the smells. And then recall Wellington's statement after he had finally, at long last, vanquished

Napoleon Bonaparte, the scourge of Europe: 'Next to a battle lost, the greatest misery is a battle gained.' And give me thirty-five hundred words, if you would be so kind, striving to make sense of that sentiment."

She gathered her materials, slipped out a side door before the inevitable grade-grubbers could swamp the podium, and began walking briskly across campus. The afternoon was overcast, fitting her mood. Her worst self was coming to the fore, trying to rub her students' noses in something ugly. Few to none of these privileged children would ever serve. Of course, a refusenik such as herself should be gratified by that. Less grist for the military-industrial mill. Still …

When the silver Altima pulled up and a rear door opened, she felt surprise—the original ground rules had made clear that she was never to be seen with the Israelis anywhere near campus. Then she felt hope: they must have discovered something she could give Horowitz, something that could not wait.

David Feigenbaum sat behind the wheel. Gavril Meir slouched in back. Dalia slipped onto the creaky brown vinyl upholstery and closed the door quickly behind her as the car pulled back into traffic.

Meir handed her a digital notebook. A scanned Mossad dossier: a black-and-white picture of a pretty girl staring boldly back at her photographer. JANA DAHAN. The photograph was six years old, dating from the girl's enlistment. She would now be in her midtwenties—about Zvi's age, Dalia could not help thinking.

Jana Dahan had scored high on her *bagrut*. She had trained at Batar Zikim and spent ten months at a checkpoint in Haifa. Then she had become the target of an al-Aqsa bomb. Her wounds, pictured in another photograph, had been serious but not fatal. Upon release from the hospital, she had transferred to intelligence. From there, out of the IDF and into the Mossad.

Someone with initials *YY* had made notes on the Mossad file. Jana's father had died of heart disease almost two decades ago. The mother had never remarried and still lived in Ramat Denya. There were no siblings. Jana had spent her childhood summers with an aunt in Manhattan. This last fact had qualified her for a classified program called Di Yerushe—apparently, an undercover operation featuring an American arm. In a third and final photograph, the girl's expression was darkly amused, crackling with acumen and self-awareness.

Meir took the notebook, worked it, and handed it back. A fringe website now. An article datelined yesterday: "Promoting Israeli Democracy by Exposing Secrets of the National Security State." The author opened with a brief attack on Israel's mainstream press for not daring to write a similar piece. Then she or he described a funeral of mysterious provenance and major significance, which nevertheless went unreported around the world. Naomi Orenstein, sixty-one years of age, the Mossad director's wife of four decades, had died two days ago in a single-vehicle crash on the road between Tel Aviv and Jerusalem. Alone in the car, she had lost control for unknown reasons, hit the guard rail, and perished instantly—or so the official story went.

Dalia remembered the amateurish recording: muffled clattering, muted wind. "Shookran*, Naomi.*"

"*Vilde chaya*," she murmured to herself. Wild animals.

They turned a corner. Meir lit a Noblesse and cracked open a window. "This was our ally within the Institute." His lack of affect struck Dalia as exaggerated, compensatory. "We'll have no further help from the inside."

Even as Dalia struggled to process the words, he was taking back the notebook and handing her something else. The gun was small but surprisingly heavy. A revolver: wooden grip, nickel finish, four-inch barrel. She could picture John Wayne holding this gun.

She hefted it, getting the feel. Once, long ago, a fellow professor had tried to embarrass her in front of an all-male department by inviting her to a shooting range. He had thought that because of her gender and her *sarvanim* deferment, she would demur. Of course, she had no better option than to agree—and then had found the experience startlingly pleasurable: the Uzi liquid in her hand, light and easy to handle, with very little recoil; the sense of power coursing up from her heels, filling her entire body.

Meir reached over, thumbed the lever, and swung out the cylinder. “Five rounds, and one beneath the firing pin.” He closed the cylinder. “Just remember, safety first. Have you ever fired a gun?”

“Once.”

“Then you know it’s not as easy as it might seem. But you can handle it if need be.”

She smiled wryly. “Playing with guns. What could go wrong?”

But after a moment, she slipped the weapon into her purse. After another moment, she gestured that she wanted a cigarette for herself. Fourteen years had passed since she last smoked. Her throat burned on the first drag. She coughed on the second. On the third, she cracked her window, pitched out the cigarette, and watched it roll sparking into a frost-caked gutter.

They turned another corner. “You’re it,” said Feigenbaum from the driver’s seat. “Our last best chance.”

Meir nodded gravely. “Dalia: we’re counting on you.”

In her mind’s eye, Zvi turned to look back as he climbed the hill to the gate of the base. He had been counting on her, too.

GALLERY PLACE STATION, WASHINGTON, DC

Currents of Friday evening shoppers circulated: spending money at Urban Outfitters and Aveda Spa and AT&T Mobility, consuming calories at Thai Chili and Sushi-Go-Round and Häagen-Dazs.

Jana hung back, letting herself briefly lose her targets before reacquiring them. Thanks to a remotely installed keystroke logging program, she knew that Lydia’s mother would be picking them up at eight sharp. That left her twenty-five minutes. Plenty of time. Didn’t want to spook them. It had to seem breezy.

The two teenaged girls drifted toward the ice cream parlor. Lydia Thompson was coltish and long-legged. Her friend was chubby, with bright metal braces. Jana fell into line just behind them. "If I ever had a boyfriend who did that," Lydia was saying, "I would so totally bust him."

"I would so totally get Brett to beat him up," said the chubby one. "Brett's, like, really protective of me."

"Boyfriends," Jana said. She smiled. "They're like dogs. They can't even help it."

An initial reluctance to engage, hardwired into any young woman's brain. "Totally," Lydia said then.

"When my boyfriend cheated on me," Jana said, "I hooked up with one of his friends. Just to get him back."

"Oh, my God," said the chubby one.

"Once," said Lydia, "my boyfriend was hanging out with one of my best friends? And I felt sorry for her, because she didn't even know what kind of game he was playing? But I didn't say anything, because I wanted to, like, take my time and really get back at him. Which I totally did: I hooked up with his brother."

The line moved forward. Lydia ordered Pralines and Cream, and her friend got Rocky Road. Jana considered her options, settling on Cookie Dough Dynamo.

They took their ice cream to a bench. Jana told a story about the time she caught a boyfriend spying on her, reading her texts. So she had written messages implying that she was going to get him a PlayStation for his birthday. Then his birthday came, but of course, no PlayStation. And he couldn't say anything or he would be totally busted. But the look on his face …

Lydia laughed. Clearly, she was the leader between the two girls—the Miriam, if you liked. One time, Lydia said, she and a friend had been walking around Veterans Plaza when a guy came up and offered to buy them drinks. This had been, like, two years ago. She was twelve years old, but the guy had treated them as if they were grown-ups. He said he was a casting director for a film company and was always looking for pretty young girls, and had Lydia, like, done any modeling? And she had totally realized he was a con man. Her friend had wanted to go with him, but Lydia put her foot down and said no way.

They shared tastes of their ice cream, and Jana wandered out front with them. Within sight of Chinatown's Friendship Archway, a Toyota 4Runner idled. "That's our ride," Lydia said. "It was nice meeting you."

Jana peered through the smoked side window of the Toyota. Christina Thompson sitting behind the wheel. The dark hair that had puddled so fetchingly on the hotel pillow was now pinned up above that smooth, elegant neck. The woman's gaze brushed Jana's face. For an instant, she gave no sign of recognition. Then it clicked, as clearly as a rifle bolt sliding home, and she did an almost comical double take.

The girls were piling into the 4Runner.

"Hey, Mom!"

"Hi, Mrs. Thompson!"

The eyes remained on Jana's face. "Hi," Jana said evenly through the open door.

Christina's mouth hung open. Jana winked. "Nice to meet you guys," she called to the girls.

She turned and walked away just as the car door closed.

* * *

In the Columbia Heights apartment, she texted the number and waited.

Nine o'clock. Nine-thirty. She sat at the kitchen table, sipping cold tea. A cockroach skittered across the linoleum floor and disappeared under the exposed radiator.

Evidently, the woman had not received the message. At a quarter of ten, Jana had just decided to force the issue, when the phone rang. The caller ID read THOMPSON, CHRISTINA.

"Christina," she answered.

A brief pause. "Who is this?"

"You don't remember me?"

Another pause—longer, heavier.

"I have video," Jana said. "From the hotel. Do you want me to send it to you? Or maybe I can just show you next time we run into each other—at church, I think. Grace Episcopal, yes? With your family?"

"What do you want?" the woman asked.

"Listen closely, Christina, because I'm only going to say it once."

TRENTON, NJ

They moved carefully through the late-night hush, picking their way over scattered toys in the hallway.

Still not quite the lead-lined subterranean room in Langley, Dalia reflected as she stepped into the study, but getting closer. A bulletin board on casters had been rolled out before the wall of diplomas. The desk was mostly cleared, making room for a large flat-screen monitor. Shades had been drawn over the windows, blocking out the moonlit suburban street, and the Buddha on his high shelf had been turned away, as if to spare him an offensive sight.

Following behind her in the hallway, McConnell stepped on a toy, which chirped brightly, "Hi, I'm Emmy, and my favorite food is bananas! I love you." With a peevish look, he closed the door.

Horowitz paid no attention. He turned around the bulletin board to reveal a three-tiered pyramid of thumbtacked placards connected by strands of black yarn.

Up top was the ramsad, looking resolute behind a podium. The photograph had come from the man's previous life with the IDF General Staff. The prime minister and the defense minister stood behind him, before a blue Star of David on a white field.

A strand of black yarn ran down one tier, connecting the director to a young man standing on a street corner, perhaps waiting for a traffic light to change. Enlarged and pixelated and bearing a CIA watermark in one corner, the photo showed a handsome man with mirrored sunglasses and black curly hair. Block letters declared him to be one Yoni Yariv.

"The initials in the dossier," said Horowitz, "match only one known Mossad operative: Yoni Yariv, the other voice in the recording."

Below Yariv, the yarn forked into three branches. One led to the most recent photograph from the file: JANA DAHAN, with wicked merriment and suppressed fury gleaming in her eyes. The other two led to placards bearing typewritten bullet points but no names or pictures.

"Our mystery man." Horwitz tapped the leftmost unlabeled card. "Who, we are told, 'will see it through'—at least, according to the psychologists. A veteran who 'suffers from PTSD, misdiagnosed as mere combat stress.' Who has recently suffered a failed marriage. And who can get 'close enough to whisper a secret. Within an arm's length of countless secondary targets.'"

He thumped the last card. "This is 'the woman in charge of the event … a trusted pillar of her Washington community.' Married mother of four; a churchgoer. Yet she is 'completely *farmisht*'—dysfunctional. She keeps a secret. Our conspirators see an opportunity here. Which brings us full circle, back to …"

Another thump of the index finger. "Jana Dahan, who has already been moved 'into position' and 'awaits only the final order to proceed.'"

"You've been busy," Dalia said. She had sent along the file, via McConnell, only eight hours ago.

"I asked for a name and a face, and you came through. Just holding up my end."

McConnell's green eyes focused intently on the board, the way a cat might look at an unsuspecting bird. In that grim determination, Dalia could see the younger man, lean and ambitious, hidden beneath the slack, pink jowls.

Horowitz rapped Jana's photograph again, with a knuckle this time. "As of this afternoon, she's been scanned into facial-recognition software. Cross-referenced with tollbooth cameras, INS, DMV, every database we have. She's on TIDE, the Terrorist Identifier Datamart Environment. That means watch lists, and cooperation, if needed, from Homeland fusion centers, which means Customs and Border, TSA, Coast Guard, ECHELON, and EEC. Local and state police. FBI, CIA, NSA, DOJ. The whole damned alphabet. All on the US taxpayer's dime. And no pesky red tape to tangle us up. I haven't given any one entity enough information to put the pieces together—which means I haven't given nearly enough to justify the expenditure. Congressional committee comes sniffing around, heads will roll, starting with mine."

He read the question in Dalia's furrowed brow. And she read the answer in his. He had put himself so far out on a limb for the same reason she had: because Jews needed Israel, flaws and all.

"Yariv's last note on her file came about three years ago. So I looked at a four-month window of US Customs surveillance at major airports … and found this." He reached for the computer's mouse. Grainy black-and-white footage appeared on the monitor: a three-quarters top-down view of a customs station, crowd-control lanes, haggard international travelers. A green time code in one corner scissored off fractions of seconds, starting at 04:06:18:41 on 11/11. "JFK. Three years ago, almost to the day."

A young woman stepped forward and slid a passport across a desk. Horowitz paused the footage to open another window alongside: the most recent photo from the dossier. A sudden outbreak of red dots on the two faces. "Eighty-two nodal matches. We consider twenty an actionable hit. The flight was a red-eye from Paris. Now, stay with me …"

Minimizing the images, he opened another camera feed. Watermark HERTZ, time stamp about an hour after the first. Another grainy top-down view. No need now for the computer to identify common nodal points. The pretty young woman was filling out paperwork, then offering a credit card and driver's license. "Her passport belonged to one Carine Fournier—who vanished off the face of the earth, far as I can tell, the instant she passed through immigration. She rented the car as Tiffany Watson, giving a fictional address in Rhode Island. Nine days later, she dropped the car off just north of San Francisco. Electronic toll information lets us track her progress …" He opened a satellite map of the United States, with date/time balloons in northeastern states connected by a zigzagging red line. "… as far west as Illinois."

Jana's slender, foxy face watched dispassionately from the bulletin board.

"She pops up again fifty-two days later—in Portland, Oregon, applying for a job at a local drugstore." He shrank the map for a moment and opened a .jpg screen capture from another security camera. And again their quarry. Even hunched over an application inside a tiny office, there was something insolent in her carriage.

"She gave a legal residence near West Hills." He clicked back to the map. "So I called a buddy in the Oregon DHS field office. He has a friend in the local PD. You think *I've* had a busy day. First they spoke with the super of the apartment, who says he last saw Tiffany Watson on October eleventh. He didn't go inside until last week, after the grace period for overdue rent expired. But all activity in the apartment, according to water, PSE&G, Verizon, and the post office, stopped around the eleventh. Plenty of fingerprints and genetic material inside. Prints match Jana Dahan's military personnel file. Remains of an iPhone recovered from the garbage disposal. And I do mean 'remains.'"

McConnell and Dalia exchanged a glance.

"As it happens, the young lady was well known to local PD. She spent most of her after-work evenings in bars—rough ones. Militia types, survivalists, white power. Scrapes with the law here and there, but never any charges. Maintained as low a profile as possible, considering the company she kept. All of which jibes, of course, with this undercover operation, Di Yerushe. One of these bars, called Shaky Ground, was already on PD radar because of a man named Luke Harris. A local, last seen there—his regular watering hole—on the night of October tenth."

He clicked. Coarse black-and-white CCTV footage played: a

rough-looking bar, neon beer signs, crowded tables. An unoccupied drum kit tucked off in one corner. Coolers lining a wall. Horowitz paused the video and used the cursor to point out two blurs, barely recognizable as a man and a woman. "Here's Harris. Hard to see his dance partner's face, but ten to one it's our Janala. On the seventeenth, one week after this video was taken, a girl from the bar finally wondered where Harris had been. Visited his cabin on Mount Hood. Noticed his truck missing. Front door locked. She found a broken padlock out back and opened the cellar door. Smelled decomp and called the law. Next thing you know, Hood River County Sheriff's on the scene. They found a body and a murder weapon—pair of bolt cutters from the toolshed. Official cause of death is penetrating head trauma to the occipital bone. October out there is cold nights, warm days; inside a cellar, somewhat open to the elements, but closed for the most part to varmints. Decay consistent, according to the pathologist, with death around the tenth or eleventh. So our story comes together. On the night of the tenth, Tiffany Watson goes with Harris from Shaky Ground to his cabin on the mountain—where none of her fingerprints or DNA were recovered, I should mention, because the scene had been washed with bleach. The next day, she goes back to her apartment, where she's seen by the super in midafternoon. One neighbor also reports seeing a red Ford pickup briefly parked by the curb. Harris owned a red 2014 Ford F150. As of ninety minutes ago, we've got a Be-On-The-Lookout in the entire lower forty-eight."

Dalia pursed her lips thoughtfully and said, "She's already been 'moved into position.' That means within striking distance, I'd guess, of this 'pillar of her Washington community.'"

"The BOLO includes MPDC. Washington State Police, too, although I find that a less likely target. Unfortunately, we can't scan every face picked up by every security camera in the DC metropolitan area—at least, not without using so much computer time that we're guaranteed to get the wrong kind of attention. On the other hand, we've got one hard address: the apartment in Manhattan where she spent summers growing up. The cousin, Miriam, died six years ago—leukemia. The uncle died of bladder cancer fifteen months later. But Aunt Becca still lives in the same apartment on Eighty-Eighth and Madison. We're watching landline and mobiles, looking into phone records for the past three years; also intercepting network packets, monitoring Internet activity and email. No FISA warrant or District Court approval, by the way, for any of this. But until someone catches on, I say push ahead. Desperate times." McConnell scratched absently at a pale scar that curved around his forearm. "Facial recognition's linked up to street cams within a five-block radius. If she contacts the aunt in New York, we'll see her or hear her."

"And then?" McConnell asked.

"That gets tricky. She's trained in field ops, hand-to-hand. My feeling is that once we make a positive ID, we let a tac team do the heavy lifting."

"Talk about getting attention."

"Let's be honest," said Horowitz. "This only ends one way. It's just a question of when. I'm willing to go down with the ship, but only after we get Jana in custody."

A few moments of quiet as they absorbed this.

"This pillar of the community ..." McConnell stopped scraping one thumbnail with the other and looked up. "... who has 'worked hard to keep her secret.' What's the implication? Crime? Infidelity? Drugs?"

"Great minds," said Horowitz. "No lack of professional ratfuckers in DC. These guys live by sniffing out dirty secrets. I've got some calls in."

Quiet again.

"You haven't even heard the best part yet," Horowitz continued. "Along with the body in that cellar on Mount Hood, the county sheriff's office found a dozen crates. White-power pamphlets, gun parts for full-auto conversions, knives, hand grenades. Standard-issue asshole gear. Frankly, nobody was all that surprised—or all that sorry—to see this guy go. Live by the sword, et cetera. But unlike the Hood River sheriff, I know that Tiffany Watson, a.k.a. Jana Dahan, is involved with something big and bad. So after my buddy interviewed Tiffany Watson's neighbors, I asked him to head out to Mount Hood. A little grumbling, but he did it. Went in right under that police tape with a putty knife and a razor blade. Scraped some samples into Ziploc baggies. Fast-tracked analysis at the DHS lab. What do you think he found?"

Dalia closed her eyes. Suddenly her scalp was crawling again.

"*And he can get how close?*"

"Close enough to whisper a secret. And within arm's length of countless secondary targets. We'll reach dozens. Maybe more."

"The samples from that cellar," Horowitz said, "tested positive for cyclotrimethylenetrinitramine—that's plastic explosive. Also for isopropyl methylphosphonic acid." He let that hang in the air for a moment. "Sarin. Specifically, the compound into which sarin degrades."

The irony was appalling. Not just a bombing attack, but chemical weapons. Outlawed by Geneva, embraced by Saddam and al-Assad—and, of course, by the architects of the so-called Final Solution: Himmler and Eichmann and *der Führer* himself. Dalia's eyes opened again. A distant bell rang inside her skull. There was no depth, she thought bitterly, to which her people would not sink in their frantic scramble to become no better than their enemies.

Jana would not go through with it. In the girl's face, Dalia recognized an essential, undeniable humanity. Compromised, angry, complicated, hurt, scarred … but still human.

But the body in the cellar; the bolt cutters, the penetrating head trauma. Fewer than one-fifth of soldiers, she taught her students, actually fired their weapons at exposed enemies. Man was not by nature a close-range killer. Usually, he took another life only to save his own. In fact, no species killed its own willingly, as a general rule. In territorial and mating battles, combatants threatened and postured. They bit, stung, clawed, and butted horns. But only when fighting other species did they gut, gore, go for the kill.

But Jana Dahan was one of the minority: a natural-born killer. When the moment came, she had not hesitated.

A sudden shadow came fluttering across the study: a night bird arrowing outside the shaded window. When it thumped against the glass, Dalia shrieked aloud.

CHAPTER SIX

HOPEWELL, NJ

Yoni Yariv pulled off the woodland road into a misty shaded glen.

He donned a black tactical field jacket, thin nylon gloves, and a dark knit cap. Getting out of the rented black Cadillac DTS, he released the trunk latch. From the gray duffel he had taken from a storage unit in Queens, he removed a Jericho 941 pistol and belt-loop holster, suppressor, extra magazines, tactical folding knife, Vortex Viper HD night-vision binoculars, and a rucksack containing eight insulated squibs. And finally, a black hardside case with shoulder strap, containing a PGM Hécate II sniper rifle.

After consulting his phone, he tested the breeze and struck off upwind. Not quite one in the morning, and the forest was alive with drips, murmurs, hoots, and rustles. *Druchus*—way out in the wild. Ground slipped and squelched underfoot. Silver moonlight picked out branches weighted with ice. A cataract of weird light hung above the horizon. He found the North Star and then, working backward, the Big Dipper.

Once, at the ramsad's behest, he had spent two weeks with a Bedouin tribe in the Sinai, digging up weapons caches and then reburying them elsewhere for reasons that had remained obscure. During long nights around spitting campfires, a sheikh had shared with him millennia-old secrets to survival in the desert. The Great Bear pointed north, said the sheikh, but if the Great Bear was beneath the horizon, Cassiopeia could serve the same purpose. Sand dunes formed at ninety degrees to the prevailing winds, meaning they ran north-south—except for the shallower crescent-shaped dunes, which pointed west. Camels were sources not only of milk and meat and labor, but, in a pinch, of water as well. The beasts could consume a hundred liters in less than ten minutes, and the water stayed in their stomachs for two weeks. But the most important lesson of all had been *shvoye*—patience. "*You need less than you think, and you think more than you should. The desert eats alive men who run in circles. When you start to chase your own tail, count back from five.*"

Now Yoni approached the safe house slowly and carefully, pausing regularly to correct his course, to scan the forest and recheck the direction of the wind and listen to the music of the night.

When the GPS indicated that he was within a thousand meters, he turned south-southeast. Two hundred meters later, he reached a clearing. A smear of Milky Way twinkled above low mountains. In a far corner of the field, shrouded by fog and almost invisible against the backdrop of forest, he found a small stone cottage with dormer windows, a brick chimney, and an old-fashioned well. A long unpaved driveway ran back through old-growth forest, toward a distant country road.

Yoni peered through the Viper infrared goggles. The cottage's windows were curtained, cold. The Nissan Altima parked in the driveway was sheathed in frost. But heat swirled at the base of the chimney, running through pipes, collecting in several mysterious clumps. He could see the line halfway up a toilet tank, where the water stopped. He lowered the binoculars and checked his watch. Twelve minutes past 2:00 a.m.

He might conceivably thunder into the cottage and catch them off guard as they slept. But who knew what precautions they may have taken? And one of the mysterious clumps of heat might be a dog.

Shvoye. Patience.

The suppressor threaded smoothly, quietly, onto the pistol's barrel. He crept closer to the house, stopping frequently to scan for cameras, animals, traps. He came near enough to the east side to discern individual bricks in the chimney. Taking one of the insulated squibs from the rucksack, he set it within twenty meters of the front door. Retreating, he counted ten paces and left another in frozen grass. Circling around the cottage, he set squibs at regular intervals.

East again, calculating the point on the horizon where the sun would rise. Near the edge of the field, he found a suitable ridge. Range about seven hundred meters, less than half the rifle's effective reach. Time it right, and anyone observing the position from inside the house would be dazzled by the breaking dawn. His shoulders rejoiced when he shrugged off the black hardside case.

To prevent glare, he dropped a hood over the Scrome LTE J10 F1 scope. Then he unfolded the rifle's front bipod, planting it firmly in the crunching frost, took up position—facedown, right leg bent at the knee—and focused on the cozy little cottage's front door.

Centering the knob in the mil-dot reticle, he adjusted windage and elevation controls. Then, to eliminate reflection that might spoil his shot, he dropped on a honeycomb filter.

Lifting the rear monopod, he tracked left and then right, to one curtained window and then the other, and mimed pulling the trigger. He preferred not to kill both men right off the bat, but to kill one and disable the other, for purposes of interrogation. Seven rounds in the detachable box magazine, another full magazine in the case if necessary.

He double-checked the silenced pistol, then readied on his phone the presets with which he would detonate the squibs. He scooped up some sleet and moved it around in his mouth, moistening his tongue.

And waited.

Discomfort, cold, thirst, hunger—a small price considering what hung in the balance. And nothing compared to what his ancestors had gone through. *You, my boy, are hard.*

The desert eats alive men who run in circles.

Shvoye. Patience.

* * *

Around 5:00 a.m., the sky grew pink and quickly turned to rouge. The fog began to burn away, and the frosted trees to steam.

Gooseflesh prickled beneath Yoni's coat. Ice melting, dripping and trickling. He had been looking through the scope for the past twenty minutes without a break. The small of his back, his elbow and knee joints, throbbed. He gave his head a small shake and clambered to his feet.

He relieved himself behind the nearby copse of balsam fir. Just as he was zipping up, he caught a flashing shadow behind a cottage window. He scampered back to his post, grabbing the binoculars.

Behind a curtain, a heat signature moved. Another swirled in the other direction—an endless Möbius strip, a magic trick with no start and no end. Then came a waist-high spurt of color—a stove, perhaps.

He assumed position again: facedown, right knee bent. His left hand picked up the phone, and he found the number corresponding to the squib nearest the front door.

He conducted a last quick inventory: backup magazine, Jericho, knife.

Ready.

He triggered the first preset.

The squib popped, spattering dead grass and frozen mud.

His right cheek spot-welded to the stock, gooseflesh gone now, nerves alive. Front door square in his sights. First shot would be to center mass. Then the head shot. The kill.

The door remained closed.

Five, four, three, two, one.

Lifting the rear monopod, he tracked to a window. The stirring shadow again. A moving corner of curtain. A glint, a pause. Another glint. Binoculars? Rifle scope? Mirror? Then a glimpse of a face. An intellectual's wispy beard. Cigarette burning between clenched teeth.

Yoni fired.

The rifle kicked, but less than one might expect, thanks to the high-efficiency muzzle brake. Cold shot, but bull's-eye. In the half-instant before the curtain fell closed, through the scope, Yoni saw the air behind the man's head blossom in pink mist.

The flat, dry echo rang back off the wall of forest. Birds startling into flight as Yoni worked the bolt, jolting another cartridge into the chamber. He took aim again. In the zone. Ready for anything. He couldn't miss.

His ears were ringing. He had forgotten earplugs.

No sign of the other one.

He traded the rifle scope for the Viper and found confusing heat signatures: another man or even two besides the one he'd hit, on the move. The spreading pool of blood was a purple infrared swirl.

He considered taking another blind shot through the window. But the angle was chancy. He stood, keeping in a crouch. Taking the phone, the Viper, the Jericho, the knife, and leaving behind the rifle, he moved away in a clumsy loping squat.

He caught a glint of brass. *Later.*

He circled around toward the far side of the house. Gavril Meir would never know what hit him. Yoni had met the old man once, years ago. A conference at a seaside resort. The water blood-red beneath the setting sun. They had just found evidence of a nuclear reactor under construction at Deir al-Zur. The argument had grown heated, but Meir had stayed calm and counseled back-channel diplomacy. In that instant, Yoni had lost all respect for the man. The schmuck cultivated a hard reputation, but beneath it all, he was soft. Look how easily Yoni was sneaking up on him now—coming around the back of the cottage, glissading down slippery frozen mud, between trees, skittering toward an outdoor oil storage tank.

His ears filled with a thin, singing ring. No matter. He was doing it. Burning away the deadwood, cutting away the necrotic flesh. Dragging the older generation into the only possible future. Nearing the back door, he raised the Jericho in his right hand, the phone in his left.

A back window was cracked open. And the back door was swinging ajar, as if caught in a breeze. Almost lazily, a realization surfaced in his mind. Window open despite the wintry morning chill, back door flapping in the breeze. Put the pieces together, and what did you get? His surprise attack from the rear was not such a surprise after all.

Something fast and heavy came blurring out the back door. Low to the ground, snarling. The gun jerked up and fired. Blood arced into the air. But the German shepherd still had momentum, even in death. Slamming into Yoni, it knocked him off his feet.

He rolled the dead dog off him and sat up. A needle pricked him in the left shoulder. He grunted, more surprised than hurt, and saw in retrospect the muzzle flash behind the gapped window near the back door. Another shot cut the air a centimeter from his right ear. He returned fire, emptying the magazine, all nine shots, each jolting the gun in his hand. Window glass turning white. Splinters of stone exploding from the cottage facade and whining off into the trees. The oil tank rupturing, not exploding.

Yoni half-crawled back up the slope and slipped around the thick trunk of a hoary old oak. He dropped the gun, the barrel steaming against the ice. He had not heard a single shot. The ringing ears. *God damn them all to hell.*

He was shuddering. Going into shock? *Motherfucker.* Where was the bullet? His fingertips searched his right flank. Then his left. There was a lot of blood but still no pain. And no bullet. Maybe it had passed through. Maybe he had imagined it in the first place. He had never been shot before. He had expected it would feel like a kicking horse, not a jabbing needle. And had the dog bitten him? He could not find a wound beneath the coat, but the entire right half of his torso was a numb, glutinous mess. He smelled cordite mixed with blood mixed with shit. He could feel his breath bubbling, feel himself panting and grunting. But his ears conveyed nothing except that annoying tinnitus ring.

He picked up the Jericho—still warm but not hot—ejected the magazine, and jammed in a fresh one. He used the mirror on the grip to look at the house. Hand shaking. Trembling and tilting. Leaking oil storage tank, spiderwebbed window, dead dog. No sign of Meir.

The phone was somehow gone. There, in a puddle of spent shells and melting ice. He picked it up and set off every squib he had planted, out front and on both sides, in quick succession. Make the goatfucker think he was surrounded.

He pushed up. Leaned against the tree. *Steady.* Two-handed grip on the pistol, keeping low, moving again toward the house. Quickly, quickly, before his trembling legs failed him.

He stepped through spilled oil. No one fired. He could see curls of smoke from the squibs drifting over the snow-crusted chimney. The back door was eight meters away. He passed the dead dog. Now six meters. No trees between here and there. He reached the door. Still ajar. Still no pain, but legs dangerously weak. Glancing back, he saw the trail of blood he had left. Lots of blood.

He pushed the door open with one foot. Went in gun blazing, like John fucking Wayne. Something flicked the collar of his coat. Something punched him in the chest. Returning fire, he emptied the Jericho again. Something fell heavily—he felt more than heard it.

He pushed forward to find Meir, facedown in the narrow hallway. Fat, gray. There really was a tremendous amount of blood. His, Meir's, maybe Feigenbaum's mixed in. The hallway was dark. How much of the darkness was in the corridor and how much in himself, he could not guess.

He slumped against the wall. His right leg was touching Meir's face. A wire in his brain slipped. Darkness. Reconnected. He had to get moving. Cover his tracks. Gather the shells. Get the dead men into their car. Make them disappear.

Flicker. The hallway. Flicker. The ramsad lighting a Gauloise. Jana on the balcony in Herzliya, naked, beautiful. Sweet plum wine. Dusk just falling. Jana. She would finish what he had started.

Dead batteries. Empty glasses. Fallen trees. Dark hallways. Fading. He moved his right leg away from Meir. He didn't want to be touching the man when he died.

Flicker. Graveyards. Murky swimming pools. Wheeling vultures. Pits filled with dead children. His mother vacuuming in the next room.

Flicker. Another hallway. Bright chrome. Flooded with light.

Flicker.

One last effort, pressing against the wall, to regain his feet.

He managed.

Then he moved forward, into the bright hallway, into the blinding light.

NORTH OF TEL AVIV, ISRAEL

An old school friend of Naomi's was telling a story.

Once upon a time, he said, he and Naomi had raided her parents' liquor cabinet. Hoping to conceal the theft, they had taken just a taste from each bottle and mixed it all together. The resulting concoction had gotten them plenty *fershnikit*. Then they spent the rest of the night puking their guts out. And even as Naomi became the sophisticated woman they all had known and loved—a boldface name in the papers, a familiar sight at extravagant government functions—he had remembered with great fondness that young girl with vomit crusted around the corners of her mouth, moaning ruefully that she would never drink again.

People laughed quietly. The ramsad forced a chuckle. Then he stood, murmuring an apology, and moved toward the kitchen.

Past covered mirrors, past the folding bridge table covered with casserole dishes and Tupperware, paper plates and plastic utensils.

In the bathroom, he washed his face. According to the rules of shivah, bereaved were not allowed hot baths, so for the past few days he had been making do with an occasional splash from the sink. He itched. He smelled. Superstitions, he thought resentfully. They should have long since left such rituals behind. But the *kippah serugot*—knitted yarmulkes—had influence beyond their number, and appearances must be maintained.

Leaving the bathroom, instead of turning left toward the living room he went right, toward his study. He had almost made it when a woman cried loudly: "*Gevaldikeh zach*!"

It was Sheba Zingel from the hair salon. She hugged him hard. "Poor thing. We were just saying how terrible you look. How are you holding up? Hard to keep it together, I bet. Behind every great man is a great woman, nuh?" Her voice lowered conspiratorially. "Or a great crime."

"Thank you for coming, Sheba. It means so much. Please forgive me ..." He disengaged as gracefully as he could and continued toward the study.

"You're not working now," she chided. "Shivah and Sabbath to boot."

He gave no reply.

"A good man," Sheba declared as he closed the door on her, "whatever anyone says."

His phone sat on the desk beside the plastic photo cube. Pushing aside the cube, he picked up the phone. Four missed calls. Condolences. A telemarketer. More condolences. And still more condolences. He checked text messages and email. He unlocked drawers, checked second and third phones. Not a peep from Yoni.

Had there been trouble?

Frowning, he locked the drawers again. In the direst scenario, the boy was expendable. Inside this very desk was contact information for the operation's key players. But of course, the ramsad preferred to maintain a layer of insulation between them and himself.

A polite tap at the door. Before he could react peevishly at being interrupted, hinges creaked.

The prime minister of Israel came into the study, gesturing behind him for someone not to follow. He closed the door softly: a large man with an expensive haircut, wearing a suit impeccably tailored to his broad build, and a sorrowful smile.

As a child, the ramsad recalled, the boy who would one day become prime minister had worn his hair in a homemade bowl cut. His secondhand clothing had hung loose, concealing a posture suggestive of a question mark. He had been an infamous bully—on the playground, in back alleys after school—sending many a weaker child home with a bloody nose.

They embraced, kissed cheeks. The prime minister drew back, hands on the ramsad's shoulders. "How are you holding up, my friend?"

"All things considered, okay."

"She was a special woman. She was *heylik*." Sacred. "*Aleha ha-sholem*." May she rest in peace.

The director nodded.

"Leah sends her love. She'll stop by tomorrow with some food." The man gave a final squeeze of the shoulder, hard enough to hurt, moved a step away, and looked at his watch. "I wish I could stay ..."

"It means a lot that you came."

"You'll let us know anything we can do."

"You've done it already."

The prime minister nodded. He turned to leave, then, as if having a last thought, turned back with his hand on the knob. "You should know, my friend, that the yentas are talking."

The director said nothing.

"The scratches on your face ... Of course, I trust you implicitly. But if you find yourself in over your head ..."

"Everything's under control."

A thoughtful pause. "I believe that you know what's best, in the long run. And I do count on you not to … burden me."

The director suppressed a lopsided smile.

"I'll keep the Mishteret off your back," said the prime minister. "The least I can do during this difficult time."

A tight nod. "*A shaynem dank*, my friend." Many thanks.

One last awkward moment. The door opened, then closed. Left alone in the study, the ramsad stood still for a moment. He picked vaguely at the torn black ribbon tied around his left arm. The ribbon chafed. He wanted very much to take it off. But appearances must be maintained, now more than ever.

He took a last moment to arrange his expression. Then he went to rejoin his guests.

ELLICOTT STREET NW, WASHINGTON, DC

"So. What else are you thankful for?"

Silas pondered. A small ridge formed between his eyes. For a few moments, he looked every bit his mother's son. "TV," he said finally.

"Well, that one you can definitely spell. The letters are part of the word."

Silas nodded. His pink tongue poked out with concentration as he bent over, laboriously embarking on a letter *T*.

The phone rang. Michael went into the kitchen. He didn't recognize the number—local 202 area code. "Hello?"

"Michael? Christina."

It took him a moment to make the connection. Christina Thompson from work. Calling him at home at seven thirty on a Saturday night. Was he in trouble? "Hey, Chris. What's up?"

"I hope I'm not interrupting."

He looked into the dining room, where his son had just finished the cross of the *T*. "Nope, nothing special."

"I know you're busy, so I'll get right to it. I'd like to put you on the pool feed at this year's State."

He blinked. The State of the Union was his profession's Super Bowl, Academy Awards, and first moon landing, all rolled into one.

"Michael? You there?"

"Yes. Thank you. Thank you, Christina. I appreciate the opportunity."

"You've earned it, Michael."

"I won't disappoint you."

"First rehearsal tomorrow at 9:00 a.m. Okay? I know it's kind of last-minute."

Stacy was picking up Silas at eight. "I'll be there."

"You can say goodbye to your weekends through January. The good news is, it's double time and a half."

"Thank you, Christina." He felt himself smiling foolishly.

"Like I said, you've earned it."

When he went back to Silas, the boy was working on the *V*. Together they Scotch-taped construction paper feathers to a teardrop-shaped body, fanning out wings. They surveyed their work:

I AM THANKFUL FOR TOYS, dAddY, MOMMY,
SCHOOL, HOUSE, LICORICE, NINJA TURTLES, TV

And the pool feed, Michael thought, not quite believing his sudden stroke of luck. Christina could have chosen any of half a dozen operators for the job, but she had chosen him.

He *had* earned it. He worked hard. And he was good at his job. And the missing leg surely hadn't hurt. "Good optics," as they said on the Hill. War heroes played well on camera for the inevitable behind-the-scenes C-SPAN special.

He pulled his son close, burrowed into soft hair with a kiss. "I love you," he said.

"Love you, too," Silas said absently.

They pinned the paper turkey to the refrigerator with a magnet, spooned ice cream into bowls, and sat together on the couch, watching the "heroes in a half shell" travel back in time to stop the Triceratons from making a black-hole generator. Afterward, they snuggled side by side in Silas' bed, reading *Charlie and the Chocolate Factory* as the cat kneaded a blanket with her front paws. "We are all a great deal luckier than we realize," Michael read. "We usually get what we want, or near enough …"

* * *

Waiting in line at a quarter of nine the next morning, he found the card:

THE OWNER OF THIS CARD HAS
A PROSTHESIS THAT MAY ACTIVATE A
METAL DETECTION DEVICE

On the flip side were his name and photograph, Phil Eggleston's credentials, and the hospital's telephone number. After showing the card, he submitted to a pat-down and wand search. The wand buzzed at his leg. The Secret Service agent operating it gave an apologetic shrug and waved Michael through to take his place in another line before another metal detector.

Ten minutes later, he joined the milling crowd inside Statuary Hall. Bronze and marble sculptures—Helen Keller, Barry Goldwater, Ronald Reagan, Dwight Eisenhower, Samuel Adams, Daniel Webster—lined the chamber's arcing perimeter. Beneath the coffered ceiling, the voices of several dozen men and women echoed and overlapped.

But there was a sense of loose camaraderie, an early-morning coffee-klatch vibe, among coworkers who often socialized in their leisure time. Matt Gutierrez, on the far side of the room, saw Michael and waved but was drawn into conversation before they could make their way toward each other. Moments later, one of the Capitol's two sergeants at arms cornered Michael with a story about a movie he had watched last night—something about a scandal in the church, an investigation, dogged journalism.

With so many people pressing close, Michael had trouble listening. His fight-or-flight reflex kept trying to engage. He remembered a crowded public square in Kirkuk, Iraqis jostling him as his brothers in arms tried to clear the area. Rubbing his eyes, he had refocused on the robot camera. Through the viewfinder he had studied a nine-volt battery, an electric blasting cap, a 120-mm mortar shell. All wired to a Motorola 8530 radio. But no timer. Because somewhere nearby, the bomber was watching. A man Michael had never met—or a woman, or a child—was waiting to trigger a blast, without a thought for wives or husbands who might be widowed, children who might become orphans. Put on a uniform and you became a symbol, both more and less than a person. After Michael had come home, the same uniform that had made strangers want to murder him overseas had made strangers walk up to him on the street to thank him for his service.

At last, Christina Thompson took her place near the entrance to the House Floor. The gabbling took a long moment to subside as she waited with strained patience. In her simple black top and gray pants, with her long dark hair pinned up, she was all business.

"Nice to see everyone," she said at last. Unamplified, her voice nonetheless rang clear and true. The dome's acoustics were legendary—so good that, according to myth, John Quincy Adams had used them to eavesdrop on rivals two centuries before. "You all know me, and most of you know each other. But for the record, my name is Christina Thompson, and I am director of media in the Capitol. For the past four years, I've also had the honor of directing the State of the Union Address. I don't have to tell anyone that this is our moment to shine. Or that it is a logistical nightmare. Or that by the moment of truth, we'll have it down pat. You'll be orchestrating coverage in your sleep. I beg the forgiveness of patient spouses and children in advance."

A ripple of pro forma laughter. Christina smiled. "Today, in this room, we see only the bare bones of the operation. On the day of truth, it will include hundreds of outside broadcasters and journalists and thousands of VIPs. Our responsibility is not only to keep the entire machine running smoothly, but to capture every bit of pomp and circumstance and broadcast it, uninterrupted, to a live audience of forty million people. It is a challenge, but also a thrill and an honor. And everyone is here this morning because I know they can do their job better than anyone else. Please welcome now Special Agent in Charge of Presidential Protection Bob Sykes—his first year handling this detail."

The Secret Service agent looked funereal in black: tall, bald, and so thin that the knobs above and below his temples gleamed beneath the dome's skylight.

"Good morning," he said. "It goes without saying we've got our plates full with this event. Someone asked me yesterday if that means we need to strike a balance between security and expediency. I'll tell you what I told him: No. Conclusively, decisively no. *Our concern is security.* We are good at our jobs, so we will be as unobtrusive as possible. Director Thompson will hit all her marks. Camera timing and cues will not be interrupted. We will coordinate a tremendous joint effort between agencies: USCP, FBI, military, and, of course, Secret Service. We will practice and practice and practice again. We will stay out of your way as much as we can. But our primary concern is security, and on this *we will not compromise*. On the night in question, we'll see an unprecedented number of high-profile protectees clustered together: the president, vice president, Supreme Court, Congress, the entire Cabinet, leaders of industry. And the entire world will be watching."

He made a small bow and stepped aside. A moment of awkward silence before Christina stepped back into place.

"Uh, yes. Thank you, Special Agent in Charge Sykes. So. Assignments. Antry, Cavanaugh, Damplo, Dewese, Liemandt, Leppik, Randall, Robinson, Tomber, Zingarelli, stay here in Statuary. Anker, Cloman, Dixon, Lampkin, Melendez, Rambeau, Reina, Wiechetek, follow Richard—raise your hand, Richard—to the Cannon Rotunda. Carr, Davis, Fontanarosa, Hall, Isaacson, Kinney, Moore, Porter, Samarin, Shaw, Timpe, Venugopal, go with Glenn to Russell. Abendroth, Boligan, Byerlee, Fanzo, Gutierrez, Geringer, Joffrion, Mastelli, Pincus, Tomko, follow Mr. Brooks to the Triangle. And with me on the Floor: Davidson, Flanagan, Fletcher, Jaworski, Jusino, Knorr, Muzzey, Oesterling, Quedens."

Ten minutes later, Michael stood in the House's narrow central aisle. Breathing shallowly, jostled by elbows from every side, feeling like the inside of a rapidly collapsing cake, he tried to keep his facial expression relaxed and neutral.

Putting hands on shoulders, Christina positioned people to his right and left, in front and behind. All standing so close he could smell their deodorant and the coffee on their breath. And today nobody was even holding cameras, which would make everything even tighter.

On Christina's signal, Sergeant at Arms Brian Larkin declared loudly: "Mr. Speaker: the vice president of the United States!" Playing the role today was Mary Davidson of *Daily Press*. She entered the chamber from Statuary Hall, smiling, doing a tight-wristed Queen Elizabeth wave, mouthing *thankyouthankyouthankyou*. Michael mimed raising his kit to his shoulder. He backed up, surrounded by a dozen people: official photographers of House and Senate and White House, members of the Secret Service, FBI, and Capitol Police. Mary proceeded slowly down the aisle, smiling *thankyouthankyouthankyou*. Michael bumped into Assistant Chief Gibson of the USCP, tripped, and went sprawling.

Christina helped him up. "You okay?"

He nodded, blushing, wanting to tell her that his leg had had nothing to do with it. Before he could speak, Gibson said, "Sorry, buddy. My bad."

"There goes the pool feed," Christina announced loudly. "And every major news organization in the country cuts to black. Places."

They tried again. This time Michael bumped into Gibson again but managed to stay on his feet until Mary reached the lectern. "Good," Christina rapped. "Places. Sergeant!"

"Mr. Speaker, the dean of the diplomatic corps!"

The dean was played by a mousy woman from administration. They backed inelegantly down the aisle. House and Senate photographers tangled, muttering in colorful terms.

Christina clapped briskly. "Let's try again. Places."

* * *

Before starting on his two hot dogs, Michael looked around in vain for Matt Gutierrez. No sign. After a moment, he gave up and unwrapped the first one.

Too cold today to sit on the reflecting pool steps, so he bolted his lunch on his feet, keeping warm by juggling his weight from onc to the other. He covered a belch. A shadow made him turn. Not Gutierrez, as he'd expected, but Christina Thompson, ruddy cheeked, with the sharp wind tugging strands from her pinned-back hair. "Hey," she said. "Doing good in there."

He toasted with his Diet Coke. "Credit the leadership."

"About that tumble …"

"Won't happen again."

"Ah, but it will. That's why we rehearse." She tucked back a flyaway strand, then fondly picked a cat hair off his jacket. "Just wanted to say, Michael, I'm really glad to have you on the shoot. First of many, I hope."

"Thanks, Chris. I appreciate it."

"*De nada*." For an instant, he had the feeling she was studying him, looking for something on his face. Then she said, "See you in the trenches."

She left him alone by the reflecting pool. He drained his Diet Coke and pitched it at the wastebasket. Two points.

He turned, and the ankle flexed easily, taking his weight. At that moment, the clouds parted, light peeking through. He walked through good sunshiny air, toward the first checkpoint leading back to the Capitol dome.

HOPEWELL, NJ

Turning into the long driveway, Dalia sensed something on the wind: a premonition, a predator.

Her foot lifted off the gas. Keeping one hand on the wheel, she reached into her purse with the other. Digging past linty Kleenex and sugar-free Trident, phone, antibacterial wipes, and lipstick, her fingers closed on hard, comforting steel: the Colt Python given her by Meir. She moved the gun onto the passenger seat.

A pleasant midafternoon, autumn just tilting toward winter; sun-dappled woods crowding close, late-migrating birds chirping away. And yet, two stone feet, a golem from legend, stood squarely on her chest. She felt a sudden, almost overpowering urge to turn around, floor it, and not stop again till she reached the airport. Fuck all of it. Dalia Artzi was going home.

She held perfectly still, letting the urge pass through.

Her tongue scraped dry lips.

She put her foot back on the gas pedal and rolled forward again.

Shadows long and deep. Keep the Prius below thirty miles per hour, and the engine stayed silent. She ghosted through shadows.

The Nissan Altima was parked by the front door. Everything about the cottage appeared normal. But something was slightly *off*, in a way she couldn't put her finger on.

She pulled up behind the Altima, yanked the emergency brake, and sat listening, waiting. Nothing.

Except that feeling.

The breeze picked up, swirling a patter of dead leaves across the windshield.

She killed the engine, opened the door; sat for another moment, and then picked up the gun. Her hand barely shook.

She got out, and her eyes immediately found a glittering puddle beneath a curtained front window: broken glass. She thought of one of her dear departed Nana's favorite sayings: *If God lived on earth, all his windows would be broken.*

Her mind wanted to lock up. She would not allow it. Instead, turning in a slow circle, she opened herself to the afternoon. Look around. Listen. Don't just look, but *see.* Don't just listen. *Hear.* What was out there? The disused well, pail and spindle creaking. A faraway glint in a corner of the field. She started instinctively to move behind the Prius, to take cover. But the glint was inorganic. Dead as the leaves. Dead as the silence. A piece of abandoned equipment … but one that wasn't there a few days ago.

Fine hairs rising on the back of her neck. A chill trailing down her spine. Nostrils twitching, registering for the first time a slaughterhouse smell on the air.

She moved toward the front door. Frosty ground slipped treacherously underfoot. She was glad to be wearing flats. She tried the knob. Locked.

She began to circle the cottage. A small, charred circle in dead grass. She poked it with one toe. Could make no sense of it. Kept moving.

Then she could see a swath of backyard; wooded, sloping upward. She caught herself whispering stupid reassurances under her breath and made herself stop. Hands shaking worse now, she peeked around the corner of the house.

Gleaming spent shells littered frozen ground. She saw more of those strange charred circles, then a pool of viscous black liquid. At first she thought it was blood. Her nose twitched again—Rabbit Dalia—and she registered heating oil.

She looked from spent shells to charred circles, to the pool of oil. And again: shells, circles, oil. At last, something seemed to tug her forward. An invisible rope, tied around her waist. She gave in and let it pull her.

A dead dog came into view. She paused again. The German shepherd, a hole under the jaw, wider where it came out behind the opposite ear. She waited to see if she would throw up. When her stomach settled, she kept moving.

Oily footprints led from the puddle to the back door. She saw a storage tank with several holes in a curving line. The back door was ajar. Drawing closer, she saw another slick footprint right beside the knob.

Now the smell of death—coppery, rank—made her gag. Holding her breath, she pushed open the door with one foot and stood for a moment, letting her eyes adjust to the dimness.

Two figures sprawled to her right. She approached them.

Gavril Meir lay flat on his back. His good eye stared at the ceiling; the glass one canted off into shadow. His face was gray. Propped against the wall beside him was a young man in all black, jacket and gloves and watch cap, sightless eyes wide. She recognized him from the corkboard in Horowitz's study: Yoni Yariv.

When Meir moved, Dalia's heart jumped like a trout in a creek.

He murmured something, his voice filled with gravel and liquid in a way that made her stomach protest again. She shrank back reflexively, and her feet made faint tearing sounds against the tacky floor. Forcing herself to come closer, she gulped a shallow breath: "Gavril … I'm here."

"Dalia." His massive hand, searching. She knelt and took it. She could smell tobacco on his fingertips. Or maybe it was gunpowder. On the floor beside him, she saw the handgun, slicked with blood. Blood inside the fine knurling of the grip, inside the stamped serial number.

"Can't …" Thick, slurring Hebrew. He drew another breath. "Make …" He released her hand, tried to wave.

He needed a doctor, but he would be dead before they reached one.

"Down …" He labored to draw another bubbling breath. "The well." His hand found hers again and tightened with surprising strength. "*Lashom harah*," he said. Evil tongue.

Later, looking back, she thought that maybe she had nodded.

She stood, her knees pulling free from the sticky blood, and backtracked into the small kitchen. Leaving bloody-oily footprints, she passed through a low-ceilinged hallway and came out into the living room. David Feigenbaum lay on his side, on the floor near a broken front window, a pair of binoculars clutched in his pale right hand. The gold-foil filter of a burned-down Noblesse lay near his bloodless lips. Red froth had collected in his thin, silvery beard. An ugly round black spot near the center his forehead. She considered listening for a pulse or closing his eyes, but this was not a movie.

Instead, she went back to Meir, tempted to say something else, to argue. But of course, he was right. If an inquiry started, it would not stop until all had been exposed. And all their efforts would be wasted.

A dull headache was starting behind her temples.

Thank God, she thought as she went to work, that none of this was real.

She started with Yoni Yariv. Getting her hands beneath his arms, with a wheezing grunt she dragged him toward the open back door. He seemed impossibly heavy. The world grayed, then came back sharper than ever. Not real sharpness, but artificial, hyperreal sharpness. *All the world's a stage.*

The young man's sightless eyes seemed to follow her. There was a lecture in this, she thought. Give me three thousand words on the psychological cost of removing casualties from a battlefield. Note how the sightless eyes seem to follow the living …

The dead body breathed, the rank, juicy smell coming in waves, freed by every bump as she manhandled it down the hallway, over the threshold, toward the well. Not real. *Make note, in your essay, of the strange awkwardness of death. The entangled limbs, the way the tissue lumps ...* Panting, heart thudding, she reached the well and rested for a moment before lifting off the wooden cover. Deep, echoey blackness.

She searched the body. In one pocket, night-vision binoculars with one lens shattered. Folding knife. Phone. Setting them aside, she humped the corpse up onto the round brick wall. It balanced there for a moment, then tipped. One dead leg sent the bucket swinging, one dead arm slithered over the rim, and Yoni Yariv vanished into the void. She heard a wet, meaty *thump* and a splash.

The others would be even heavier.

The headache was white hot, almost blinding now.

Back throbbing, hips creaking, she trudged back toward the house, taking note of the metallic glints scattered about the yard. She would make it all disappear. Right down the well. If she knew Feigenbaum, the wily old *yekke* would have leased the safe house for at least six months in advance to ensure privacy. No landlord would come sniffing around anytime soon. And the well was just a rustic artifact anyway. The real one was in a shed behind the house, connected by modern plumbing.

In the back hall, on her way to Feigenbaum, she realized that something about Meir had changed. Something had left him. *Yom asal, yom basal.* A day of honey, a day of onion.

She looked in stupid wonder at the corpse. Nothing was less elegant, nothing less dramatic, than death.

Class, give me three thousand words on the meaninglessness of death.

She stood looking at Meir for a long time. Then a bird twittered. Another shrilled a response. Dalia bit her lip and went back to work.

CHAPTER SEVEN

TRENTON, NJ

In the image, bright sun heliographed off the hood of a rust-colored Mercury Grand Marquis. The glare stopped just short of obscuring the driver's face. Horowitz zoomed in, opened another window on the monitor. Red dots appeared as the computer found common nodal points; a counter ran up to sixty-six.

"October twenty-first. A tollbooth camera on I-80, twenty miles west of Youngstown, Ohio. Note the black wig. Happily, that doesn't throw the software." He zoomed out, then in again on the Utah license plate: 711 XPC. "The car was reported stolen three days earlier, from a driveway near Salt Lake. Last night, I spoke with the South Salt Lake City Police. I mentioned our missing red Ford. They found it this morning in the parking lot of a Chinese restaurant. Probably been sitting there, ignored, for a month." He clicked the mouse again, and a map of the United States appeared. "Draw a line from Portland through Salt Lake, and … I'm sorry, Dalia, are we disturbing you?"

Studying the photograph of Yoni Yariv on the corkboard, absently massaging the still-aching muscles of her shoulders and neck, she did not respond immediately. She wasn't thinking of the dead men, the blood, the guns, the shells, the hungry old well that, three days ago, had consumed them all (except for a single casing she had taken as a souvenir—it would fit nicely on her shelf, beside the fragment of German 5.9-inch howitzer shell recovered from Ypres). Nor was she thinking of Yoni Yariv's phone, which had contained GPS information about the Hopewell cottage, electronic triggers for the squibs—the mysterious charred circles of grass—and nothing else. And she wasn't thinking of the sketchy neighborhood in South Brunswick where she had left the Altima to be stolen and stripped, *Inshallah*—God willing. Instead, she was thinking of Napoleon Bonaparte, who, on the morning of June 18, 1815, the morning of the rout that would forever be known as Waterloo, had ordered the capture of a farmhouse on a low hill near Wellington's right flank. *Le petit caporal* had assumed that his opposite number would respond by funneling reserves from his center—whereupon Napoleon would make his real approach, driving through the now-weakened British ranks near La Haye Sainte. But the initial French sortie had failed to capture the Château d'Hougoument. And as the day progressed and the farmhouse remained in British hands, Napoleon had appeared to forget his original plan, committing ever more forces to the enterprise, refusing to abandon it even as his strategy backfired, as *he* became the one overly committed to the flank, fatally weakening his main force. Why? Dalia explained the mistake to her students via a simple colloquialism. Despite his renowned steely will and peerless intellect, Napoleon had made the most human of errors. Caught up in the moment, he had lost sight of the larger goal. He had missed the forest for the trees.

"Dalia? I said, 'Are we—'"

She shook her head. Clearing away the tangled undergrowth, refocusing on the monitor, the map of the United States. The larger goal. The only thing that mattered. *Jana.* "Not at all."

His mouth tightened, but he didn't comment.

In the kitchen down the hall, pots and pans clattered and banged. After a few seconds, Horowitz turned back to the computer. "Draw a line through …"

His phone vibrated, jittering toward the edge of the desk. He caught it just in time, checked the display, and raised an index finger as he answered. "Jacob Horowitz." He listened, reached for a pen. "Did you …" Writing. "And …" Writing again. "Okay …" Listening without writing. He checked his watch. "Call off the dogs. I'll take it from here." A tight smile. "I owe you for this." He laughed shortly. "Back atcha."

He hung up, the smile vanishing. "Friend in DC." Opening the desk drawer, he took out a semiautomatic pistol with an inside-the-waistband holster. "Had his feelers out for our 'woman in charge' …"

Strapping on the holster, he turned again to the laptop. An email attachment opened into a photograph of a birdlike woman in her early fifties, seated on a park bench and holding a sandwich, looking somewhere off to her right, wearing glasses connected to a rhinestone chain.

"One Connie Lubelchik. Heads a civil works program under USACE. Married, two sons of her own, two step. Been some talk of a future in politics. Which means that some not-very-nice people have been watching her. Which includes friends of my friend, who found out that during the past three months she's taken just shy of ten grand from her bank account—just below the legal threshold where banks have to report to Treasury—six times."

He clicked, and a new image appeared: a telephoto lens capturing the woman inside a fast-food restaurant, sitting with a fair-haired woman whose back faced the camera. "Every Wednesday evening for the past four weeks, she's gone to Burger King to pick up dinner for the family. Inside, she hands over an envelope to a young lady. They meet between six thirty and seven. There's no going back if we call in the tac team, so I say we suss it out in person. If it feels right, then call in the big boys."

He packed up the laptop. On the way out, he detoured to a closet and grabbed a brown leather satchel. Reading the question on Dalia's face: "Directional antenna. We'll spoof her."

"Which means what, exactly?"

"In effect, we set up our own miniature cell network tower. Any phone the antenna finds connects automatically. Then we send a command to the baseband chip, access the microphone and camera, and sit back and enjoy the show."

"Unless," added McConnell, "she's got a signal-blocking phone case."

"Or a DFU to bypass the standard operating system. Or she's pulled out the battery."

Horowitz stopped in the kitchen to exchange a few words with his wife. Dalia and McConnell, not yet having been officially introduced, waited self-consciously by the front door. On a TV in the living room, SpongeBob and Squidward were trying to deliver a pizza.

They went down the concrete walk to the driveway. The shotgun seat of the Lincoln Navigator was overflowing with papers and junk. Dalia and McConnell squeezed in back beside a child's car seat as the neighbor's dog yapped.

Horowitz called ahead to Trenton Mercer Airport. Traffic was heavy on the day before Thanksgiving—the most brutal travel day of the year. Twenty-two minutes later, they entered the airport through a back gate. Forsaking the terminal, Horowitz parked beside a tiny warming Cessna in the shadow of a huge Frontier Airbus. He exchanged words with a mechanic, handed over the car keys, and climbed into the pilot's seat. As he adjusted the aviation headset, McConnell joined him in front, leaving Dalia alone in back. Cold air seeped into the cockpit. She fastened her seat belt, then the top button of her coat.

Horowitz ran briskly down the preflight checklist. They taxied, turned around on a small apron, and lifted off. Dalia closed her eyes. The flight lasted forty nail-biting minutes. Her stomach rose as the airplane descended.

"Final approach," Horowitz yelled.

By the time they bumped to a stop, she was sweating despite

the chill. McConnell offered a sympathetic smile, then a helping hand. She shook off both, then took a moment before climbing out, puffing, from the tiny Cessna.

A police cruiser was waiting on the twilit tarmac. No handles inside the rear doors, Dalia noted after sliding into the backseat. Prisoner screen between her and the driver. McConnell followed her into the backseat. Horowitz went up front.

A navy captain in uniform craned around from behind the wheel and smiled at her. "Ma'am." Gentlemanly, touch of a Southern accent, beginnings of a double chin.

They drove past avgas tanks, through another back gate in another cyclone fence, and onto an access road, merging with civilian traffic, using the strobes and siren strategically to press through the worst of the traffic. Horowitz and the navy captain talked intently, low enough that Dalia could make out only the occasional word. Then Horowitz got on his phone, brought up Google Maps, and showed them through the prisoner screen.

The satellite image showed a neighborhood of red brick duplexes, attached mother-in-law basement apartments with separate entrances. Toggling to street view, he panned 360 degrees to reveal cars parked alongside curbs, bikes on porches, a playground and baseball diamond, a funeral home, a church, a Burger King.

"If it feels right, we call in the heavy guns. Jim, promise me a reference when I'm job-hunting?"

"I make no promises," said McConnell dryly.

They left the Beltway and got on US-50, then MD-410. Then they were in a neighborhood of row houses, fire hydrants, nail salons, and chain drugstores. They turned at a mailbox, onto a block Dalia recognized from the satellite image: playground, baseball diamond, funeral home, church.

They parked across the street from Burger King, before a house with a low retaining wall, and the captain killed the engine. A cluster of teenagers smoking blunts in the restaurant parking lot, embers burning in the dusk, eyeballed them suspiciously.

In the passenger seat, Horowitz opened his laptop. From the leather satchel he unfolded a directional antenna. He powered up the IMSI Catcher 4.5 software. When he cracked his window, the gust of bracing air made Dalia shiver.

He aimed the antenna at the Burger King, and they watched the program search for signals. Twenty-one hits registered: twenty-one active cell phones inside.

It was 6:12 p.m. "We're looking for a beige Subaru Outback," Horowitz said, "license EL-5772."

They waited.

Traffic came and went. As the line at the drive-through lengthened and shortened, the count of cell phones went up and down.

At 6:37, a beige Outback turned into the parking lot. The plate read "EL-5772." The antenna picked up one mobile phone inside the car. Horowitz sent a command to the baseband chip. It was enough to make Dalia pine for the good old days, when the CIA's seventh-floor executive suite had run roughshod over all corners. At least, back then you knew who was spying on you. But the massive organizational reshuffling that followed 9/11 had left an accountability vacuum—a bouillabaisse of high-tech surveillance and data mining, with exotic new vistas of plausible deniability.

The Outback parked, and Connie Lubelchik emerged: birdlike, glasses on a rhinestone chain, brown purse, faux mink over a teal blouse. She went into the restaurant. Through the laptop speakers, they heard, via the mike on the cell phone in her purse, background music, crinkling wrappers, orders being called.

The woman went to the counter, where they heard her order enough food for an army: bacon double, Rodeo burger, Crispy Chicken Jr., three Whoppers, four orders of fries, two onion rings, a side salad, two Cokes, two Diet Cokes, a Dr. Pepper, and a Tropical Mango Smoothie.

If Jana Dahan was in this restaurant right now, she was well camouflaged. Dalia's weary eyes roamed, though from this distance, they couldn't make out many details: two adolescent boys playing some sort of card game amid the remains of a meal; a man wearing a cowboy hat, and another with an extravagant mustache; an already well-nourished woman in skintight Lycra folding half a Whopper into her gaping mouth. No sign of a young woman or even a teenage girl, other than the one behind the counter.

But here, crossing the street from the Exxon station. Caucasian, youthful, reddish hair in a pixie cut, baggy army jacket. As Connie Lubelchik accepted grease-laden bags from the counter server, the younger woman came in through a side entrance and slipped into a booth. Dalia glanced at Horowitz. He had seen her, too. McConnell seemed fixed on Lubelchik. The Navy captain seemed to be examining the layer of dust on his dashboard.

Lubelchik carried her greasy bags to the booth, and they caught a snippet of the two card players' conversation as she passed—something about *deuces, one-eyed jacks, suicide king.* Lubelchik slid into the booth, across from the younger woman. An envelope came from one faux mink pocket, glided across the table, and vanished into the army jacket.

They watched as Connie Lubelchik reached out and took the young woman's hand. No sound of tears came through the phone, but the young woman's shoulders heaved.

"It's okay, Berry. Really."

Faintly: "You don't … I didn't want to …"

"Shh. It's okay."

Horowitz looked back through the screen at Dalia, who shook her head. She didn't know just what this was, but it was not Jana.

"It's so much," the younger woman said. Now they did hear a sob. "So much. It's just …"

"I can manage it."

"It's enough to buy a house. You put it all together."

"I can manage it."

"I feel like I'm—"

"You're not doing anything. *I'm* doing it, Strawberry. And I wouldn't have it any other way. I love you."

"We'll pay you back, I promise. Once Benjy gets back on his—"

Horowitz killed the connection. McConnell leaned back in his seat with a sigh. Dalia said nothing.

"We take a mulligan," Horowitz said. "Just a first try. We'll get her."

He sounded to Dalia as if he was trying to convince himself.

IRVING STREET NW, WASHINGTON, DC

FOR A GOOD PRIME CALL 555-793-7319

Beside the graffito, Michael Fletcher found a fourth small cross scratched into the molding.

He gave no visible reaction as he finished, zipped, and turned away. The urinal flushed automatically. The sink spritzed out soap automatically. The faucet ran automatically.

He left the bathroom. At 7:00 p.m. on the day before Thanksgiving, the pub had recently turned the corner between happy hour—younger drinkers alone and in pairs—and dinner. A knot of patrons waiting to be seated had formed by the door. A mother struggled with the zipper on a baby's plastic orange sheath. An elderly man leaned against a cane. A flat-screen TV played cable news with no sound. Cutout paper turkeys and pilgrims festooned a ledge, sharing space with plastic sprigs of mistletoe and holly. Not even Thanksgiving yet, and already Christmas was elbowing its way in. But of course it was. It was all about Black Friday now. Capitalist hog heaven: this was what he had fought for.

He moved past crowded red banquettes, buxom waitresses in low-cut blouses. The air smelled of potato skins and pot stickers. He stepped outside, into a fresh, cool breeze. Inside the deserted Metrobus shelter, he pretended to study a map of tangling routes.

A red, white, and blue bus wheezed to the curb and decanted a thin stream of passengers. Michael climbed aboard, swiped his fare card. The bus was nearly empty. He moved toward the back, using seat-back handholds to keep his balance as they lurched into motion again. He dropped into a seat and waited. Thinking of nothing consciously, but feeling a trickle of mingled excitement and dread in the back of his throat.

At the next stop, a young woman came aboard. Blonde, attractive. After paying her fare, she passed several empty rows to sit beside him. Their gazes met briefly. She had cool gray eyes flecked with harlequin sparkles, and wore jeans and a navy pea coat, no makeup. Suddenly, he remembered arriving home for his first leave and liberty, his wife waiting on the airfield to meet him, cheeks rouged and lips painted bright red. Stacy looked like a clown, he had thought in that first instant—or a corpse.

The young woman looked away. He followed suit but kept stealing glances from the corner of his eye. She was almost beautiful. Complexioned in a way that suggested her blond hair might be a wig. And something else. He had seen enough burn scars at the DC VA to recognize those on her right cheek, skillfully grafted though they were. They continued down onto her slender throat and, by implication, at least partway down the right side of her body.

At the next stop, she stood up without even glancing at him.

He followed her from the bus to a residential block of low brick-and-stucco buildings. Boarded-over windows, garage doors tagged with spray paint, splintering wooden balconies. Approaching a narrow single-family house, she took keys from her purse. Smoothly she opened the door and stepped aside, letting him lead the way in. He hesitated for only an instant.

The dim entryway smelled of fresh paint. She brushed against him as she reached for a light switch. A narrow staircase led up. He saw a drop cloth overhanging the top riser and guessed that the upstairs was not in use.

The sitting room had a small sectional couch, cheap IKEA coffee table, wooden blinds covering the windows. A single small lamp. A closet door. She gestured for him to sit. "Mr. Fletcher. Call me Kristen."

She spoke pleasant, unaccented English. Michael sat carefully on one end of the couch. She sat on the other and spent a moment looking him over.

"I understand you recently received an important assignment," she said. "Congratulations are in order."

It took him a few seconds. Then he realized that not only had they been watching him, their role had been more active. They had pulled some string to get him the job. But why?

For access, of course. Access to VIPs, perhaps even to POTUS.

He remembered Christina finding him by the reflecting pool during the lunch break. The feeling that she'd been studying him, looking for something on his face.

Keeping her own face expressionless, she watched the thoughts play across his face.

His hands wanted to fidget. He held them tightly in his lap. "Am I …"

She waited.

"Will I be …"

"You will be serving a crucial role in a historic operation."

He said nothing.

"Future generations will sing songs about you."

He said nothing.

"I envy you," she said.

He felt her sincerity, and said nothing.

She looked at him for another few seconds. Then she stood, went to the closet, and opened it. She took out two stainless steel Ohaus Navigator balance scales and beckoned him to join her.

Each scale was accurate to one one-hundredth of a gram. He stood on one, then the other. The first read 2.2 grams heavier than the second. She made notes on her phone and then said, "Remove the leg, please."

Returning to the couch, he sat down again and started clumsily taking off his pants. The pin clicked nine times as he untethered the liner from the housing mechanism. She indicated that he should leave the leg on the couch and weigh himself again. He did, balancing on his right foot. She noted the weights again on her phone, then carefully photographed the leg from every angle. As she worked, he examined her scars and wondered what her story was. Wondered if everyone involved in this fight was somehow mutilated.

* * *

As Michael was pulling into the garage of the house on Ellicott, headlights splashed behind him: the red Mini Cooper Stacy had gotten shortly after the split—thanks, he suspected, to a financial assist from her father.

They met on the front stoop. A snapshot of happier times, worthy of the staircase wall: the whole family together, wearing forced smiles. But the illusion was fleeting. "Happy Thanksgiving," Stacy said. She knelt, kissed Silas, ruffled his hair, and trotted away. Back to her own life. The new normal.

Michael found the key for the door. "Have fun, buddy?"

Silas shrugged.

"What'd you do?"

"Don't remember. Can I watch TV?"

"Change into your pj's, brush your teeth. Then one episode before bed."

As Silas watched *Teenage Mutant Ninja Turtles* in the living room, Michael worked in the kitchen. At the supermarket, he had found the world's smallest turkey, which reminded him of that old Waitresses song. He set it on the counter. Pepperidge Farm stuffing. Ocean Spray cranberry sauce. Chicken stock, measuring cup, onions, and celery. Licorice jumped onto the countertop, nose twitching. Michael picked her up, kissed between the flattened ears, and set her back on the floor. A ribbon of disembodied laughter trailed over from Wisconsin Avenue.

Working the dripping cheesecloth bag of guts loose from the

chest cavity triggered a memory of chemical orange sky. Distant small-arms fire. A screaming haji civilian. Female. Clutching her belly. Gut shot—the worst. Slow, painful death. The woman's own intestines slipped through her fingers. He had felt an urge to put her out of her misery, as one might a rabid dog. But he had turned away, pretending not to see. Not his problem.

He came back to himself some time later. Still holding the dripping bag of turkey giblets. Pot frothing, hissing against the stove. Tears rolling down his cheeks. *Please, God, don't let my son come into the kitchen now and see me like this.*

He switched off the burner and stood there, quaking. A fucking mess—that's what he was. Silas would be better off without him.

He sniffled, wiped his nose on his sleeve. That set off another memory: lying awake sobbing in his childhood bed shaped like a race car. His brother peeking into his bedroom. Backlit, haloed. Michael turning away, covering his shame. Seth coming into the room anyway, settling gently on the edge of the mattress. Bedsprings creaking. "*What's wrong? Let me help.*" They had stayed awake half the night, studying together. And at the seder the next night, Michael had recited the Four Questions with flying colors. Seth watching with an approving smile. Father beaming from the head of the table. Then Father had moved on to the next part of the ceremony, explaining how the Lord, Blessed be He, King of the Universe, with a strong hand and outstretched arm, and with great terribleness, and with signs and wonders, had avenged the Jews upon their enemies, delivering unto the Egyptians ten plagues, culminating with the slaying of the firstborn sons.

Future generations will sing songs about you.

Michael dumped out the chicken stock, which had mostly boiled away. Measured more, put it back on the stove, and started dicing vegetables. Knife rapping fast against the cutting board. Tears drying up now. Back to reality. Work to be done.

Tomorrow was Thanksgiving.

COLUMBIA HEIGHTS, WASHINGTON, DC

Looking at the message, Jana puckered her brow.

Yoni had played her like a violin, but he at least had bothered to play her. The director was all cold formality and entitled assumptions. *Await further orders.* Not even a cursory, *Well done.*

The message deleted automatically when she closed it. Brimming with nervous energy, she paced the length of the apartment for a few minutes. Eventually, she shucked on her navy pea coat. Before descending to the street, she checked herself briefly in the mirror. At the ramsad's suggestion, she had worn no makeup while rendezvousing with Fletcher: *Let the scars show. You look on the outside the way he feels on the inside.* Now she brushed over the scars with light blush, then applied lipstick.

She walked down four flights, through stronger-than-usual pockets of cooking smells—preparations for tomorrow's holiday. Reaching the front stoop, she picked a direction to walk, clear her head. *Where* hardly mattered. As she struck off, someone gave a piercing wolf whistle. She paid no attention.

Fingers working against the phone in her pocket. Just to hear the sound of a friendly voice would do wonders, but there was no one to call.

For a moment, she dared think of Yoni. Maybe she had misunderstood, during her brief conversation with the director a week ago. Hearing that voice on the other end of the line had caught her off guard. (And she had been impressed, despite herself, as any girl from a shabby old Jewish Agency house would surely have been.) "*Our mutual friend is indisposed. From now on I must contact you directly, using the alternate number. You should take care. Watch your back. We may have suffered a ... lack of sanitation.*"

Angrily now, she shook her head. She knew what "indisposed" meant. Yoni, who had been so alive, so passionate, so vital, was dead. Gone. Worm food. And that was okay. He had known the risks. She was the unfortunate one. Still alive, still fighting. But alone now. And more homesick than ever. She wanted to be back in Jerusalem, in the bazaar, surrounded by Israelis in jeans, Arabs in colorful kaftans, soldiers in crisp fatigues, clerics in flowing black robes. Hanging Persian carpets and clouds of burning incense, awnings and umbrella-covered food carts, honking taxis and pecking pigeons. Dusty olive groves beyond red-tiled roofs. Hazy blue mountains sleeping in the far distance. Home.

Maybe Mom.

She snorted aloud. The last time Jana spoke with her mother had been to announce that she would be staying with military intelligence beyond her mandatory service. (In fact, she had been preparing to make the switch to Mossad, but that detail one did not tell even one's own mother.) And suddenly, Mom had lit into her: "*You're a follower, Jana. You've always been a follower. You don't think for yourself. You don't stand on your own two feet.* Nit ahin, nit ahir. *Neither here nor there. You're drawn to strong people because they give you a sense of purpose. But it's only skin deep. My own daughter, a professional hanger-on. A lifetime* nokhshlepper."

No, she would not be calling her mother.

She walked past laughing families, bickering couples, feeling a certain festivity in the air. The night before Thanksgiving. More evidence, she thought darkly, of American hypocrisy. They wagged their fingers at Israelis, told them to give back the land they had stolen. Even as they celebrated their own epic land grab, adding insult to injury with cutesy little paper turkeys, buckled Puritan hats, war feathers, and Indian headbands. Government-sanctioned alcoholism had finished the job started with smallpox-infected blankets. And so the question of giving back the land had become moot. Wasn't that convenient. But if Jews were to try the same approach, watch the world scream.

Dark thoughts. She needed human contact. But Yoni was gone. There was nobody else. She was reaping what she had sown.

Cousin Miriam, maybe. Aunt Becca …

She took out the phone, deliberated, then returned it to her pocket.

"*We may have suffered a ... lack of sanitation.*"

Turning a corner, passing boarded-up windows, she quartered the street, checking her six. No one followed her. But it paid to be cautious.

Half a block farther on, she stumbled across what may have been a drug deal: two teenagers jamming hands in pockets, melting away into shadows. All within a stone's throw of the White House, with its private chef and underground bowling alley. Yet the White House dared criticize Israel. For what? For defending itself. Truly, Americans had made an art form of hypocrisy.

Her mind turned back to Cousin Miriam, to Aunt Becca. She could picture them just sitting down to dinner. A rich dinner, no doubt. In that apartment, every dinner had been rich. Compared to the house where Jana had grown up, with its concrete walls and weeds and cockroaches and paychecks stretched thin, the Upper East Side doorman building had been a fantasy straight out of a children's book. Speaking of which, Miriam's bookshelf had featured every Eloise title: the original, and *Eloise in Paris*, and *Eloise in Moscow*, and even *Eloise at Christmastime.* Because in America, even Jews celebrated Christmas. Over dinner in that apartment, they didn't talk about gas masks or bomb shelters or what to do if you inhaled anthrax. They talked about reality TV shows, and how Miriam's private school, whose annual tuition exceeded those of many universities, was nonetheless always trying to squeeze still more money out of the parents. Miriam's father had announced that he would not even go into that school without keeping one hand on his wallet. Chuckle, chuckle. But what if New Jersey had been lobbing rockets at that fancy school? What would they do then?

Americans. They saw no reality except their own. They could not see that the Mideast was not Ellis Island, that there was no *melting pot* in the Mideast. Sunni, Shia, and Kurd would not fight alongside each other in some jury-rigged army, arms linked, tra-la-la, just because it suited Americans to believe they would. Their "Middle East" was the result of lines drawn almost at random by French and British diplomats who had not troubled themselves to understand the first thing about local history. Here, let's call this "Syria." And let's call this "Lebanon." This we call "Iraq." So what if it contains the very different people of Kurdistan, Baghdad, and Basra? So what if our Anglo-French manufactured national consciousness is but a century old—despite Saddam's speeches about eternal Iraqi empires—and so there will always be fighting until the bitter end? Ever since the fall of the Neo-Assyrian Empire, the Middle East had been unstable. And it would continue to be so until one side or the other delivered the killing blow. But no, that makes us uncomfortable as we eat our fine rich dinners and celebrate our whitewashed version of our own history, so we will reject it. Even as we kill more babies with more bombs and more flying robots and, with each dead child, drive a new generation into the arms of radical fundamentalists, we will happily throw Israel to the wolves and claim to be above it all.

They deserved everything they were going to get. Everything and more. Fucking hypocrites.

She would call Miriam. Give whoever answered a long-overdue piece of her mind. She took out the phone again. She still remembered the number of the apartment. Funny how long-term memory worked. She keyed it in, and her thumb hovered over the call button.

* * *

On Eighty-Eighth and Madison, two hundred miles north, the StingRay technology used by Homeland Security to extract stored data from mobile networks waited, humming, poised to reverse-trace the call.

* * *

But of course, Jana thought, a decade had passed since her last visit to New York. Miriam would be a young woman now, as she herself was. Not living at home and eating with her parents.

She lowered the phone and kept walking, hands jammed in pockets, head lowered against the cold wind, alone.

NORTH OF ANDOVER, VT

At seven on Thanksgiving morning, George Rockaway closed the side door gently behind him and fell into a loose, loping jog, through frozen forest striped with shadows. Finding a good, steady rhythm, taking care to pace himself, to avoid twisting his ankle on leaf-hidden roots or treacherous ice.

Feet pounding, heart thumping. Clear blue sky, dark mountains. Reaching the end of the long gravel driveway, he turned right without slowing. The same route he had followed back in high school when he joined the Kearsarge Regional High track team. Back then, trapped every night beneath his father's roof, he would run six or eight or ten miles at a stretch, pushing himself to exhaustion and beyond. Then he would come home, wolf down dinner standing at the kitchen counter, and crawl into bed.

Having everyone back together under the same roof for the holiday brought all the old dysfunctional dynamics bubbling up with a vengeance. His sister, Judy, who had always been a whiner, complained incessantly. His brother, Jack, a lifelong mama's boy, turned childlike and helpless. For her part, Mama fretted, for she was a born fretter. And, of course, Daddy drank. Hiding bottles in cupboards, on high shelves, under couches. And when Daddy got sufficiently drunk, his simmering irritation boiled over. As the baby of the family, George usually took the brunt.

But he would survive. And on Sunday afternoon he would escape back to the city, to his dorm room and the new life he was carving out for himself, very far from here. The next four days would be a pisser, yes they would. But he would make it through.

And the woods were beautiful. No denying that. And after a few months in the concrete jungle of Manhattan, he did miss this towering forest, the yawning sky, the watchful mountains.

Reaching the old fire road, he turned right. *Once around the lake.* If he had enough energy, maybe twice.

Cranking up his lungs, he hawked up a plug of phlegm. He pushed harder, extending his stride. Back in the old days, he would run until his mind turned white, washing away all the family dysfunction. Running, running, running, and nothing else. Now he was out of shape, and his chest already burned.

He reached the lake, following a rough natural trail, drawing toward and away from the banks as terrain dictated. Thin ice near the shore, but open water farther out. Winter birds calling querulously, morning songs echoing. Land climbing and dipping. Dark hollows, slashing ravines, open fields, wild country.

A glint in the water. *Ice*, George thought. Then it flashed again, and he knew it was metal. He drew to a stop, panting, hands on knees, squinting across the lake, into the sun.

Metal indeed—and a lot of it, from the looks—there beneath a scrim of ice near the banks.

He straightened, spat again, and cautiously picked his way closer.

Shadows were lifting now as the sun climbed higher. The only sounds were the birds, the soft wind, the slow drip of a warming day. George shielded his eyes with one hand. The metal was mostly underwater, reminding him of an iceberg, just peeking above the surface. The color of rust, giving way to shining chrome. A fender.

A car, he thought.

He took out his phone. But there was no reception out here.

After another moment, he turned, spat again, and began running back toward the house as fast as his lungs would let him.

TRENTON, NJ

"October twenty-first." On the left side of the screen, Horowitz opened the image of the Grand Marquis, captured by a tollbooth camera near Youngstown, Ohio. "And, this morning ..." On the right, he scaled to size a top-down image of a claw dredge and an industrial tow truck, parked near the edge of a wooded lake outside Andover, Vermont. A loose throw of men and patrol cars. At the end of a winch cable, the Grand Marquis emerged, streaming water.

"Jogger called it in at half past eight. Local kid, home from college for Thanksgiving. No human remains, no sign of foul play, no contraband; so the case becomes a less-than-alpha priority, especially on Thanksgiving Day. Upshot: the car's sitting in the Merrimack County impound lot, where nobody will give it another thought until Monday."

McConnell scratched one ear. Horowitz worked the keyboard, and the image zoomed out. Not standard Google Maps, Dalia noticed, but EEC satellite, doubtless accessed via a "fusion center," providing current real-time footage. She thought again of the days when only top-level spooks had possessed this technology. There was a plus side to the democratization of surveillance. Yet the downside was terrifying. Technology had a mind of its own, but no conscience, no moral center. What it could do determined what was done.

"The EEC cache dumps after sixteen days. No sign, during that time, of the car going into the drink. However …" The cursor moved to the far end of a clearing. "Must have driven in from this fire road. Mother Nature has long since covered the tracks—three heavy rains in the past sixteen days, and five since we saw her in Youngstown. But …" The image pulled back again, revealing a toy patchwork of lakes, ponds, trees, fields. "Where did she go *after* dumping the car? I see four possibilities. One: she's still roughing it somewhere nearby. Two: she had access to another vehicle. A bike stowed in the Mercury's backseat, a car or motorcycle hidden beforehand. Three: an accomplice gave her a lift. Four: she went somewhere on foot."

"*Lex parsimoniae*," Dalia said.

McConnell nodded. "Also known as Occam's razor. Among

competing hypotheses, the one with the fewest assumptions should be selected. Or, as my freshman logic prof put it, 'The simplest answer is usually correct.'"

"So, in order …" Horowitz tapped one fingertip against the cleft in his chin. "She's not nearby; we know she was 'moved into position' around Washington. Another vehicle, then. But we're talking about a woman who's driven from Oregon, probably straight through, to Vermont. She's exhausted. In a stolen car. Carrying explosives and sarin. Where does she find the time to hide another vehicle beforehand? Where does she *get* the vehicle? We'll check local police reports during the dates in question, but I'd be surprised if we find anything."

His fingers flew across the keyboard, and the display switched to a data cube—a three-dimensional array of values used to describe a time series of information. Multispectral insights for the past sixteen days revealed no event outside usual parameters. Heavy November rain had covered any tire track, footprint, or heat signature. "We also won't find any evidence of an accomplice. Which doesn't mean there wasn't one."

He pulled out again, higher this time. "But if she went on foot …" Still higher. The nearest area with any population density was the town of Andover. "Only three houses within five miles of the lake. Per the Merrimack assessor's office …" A website filled the screen: lot numbers, square footages, valuations, property taxes, sales histories. Two of the houses had been resold within the past seven years; the third, not for twenty-five. A toggle provided names to go with the addresses: Fisher, Klein, Rockaway. "Rockaway—that's the jogger. Still, doesn't mean someone in the house isn't working with our Janala."

"Spoof 'em," said McConnell.

"Feasible. But we need someone on the scene to run the equipment. I've got nobody I trust closer than Boston. And my wife's been cooking for two days. Maybe tomorrow I could get away …"

"I'll go." Dalia had no classes until next week. Thanksgiving was not her holiday anyway. Both of which Horowitz had no doubt already guessed.

"Shotgun," McConnell said. "Beats the Hungry Man Bachelor's Special."

* * *

Traffic on the holiday was as light as yesterday's had been heavy. Even stopping for gas and a rest-stop meal that tasted like freeze-dried cardboard, they reached the first house on their list—the Rockaway address—at 7:22 p.m.

They parked on a frozen dirt shoulder near the driveway's mouth, behind a compact thatch of evergreen. McConnell opened a laptop in the passenger seat, fired up IMSI Catcher 4.5, and extended the directional antenna.

The program found four hits within two hundred yards: four cell phones inside the house. He sent a command to the first baseband chip. The view on the laptop was of a blank ceiling. Audio as crisp as if the conversation were occurring beside them in the car:

"*I don't approve.*" A man's voice, with a petulant edge.

A woman responded from the background:

"*She deserves a reward. And a girl can only eat so much ice cream.*"

"*Did she like it?*"

"*After I put enough sugar and milk in.*"

"*So she had sugar milk, really, not coffee.*"

"*Can't have it both ways, Jack. Either I'm a bad mother because I gave her coffee or—*"

"*No, you're a bad mother either way.*"

"*Nice.*"

"*Well, you asked.*"

"*Actually, I didn't.*"

"*Actually, you did. You said 'Do you think it's bad I gave Holly coffee?'*"

McConnell killed the link and went on to the next phone in the house. Blackness; an echo of the same conversation, now a room removed:

"*Maybe if you had your own kids, I'd value your opinion. But it's too fucking easy to just sit in the peanut gallery and lob—*"

He killed the connection. Dalia released a breath as he went on to the third signal. A TV soundtrack played:

"*Gee, I never thought of it like that. Do you think I hurt ol' Chuck's feelings? I bet I hurt his feelings, huh? Golly, why can't I act right outside—*"

McConnell smiled. "*A Charlie Brown Thanksgiving.*" He used a church voice, soft and guilty. "What do you think?"

"I think it's an average, innocent family. And I feel dirty."

"Ditto. But this is why we're here."

The fourth phone was either facedown or covered, in a quiet room. He brought in the antenna and powered down the laptop.

She programmed the next address into the Prius' GPS and swung back onto the road.

The Fisher house, a mile and a half distant, perched atop a small hill. Evergreens screened the home on every side, allowing no clear signal. Dalia drove to the next intersection and doubled back on a higher road, coming at the house from above. They parked in relative openness, stars blazing cold overhead, and aimed the microphone.

Two signals inside the house. The first, silent and dark. The second afforded both a soundtrack and an upside-down image: a skinny man with receding hair sitting shirtless before a computer, monologuing, while a golden retriever sprawled on the floor beside him:

"*Of course, you don't even have proof of concept yet. While we've got several promising HAMLET drugs nearing the end of trials. Attacking all at once mitochondria, proteasomes, and histones while interfering with macroautophagy and decreasing mTOR ...*"

McConnell pulled in the antenna as Dalia reached for the GPS.

The third address, Klein, was another mile away. They pulled up to the end of a long dirt drive. The house was concealed by tall woods. McConnell tried and failed to find a signal, reangled the antenna, bombed again. "Closer."

Headlights dead, Prius humming on electric power, they whispered down the driveway. Towering trees blocked icy starlight. A nearly full moon peeked through branches. They drew within a hundred yards of the house, close enough to achieve an uninterrupted sight line. Two stories, white trim. Peeling paint, roof needing work. Garbage cans. A downstairs light burning. Before a garage door, a parked black Chevy Sonic. McConnell worked the laptop again. "Nothing. No phone—or it's blocked."

She put the Prius in reverse. At the end of the driveway, she parked behind trees, fished through her purse, and came out with the gun. "What are you doing?" he asked.

"Going to look around." She opened her door. "Who doesn't have a phone these days? Be careful. If anyone comes, loop back around and pick me up here in half an hour."

She left without giving him a chance to argue. Cold but adrenalized, she stepped off the driveway and moved through forest. Twigs crackling underfoot. Night animals stirring nearby. She saw a flash of movement—perhaps a fox. Then a deer, startlingly close. Dalia stopped, and they regarded each other. A buck. Ten points. Others milling behind it. As she resumed walking, they calmly watched her pass.

This was the place. A feeling on the air, an intuition vibrating in the moonlight. The house was remote—deep in the sticks, by the standards of the American Northeast. The phone was blocked. With today's technology, you could see everywhere. But not here.

Because this house was safe. A safe house.

Jana had been here. She had walked beneath these same trees, across this same frozen woodland floor. This forest, these trees. Not so difficult, Dalia thought, to get into the girl's mind-set—not when she herself was frightened. Exhausted, too. Here in the night forest, survival went to the fastest prey, the most cunning and brutal predator. Israelis lived every day by the same code, surrounded by enemies who wanted them dead: Syria, Lebanon, Saudi Arabia, Libya, Iraq, Jordan, Sudan, Iran, Kuwait, Yemen. Even their so-called allies, Egypt and Germany and France and England, would not truly mourn their destruction. With friends like these …

She focused on approaching the house, avoiding wires or cameras or dogs.

A silhouetted form appeared in the lighted ground-floor window. Dalia froze. An unpleasant tingle moving up her backbone, raising the tiny hairs on her forearms. Her palms felt clammy as she adjusted her grip on the gun.

An outside light came on. Dalia's bladder clenched. She retreated deeper into branches, into darkness.

A side door opened. A man emerged—heavyset, wearing only a T-shirt and jeans. Carrying a white trash bag. Jack Klein, according to the assessor's report. Purchased the property seven years ago. He walked to the garbage cans, lifted a lid, frowned, replaced it, tried the second can, deposited the bag, retraced his steps. The side door closed, and the outside light went off.

Dalia watched his silhouette move past the ground-floor window again, then abruptly disappear, in such a way that she knew he had flopped down—onto a couch, likely as not. His physique spoke of many hours spent flopped down on couches.

A pure exhilaration flooded her. She was moving forward again, stepping into the jaws of the beast; close enough to the house now that should the outside light come on again, she would be caught dead to rights.

She approached the window and confirmed that the man was

indeed sprawled across a couch, watching something on a laptop. And next to him, clearly visible on an end table: a mobile phone. Blocked somehow. But of course.

She moved again, lighter on her feet than she had felt for a while. A girl again—inside, anyway. She circled the house. A patio with a grill, buttoned up tight in anticipation of snow. A snow shovel standing ready by the back door. An empty plastic bucket turned upside down. Around the other side, dark windows. A kitchen, she assumed. No sign of another living soul.

Back around front. A patch of petrified yellow weeds. A ringbarked tree in the last stages of Dutch elm disease. Moon smiling down between dark clouds. What now? What had she really found? Nothing except that feeling, that intuition all atremble.

The garbage cans. He had not replaced the lid flush. She moved it gently aside. Moonlight beamed down, illuminating a banana peel, a twist-tied Hefty bag. She poked aside the banana peel. She loosened the twist-tie and got the bag open.

Coffee grounds. Egg shells. Her nose wrinkled. A fishy smell. She dug deeper. KING OSCAR SARDINES IN EXTRA VIRGIN OLIVE OIL. Empty bag of hulled sesame seeds. Empty bottle of grape-seed oil. Mediterranean food. A taste of home.

Peanut butter. Muesli.

Then the distinctive orange-and-white packaging of Manischewitz: matzo ball soup mix.

Her brow creased. For an instant, she closed her eyes, listening to the muffled drumbeat of her heart. *War drums.*

Her eyes opened. Gingerly, she put the lid back in place, then retreated, moving backward, facing the house so that nothing could leap out and catch her unawares.

PART THREE

CHAPTER EIGHT

NEBRASKA AVENUE NW, WASHINGTON, DC

"You don't understand," Alana Matthews said in her most reasonable and patient voice.

Outside, the December morning was sunny and cloudless, the sky a cold hard blue. Inside, the carpet was moldy and the lead-based paint was chipping off the walls. The dilapidated building had once been a psychiatric hospital—a perfect headquarters, Alana had reflected on seeing it the first time, for an agency suffering from multiple-personality disorder. Twenty-two different bureaus, each with its own established culture, had been crammed haphazardly under a single ragged bureaucratic umbrella. Two crumbling madhouses, made for each other.

From the fraying chair before the desk, Jacob Horowitz said nothing. For the past week, over the phone, he had been the polar opposite of forthcoming. Finally, she had insisted that he come to her sad office on the wrong side of Washington to speak in person. She hoped that upon seeing what she had to deal with, he would relent. Deep down, she knew better.

"You don't understand," she said again, her reasonable, patient tone holding steady. A four-foot-eleven-inch African American woman in a predominantly white, male world got a lot of practice at being patient. “At the end of the day, *I’m* held accountable—personally.”

He looked back at her blankly.

She got up from behind the desk and walked over to the window, with its view of tangled scrub brush. “You’ve coasted this far on your reputation, Jake. And, frankly, because you’ve built up a lot of goodwill around here. But now … need I say it?”

She turned expectantly. He affected weariness. Once they’d spent a tipsy night together at a conference in Virginia. She still remembered his embrace in the dark Hyatt suite. For such a wiry man, he had proved surprisingly strong. “Jacob.”

He smiled. “Alana.”

“I don’t want to waste your time.” Her impatience was seeping through. She took a moment to reassemble the seamless front. “I need *some*thing.”

“Do you trust me?”

“It’s not that …”

“But it is.” He was still smiling gently. “Alana: I *do* understand. I know what you have to deal with. And when it comes around—which it will—I’ll take the hit. Because it’s necessary. It’s worth it. But you have to trust me.”

“Mother-loving Christ.”

“You want to listen to me on this one.”

His calmness was infuriating. She strove to match it. “One more week.”

He said nothing, sitting in the bright clear sunlight with the self-possession of the Buddha.

IRVING STREET NW, WASHINGTON, DC

Jana watched as Michael Fletcher opened the messenger bag.

He scowled at the contents, then lifted out the prosthesis and turned it over in his hands. He wore a weird, thorny expression.

She tried to sound informal. “Try it on.”

For a few seconds, she thought he hadn't heard. Then he nodded, as if to himself. He took off shoes, then socks, then pants, all without the least embarrassment. It occurred to her that he had forgotten he even had an audience.

He removed his left leg below the knee, setting the modular prosthesis on the floor, near the IKEA coffee table. He hefted the replacement appraisingly, then fitted it into the liner and forced out the excess air before pushing the pin back into the housing mechanism. She heard nine clicks. He stood, tested his weight. Wincing slightly, he adjusted the leg and tested again. This time, he nodded guardedly.

"It'll be heavier," she warned, "once it's …"

He looked at her and nodded again.

He circled the small sitting room like a man trying out shoes in a store. Around the sectional couch, around the coffee table, past the lamp, the closet, the shuttered window. Back to the couch, where he sat carefully beside her. His brown eyes glistened, but he wasn't crying.

She let a moment pass, then reached again into the messenger bag. Arranging papers on the coffee table, she ran through the backdrop worked out by Mossad's Research Department. The disclosure was a calculated risk. He would not like what he heard. But no one doubted Michael Fletcher's intelligence. If he sensed a trick, a withholding, he could ruin everything.

The story, like all good stories, had a firm basis in reality. In Hawija and Kirkuk, Michael Fletcher had been friendly with a Shiite interpreter named Mitri. Interviewing former comrades-in-arms after the State of the Union address, investigators would quickly hear of the unusual camaraderie between the soldier and his terp. But upon visiting the Shiite's home in Habbaniyah, they would find signs of a hasty departure—so hasty, in fact, that a simple system restore would salvage an entire hard drive's worth of incriminating evidence. Indicating that Mitri Chalabi had in fact worked for Unit 400 of the Quds Force, the Iranian special-ops division devoted to planning and conducting attacks outside the country. Aiding and abetting Shiite militias in Iraq while undercover as a translator, Mitri had stumbled across a prospective American asset—friendly, emotionally troubled, marriage on rocky ground—who offered much greater potential. They had shared women, drink, drugs. Then Michael Fletcher lost the leg. He turned embittered, unbalanced. And Mitri Chalabi sensed an opportunity.

The operation had been code-named Vadaa, Farsi for "farewell." Questions—Mitri's fate, exactly how the sarin got to America, the precise techniques used to push Michael Fletcher into making the ultimate sacrifice—would linger. For if investigators found too neat a puzzle, their antenna would begin to quiver. But there would be no missing the significance of the schematics calculating blast radii and aerosol dispersals. Names known to the CIA would be found: Iranian engineers who had converted obsolete Pakistani centrifuges, P-1s and P-2s, to functioning cascades, who might credibly design a vacuum-sealed false leg to be filled with nerve agent. And then the smoking gun: diagrams of Capitol Hill security, drawn by Michael Fletcher's own hand, annotated in Farsi.

She finished speaking. The last words hung in the air. She watched Michael closely, waiting for his reaction.

"But …" A narcotic blink. "You said …"

She waited.

"'Future generations will sing songs about you.' That's what you said."

She nodded. "But that comes later. At first, it must be this."

"But …" Blink. "My son."

"He'll know the truth. When he's old enough."

"How?"

She touched his shoulder. "I'll make sure."

"What if they find Mitri? He'll tell them …"

She shook her head.

He said nothing. Still sitting there in his boxer shorts. Barefoot, like an overgrown kid, his brown cowlick standing on end. A muscle worked in his jaw.

She reached for him. Stripped off his shirt, laid him back on the couch. "You're strong," she breathed into his ear. "You're brave."

His hands removed her blouse mechanically, exploring the double-fin of her shoulder blades. His gaze searched her face. She tipped her hair self-consciously forward, covering the scars. Felt the color rising in her cheeks. Slowly. Slowly. And then faster, his fingers digging into her hips, hard enough to leave bruises.

Afterward, she kissed him. Gently. His lips parted invitingly, but she was already climbing off him.

She dressed facing away from him. For a few seconds, he sat watching; then he started putting his clothes on. Neither spoke another word.

NORTH OF ANDOVER, VT

In the day's last light, Dalia parked between an EMS vehicle and a Lenco BearCat and climbed the splintery porch steps.

She paused for a moment in the doorway, taking in the bustling common area beneath the gambrel roof. Little had changed during her four-day absence. The linchpin of the command center remained the large monitor above the flagstone fireplace: a terrain map with digital green crosshairs and endlessly changing data displays. The Autonomous Real-Time Ground Ubiquitous Surveillance Imaging System, ARGUS-IS, offered more than just a clever acronym referencing the all-seeing mythological Greek giant Argus Panoptes. At 1.8 billion pixels, ARGUS used the world's highest-resolution camera. Unlike most airborne systems, which provided either a wide-field view for surveillance or a narrow-field view for target acquisition, the drone could do both simultaneously. From twenty thousand feet above Klein's house, the device gave an overview covering thirty-six square miles, and an option to open a window focusing on a select field with a resolution of ten centimeters. Sixty-five such windows could be opened at once. A processing subsystem streamed live footage while storing one million terabytes of video per day, meaning that military or civilian operators—not that the United States government would admit that this technology existed, let alone had been implemented by domestic law enforcement—could record everything that happened in a target area. And then they could cherry-pick a time after the fact, go back through their archives, and view any given street corner from the past month, with enough resolution to identify a human face.

After a moment, Dalia proceeded forward. Her arrival was roundly disregarded by a roomful of young men and women monitoring ARGUS and StingRay, feeds from parabolic microphones, and infrared and ultraviolet video. An analyst sitting slightly apart from the others scrolled through incoming police reports. Coffee mugs and cans of Red Bull populated every horizontal surface. A handheld police P25 radio lay flat on a bridge table near a laminated field map into which Jim McConnell was sticking a red pushpin.

Horowitz appeared at her left elbow. Before she could ask, he shook his head.

In the small kitchen, they brewed tea and sat in moody silence. A scented candle—a relic of the lodge's previous incarnation—rested on the table's green-and-white-checkered gingham: COUNTRY COMFORT COLLECTION. Dalia picked at the label, frowning. Idly picking up the small box of Diamond matches beside the candle, she tapped it against the tabletop. Tens of millions of dollars' worth of equipment at their disposal, yet she did not feel hopeful.

She shook out three matches, arranging them in parallel near the edge of the table, and thought of Hannibal at Cannae: the textbook example of the futility of superior technology and manpower. Two centuries before Christ, the Romans, ninety thousand strong, had cornered Hannibal, whose force numbered less than half that, against the Aufidus River. Most of the Carthaginian troops were inexperienced—an untested hodgepodge of Iberians and Gauls with shoddy arms and poor armor. And the Roman consuls knew it.

Lazily they had arranged their superior numbers in three ranks—the three parallel matches—believing that the untried and outnumbered Carthaginian army, with no room to maneuver against the riverbank—the table's edge—would be cut down in panicked disorder as the massed legionnaires drove relentlessly forward.

In response, Hannibal had deployed his weakest men in front. Dalia broke a fourth match into four pieces, which she arranged in a shallow convex crescent facing the three parallel lines. Offering his soft white throat to the enemy. Goading the superior Roman infantry to continue its advance, he placed his few battle-hardened troops—African infantry—far at the flanks. Hannibal himself had stood in the center among his inferior foot soldiers, steeling their courage while personally leading a controlled retreat, step by step, foot by foot, slowly and methodically, in the process turning the Roman position inside out. With a fingertip, Dalia inverted the arrangement of the broken match fragments, turning the convex formation concave. Then she pushed the three unbroken matches closer, filling the open space inside the semicircle. Now the outermost bits of broken match flanked the ends of the three unbroken matches.

And then, with whipcrack timing, the veteran African infantry had wheeled on the flanks of the now-disordered legionnaires, who now faced east, into glaring sun and windblown sand. A devastating double envelopment—history's most effective pincer movement. And the Romans, suddenly enclosed in a pocket, packed tightly together, entangled and half-blind, were cut down like wheat. Every minute, six hundred legionnaires perished. Seventy-five thousand had died before nightfall put an end to the slaughter. Barely three thousand escaped. Hannibal at Cannae had turned the tables on a force that outnumbered him more than two to one—and exacted casualties at a rate of *ten* to one. And yet, military leaders still insisted on seeing as counterintuitive, despite ever-mounting proof, the lesson that maneuverability trumped force. Alexander crossing the Danube on improvised rafts where his enemy thought the river uncrossable; MacArthur, during his

South Pacific campaign, seizing only the islands he needed as stepping-stones northward; the Russians implementing their Deep Battle Doctrine during Operations Bagration and August Storm. And *still*, for the West, might and firepower reigned supreme, always and forever. And so they would deploy their priceless equipment, their bottomless resources of manpower, and still a lone girl would prove faster and more maneuverable, ultimately leaving them with nothing.

She rubbed her eyes. Horowitz was looking at her. "You okay?"

She shrugged. "*Hafookh.*" Beat.

"Get some sleep." He reached out and patted her hand. "Anything develops, I'll let you know."

WISCONSIN AVE., WASHINGTON, DC

Browsing through Bath and Body Works, looking for gifts for Mommy and preschool teachers and grandmas and grandpas, canned Muzak piping through speakers, and suddenly a voice inside his head voice spoke up from nowhere: *Funny how life works out, innit it, Mikey?*

The voice had been triggered by the Muzak, which evoked Kirkuk mosques broadcasting propaganda through their crackly PA systems. The United States was in Iraq only to seize the oil and wealth of holy warriors, and so on. *But now* you're *the holy warrior. And when the time comes, you'll strap on your suicide vest and Allahu Akbar your way to paradise right alongside the rest. Funny, innit?* Wink, nudge.

The voice sounded a lot like his dead brother's. But Seth had been a soft-spoken young man—polite, conscientious, kind. This voice was obnoxious, lewd, sardonic. Michael decided to pay no attention.

After shopping, they grabbed a pizza to go. Stacy was coming to pick up Silas after dinner. They sat at the dining room table on Ellicott Street, working their way through half a plain pie. And as

Michael watched his son chew, the voice turned somber. *Gonna leave this kid without a father, Mikey. And once you're gone, you know what he'll hear about you? That Daddy was a crazy vet fuck. An enemy of the people. And don't believe for a second, Mikey, that the bitch is going to come tell him the truth like she promised. Why would she? I think we've been around the block a few too many times to believe—*

Shut up, voice. Leave me alone.

Silas chewed pensively. "Daddy, what's pizza made out of?"

"Bread and cheese and tomato sauce."

"I love cheese. I love it five thousand times."

Michael smiled. "I love it five thousand plus one."

"I love it five thousand plus infinity plus one."

"Everyone loves cheese, I guess."

"Lou doesn't."

Michael kept his face pleasant. "Who's Lou?"

"Mommy's sleepover friend."

There it is, Mikey.

"Huh," he said.

Too old, he guessed, to get consumed by jealousy—been around the block a few too many times, as the voice had pointed out. Still, he might have expected to feel *something*. His soon-to-be ex-wife, mother of his only child, shacking up with Lou, who didn't care for cheese.

But he felt nothing. Nothing at all.

"Huh," he said again. And that seemed to cover it.

"Can I go play?"

"Sure. Go play."

Silas bounded away, and Michael sat alone at the table, looking dully at his half-eaten slice of pizza.

He knew a dozen grunts who had gotten hitched at courthouses the week before deploying, just so someone would get their benefits if they came home in a box. And while his own effort at matrimony had risen slightly above that dismal standard, half of him, he guessed, had never really been invested in the union with Stacy. He had gone along with the program, sure. But he had been a passenger, a bystander. Just look at the honeymoon picture hanging by the staircase. His body had been at Niagara Falls. But his eyes, his mind, his heart, had been somewhere else. He remembered the wedding day: tinted sunlight coming through stained-glass windows. A church wedding: psalms and pious murmurs and lacy white. And what had he thought at the time? One word. *Bullshit.*

At last, he carried plates into the kitchen. He dumped half-eaten pizza into the garbage and stood, looking at nothing, as the cat wound around his ankles. The house was quiet. Silas was quiet. The block was quiet. Even the voice was quiet—for now.

* * *

After Stacy picked up their son, Michael went into his bedroom, turned on the lights, drew the shades, and took off the prosthetic leg.

Sitting on the edge of the bed, blinking slowly like a man in a dream, he gave it the closest inspection yet. Beneath the carbon fiber shell, molded plastic casing contained six vacuum-sealed cavities. Each cylindrical cavity sloped up, with its own customized fuse and detonator built in at the base.

During their latest meeting, the woman had explained that Mossad engineers had considered two possible approaches. Speaking slowly and carefully, making sure Michael understood every word—not because she wanted him, having been made aware of the consequences of his choices, to reconsider. He knew that she did it only so that if he *did* reconsider, she could witness it happening and take action to prevent it.

The first option had been a spray device with multiple nozzles. A single drop of sarin mist, twenty-six times deadlier than cyanide, was fatal to a full-grown man. A liquid form of the substance had been used in Japan in 1995, when five members of the doomsday cult Aum Shinrikyo had boarded subway cars during Tokyo's morning rush hour, holding plastic packets wrapped in newspaper.

They had dropped the packets to the floor, punctured the newspaper and plastic packets with the sharpened tips of their umbrellas, then retreated, leaving trainloads of commuters to die. The toxin had both leaked onto the floor and evaporated into the air. Sloppy planning and cowardly execution, using no mechanism more complicated than an umbrella, and the casualties still had been high. Twelve dead, fifty crippled, and many thousands injured.

"*But our target area is much larger than a subway car. And every corner will be filled with objectives worth reaching. Our payload will be surrounded by obstacles ...*"

"Obstacles": a polite euphemism for human flesh—including, of course, Michael's own. He thought of Abdullah al-Asiri. In 2009, the al-Qaeda operative had tried to murder Saudi Arabia's deputy minister of the interior, gaining access to the man's Jiddah home during Ramadan by claiming to be a well-wisher. Passing successfully through a metal detector and a search by bodyguards, al-Asiri had waited more than twenty-four hours with half a kilo of *plastique* hidden inside his rectum. When at last he had achieved direct proximity to his target, his own body absorbed the brunt of the explosion. He succeeded only in lightly wounding Muhammad bin Nayef, while killing himself. Human flesh was an effective absorber of explosive force.

"*To achieve maximum dissemination,*" she had said, "*we must volatilize our liquid to gas.*" Unwilling or perhaps unable to disguise her enthusiasm, her cool gray eyes glinting keenly. "*Aum Shinrikyo initially planned a similar approach, hoping to spread the agent as an aerosol. But they lacked a team of talented engineers to make it happen. Of course, Israeli engineers are the best in the world. Child's play, they assure me. A small explosion to break open the ampoules and raise the temperature beyond sarin's boiling point of 158 degrees Celsius. Then dispersal occurs through natural Brownian motion.*"

Initial symptoms included running nose, tightness in the chest, constriction of pupils. Then nausea, difficulty breathing, drooling.

Vomiting, incontinence. Twitching, convulsive spasms. Death from asphyxia, within minutes.

It had to be done. A tragedy, a crime against God—but history, left unchecked, would only repeat itself.

Again and again and again, just because they were Jewish.

For no other reason than that.

It was the right thing to do.

It had to be done.

NORTH OF ANDOVER, VT

"Dalia."

A strange overlay of past and present: sitting up abruptly in bed, as if jabbed with a needle.

"Dalia."

"Mm. What time is it?"

"Four a.m." In the dimness, McConnell's eyes gleamed like obsidian. "We've got her."

Still in her nightgown, Dalia followed McConnell into the makeshift operations room. Horowitz handed her a steaming mug. She took one sip, set the cup on the mantel of the fireplace, accepted headphones.

The call had been recorded eight minutes ago. Whatever method the man called Klein had used to block the spoof apparently also worked on StingRay. They were listening to a feed from a parabolic mike—mostly high end, tinny, and hissing. Nevertheless, Dalia could clearly hear the voice, thick with interrupted sleep: "Hello."

The reply was dim but audible. "Lots of fog," a woman said. "Not safe to drive. I'm taking an alternate route."

A pause as the man no doubt processed code phrases. "Drive safe," he answered. "Ten and two."

The recording ended. The whole thing had lasted eleven seconds. Before Dalia could comment, a drone operator called breathlessly, "On the move."

Through a night-vision camera, they watched a lumpy glow leave the door of the house and climb into the car—not the blue Mazda registered to Klein, which was still MIA, but the black Chevrolet Sonic RS he had leased from a dealer in Concord six weeks ago. The Chevy turned around and eased down the long driveway.

"Dust," Horowitz said.

The screen shaded from pink to purple, from thermal to ultraviolet. The spy dust—powdered nitrophenyl pentadien mixed with luminol, sprinkled liberally onto the Sonic's door handles, steering wheel, and floor mats and now clinging to Klein's hands and feet—glowed like phosphorus.

Facing the laminated field map, Horowitz found a channel on the P25 radio. "Checking Alpha."

In response, a distant fire-team leader keyed his radio once.

"Alpha, we're warm. Tango, eight o'clock. Bravo, route two. Charlie, LCC."

On-screen, the purple smear that was the Sonic reached the end of the driveway and turned north.

"Alpha, Tango, twelve o'clock. Bravo, route three to rally point two."

He lowered the radio to his hip. Without turning from the screen, he echoed McConnell: "We've got her."

* * *

Lying prone on a high ridge, Jana watched the Chevy roll away down the long driveway.

She relaxed slightly—if they had traced her call, they would be on her already. No doubt they had left behind cameras, microphones, night-vision, drones, satellites. But they would not be expecting her here. They would expect her to rendezvous with the Chevy. She had bought herself a chance.

One last moment to steel herself. Then she clamped her teeth together, picked up the shovel, and went, hugging three layers of blankets around her shoulders. The layer nearest her coat was wool.

Then a heat-reflecting blanket of polyethylene terephthalate. Then wool again. It wouldn't render her thermal signature completely invisible—high-end imagers detected not only changes in temperature, but also the actual photons emitted by an object—but the three layers would afford her some breathing room.

In alabaster moonlight, she scampered down the ridge, using every available bit of cover. Clumsy, half-shambling under the weight of the blankets. Prickly brush tugged at the outer layer of wool. She detoured around a shallow dip, keeping thick branches overhead. She remembered moving through this forest the first time, burying the cache. And the second, coming back from the lake. The third time would be the last. Third time for keeps.

Beyond a thicket of evergreens, she spied the gnarled yellow elm she had dug beneath. Cover overhead; cover between her and the house. Still, she made herself pause, sniffing, listening, searching the night. She found a glint of moonlight off metal, almost close enough to touch. A camera. She had nearly blundered right through its sight line. Holding her breath, she backed away slowly and circled carefully, approaching from a roundabout route. *Slow down, god damn it. You'll ruin everything.*

The freshly turned earth, the branches and leaves and pine needles, was still distinguishable two months later. After looking one last time for cameras, she raised the shovel—fiberglass, $19.98, from Lowe's—and jammed the blade into hard soil. Frozen. Like digging through rock. *Put your back into it. Hurry.*

No. *Shvoye*, Yoni had taught her. Patience. The Chevy would lead them all the way to Burlington. Two hundred miles round trip. Her contact would linger for at least an hour before giving up. Altogether, she could reasonably expect five hours in which to work. Her task would take a fraction of that. She felt exposed, vulnerable, but she must slow down, stay aware, notice every little thing.

We may have suffered a lack of sanitation.

That was one goddamn way of putting it.

Crunch. A centimeter's give this time. *Hurry.* Crunch. *No. Slow down.* Crunch. *Pause*, crunch, *look*, crunch, *listen.*

She rested, breathing hard now. Looked, listened, dug again. A faraway red light atop a radio tower pulsed like a heartbeat. Watery predawn diffused the moonlight. Just as she had timed it. As she labored, her heat signature would surge, eventually becoming visible to heat sensors despite the blankets. But so-called thermal crossover, the axis of night turning to day, would smear the data and help keep her concealed.

Somewhere very far away, the howl of a police siren. She straightened, cocking her head. Back throbbing. Sweat pouring down her temples, pooling beneath her collar, collecting in the small of her back. No siren. Just her imagination.

Hurry, for fuck's sake.

No. Shvoye.

With a grunt, she went back to digging.

Wind picked up, sailing a rack of clouds in front of the moon. Chilling the sweat, making her shiver. The clouds sailed on. She became aware of her shadow lumping behind her, squat and distorted, a laboring dwarf. *We dig dig dig in our mine the whole day through. To dig dig dig is what we really like to do!*

Deep enough now to penetrate below the frost. Softer soil, easier going. Blisters forming on her palm and the pad of her thumb. Dank smell of fresh dirt, rising in wafts. The smell of gardens, of life, of graves, of death. Close now. Had she missed it? Did she have the wrong spot?

The breeze sang darkly through the trees. She tossed yet another shovelful of gravelly earth, pitter-patter, to one side. Half a minute later, she paused again to catch her breath. Took advantage of the pause to look, listen, sniff the wind. Felt her ears lie back like a cat's. Forced herself to dig again. *We dig dig dig ... Let the wild rumpus start!*

Then she was lifting the faded black briefcase on the shovel blade. More faded than ever, earthworms writhing atop the fraying leather. She stared at it in dumb astonishment. Apparently, she had dislodged the case without realizing it, and then kept digging. But now here it was.

The shivers were back, from scalp to tailbone. Delicious and terrifying, the all-over tingle one felt after almost stepping in front of a bus. In her headlong race to dig, hammering away with the shovel, she might easily have broken one of the ampoules inside the case. Yes, she very easily might have done that. And then she would be dead.

Her knees buckled unexpectedly from the fatigue. She straightened and gave herself a minute, leaning against the shovel, to regain control of herself. Setting aside the wormy black case, she resumed digging. *Plastique* now. The shovel could not set it off by mistake—you could grind out a cigarette in the stuff; it was that stable—but a strange kind of superstition had fallen over her, and now she dug softly, gently.

When she uncovered the first block, the motor-oil smell summoned the old flashback: the boy wearing the checkered kaffiyeh, the earthy-oily whiff of RDX … She forced the memory away. Uncovered the Saran-wrapped chunk. Then another, and another.

She paused again, calculating. She would need only a fraction of this amount—no more than could fit inside the black valise. The vacuum-sealed prosthesis contained its own customized fuses and detonators. That left her some extra explosive, some unnecessary blasting caps …

They would realize soon enough that she had been here. Why not leave them a little surprise—send a message and perhaps, in the process, buy herself some more time to maneuver?

She set aside a block of explosive: enough to serve her purposes with Michael Fletcher, with some extra left over for safety. The remaining blocks she prepared with Nonel tubes and electric blasting caps. Checked connections, programmed the numbers. She reburied the bulk of the C-4, but poorly. Left the shovel sticking out from beneath cover, where they couldn't miss it.

As she made her way back to the high ridge, a mountain intervened between her and the rising sun. And for a few moments there in the breaking dawn, she cast no shadow at all.

* * *

The operations room had become a cauldron of activity.

Horowitz had pulled out all the stops, and to good effect. Klein would lead them to the girl. Two tac teams, with a third on reserve, would pounce. All-seeing ARGUS could not be escaped—a sure thing if ever there was one.

But Dalia Artzi had devoted her professional life to the thesis that maneuverability trumped force. The illusion of overwhelming advantage was just that. Take things at face value, and you risked losing the forest for the trees, just as Napoleon had done at the Château d'Hougoument.

These trees. This forest right here, portrayed in scintillating digital bits on the monitor above the fireplace.

The woman's voice had been unexpectedly young, girlish. "*Lots of fog. Not safe to drive.*"

How had she known that it was not safe? Because Yoni Yariv was at the bottom of a well. Because Yoni had missed some prearranged signal, some expected communiqué, and so Jana had realized that something was amiss.

And why should Dalia have been surprised by the youthfulness of the voice? The voice fit the face. Just a girl. But make no mistake: a killer. Savvy, cunning, and utterly ruthless.

Jana knew they were onto her, which meant she knew, or at least suspected, that her contact had been compromised. Yet she was still delivering herself to them?

No. Jana was using Klein as a diversion.

On the monitor, ARGUS depicted thirty-six square miles of terrain via 1.8 billion glorious pixels, with Klein's house increasingly off center—the bullseye following the Chevy. "The house," Dalia said aloud.

Horowitz turned. "What about it?"

"She's drawing us away. We've got to *watch the house.*"

Horowitz frowned, gestured to a tech. Seconds later, another window opened on-screen, close on the house. Dalia regarded the roof in need of new shingles, silvered in the dawn light. The snow shovel standing ready. Garbage cans, the lids propped on loosely again.

Her gaze moved. To the girdled tree near the driveway. That same intuition vibrating. Jana had been here.

She found a glint.

Suddenly, Horowitz was beside her. Gesturing again. The camera zoomed closer. They were looking at several centimeters of metal: a pipe, a handle, barely exposed beneath an overhang of branches. "What is it?" he murmured.

Dalia shook her head. The resolution sharpened. Not metal, she thought. Some kind of metallic-sheened polypropylene. A black plastic link handle … "A shovel."

Horowitz turned to the tech. "Was that there before?"

A moment of fumbling; then an earlier image of the same patch of forest appeared. 05:44:30. The glint was there.

"Earlier."

05:22. The glint was gone.

But in its place was a flesh-colored smudge.

"Enlarge," Horowitz commanded.

The image enlarged, resolved. A sliver of cheek, smudged with dirt, barely visible through the branches, peeking out from beneath a brown covering, perhaps a blanket.

Dalia closed her eyes. The world seemed to be falling away behind her.

Less than an hour before. Less than five miles away.

A final, frozen instant. Then Horowitz went back to the radio. "Charlie. Checking Charlie. Charlie, rally point one ASAP."

"I'm going," Dalia announced, already turning for the door.

* * *

The sun climbed higher.

Birds twittered. An early rising woodpecker hammered. Jana could have been using these minutes to make her escape. But she equivocated, lying prone on the ridge beneath the three layers of blankets, phone in hand.

Just when she was about to give up and not throw more good minutes after bad, she felt a change in the forest. Birds quieted. Her ears twitched. A distant, muffled engine approached.

And another. They stopped far away. Jana held still, blisters stinging, back aching, finger hovering.

She heard the dogs. They kept quiet, as they had been trained to do; but they were eager, snuffling and nosing excitedly through the forest undergrowth. Then she saw them: pulling against a tangle of leashes. Something inside her went slack. Fear of dogs was primal. But her rational mind elbowed past it. The wind blew into her face, so they would not scent her, and in a moment they would no longer exist and she would be on her way.

Patience.

The forward member of the team appeared, working to handle the leashes. Another man came up alongside him, signaling. The point man stopped. The second man moved ahead and found cover behind a tree, checked the mirror on the grip of his pistol, and signaled again. In this method, spilling forward and then drawing up tight behind, reorienting, moving again, the tac team advanced. Toward the bait, the gleaming shovel handle.

She had killed before. A man with whom she'd just been intimate. Up close, with her hands. Now she would kill from a distance. Men she had never even met. The push of a button. Nothing at all.

She licked her lips.

One dog gave an eager little yip; scenting the explosives, launching toward the mound from which the shovel protruded. Jana started to push the button.

Then she registered another approach—a civilian, blundering noisily through trees. With a fraction of an ounce still left to exert on the key, she paused.

The newcomer was a woman. Flat-footed carriage, broad, heavy shoulders. As old as Jana's mother, maybe even older. Wearing a cheap, tacky coat. And—*really?*—a powder-blue nightgown. Drawing up close behind the tac team. A few more steps, and she, too, would be within the blast radius.

But the woman had stopped. She was talking with the team leader. The wind carried the words to Jana. Phlegmy fricatives, rhonchial consonants. An Israeli. Urging the team, it seemed, not to get too close. The woman had sensed a trap. Who was this bitch in her tacky nightgown?

Then they were starting to withdraw—yanking leashes, doubtless planning to regroup at a safer distance.

Jana pressed the button.

Next thing she knew, she was on her back. The echo of the explosion rolling away, bouncing off mountains, coming back mockingly. Ears ringing. *Déjà vu.* Heat on the air, daggers of fire.

The bitch with the big shoulders was also on the ground, surrounded by tongues of flame. But moving. Most of the men moving, too. Crawling. Except one. Blackened, lifeless. Dogs yowling, others inert.

Shaking beneath the burden of the blankets, Jana found her feet again. The detonation had been much more powerful than expected. She had dropped the phone. She hunted for it, but her eyes wouldn't focus. The forest floor swam and heaved crazily. Her entire body was trembling.

Fuck the phone.

But the valise …

There.

She snatched it up, then turned, legs quivering, ears singing, and began working her way back toward the Mazda on the fire road.

CHAPTER NINE

NORTH OF ANDOVER, VT

She drove twenty miles before the car suddenly felt unsafe.

The nearest mass transit was another thirty miles. But if she stayed in the Mazda, she would never make it.

Just a feeling, but Jana trusted her feelings.

Half a mile later, in the brightening dawn, she reached a frozen mud track rolling away from the main road. Broad tractor treads herringboned into petrified mud. During December, the farm track would see minimal use. Turning onto it, she bumped past a silo, a cowshed, a fenced-in pasture where bovine heads turned to follow her progress. She drove another hundred yards. Reaching an orchard, she pulled behind a stand of bare fruit trees, locked the car, and hiked back to the road.

She continued on foot in the direction she had been driving. A ceaseless high tone, thin and sharp as a blade, still buzzed between her ears.

The first car she heard sounded wrong. A big, powerful engine grinding along in a low gear: a military vehicle, maybe a half-track. She hid behind a stand of pines and watched it pass. Not military after all. A civilian three-quarter-ton pickup, driven by a girl who looked too young. If Jana's hearing had been right, she would not have made the mistake.

She walked again. A quarter-hour passed before she heard another a car. This time, with the buzz receding at last, she parsed the sound carefully. Four-cylinder engine, traveling at a good clip. Time to take a chance. She thrust out her thumb.

The lime-green Toyota Camry had Vermont plates. The driver was in her midfifties, with tangled gray hair falling around a blue windbreaker. She pulled over and leaned across to open the door. The well beneath the glove box was filled with coffee cups, empty cigarette packs, coleslaw containers.

"Going my way?" the woman asked.

"Going *any* way," Jana said as she slipped in, "long as it's going. Thanks for stopping."

"My neighborly duty. Car trouble?"

"No, ma'am."

They pulled back onto the road. "Hitching?"

"Yes, ma'am."

"You travel light." She nodded at the black case.

"Try to," said Jana easily.

"I'm Steph." The woman shook hands, not paying much attention to the road.

"Skye."

Steph pulled a joint from behind one ear, fished a plastic lighter from the ashtray, and, though it was not yet 8:00 a.m., offered both. Jana accepted politely and lit the joint, puffed twice, and handed it back.

"Thumbed cross-country myself." Steph held in the smoke, exhaled, and cracked open her window. She took another hit and passed the joint. "'Course—*phhhaugh*—that was a long time ago. Different world. Everybody …" She covered a racking series of coughs. "Did it then. These days, you never know." She spat out the window. "Had much trouble?"

"I can take care of myself."

"Where you coming from?"

"Originally, Scranton. But I headed west first."

"You got it backwards. Ought to head west for winter."

"It *was* winter. Last year."

"You a Libra?"

"Taurus."

"Could have sworn you were a Libra."

They drove without speaking for a few moments. Jana watched the side mirror. No sign of pursuit. She could feel the marijuana fuzzing her edges.

"I can take you as far as Coolidge," Steph announced. "My ex-husband lives there. Technically, I guess, still my husband. We never signed the papers. But it's been, oh, God, fifteen years. He's sick now."

"I'm so sorry."

"Part of life." Steph tried to smoke, found the joint had gone out, and put it in the ashtray. "Part of life," she said again, and lit a Merit without offering the pack.

"Mind if I close my eyes? It's been a weird couple of days."

"Sweet dreams, angel."

Jana closed her eyes, then surreptitiously cracked one lid, checking the side mirror again. Nothing except receding landscape. Her fatigue was immense. The digging, the sleepless night, the stress, the weed. Maybe a concussion. She closed the lid again, felt her head roll loosely on her neck. Surely she would not actually fall asleep in these circumstances.

She woke to a hand on her shoulder and only just caught herself before twisting it back reflexively into a submission hold.

"Wake up, angel. We're here."

One- and two-story red-brick buildings, a single stoplight, old-fashioned clock tower—quarter past eight. Like a Hollywood movie set from the 1950s, Jana thought. A bakery proclaimed, We Deliver Fresh Daily. Beside it, a barbershop's red-white-and-blue helix was the only thing moving on this side of the street. Signs pointed to nearby interstates 89 and 91. She could picture the Beav trotting down this sidewalk.

Steph smiled. "Good luck, traveler."

Jana considered killing her and taking the car. But satellites might have seen them; the Camry might be compromised. And there was a witness, a man soaping windows across from the bakery. So she returned the smile. "Thanks for the ride."

Standing on the sidewalk with her small case in hand, she watched the Camry drone away, then looked up into the cloudless blue sky. *Say cheese.*

She turned a tight circle, contemplating her next move.

Beyond the brief main street, a residential neighborhood unfolded: square Georgian architecture, sun-kissed cupolas and gables and steeples, cars parked in driveways. But even if she could steal one without the satellite noticing, the theft would quickly be reported.

She found a train station. PARK AND RIDE. A shining dome topped with a rusted weather vane. Just opening, shutters swinging back. Beyond the station, railroad tracks with the occasional missing tie, weeds and brambles, weathered utility poles, all receding toward a distant vanishing point.

Safest way to travel. But again, there were satellites to consider. At the first stop, she might find a small army waiting to take her off.

She looked the other way. Far down the street, a discolored Greyhound logo.

Her stomach growled at the smell of fresh bread.

A quiet bell announced her entrance into the bakery. Vivaldi's lilting strains mingled with the scent of baking bread. Loaves and muffins and rolls and croissants on display, soft in the morning sunshine. A kind-faced man in a dough-stained apron stood behind the register. He smiled, tipping an imaginary hat. She smiled back. A small town, but also a transit hub in an area populated by aging hippies. An unknown young woman was nothing out of the ordinary.

After buying a roll and a cup of coffee, she left the bakery.

She paused briefly, then continued down the street toward the bus station, staying in plain sight. Giving any satellite plenty of opportunity to find and photograph her. Giving them plenty of rope.

Chewing hot buttered bread, she passed American Legion Post 26 … a cigar store … a stationery store. Upper Valley Food Co-op, EVERYONE WELCOME. The coffee was strong and good.

A dog barked; her heart tripped. A long, rangy poodle on the far side of the street pulled at the end of a leash, straining after a fluttering pigeon. As the owner heeled it, Jana's heart found its regular rhythm.

She reached the bus station. Except for a blue-capped woman behind a ticket window, the place was empty. It smelled of Lysol and clay mud. A security camera goggled beneath a large IBM wall clock. In plain view of the camera, Jana walked to the counter and waited where the gray Formica had been worn almost white by decades of elbows. On being told the next bus to Portland, Maine, left in two hours, she bought a ticket for forty-two dollars plus tax. When asked for ID, she produced a driver's license she had made with a color printer and thermal laminator. Lacking a biometric chip and magnetic bar code, it would not get her across any international borders, but it should get her across a couple of state lines.

In the women's room, she set the coffee and black valise on the enamel edge of a sink, shucked off her pea coat, and turned it inside out, changing the color from navy blue to pale yellow. The fraying liner would pass superficial inspection. Examining her reflection in the mirror, she saw an unappealing young woman: underfed, underrested, with a bad dye job. The scars seemed to stand out, making her face look vaguely asymmetrical. Cheap jeans and a peasant blouse and a threadbare, inside-out jacket. She touched the hair, then took off the coat again. Tearing a strip from the back of her blouse, she fashioned a ragged kerchief that, seen from above, would cover most of the blond. She tied it under her chin. It was the best she could do for now.

She put the coat on again, slipped the case beneath it, and left the restroom and the bus depot without looking back. Retracing her route back up the street, she kept beneath the shop awnings as much as possible. At the stoplight, she waited for a small knot of pedestrians to collect and crossed with them.

Before entering the train station, she scanned from the doorway. No obvious cameras—in this day and age, hard to believe. Maybe a better class of passengers rode the train than the bus.

There, an opaque black dome half-hidden by a sprinkler head. Probably with a 360-degree field of view. She made her eyes keep moving, as if looking for a friend. After quickly scanning the departure board, she turned casually away and walked a few yards down the block. She found a bench beneath a sidewalk awning and sat, tucking the case beneath her legs, and enjoyed her coffee.

Ten minutes passed. Laughing children bought doughnuts at the bakery. Two dog walkers gossiped about a yoga class. *Thud, thud*, went her head. She wondered again about a concussion. No. Just the exertion of digging, and the stress, fear, and fatigue. She was okay.

She closed her eyes. The case beneath the bench contained enough sarin to kill hundreds, maybe thousands. She opened her eyes.

No cops. No soldiers. No sign of the old Israeli woman in the woods. A bucolic small town, cut and pasted directly from the Universal Studios back lot.

The blister on her thumb felt puffy and tender. She rubbed it absently.

The old woman had sensed the trap. A civilian, crashing like a boar through the forest, yet she had sensed the trap where the military team had failed. Who was she? An Israeli. Yet working against Israel. Working for the Americans. *We may have suffered a lack of sanitation.*

A group of kids, not much younger than she, were coming down the sidewalk. Backpackers, redolent of patchouli and body odor, each lugging half their own weight in gear … and heading for the train station. She would not find a better chance. She stood, case and coffee in hand, and mingled good-naturedly among the backpackers, slipping into the station under their cover.

Inside, they formed an unruly line at the ticket window. She waited her turn, sticking close, and bought a ticket aboard the 57 Vermonter on the Northeastern Corridor. Using a fresh driver's license, she splurged on a business-class seat—a hundred and sixteen dollars.

Then she found a seat on a hard wooden bench near the kids and blended in. Twenty-two minutes until the train departed. Surely they would board a few minutes earlier.

Holding the empty cup in her lap, she waited, counting down from five again and again.

NORTH OF ANDOVER, VT

Fifty miles away, Jacob Horowitz scowled at the monitor above the fireplace.

"Boss." A small woman with a pale, strained face, whose body seemed to float inside a large fleece parka that she kept zipped nearly to the top. She had called Horowitz "boss" since their first day in the lodge. Dalia suspected that he appreciated the implied authority, even though—perhaps *because*—it was not strictly true. The real boss of this outfit was Operations Coordination in DC. Led by a woman named Alana Matthews, who held twice-daily phone conferences with Horowitz, after which he always looked as if he had received the telephonic equivalent of a particularly distressing suppository.

Frowning, he moved to the tech's console. Dalia drifted behind so she could see, too. She had taken four Tylenol with codeine, supplied by a medic from the EMS vehicle. Now the pain of the bruised leg and hip were gone, and the throbbing in her forearm had faded to the smart of a bad sunburn. But the codeine had set her head mizzling like a spring rain. Her ears still rang with a loud electronic tone, which came and went in waves.

Now the tone came again, and she missed the woman's next words. But she saw Horowitz lean closer to the screen. The live feed portrayed thirty-six square miles, centered on Klein's house, where one member of the tac team had been killed and three severely wounded by the young woman's booby trap. A highlighted off-center square had been enlarged twentyfold: cowshed, silo, orchard, barn, rustic farmhouse, pasture dotted with cattle.

The view of the orchard inflated again. A rutted dirt track; a metallic blue dot hidden in a row of bare trees.

On the monitor above the fireplace, the image appeared and then enlarged yet again, to a resolution of ten centimeters. They were looking at a blue Mazda 3 hatchback—Klein's missing car—expediently abandoned in an apple orchard. New windows popped up as techs struggled to find workable views of the license plates, which had apparently been slathered with wet mud and then left to dry.

Someone to Dalia's left asked a question. She missed it—the tinnitus still—but caught the answer. "Waterbury, Montpelier, Randolph, Coolidge, White River Junction, Windsor. Trying to get access to their systems. Charlie's ready to roll. But not till we've got something solid."

The satellite pulled away to a relatively medium shot. Other windows closed. The feed flickered, switching from real time to cached video, then began to run backward. A time code counted down from 09:18. A crow flew backward. Cows remained mostly motionless. On the country road intersecting the rutted track, a pickup truck rolled the wrong way. Daylight darkened slowly toward dawn.

At 07:53, a lime-green compact car with Vermont plates rolled backward down from the top of the screen. It stopped, discharging a passenger who moved backward on foot. The image froze, expanded. The discharged passenger was a slender bleach blonde, wearing a navy pea coat and carrying a small black valise.

The footage zoomed out, resumed in reverse. The lime-green compact vanished off the bottom of the screen. The woman on foot hid behind a stand of pines as a full-size pickup passed. Then continued backtracking, off the road, past the cowshed and silo, to the waiting blue Mazda. Climbed inside. The Mazda retreated from the orchard, reversing down the track, to the road, and away.

Forward now. Day brightening; blue Mazda hatchback coming up the road, turning onto the rutted farm track, driving into the orchard. Woman abandoning car, walking to road. Woman hiding as pickup passes. Then—zooming closer again—woman walking, extending a thumb. Lime-green compact stopping to pick her up.

"Toyota Camry," said a young man. "Got the plate."

"BOLO," said Horowitz.

On-screen, the Toyota kept driving, and the field of view followed it: up the road paralleling Route 5, along the Connecticut River, dividing Vermont from New Hampshire.

Fourteen pairs of eyes watched.

The time code sped forward: 08:02, 08:04, 08:06. At 08:09 the Camry skirted a looping tangle of interstates—89 and 91—and eased into a small business district. Past a clump of car dealerships and fast food, motels, and a medical center; closing on the junction of the Connecticut and White rivers. Then turning more directly north, traveling through another short stretch of countryside. At 08:14:17, the Camry hit the main street of a small town and pulled over. The woman left the car, exchanged brief words with the driver. The car pulled away. ARGUS divided, one view following the Toyota, the other focusing on its former passenger.

"Coolidge," reported the young man who had identified the car's make and model.

At 08:15 exactly, the woman on-screen started walking. "God damn it," Horowitz said, "I want local feeds."

As if on cue, the image on-screen split seven ways: the bird's-eye ARGUS perspectives of Camry and woman, plus street-level views of a traffic intersection, two interstate toll plazas, and security feeds from bus and rail stations.

A moment of confusion as techs rolled forward and back, synchronizing the time codes. Then all seven ran in sync, moving forward from 08:15:30.

The young woman came into view on the traffic cam. Still holding the small black case. As she turned toward a bakery—WE DELIVER FRESH DAILY—another tech brought up Jana's dossier photo. The computer squared her face, scanned for common nodal points, identified sixty-three.

Jana entered the bakery, disappeared. Dalia's eyes ticked from one window to another. Traffic cam, toll plazas, darkened railroad station, shabby bus station. 8:16. The clocks crawled forward in real time. After an eternity, 8:17. Dalia made herself release a breath. Horowitz said, "Run it forwa—"

At that moment, Jana reappeared, holding coffee and, in the same hand as the black case, something else.

The radio clicked. Horowitz picked it up as the woman on-screen moved down Main Street. "Go ahead."

"Tango's warm again," a voice squawked. "No sign of primary."

"Take him," Horowitz said. He announced to the room at large, "We're taking Klein."

They focused again on the screens. The traffic cam lost Jana as she left its field of view. But ARGUS stayed with her, following as she moved down the street. A dog barked, and she recoiled visibly. McConnell made a sound in the back of his mouth, almost a snarl.

Jana vanished from the ARGUS feed and, at the same instant, appeared on the bus station's CCTV. She walked to the counter, giving no sign of awareness of the camera.

Dalia's mind, sharpened by the thrill of the hunt, cut right through the codeine fog.

Jana exchanged words with the cashier and dug cash from a hip pocket.

"Anybody catch it?" Horowitz asked.

Only silence in return.

Jana accepted a ticket. She left the CCTV's view, but not the building. "Where the hell did she go?" Horowitz demanded.

"Bathroom," McConnell suggested.

"Get me the goddamn bus schedule. Get me that cashier. Get Charlie on standby. Get me a goddamn lip-reader. And get that goddamn Camry."

As people broke off into their various activities, Dalia hooked Horowitz's elbow and brought him aside. The P25 was clicking again. He looked at it longingly. She put a hand on his cheek, drawing his attention to her face. "It's a trick."

Gazing distractedly over her shoulder, he didn't answer.

"She knows we're watching. Don't believe everything you see."

"We've got her," Horowitz insisted.

"I've heard that before."

"Let me do my job, Dalia." He pulled away. Meanwhile, on the bus station's CCTV, a man with a beard had approached the ticket counter. A kerchiefed woman in a pale coat passed beneath the camera. ARGUS zoomed in on the rear of the building, to catch Jana if she left through a bathroom window. Three long Greyhound buses sat parked like beached whales. On another monitor, pedestrians crossed at the town's sole traffic light. At the interstate toll booths, Saturday morning traffic remained thin.

A man said, "Only one bus so far today. Left five minutes ago. 10:17 to Portland."

"We've got her now, god damn it. Charlie will get her."

Powerless, Dalia looked on.

COOLIDGE, VT

The train left the station.

Past the leaning utility poles, rocking, gaining speed. Jana's business-class car empty except for a pretty woman of around her own age, plugged by headset into a phone, and a chubby straw-haired man a decade older, wearing muttonchop sideburns and a denim jacket, reading a dog-eared science fiction paperback.

She closed her eyes, relishing the warm sunshine on her face. The faded black case nestled beneath her seat like an obedient dog. Every once in a while, it nudged against her calves as if to reassure her of its presence. All things considered, she felt remarkably calm.

Yet fewer than ten minutes passed before the train was slowing, whistling, and then rolling into the next station. A heavily pierced teenage girl came into the car and sat across the aisle, two rows ahead of Jana. A few moments passed. The whistle blew again. As they jerked forward, the girl tossed Jana a look over one shoulder.

And suddenly Jana's eyelid twitched. Something about the way the girl had looked at her …

A teenage girl was the least of her concerns. Military task forces with Kevlar and CS grenades, gas masks, and automatic weapons—those would be cause for alarm. Not surly adolescents with cheap piercings and too much attitude for their own good.

Now the conductor was coming down the aisle. Jana watched the teenage girl hand up a ticket. Then she handed up her own. Legitimate passage, she reminded herself as the conductor inspected it closely. No reason to be nervous. *Five, four, three …*

The punched ticket came back, and she smiled thanks.

Making good speed now, countryside rocketing past the window. Almost exactly the same countryside she had driven through two months ago, during her initial foray south. Leering scarecrows, rolling brown cornfields. Back then Yoni had still been alive. Back then she had never met Michael Fletcher. Back then she had never had direct contact with the ramsad. What a difference two months made.

Her mind skipped to the heavyset Israeli woman who had come barging through the woods, sensing the trap. *Di yuchna*, she thought derisively. Fishwife. Something about the woman reminded Jana of her own mother. Loud, boorish, nasty old bitch. "*My own daughter, a professional hanger-on. A lifetime* nokhshlepper."

A signal box flew past her window. Then a railroad crossing, with cars waiting behind the gate arm, sunlight flashing off hoods. Then countryside again. Forest, blue sky, distant low mountains. Moving faster than ever, the case nudging against her heels.

The kid had not looked her way again. Instead, she had taken out a knitting bag—*knitting*, of all things. She dug past a pair of scissors with pink plastic handles, found needles and yarn, and cast on.

Before she could overthink it, Jana stood. Leaving the case beneath the seat, she nonchalantly plucked the scissors from the bag as she passed, slipping them fluidly beneath her coat. She went to the bathroom at the end of the carriage: OCCUPIED.

She waited. The band of red beneath the lock turned green, and the bathroom door opened. The man with muttonchop sideburns emerged, gave her a shy smile, and moved back to his seat.

Jana stepped inside and latched the door. The rhythmic sound of wheels against track reverberated, strangely amplified in the small space: *WICKwickaWICKwickaWICK.*

Everything was metal: sink, toilet, mirror, refuse container lid. PLEASE FLUSH TOILET *AFTER EACH USE* EXCEPT WHEN TRAIN IS STANDING IN STATION. No windows, and only a tiny ventilation grate. A fluorescent lightbulb safe inside its metal cage. Facing the mirror, Jana untied the kerchief from her chin. She wet her fingertips, then her hair. Quickly, using small snips, she trimmed. The dye job had been almost five weeks ago; get right down near the skull, and the roots were dark.

She shook her head, dislodging remnants. What little hair remained, unevenly cropped, would not win any beauty pageants. But it would serve her purpose. A bleach blonde in a ragged kerchief had gone aboard the train. A brunette with a crew cut would get off. Under the right light, the coif might even pass for stylish—no one could say it wasn't daring.

She cleaned up as best she could and went back to her seat, returning scissors to knitting bag en route, and pushed the black case farther beneath the seat with her heels. No one paid her the slightest attention.

She stared out her window, at harvested fields and pale winter sun.

NORTH OF ANDOVER, VT

"License plate is different—looking into that—but VIN matches Klein's missing Mazda. Inside the trunk, blankets: two wool, one space. Which, if you asked me how to throw off thermals, would be my recommendation—that plus timing a crossover. Fingerprints and DNA match the dossier and the phone—burner, by the way, only made two calls: the one we recorded to Klein and the one that triggered the charge."

Horowitz and McConnell were giving the tech their full attention. Dalia was looking at the monitor above the fireplace, picturing now the Greyhound bus heading northeast on Route 91. The bus had both northbound lanes to itself. On the southbound track, a single red VW Beetle whipped past.

"Intercept in ten," a woman interrupted. "Nine … eight …"

Charlie team's armored Lenco BearCat appeared in the monitor's lower right corner. Sirens off, blast shields lowered, battering ram detached. But thermographic camera operating. And as Horowitz and McConnell turned to the monitor, a smaller window opened, displaying a view of the bus from the rear as the BearCat drew into the Greyhound's blind spot.

"Seven … six … five …"

On the ARGUS feed, the roadblock came into view: eight green-and-yellow Vermont State Police cruisers blocking the highway in four staggered rows. A dozen troopers under cover, handguns out.

"Four … three …"

The bus slowed uncertainly. A trooper came forward and waved it to a halt. The BearCat pulled around on the left, boxing it in, and slued to a stop.

"Charlie, breach and clear."

The SWAT team deployed, wearing helmets and gas masks, desert camo and tactical body armor, brandishing semiautomatic handguns and M4 submachine guns. Two men in the rear guard wielded clunkier weapons: an ARWEN-37, set to fire multiple tear-gas canisters, and an LRAD, or long-range acoustic device—a sonic contraption that created agonizing pain, traditionally used to disperse crowds.

Overwhelming force. Yet Dalia, watching from two angles at once as the team took up positions surrounding the bus, thought of Cannae and despaired.

A concussion grenade exploded just below the driver's window: soundless on the monitor, but shaking the BearCat's camera. At the same instant, two men with knives slit the Greyhound's rear tires down to the rims.

Then agents were on board, subduing passengers and handing them back out through the door to be handcuffed, searched, and detained.

By the time the all clear had come, nine people stood in handcuffs by the side of the road. A traffic jam was forming, and a news copter hovered overhead. Two troopers hurried to set up sawhorses, closing off one lane and funneling traffic into the other. No one had thought to bring a tow truck to move the Greyhound with its slit tires. A pair of agents cleared out the baggage compartment, peering into the shadows with baton flashlights, as another pair watched with machine guns ready.

Of Jana Dahan, there was no sign.

NEW HAVEN, CT

At New Haven, the platform was packed.

Two young women, chattering animatedly in Czech, squeezed into the seat beside Jana. A man traveling with a brood of children took up a block across the aisle. Someone had a dirty diaper.

"Next stop Stamford," the conductor droned. "New Rochelle, then New York Grand Central."

Jana settled back into the seat. If they knew where she was, they would have intercepted the train already. In New York, the biggest and busiest city in the country, she could melt away.

She half-dozed. Maybe she would give Miriam a call, since she was in Manhattan. Miriam was a woman now, of course. Long gone from the old apartment. Life had moved on. But in the ensuing fragmentary dream, Miriam still lived at home, and answered the phone eagerly. They went for a walk together for old times' sake. Into the park. Down the Fifth Avenue side, to the zoo. But zookeepers followed them, approached them outside the monkey house. *Ticket, please*, one asked. *May I see your ticket?* Jana tried to find her ticket. What she found was a postcard of the Capitol dome. She tried frantically to hide it, but the zookeeper had already seen. So had Miriam, who looked at Jana sideways, frowning, and then checked her watch and said it was time she headed home. But she was not wearing a watch. And she then gave a surreptitious signal to the zookeeper, who returned a secret nod.

Jana sat up, blinking. Mouth dry. The children across the aisle had fallen asleep. The young women beside her had lapsed into thoughtful silence. Either the diaper had been changed or Jana had gotten used to it. She slowly settled back again.

Some minutes later, they pulled into Stamford. By now Jana had started feeling nervous again, the anxious feeling of the dream clinging stubbornly even as the details vanished.

Her ruse had worked, yes. But they would not give up so easily. The damned fishwife: stubborn, you could bet on it. By now the woman would be combing back over satellite footage, searching, putting it together.

But the Stamford platform was deserted. Saturday afternoon ripened toward evening, but no one was heading into New York City yet. Even from where she sat, Jana could see two separate cameras. Leave the train here, and she would stand out like the proverbial sore thumb.

She hesitated. They moved again.

"New Rochelle," said the conductor, coming up the aisle. "Next stop New Rochelle."

NORTH OF ANDOVER, VT

The footage played again.

Jana Dahan entered the bakery at 8:16 a.m. Ninety seconds later, she reappeared on the sidewalk, holding coffee and the black briefcase, and something unidentifiable. Dalia, having seen the receipt, knew now that it was a buttered roll.

Next Jana stepped out of view of the traffic cam ... but not out of the view of ARGUS. She strolled casually down the sidewalk, apparently in no rush, enjoying the sunshine. But in her carriage Dalia detected the same hint of audacity she had picked up from the security footage of the Portland drugstore. The girl could pretend casualness with dazzling ease, but she could never completely mask her insolence.

The dog barked; Jana recoiled. Another crack in the facade. Then she vanished from the ARGUS feed, appearing inside the Greyhound station, betraying no awareness of the CCTV. But that was another ruse.

She spoke with the cashier. Dalia had seen this receipt, too. For the price of forty-four dollars and fifty-two cents, Jana had bought passage on the 10:15 Greyhound to Portland, using a Florida driver's license in the name of Erika Mallo. The casual stroll down the avenue had been the hook, the heedless presentation before the station's security camera the line, the ticket the sinker.

Jana disappeared. With the benefit of hindsight, they had reconstructed ensuing off-camera events. Inside the bathroom, she had turned her navy pea coat inside out, tied a colorless kerchief around her head, tucked the black valise beneath the coat. Two hundred and twelve seconds later, she reappeared: leaving the bus station the same way she had come in: right in front the camera, right under their noses. Hiding in plain sight. They would not have missed it the first time, thought Dalia, had Horowitz not been so eager to take her bait.

Stepping onto the street again, Jana then did the opposite of courting surveillance. She found cover beneath awnings, in shadows, amid Main Street's surprisingly robust crowd: tourists, locals, baby strollers, dog walkers, breakfasters, cyclists, weekend warriors on Harleys, all trying to make the most of a relatively mild Saturday. The traffic cam, facing endlessly south, offered limited help, and the top-down view from ARGUS was not much better. Clusters of pedestrians swirled, showing the camera baseball hats, hoods and hoodies, bald spots, man buns, and ponytails, but no clear views of faces for the computer to count nodal spots. Technology had hit its limit.

"Back," Horowitz ordered.

A tech rewound. Jana emerged again from the Greyhound station, vanished again beneath an awning. Horowitz ran a finger up and down the cleft of his chin, whistling air in between his front teeth.

A new group walked into the Greyhound station. A brunette in their midst drew Dalia's eye. Jana might have quickly dyed her hair in the bathroom—in which case the kerchief had been yet another ruse—and then doubled back, buying a second ticket on a later bus. The Greyhound cashier, now in custody alongside the baker and the man calling himself Jack Klein, had offered no insight. Nor could he, Dalia thought. The girl had covered every track.

They looked from one feed to another. In the train station, a broad-shouldered man in a corduroy jacket was pushing a broom across the floor. By the interstate, a trucker was climbing down from his cab after his E-Z Pass malfunctioned. On the town's traffic cam, a clutch of pedestrians crossed the street. In the bus depot, the brunette reached the ticket counter. For an instant, she presented a three-quarters view to the camera. Impossible to be sure. Dalia opened her mouth, but Horowitz was faster, jabbing a finger at the image. "Scan it."

The computer scanned and found only six nodal points in common with Jana's dossier—fourteen below the minimum considered to be a hit.

Behind the American Legion Post, two kids on bicycles pored over a glossy magazine. Near the town square, joggers pedaled in place while waiting for the light to change. A woman pushing a stroller collided with a man leashing a dog to a lamppost. 8:24 a.m. A man tossed breadcrumbs to pigeons. Thickening traffic circulated through the bus depot, the train station, the toll plaza. 8:25. Dalia covered her eyes, lost herself for a moment in comforting blackness. She lowered her hand. 8:26. Children burst laughing from the bakery. A woman cleaned up after her dog. A man turned away from his family to take a clandestine nip from a pocket flask.

8:27. A van dropped off a group of backpackers, who headed for the train station. A woman inspected a hairline crack on the windshield of a parked car. An immensely obese young woman struggled to get through the door of the stationery store. 8:28. Two dogs by the traffic light barked at each other. A woman carried garbage out the back of the American Legion Post and ran off the boys with their magazine. A youngster chased a windblown hat down the sidewalk.

8:29. A pair of tourists took selfies before the clock tower. In the train station, the backpackers were queuing up. A couple directly in front of the traffic cam kissed, then hugged. Inside the bus station, a woman lit a cigarette. The cashier came around the counter, gesturing angrily, and the woman retreated to the sidewalk. Back in the train station, the backpackers …

Dalia moved closer. One wore a dun-colored kerchief around her head, a lock of blond hair peeking out from beneath it. Face averted from the camera. And now that Dalia looked carefully, this one had no backpack.

8:30. After buying her ticket, the woman in question sat with the other hikers, but not quite *with* them. Close, but apart. Still averting her face from the camera.

Holding the empty coffee cup in her lap.

CHAPTER TEN

NEW ROCHELLE, NY

The platform was clogged with police. Some wore local uniforms: a gentle shade of blue that looked all the gentler in contrast to their glistening black boots and belts. Some were NYPD, familiar in dark navy. Some wore plain clothes, and expressions of jaded watchfulness. And some, Jana thought, were feds: DHS, FBI, in sports coats or off-the-rack pantsuits, with the telltale bulges of guns and radios and plasticuffs.

As the train pulled into the station, the uniforms dispersed along the length of the platform, leaving the suits behind to block turnstiles and staircases. Cops came onto cars in pairs, from both ends, weapons holstered, checking faces against their digital tablets. The man who looked at Jana was middle-aged, well fed, pouchy. As his eyes grazed her, she felt a trapdoor open in her stomach. But she rinsed her face of fear and looked back at him warily, a touch resentfully: *What's going on, sir, and will it prevent me from getting home in time for dinner?*

His eyes moved on without slowing, to a blonde two rows back.

He rendezvoused with his partner in the middle of the car. Words were exchanged. Still the train remained in the station.

Passengers began muttering, grumbling.

Conductors, feds, and plainclothesmen held ad hoc palavers on the platform. The Czech pair sharing Jana's seat angled their phones to catch their own faces backgrounded by the activity through windows—Jana wriggling to get out of the shots as much as possible—and then posted selfies.

Four minutes passed. Another pair of cops came through the car, wearing civilian clothes, concentrating on young women. Again Jana, with her blunt dark haircut, didn't merit a second glance.

As the passengers grew peevish, the conferences between authorities took on a more harried air. At last, a signal was passed down the length of the platform. Two NYPD officers, a man and a woman, positioned themselves at the front of Jana's car. A whistle blew. Air vented, doors closed, and the train jagged again in the direction of New York City.

This time, no conductor came through to announce the next stop. But Jana knew that about sixteen miles remained between her and Grand Central. Between her and freedom.

NORTH OF ANDOVER, VT

Security feeds from railroad platforms in Springfield, Woonsocket, New Haven, and Stamford had been divided among analysts, broken into sections, and scanned in fast-forward.

But the computers, thought Dalia, would find nothing. Not pessimism, but realism. The girl was a step ahead of them and had been the entire time. She had not come this far by exposing herself carelessly to security cameras.

Horowitz appeared by Dalia's elbow. "What do you think?"

"I think she's still on the train," Dalia said. "But I'm not sure."

"Me neither."

"How long till they reach Grand Central?"

"Twelve minutes," he said. "Twelve minutes."

GRAND CENTRAL STATION, MANHATTAN

As the train entered the tunnel, passengers began collecting their belongings and standing, eager to be first to the doors when they reached the platform.

"Please stay in your seats," ordered the policewoman at the front of the car. A few years older than Jana, she wore her auburn hair neatly pinned beneath her peaked cap. She started down the aisle, leaving her partner to cover the door at the carriage's end. "*Stay in your seats.*"

As soon as she had passed, Jana stood, taking the case, swiftly crossing the territory the woman had just covered. The partner, a hefty man with a close-trimmed goatee, thumbs hooked through belt loops as if to frame his genitals, gave her a look of frank disbelief. "You don't hear so good?"

"I need to use the bathroom." She did a Betty Boop little-girl dip, crossing her legs. "Real bad."

"Back to your seat."

"Officer, I swear, it's an emergency." The policewoman looked around, gave her partner an eye roll, and continued her sweep down the aisle. "If I could—"

"Back to your goddamn seat." He raised his right hand threateningly.

Jana covered his fingers with her left hand, gently. Passengers on every side watched as she bent back his wrist, leaning forward and down. Krav Maga, the hand-to-hand fighting style taught to Israeli special forces, emphasized that leverage trumped size—and that once battle had been joined, it should be ended with all possible dispatch.

As the man's jaw opened in surprise she brought her right elbow around hard into his left temple, and he went down without so much as a grunt.

In an eyeblink she was past him and through the door, before witnesses could even process what they had seen. The space between cars was dim and dank. The train was moving slowly through the tunnel, at about five mph. Turning the lever, she ratcheted open the heavy door, spent a fraction of an instant examining the passing gravel below, and leaped down, running alongside the coach to spin off momentum. As she kept running, she spied a glow ahead—a fluorescent-lit subterranean platform.

She was moving faster than the train. She caught a glimpse inside, of gawking faces still reacting to the violent assault they had just witnessed. But they could not see out into the darkness. They could not see her, and she had the sense that she was passing a diorama, a schoolchild's project, meticulously constructed inside a moving shoe box.

Other trains, in the process of loading or disgorging passengers, waited by platforms. Seeing the brigades of police in riot gear and gas masks awaiting her train's approach, she veered away. The next platform was too tall to climb. She jumped up anyway, boosted by the adrenaline. Doors chuffed open and passengers spilled out, and suddenly she was surrounded by a crowd.

The human tide carried her along. A loudspeaker barked orders. A child was crying. Dogs barked in the distance before being overwhelmed by the thunder of footsteps.

A staircase led up. The tide rising, floating her along. Sharp elbows on every side. People laughed, cursed, talked on phones. Excited, a little bit crazy. Saturday night. But something was wrong: a logjam at the top of the stairs. More police, barricading the exit. The tide stopped, shifting restlessly. Panic tried to take Jana in its teeth, and she forbade it.

Orders rapped again through the loudspeaker, echoing. Getting people's attention now. A blanket of apprehension abruptly smothered the festive Saturday night vibe. People noticing all the barking. Thinking of bombs and gunmen and terrorist attacks. More and more, Jana thought with dark satisfaction, they were starting to understand what it meant to be Israeli.

She elbowed her way up the stairs. Three police blocked the top: rank-and-file NYPD, holding batons and pepper spray, pistols holstered. No riot shields, no gas masks. Just three people with uniforms and billy clubs and spray cans, surrounded by confusion.

The crowd surged, pushing against the cops and then falling back. Someone on the stairs almost lost her footing. Someone else cried out. In the next few seconds, Jana realized, the police would either lose control or establish it incontrovertibly.

A woman was being jammed face-first into the cops. Jana slipped behind her. One of the cops raised his pepper spray. The crowd magically thinned. The woman's breath had been squeezed out of her, and she started to collapse. The cop stepped forward, taking her arm, opening a gap in their ranks. Jana slipped through.

"Hey!"

But she was off already, low against the wall, not looking back; and the speaker turned away, returning his attention to the throng.

A short hallway led into a seething concourse. New York City. Hitler's worst nightmare: legions of *untermenschen* walking and talking and trading and fucking and thriving. She vanished into a sea of businesspeople, artists, clergy, dancers, lawyers, pipefitters, sex workers, scientists, adults, children, elderly, alcoholics, fashion models, fugitives.

The tide kept rising, carrying her up another level, onto the main concourse. A dog on a chain leash growled. She turned the other way. Past the four-faced brass clock. The elaborate astronomical ceiling spread out overhead. The exit to the north was blocked by more cops.

To the south were ticket windows and vending machines. She might buy another ticket and board another train. Or maybe the subway … no. Up onto the street. Freedom or bust.

She consulted a mental map. She and Cousin Miriam had come through here often, on day trips to visit Miriam's friend Mark up in Mount Kisco. Jana had never liked Mark, who was older, who had ogled the teenage girls and plied them with Miller Genuine Draft. ("*Beers and leers*," Miriam had called it. Yet she had thrived on the attention.)

She moved again, toward Vanderbilt. Past a busking guitarist, a breastfeeding mother, an androgynous young panhandler with open sores, a rawboned kid selling bootleg movies on a ragged blanket. Two cops stood outside the Chase Bank. One faced her while speaking on a radio. The other faced away, studying a picture on a tablet. Fear gnawed again.

Past Zaro's Family Bakery. From the left, beyond a Rite Aid—her former employer—came a mass of cops and dogs. She hastened the other way. Crowds thinning here, which left her exposed. But exits ahead. Although, between her and them, more blue. Coming up on her right and closing ranks, soldiers: camo fatigues, automatic weapons. *Fuck.*

A nun was walking past, turning into the ladies' room.

Jana followed.

A stall door just closing. She pushed in. The woman, facing away, tried to turn, but before she could, Jana threw on a sleeper hold. Crook of the right arm compressing jugular veins and carotid arteries; right hand tucked into left elbow, locking it snug. She squeezed. The nun squeaked. Three seconds without blood, and consciousness shut off as neatly as a light switch. The woman sagged, turning surprisingly heavy.

Jana lowered her, propping the dead weight inelegantly against the toilet. A flush came from the neighboring stall. God willing, people in New York still minded their own business.

She stripped off the habit: white cotton cap and bandeau, white linen wimple, black serge tunic, rosary. The woman was larger than Jana, and older. The habit would hang loose, no helping it. Under the uniform, she found a pink V-neck rayon blouse and, beneath complex underskirts, Liz Claiborne pants.

She put on the starched wimple, the tunic, the belt, and rosary, hands fumbling with the small hooks. Then the cotton cap. She tried the underskirts, quickly gave up, and adjusted the tunic so that it mostly covered her jeans. Kicking off her running shoes, she stepped into plain black shoes two sizes too large.

The woman was aspirating rustily. One pale white hand had fallen beneath the door to the neighboring stall, which was now, happily, unoccupied.

Jana propped her back onto the toilet. She was about to leave when she saw the woman's small black handheld bag. She dumped onto the floor toiletries, phone, notepad, book, eyeglasses case, and a sandwich and celery sticks in a Ziploc baggie. From the glasses case she took a pair of rimless reading glasses, setting them across the bridge of her nose.

Her black case fit inside the nun's bag. She zipped it, then spent the barest instant checking her reflection in the mirror.

Heart pounding, she left the bathroom. Made herself slow down as she approached the police blocking the exit. Veered away from the dogs—they might smell the *plastique*—which meant moving toward a thick knot of cops. Men and women, looking at her evenly. What would a nun say? Laying it on too thick would be counterproductive.

She could see the street right behind them. Evening: cold wind seeping inside.

Five, four, three, two, one.

Easy-peasy, lemon squeezy.

A drunk voice rose not far to her left. The cops' attention drifted toward it. Jana drifted right and stepped up to a bright-eyed young man in a crisp blue uniform. He raised a hand to stop her—unnecessarily, since she was already giving him a polite smile, making no effort to get through. Her eyelid twitched.

He looked at the tablet in his hand. Back at her face. Back at the tablet. Back at her face.

Back at the tablet. Uneasy now. No one wanted to offend a nun. But he had registered something.

Back at her face.

She let her smile turn uncertain.

For a suspended instant, she thought he would take her aside. Then a dog exploded into a volley of barks, making everybody jump. Other dogs joined in. Someone was running. The cops were giving chase. The door was unguarded.

Jana walked forward, to freedom. She turned, reached the end of the block, turned again, and vanished into the falling night.

NORTH OF ANDOVER, VT

Dalia gestured for the other men to leave the room.

Now she and the man calling himself Klein were alone. She lowered herself onto a chair. It creaked. As she regarded the prisoner expectantly, a long moment passed. Beyond the window, the wind played an eerie melody through the nighttime forest. At last, he jerked the restraints behind his back, as if to remind her.

"Ah." She spoke kindly, in Hebrew. "Could you use a hand?"

He looked back at her balefully.

"Nissim Dayan. Born into the College." She had used the Israeli nickname for the fortified Mossad headquarters in Tel Aviv. "A legacy. Your father at Entebbe. Eh?"

He said nothing.

"But sometimes it skips a generation. You made a crucial misstep in Dubai. Missed some security cameras. And so your squad was documented: landing, using foreign passports, checking into hotels around the city. Renting the room opposite your target, even changing into a wig in full view of hotel surveillance ..." She clucked in disapproval. "A piece even made the London *Sunday Times*."

He glared.

"But thanks to your father's reputation, you weren't terminated. Just sent out to pasture, yes? Far away, to a remote safe house in America. Where you waited to offer assistance, when required, in a support capacity. Not much in the way of glory, to be sure. But a valuable and necessary function nonetheless."

He said nothing.

"Seven years you waited, Nissim Dayan. Leaving your wife and children back in Israel. That must have hurt."

No reply.

"Imagine how it feels for the children of the people Jana Dahan killed." She leaned forward. "The wives and husbands left behind."

No reaction.

"You went to Burlington to meet her."

He answered suddenly in English: "Who are you? What's going on? I haven't been read my rights. I haven't been offered—"

She continued in Hebrew: "You'll spend the rest of your life in a federal penitentiary. Unless you tell me how to find the girl."

"—access to an attorney. I haven't been given a phone call. I haven't seen a badge or—"

"And it won't end there. We'll make it hell for your family back home." Shrugging, she leaned away. "Hardly fair, since Jana did all the dirty work. But then, life isn't fair. So your children will suffer."

"*Lech tis dayan ve tabe kabala*," he spat suddenly. Go fuck yourself and send me the bill.

"Ah."

"I know you." He straightened with shabby pride. "From the news. Some nerve you've got. Talking to me about family. With your *Jüdische Selbsthass*." Jewish self-hatred. "I prefer Hamas to self-deluded Jews. At least they are honest."

"Tell me more."

"We've nothing more to talk about, *Jüdische Selbsthass*."

"So your type always says." Her voice climbed a mocking octave: "There's nothing more to talk about. And nobody to talk to even if we wanted. There's no one to negotiate with. Oh, woe is we. Just let us sit in the dark, in the corner, alone."

His mouth within the salt-and-pepper beard pursed tight.

"Dead children? No problem. So long as they're not dead *Jewish* children."

"Says the woman all too eager to sacrifice her own son to the Arabush."

"Dead Egyptian children. Dead Jordanian children. Dead American children."

He shook his head. "Self-loathing sow."

"Where is Jana?"

"Fuck yourself."

"Cooperate, and it will be taken into account. Withhold, and you go to Fort Leavenworth—and your children suffer. Where is she?"

He lifted his chin. "Rot in hell."

She almost reached forward, seized his cheap T-shirt, and dragged him to his feet. But what would be the point? The operation would have been compartmentalized. Nissim Dayan could tell them nothing even if he wanted to. So had she insisted to Horowitz, who nevertheless begged her to try.

Instead, she stood. Without another word, she turned, opened the door, and stepped out past the waiting guards. "While you're there," he called behind her, "say hello to your son."

In the hallway, Horowitz was on the phone. "But that's exactly why—"

Dalia joined him.

"Alana," he said with exasperation. "Obviously, we can't put the genie back into … No. But that's exactly why … god damn it. Don't. No. Alana, *no.* I'm coming down."

He hung up. His face seemed more deeply lined than usual. He shook his head. "I'm going to DC."

"They promised us a week."

"That was before we had news copters and a dead cop."

"They can't do that."

"But they can."

"But—"

"Dalia, we tried. It's over."

"'If you are planting a tree and you hear that the Messiah has come, you finish planting the tree before going to greet the Messiah.'"

His mouth quirked sideways.

"We're going down anyway, yes? Obstruction of justice for you. Probably espionage for me. But let's take that bitch with us."

"I'd like nothing better. But—"

"Where's she heading? DC, yes? So. Secret's out? Get it farther out. Make it public. Release a photo to the media. Start knocking on doors. All in … until we're all out."

Horowitz paused.

ELLICOTT STREET NW, WASHINGTON, DC

When headlights sprayed around the corner, Jana stepped back into shadows.

The blue Hyundai decelerated with a soft hum, and she watched it turn into the driveway across the street. A few seconds passed before the garage door trundled up. Then the Hyundai rolled forward, out of a cold night just starting to sleet.

The garage door closed. Moments passed. A light came on inside the house. Michael Fletcher appeared in the living room window, burying his face in the cat's ruff. Curtains open, apparently nothing to hide. No sign of the soon-to-be ex or the kid. And no pause to disable an alarm system.

She kept watching. Err on the side of caution. He had not been compromised. But she would take no chances.

Fletcher disappeared. More moments passed. A light went on upstairs. He appeared again, in a second-story window. Closed the shade and stood in silhouette, taking off his shirt. Undid his belt, let his pants fall. Sank down, as if sitting on the side of a bed. Reappeared, hopping now, and vanished into another room.

Jana shivered behind a Japanese maple. A bedroom light in a window up the block went out. At long last, Fletcher's silhouette reappeared. Toweling off his hair.

It was as safe as it ever would be.

Even so, she avoided the front door, creeping around back, past the garage, to a rear stoop. The back door was locked. Setting down the case, she reached into her coat. Straightened two paper clips. Gingerly inserted one. Applied torque, held it. She slipped the second clip below the first. Pressing up, she felt the individual pins, one after another. Raised the stubborn one until it set. Still applying pressure, she repeated the procedure on the remaining pins, twisted the knob, leaned the door open, and stepped into the kitchen.

Warm and dry. She reached back for the case, closed the door softly, and stood listening to the slap-dribble-drip of sleet against walls and roof, and the quiet hiss from heating grates. A faded, curling paper turkey was stuck by magnet to the refrigerator. In the gloom, she deciphered the words:

i AM THANKFUL FOR TOYS, dAddY, MOMMY,
SCHOOL, HOUSE, LICORICE, NINZA TURTLES, TV

A cat came padding across the linoleum floor, twining good-naturedly around her ankles. Kneeling, she scratched one ear. Then straightened, picking up the case.

She moved through the dining room, drawn to the thin yellow light spilling from beyond. At the foot of the stairs, she discovered framed photographs lining one wall. The photos portrayed a happy family, at least superficially. Young Michael Fletcher cavorted with an older boy, the family resemblance unmistakable. Building snowmen, eating ice cream, swimming in a neighborhood pool. As an awkward adolescent, Michael was bar mitzvahed. Then a graduation: mom and both boys smiling bright and clear as chrome, dad serious and macho. Some moody black-and-white studies of landscapes and windowpanes. Then the wife. Jana lingered on these, frowning. Was this his type? The woman looked like a sorority girl. One had to admit, they made an attractive couple. Ken and Barbie posed for wedding shots, honeymoon shots. A final shot of Michael, in uniform now, looking proud but deeply unsure. Then the narrative was hijacked by a swaddled baby. And the circle of life began anew: a growing boy cavorting at playgrounds, devouring cake at birthday parties.

A shadow at the top of the stairs.

He was watching her.

He was wearing sleep pants but no shirt. His skin clean and still damp. She climbed the stairs slowly.

Into the bedroom. The room he had shared with the sorority girl. But now the sorority girl was gone and Jana was here. He lowered her onto the bed. She dropped the black case. His lips were softer than she remembered. Something stirred inside her, straining to meet him.

Afterward, they lay tangled together. She murmured into his collarbone, "I need to stay here from now on."

Toying with her close-cropped hair, he said nothing. The freezing rain slapped and dribbled. The cat jumped onto the bed, purring. At last, Michael mumbled a reply. She had been halfway to sleep, pulled back now. "Hm?" she said.

"I said, I wish we could stay this way."

She thought about it. "Nothing lasts forever."

"Did you grow up speaking English? It's perfect."

"Don't worry about my English." Immediately, she regretted her tone. He was fragile, unstable. "We've still got some time," she said more gently. "Enjoy it while you can."

"I'll try."

She kissed him.

RITTENHOUSE STREET NW, WASHINGTON, DC

Three miles away, Jackie Brady stood outside her niece's room, listening to make sure Alyssa was going down comfortably—they had stopped using the baby monitor only last week.

Beneath the whispering sleet, the three-year-old was singing softly to herself, a song she had learned in preschool. "Let there be peace on earth, and let it begin with me. Let there be peace on earth, the peace that was meant to be …"

Jackie decided it was all right. She moved away down the hall, into the bedroom that had been her home for the past four months. The sleet outside made the soft circle of light from the desk lamp seem even cozier. Sis and Brad were out to dinner and wouldn't be back for two hours at least. Quiet, privacy, warmth. Heaven.

Propped up on the bed, burrowing her feet beneath the quilt, Jackie fired up her laptop. She was about to check Facebook when a headline caught her eye. Authorities had released a detailed sketch of a suspect they were seeking for questioning. The picture grabbed her attention because its subject looked—really, quite remarkably—like Jackie herself. Early to mid-twenties; short, spiky dark hair; lean pretty face. And, in fact, they were seeking the woman, who had used the aliases Tiffany Watson, Erika Mallo, and, most recently, Eve Berg, in this very same metropolitan area.

The doorbell rang. A brusque knock quickly followed. Frowning, she set the computer on the nightstand.

"Auntie," Alyssa called as Jackie stepped into the hall, "someone's outside my window."

"Go back to sleep, Lyssa. Just a bad dream."

"'S not. He's outside my window. He's on the roof."

Catching her lower lip between her teeth, Jackie proceeded toward the front door. Moving past the living room, she noticed that her phone was glowing, awake, on the coffee table. Weird. Could have sworn she had turned it off.

Before answering, she checked the peephole. These days a woman alone with a child could not be too careful. Two policemen stood on the porch. Behind them lurked a third. And she just caught a glimpse of a fourth, moving through sleety darkness. Parked by the curb, cloaked by waves of precipitation, were two squad cars, an unmarked shit-shaded sedan, and a suspicious-looking gray van with windows tinted almost black.

Her frown deepened. She worked the chain, turned the bolt. When the door opened, the nearest cop pushed past her without asking permission. Before she could protest, the other was in her face. "You're not under arrest," he said in a way that suggested this might change at any moment.

"What's going on?"

"Are you carrying any weapons?"

She shook her head. He turned her around anyway, frisking her. *Unfuckingbelievable.* The other cop watched, hand near his belt—the side with the pepper spray and Taser. And now others were coming in. More than the two lurkers she had seen—three, then four. Moving down the hall, trailing wet. One peeked into Alyssa's room, and the little girl shrieked.

The frisk turned up nothing except Jackie's lip balm. The cop's tone softened slightly. "Who else is on the premises?"

"My niece. What the holy hell is—"

"Your name?"

"Am I being charged with something?"

"Why so evasive?"

"I *live* here." Thinking of an article she had seen just last week. Some cops had gunned down a kid. Turned out the kid had only been holding a BB gun. *Un*motherfucking*believable.* "I *live* here, and you can't just come barging in—"

"You just showed up here in September?"

"Right. I'm helping my sister with her kid. Since when is that a crime? What the hell is going *on*?"

A glance passed between the cops. "We'll take a look around," said one, and disappeared without asking permission.

Something clicked for Jackie. "It's that suspect. I was just reading the article. Isn't it?"

"We're just making sure, ma'am."

* * *

The media had received only a police sketch. But investigators tracking down seventy-seven leads around the Washington metropolitan area that night had been given supplementary images—from the Mossad dossier, the tollbooth camera on I-80, the manhunts in Vermont and New York.

Targets had been gleaned from security cams, traffic cams, satellite and drone imagery, bartenders, clergy, meter readers, hotel clerks, homeless shelters, waitresses, hostesses, managers, superintendents, letter carriers. Investigators included patrolmen, detectives, FBI, INS, and members of the Washington Regional Threat and Analysis Center.

By 9:40 p.m., the initial pool of seventy-seven suspects had been exhausted. Nine had been brought in for further questioning and then released. Two had been arrested on unrelated charges.

The net was cast again.

EMERALD STREET NW, WASHINGTON, DC

On Emerald Street NW, a black van cruised slowly past the row houses.

In the rear of the van, a tech looked up from a GPS map and pointed out, through the tinted window, a house near the end of the block. Another used a joystick to aim a parabolic microphone mounted beneath a Plexiglas dome on the van's roof. Voices broken by the rhythm of sheeting ice pellets came through two sets of headphones.

Two miles northwest, a phone rang; StingRay kicked on, and inside another van, another pair of techs listened intently.

On H Street, another black van aimed an antenna at another house. Inside, IMSI Catcher located three phones. On a laptop screen, a sliver of a bedroom mirror appeared: a petite woman with cold cream on her face, wearing a thin blue nightgown.

In Columbia Heights, a pair of agents located an address, climbed crumbling stairs between a check-cashing emporium and a liquor store. Inside the foyer, shucking off their plastic hoods, they buzzed the superintendent. After repeated buzzings, the super finally banged irritably out of his ground-floor apartment. Upon seeing the agents' identification, he held his irascibility carefully in check.

The postman, said the taller of the agents, had reported a new tenant in the building within the past few months: a young woman. The super shrugged. The apartment in question, he answered, spent most of the time empty. Occasionally, someone—friends or family, he assumed, of the young couple who had rented the place years before—appeared for a few days, a week here and there. The rent was always paid on time, from an automated account at a bank downtown. There had been no complaints from neighbors, and so he had seen no reason to rock the boat.

They ascended four flights, knocked on the door, rang the bell. Waited, knocked, and rang again. When the agents requested access to the apartment, the super hesitated. Didn't they need a warrant for that? Not with probable cause, said the shorter agent.

A passkey opened the door. Their hails echoed hollowly back. They entered, switching on the overhead light. The smell of bleach was overpowering. Despite the chemical stench, cockroaches scuttled for cover beneath an exposed radiator. The apartment was two rooms, undecorated, offering a view of the church across the street. An empty Clorox jug sat on the kitchen table beside a heap of rags.

As the agents started looking around, the super told them they could find him in his apartment if necessary, and retreated.

A first pass uncovered minimal evidence of habitation. The bed was stripped, the cupboards sparsely stocked, the closets empty. A second look dug deeper: beneath the mattress, inside toilet tank and ice trays, under sinks. Passing the garbage disposal, the taller agent blinked and went back for a closer look. "Lookit this."

Using a long-handled wooden spoon, they fished fragments from the drain. Chips of quartz, splinters of glass, chunks of green circuit board.

"Computer," said the shorter.

"Someone's covering her tracks," said the taller.

They placed a call.

CHAPTER ELEVEN

BLUEMONT, VA

Michael Fletcher parked in the dirt driveway, behind a red Chevy Silverado.

He approached the house slowly, rolling his shoulders, feeling the air, double-checking the conclusions he had reached studying Google. The place was isolated, set far off a dirt road, with no visible neighbors, yet still near enough home that he would not spend too long on the highway with cargo he'd rather not explain to a state trooper. Pine and spruce, slash valley, distant cliffs. Above the horizon hulked Mount Weather, command center of FEMA, rumored to house a secret bunker for continuity-of-government purposes.

The property featured small outbuildings: woodshed, toolshed, and an ancient outhouse. All the structures looked sturdy. He veered closer, eyeballing them before continuing to the main manor. Brick and redwood, two floors—downright idyllic in the sunset light.

As he drew near the porch, the front door opened. An old man came out warily. Michael didn't blame him. You could meet some real freaks on Craigslist.

"Evenin'," Michael said. "You must be Ralph."

"That makes you Stuart."

"Yes, sir."

The old man had a firm, aggressive handshake. Eyes threaded with red but still sharp. Two days' beard, mostly gray. He wore a checkered flannel shirt and didn't seem to feel the cold. "Lemme give you the grand tour."

They entered a kitchen with a wood-burning stove, walked through a living room, past a TV and bathroom, and climbed the creaky stairs. There were two guest bedrooms and the master, which Michael sensed was occupied. The man spoke softly and evenly. "We head out most weekends. Weather warms up, we rent an RV and spend maybe a month poking 'round. So this place spends a lot of time sitting empty. Couple years ago, my daughter suggested we rent it out, and I gotta say, it works out real well."

Michael wondered whether the man was carrying a gun. Something about his carriage suggested it. A vet. You could just tell. Vietnam, probably.

"Furnace in the basement, but we usually leave it off. 'Tween the fireplace and stove, you're good. Extra blankets in every closet. Wireless, but it's spotty. Good old-fashioned landline for emergency. You said one night? Checkout's not until four, so no hurry to get going in the morning. You provide your own groceries. We provide the linens and the firewood. So there she is. What do you think?"

They'd ended up back in the kitchen, where they had started. Michael's mouth was suddenly dry. Each step brought him closer to something that he would eventually be unable to turn back from. At some point, critical mass would be reached, but you didn't realize it when it was happening. You just kept adding straw. Then, suddenly, to your surprise, the camel fell out from beneath you, broken-backed.

He wet his lips, found a smile. "I'll take it."

SIXTH ARRONDISSEMENT, PARIS

The café was filling rapidly with the lunch crowd.

Inside the truck parked out back, Ali Chamoun needed very badly to go to the bathroom. Rationally, he knew that this mattered not at all. Within the next few minutes, his underwear, soiled or not, would be vaporized along with everything else. Still, he found himself squirming, embarrassed, unwilling to shit his pants, even though no one would ever witness his humiliation.

His bowels clenched sharply, sending a cramp up his side. He grimaced. All the times he had pictured this moment, he had never imagined it like this.

He consulted his phone. 11:58 a.m. Thus began his last two minutes on earth. He should be having enlightened thoughts, divine thoughts. Instead, he was wondering if the triacetone triperoxide mixed by his brother in a damp, dingy basement would liquefy his remains sufficiently that, were he to lose control of his bowels, all evidence would be destroyed. Of course it would. But what if it wasn't?

It doesn't matter.

But in a strange way, it did.

Biting back a groan, he glanced in the sideview mirror. The view was of dumpsters, trash cans, gutters. The front of the café opened onto a quaint cobblestone street of shops, patisseries, galleries, and restaurants, but here in back you saw the real truth. It reinforced the most basic fact Ali Chamoun had discovered during his two years in Paris and Belgium: in the Western world, shiny surfaces concealed dirty secrets.

His hands were sweating. What if he could not pull the cord when the time came? What if his hand just slipped off? Absurd. He need only find enough purchase to tug lightly. His mind was serving up absurdity, nonsense.

His bowels clenched again. Moaning softly, he checked the time: 11:59.

Do it now, before you shit yourself.

No. The others would be acting at noon precisely. If he went sooner, he would put the gendarmerie on guard and might ruin everything.

He tossed another glance in the mirror. He had been afraid that police might hassle him, parking here. Dark-skinned man in a closed truck. He had a Baikal IZH-79-8 on the seat beside him, ready to answer just such an occurrence. But there were no police. He had been afraid, too, that he might see his imminent victims and lose his nerve. Pretty girls, innocent young children. Dogs and cats. He had a soft spot for dogs and cats. But there was nothing back here except garbage and rats. He hated garbage and rats.

He checked the time again. As he watched, the clock ticked down to twelve noon exactly.

Now.

His took hold of the cord, opened the small curtain separating him from the jugs piled in the back of the truck—not that the curtain would really make any difference—and braced himself.

Now. Go!

All around Paris, at this moment, two years of planning would be coming to a head. This was it. This moment was his destiny. This, now. A place in paradise, seventy-two virgins. His brother would already be waiting. This moment. This moment right now.

Now! GO!

He was staring at his own sneakers. Bright orange Nikes. When he pulled the cord, would the sneakers burn, too? They were nice sneakers. Nicer than any he'd ever had back home. But of course they would burn.

The clock read 12:01.

His body, his mind, were betraying him.

Allahu akbar! God is great!

He closed his eyes and pulled the cord.

ELLICOTT STREET NW, WASHINGTON, DC

"Silas, Kristen. Kristen, Silas."

She hunkered down to his eye level and stuck out a hand. "Pleased to meet you," she said gravely.

"Buddy?" Michael nudged the boy's foot with his toe.

Silas shook hands reluctantly, without making eye contact. "Can I go play?"

"Sure. Dinner in ten."

Silas ran away. She straightened, firing Michael a look. He shrugged: *It is what it is.*

They sat around the dining room table, eating salmon and couscous. Michael watched without contributing as she tried without success to engage his son, asking reasonable questions and receiving blunt, dismissive answers. What had he done at school today? Nothing. What did he hope Santa would bring him for Christmas? A telescope. What was his favorite food? Candy.

Afterward, they retired to the living room couch with bowls of ice cream. Michael and Silas had been watching *Superman: The Movie.* They picked up where they had left off. Gene Hackman: "Only one thing alive with less than four legs can hear this frequency, Superman, and that's you. In approximately five minutes, a poison gas pellet containing propane lithium compound will be released through thousands of air ducts in the city, effectively annihilating half of Metropolis …"

Oh, the irony! Crowing, mocking, victorious. *Lex Luthor using poison gas! This will throw the boy for a real loop, Mikey, when he's lying on the couch in twenty years trying to make sense of it all. The bad guy used poison gas; Daddy used poison gas. Therefore, Daddy is the bad guy. But Daddy's the one who showed me the movie! And sitting eating ice cream alongside his whore. You do realize, Mikey m'lad, that children of suicides are five times more likely to take their own lives. You do realize you're signing Silas' death warrant. But you're not giving him the gift of a fast death, oh, no. That one you're keeping for yourself, you selfish prick. No, you're putting Silas on the slow boat to hell, the one that twists through dark hallways of confusion and self-loathing and alcoholism and drug addiction until finally, mercifully, comes the blued steel of a one-way ticket.*

I'M NOT LISTENING!

The tree had been set up beside the TV set. Stacy's Christmas trees had been studies in glittering symmetry, with the presents artfully arranged beneath the lowest branches. Michael and Silas had done their best. The result nonetheless looked sad and lopsided, bulbs unevenly distributed, tinsel knotted and sparse. Still, there were plenty of presents. Trying to assuage his guilt, Michael had gone overboard, buying not only telescope but binoculars, skateboard, Laser Pegs, Legos, art set, Nerf sword, Razor Scooter, and Tonka backhoe.

Great parenting, Mikey. Dad's gonna check out, leaving you holding the emotional bag. But here, have some crappy plastic toys. That oughta take the sting out of it. God bless America.

He pushed up from the couch and went into the kitchen. His ice-cream bowl was still mostly full. He ran water in it anyway, washing the sweet dessert down the drain.

"Superman can just change into his costume like magic," he heard his son announce from the next room.

"I noticed that," she answered. "Weird. Usually, he has to duck into a phone booth or something."

"He just jumped out the window and, *blam*, he was wearing his costume!"

"I wonder if maybe he changed, like, so fast we couldn't see, using super speed, so it looked like magic."

Michael went back into the room. The two had closed ranks on the couch, taking his space, and watched side by side. "Will you put me to bed tonight?" Silas asked.

"My pleasure." She sent Michael another quick glance—this one of triumph.

* * *

Saturday morning, they made sure to be up before Silas, dressed, in the kitchen, sipping coffee, frying bacon and eggs.

Stacy picked him up at 8:00 a.m. sharp. She ventured no farther than the doorstep. This was no longer her territory, and she seemed to know it, although, judging from her eyes, she harbored mixed feelings about her choices. Waiting for Silas to get his shoes on, she and her estranged husband made polite but insipid small talk about the weather.

By nine o'clock, Michael was on the Hill. Rehearsal started twenty minutes late. Christina Thompson opened with a bracing pep talk about not slacking off, about leaning into the home stretch. Then the members of the Capitol's four major news galleries filed out from Statuary Hall to their various stations: Cannon and Russell Rotundas, which offered clear views of the dome, used as react locations for elected officials doing live shots; beauty-shot duty near the House Triangle or the Elm Tree; B-roll, filming arrivals whom network anchors would comment on during the long run-up to the event itself. Inside the House Chamber, the sergeant at arms made his first announcement. As Michael backed down the aisle, photographers and security moved with him in fluid lockstep: if not quite a well-oiled machine, then a close likeness.

"Mister Speaker, the dean of the Diplomatic Corps!"

By half past one, Michael was home again. By two, he had the car packed. He had been shopping all week, squeezing in forays around the edges of his schedule. By two fifteen, they were on the road. In the passenger seat, Kristen wore a cloth coat, sunglasses hiding her eyes, woolen cap pulled low around her ears. Michael wore a Full Sail hooded sweatshirt, blue jeans, and down jacket. It felt almost like a date … and, perversely, he was almost enjoying himself.

The little Hyundai rode low, suspension creaking even under

this modest burden. They headed west, following the same route Michael had followed Thursday evening. The sky blue and white, the day mild enough that his pretty passenger had cracked a window. They did not speak, but the silence was comfortable.

They left Route 7 and rolled up the dirt driveway a few minutes later. The lock on the front door was keyless, opening to a preestablished code. She waited in the car until he had confirmed that the owners were gone. Taped beside the wood-burning stove, they found a typewritten note:

> Welcome to Chez Bluemont! Checkout time is 4:00 p.m. Wireless code JY534, but connectivity is unpredictable. In case of emergency, dial 911. You are at 143 Saw Mill Hill Road in Loudoun County, Virginia. Recycling and garbage bins beneath the sink. Firewood beside the stove, more in woodshed if necessary. Circuit breaker in cellar near washing machine. Please place all dirty linens and towels into the washing machine before leaving. Please run dishwasher and return silverware and plates to proper cupboards. Please remember to lock up. Enjoy your stay!
>
> Best regards,
Hattie and Ralph
347-763-2939

They inspected the outbuildings. The woodshed was half full of mossy lumber. The former outhouse was even more cluttered: chainsaw, old Ping-Pong table broken into parts, jumper cables, ruined carburetor, dusty gray boxes of nails and screws. But the toolshed was mostly empty. They rolled out an old lawnmower. Beside it, in the yard, they set hedge clippers and WD-40, a rusty hoe and trowel, and a dull hatchet.

They unpacked the car. Clothes, groceries. Duct tape, bell jar, wire, spoons, plastic tub with airtight lid, sealed syringes, twelve-volt battery, four-thousand-watt inverter, box of latex gloves. Bleach, string, safety goggles, scissors, heavy-duty trash bags, baking rack, disposable sterile towels. The faded black case. A wire cage floored with cardboard and newspaper and hay, containing three gray rabbits with twitching pink noses and downy white tails.

All these things went into the house. Into the now-empty toolshed went turpentine, staple gun, Nonel tubes, electric blasting caps, waterproof tarps, dye, test tubes, and two burner phones.

By tacit agreement, they started with the rabbits, carrying cage and equipment down to the basement, then coming upstairs again to fetch two-liter bottles of soda and a gallon jug of vinegar. Diet Coke frothed into the sink. They rinsed plastic and returned to the basement. Finding a broom leaning against a mossy wall, they cleared a workspace between furnace and washing machine, pushed rat droppings and cobwebs and a single decomposing mouse in a glue trap against one wall. In the corner, a dehumidifier rattled and thrummed. Beyond narrow windows set high in cinder-block walls, the afternoon sky had turned a hard copper. The rabbits watched apprehensively, noses vibrating.

Kneeling on the filthy basement floor, exchanging only monosyllables, they assembled the apparatus. They worked quickly—she with God knew what training, he with skills from USAF Explosive Ordnance Disposal. Using heavy, multibraid copper cable, they wired the four-thousand-watt inverter to the battery and ran a length from the positive terminal to one end of a spoon. They ran another back from the spoon to the negative terminal but left it unattached. Then they set the large bell jar on top, making certain the insulated seal around the wires remained tight.

Michael prepared the baking rack, snipping it down to size, bending sharp wires at right angles to give it some height. He cut a sheet of paper into quarters, rolled one piece into a cone, and used tape to seal the crack. Moving aside the bell jar, he set the small cone with its base over the spoon. Then he set the rack above the cone, with a millimeter's clearance between them.

They assembled their homemade hazmat suits, more for peace of mind than for actual efficacy. They cut holes in two black trash bags for arms and head and donned them like soccer pinnies, then snipped plastic Coke bottles into masks, softening the ragged edges with duct tape. Soaked surgical towels in vinegar, stuffed them into the narrow neck at the top. Put on goggles. Tied the masks onto each other's faces with elastic string. Cut another garbage bag into pieces, covered their hair, and sealed every juncture with duct tape. The acrid smell of vinegar stung Michael's nostrils, but he didn't let himself cough.

They put on gloves. Michael moved aside the baking rack and paper cone and took a deep breath.

Kristen knelt, opened the black case, and drew out a plastic packet labeled *Handhabung siehe Anleitung.* SOMAN, SARIN, V-GASES.

Opening the packet, she slipped out one glass ampoule. Michael reminded himself to breathe.

She nodded, and he took the lid off the airtight plastic tub, unwrapped a syringe, and fitted a needle to it. She accepted it and moved beneath the window, into good light, where she snapped the ampoule at its neck. Just below the neck, the tiny hole was plugged with cork. She flipped the tip protector from the needle, pushed the tip through the cork, and slowly raised the plunger. A quivering drop, pea-soup green, rose from the ampoule into the hollow barrel of the syringe.

She lowered the ampoule carefully into the plastic tub, then turned to the spoon and knelt again. Her hands were steady.

She touched the needle's bevel to the bowl of the spoon and depressed the plunger.

The quivering green drop moved onto the spoon. She covered the spoon with the paper cone and then the rack, put the syringe beside the ampoule in the plastic tub, and closed the airtight lid. At the same time, Michael knelt and, with a tenderness that surprised him, removed a rabbit from the cage.

The animal seemed to know. Its ears lay back, and its feet pedaled desperately. During the short journey from cage to baking rack, it shat a dozen pellets onto the floor. He put the animal on the rack above the paper cone and released it. It squatted, frozen.

Kristen covered it with the bell jar and checked the seal.

Michael attached the loose wire to the battery's negative terminal. The spoon beneath the paper cone began to heat. A curl of black smoke, and the paper turned orange, flared briefly, and broke apart. The rabbit jumped, banging against the side of the jar and making Michael jump in turn. But the seal held.

The spoon glowed orange now, and the drop of pea soup danced, spat, and sizzled.

The rabbit jumped off the rack and huddled by the edge of the jar, staring at the glowing spoon. The other rabbits in the cage seemed to be watching, too.

The rabbit began to drool, and its eyes rolled upward. It leaped again, shaking the glass, and rolled kicking onto one side. Dribbling urine and bloody feces, it jerked and flopped, gave a single mighty shudder, and lay still, eyes open in death.

An evil smell came through the mask, through the vinegar. Wondering whether he had inhaled the gas, Michael braced himself for the running nose, the tightening vise in the chest. But nothing happened.

He detached the wire, and the spoon began to cool.

* * *

When they had finished cleaning up, they left the sealed hazmat tub outside, near the lawnmower. Later, they would bury the ampoule and divide the remaining contents of the tub among dumpsters in three states. They released the two surviving rabbits and chased them off into dark woods. They showered, Michael first. When it was Jana's turn, she stayed beneath the needle spray for a long time, letting it prick and scour her. She soaped, rinsed, soaped again. Rinsed again, soaped, rinsed.

She went down to the kitchen. Michael was standing there, loitering aimlessly in the half-light. He knew that it was time for the evening meal, and must feel obliged to follow convention despite his obvious lack of appetite.

She kissed him, stripping off his clean clothes, his fresh boxers. Then she took off her own clothes and pulled him down onto the linoleum floor.

Ugly, ugly. Two animals rutting on a dirty floor. Grunting and writhing, she made herself uglier still. Their bodies two sacs of liquid, gas waiting to be released, putrefaction waiting to happen. Two rutting animals, disgusting and ugly. Kidneys and bladder, liver and spleen, heart and intestines. Lust and death, Eros and Thanatos. Shameless, greedy. Avenging angels, lords of the flies.

His face in the twilight looked stricken. He had gone limp inside her. He was essentially a weak man, she reflected—soft beneath the hard corded muscles. He needed masks, walls, boundaries. He was out of his league. But he would do his job. She could push him where necessary. A steady hand on the tiller. Even as he went limp inside her, she refused to let him go, continued grinding against his pubis until she climaxed suddenly, sharply, joylessly, in a spasm like the dying rabbit's.

She rolled off him.

For the time being, she was done with him.

* * *

Later, during the night, he said, "They'll think we're all the same." His eyes slick and shining in the gloom.

She burrowed into the hollow of his shoulder, now playing the role of girlfriend, intimate, confidante. "Does it matter?"

A pause. Let him get it out. Let the wound drain. *Ubi pus, ibi evacua.*

"Security will be even tighter after Paris. They might …"

"They won't."

"But they might."

"But they won't."

She trailed a finger across his chest. Up and down and up. Playing him the way Yoni had played her, but softly, softly. All the best instruments required a delicate touch.

He released a pent-up breath. "Maybe we don't need to. So many lately … Maybe they've done it for us."

"We need to. The world forgets. They forgot the Shoah. They'll forget Paris."

His jaw grinding. Muscles tense. His entire body rigid. Then, all at once it relaxed, as if a string had been cut. "Kristen."

"Yes."

"Silas …" He fought back tears. "His mother looks after him. But …"

"Yes?"

"My cat," he sobbed. "Take care of my cat."

* * *

Breakfast was black coffee.

Inside the toolshed, icy air whistled through gaps between the slats. Frost on the wood and on the earth floor. Breath visible in narrow shafts of morning sunlight. Again they went to work without consulting, wordlessly dividing up the chores, a natural team.

Sunday morning. A hush on the winter air. How loud would the explosion be? Jana remembered the detonation on the ridge in Vermont. Its ferocity had taken her by surprise.

The *chik-chik* of the staple gun echoed off the forest as they hung the green tarps. Of course, they had come here for the isolation. But in such seclusion, the explosion would seem all the louder. For this reason, they had considered renting a place near Quantico, where endless artillery tests would cover any boom. But Michael had rejected the idea. He lacked the nerve. She had not pressed the point. One chose one's battles.

Once they had tarps stapled to the walls, ceiling, and floor, Jana readied a test tube. Same dimensions as the ampoules: seven centimeters long, a centimeter wide, the glass wall a bare 1.2 millimeters thick. She filled it with turpentine, leaving a centimeter of space at the top, and added red dye. Sarin and turpentine boiled at the same temperature. If the liquid had volatilized, the explosion would leave a fine, even red mist covering the tarps. If not, they would find fewer and heavier splotches of red. The difference at the event would be five dead—those immediately surrounding the blast—instead of fifty, maybe even five hundred. A girl could dream, couldn't she?

Meanwhile, Michael had prepared the Nonel tube, blasting cap, and *plastique*. He shaped the charge around the end of the test tube, then went outside and found a stick, which he broke to about the length of his forearm. He jammed the sharper end through the tarp, into the frozen earth floor with a strength that surprised her. Then he fixed the charge against a knurl in the wood, approximating the eventual orientation inside the prosthetic leg: explosive inside, toxin out. Choosing a burner phone, he programmed the number.

They walked fifty yards from the shed. He raised the phone.

A little dusting of snow lay evenly on the ground, unmarked by feet, human or animal. Slippery. Jana put her hand against a pine trunk, bracing herself. Not that there would be a shock wave. This explosion would be much smaller than the one that had surprised her in Vermont. That had been the biggest blast she could manage. This would be just enough to atomize the liquid.

She was excited now, her heart beating faster in anticipation.

FLOOOM!

A feeling as much as a sound—a prickling along the nape of her neck. She looked at Michael, expecting to see exultation on his face. But he looked distracted, mildly concerned, like someone wondering whether he had remembered to turn off the stove back home.

They moved toward the shed again, Jana in the lead.

At a thudding sound, she quickly turned. Michael had fallen, the prosthetic leg losing purchase against the snow. Shamefaced, he regained his footing, his North Face jacket now dusted with snow. She gave a reassuring smile. He returned it without conviction.

Inside the shed, she examined their handiwork. The tarp was an even pink: misty red dye shaded by the green plastic underneath. She heard Michael coming up behind her and stepped out of the doorway so he could see for himself.

They spent a few moments appreciating a job well done. Or at least she did. His thoughts were impossible to read. He still wore that look of distraction, of mild apprehension. Then they donned gloves, stripped the tarp off walls and ceiling, and folded it together, collecting shards of glass and other debris, and left the bundle by the sealed hazmat tub, to be disposed of later. The lawnmower, tools, and WD-40 went back in the shed.

They were about to go back inside, to pack up and make a final pass with bleach, when she heard the unmistakable crunch of tires coming up the drive.

Suddenly, she had a queer, hammering headache. The same feeling she'd had when sneaking a cigarette with Miriam, hanging out six flights above Madison Avenue, and the apartment door swung open unexpectedly. *Busted.* All the fanning hands in the world wouldn't clear away the smell before Aunt Becca came to see what was keeping her little angels so unusually quiet.

She turned. Somehow, she already knew what she would see: a police cruiser. Across the passenger-side doors was emblazoned SHERIFF: LOUDOUN COUNTY.

Michael wore that same look of mild concern as the cruiser stopped before them.

A single man inside, wide-brimmed hat in silhouette. Jana stood empty-handed, taken entirely by surprise. She had nothing with which to kill the man. Stupid. Nobody to blame but herself. She had let down her guard.

Her eyes sought Michael's, but Michael was looking away … at the hazmat bin.

Ah, fuck. Don't give it away.

She started toward the driver's side of the cruiser. The loudspeaker atop the car crackled importantly. "*Stay back. Keep your distance. Hands where I can see them.*"

She paused, head pounding like a bass drum, hands hanging loose by her side.

The cop hesitated for another few seconds, weighing the situation. Taking their measure, she thought. One of him, two of them. Michael was a big boy. Broad-shouldered, powerful. Run the plate, call it in, wait for backup. Or handle it alone?

A bird sang. Here it was December, but the bird sang sweetly, and that seemed to decide it.

The cop got out of his car.

The beat in her head receded to a dull thud. She could handle this.

One hand hovered near the holstered gun on his belt. The other tipped the wide brim back off a long, morose face. Carroty-red hair. Freckles. *Oy vey*, she thought. *It's fucking Opie.*

He took two steps forward, planting himself midway between them. Relaxing his body language, showing that he didn't consider them a threat: nice lady and her friend. He was here to help. "Mornin'," he said.

"Morning." She was tempted to drop the final "g" in imitation, but that would be slathering it on too thick.

"I see by your plate you're from out of town, so maybe you don't know." Long, droning vowels. "But there's postings all around here. No huntin', fishin', or trespassin'."

She nodded.

"You rentin' for the weekend?"

She nodded again.

He nodded back; looked at Michael, then at the hazmat bin. The breeze picked up, stirring the fine snow. Something was missing, and it took Jana a second to figure out what. Then she had it: she still expected to feel flyaway strands of hair against her face when the wind blew.

The cop kept looking around—for the rifle, she guessed. He or a neighbor had heard the bang and assumed they were hunting. That made sense. That was what people did out here. Yet he saw no gun. But, of course, the gun might be anywhere: in the house, the car, the shed. The story he had told himself still held.

His eyes ended up again on the sealed plastic hazmat bin. The gathered bundle of pink-stained tarp. Where did these fit into the story?

The headache pulsed, trying to drop a veil of red inside her mind, pushing her to do something she might regret. She squared it back and held her ground.

"Where y'all from?" the cop said in a conversational tone. Looking at Jana a little more closely now. Perhaps thinking of an attempt-to-locate he'd seen back at the office; trying to remember just what that face had looked like.

"DC," Michael answered.

The hand still rested with the thumb hooked over the gun belt.

Then something shuffled in the forest. They all turned reflexively. A rabbit. Not one of the fluffy-tailed bunnies they had released, born and raised in the tranquility of a pet store, but a wild cottontail, driven by winter to venture closer to human haunts than it otherwise might.

As the sheriff looked toward the woods, the hand drifted a few centimeters from the gun.

Jana's body made the decision. Moving in, dipping behind him to buy an extra fraction of a second out of his field of view, she swung a hard right hook into the base of his jaw, just under the ear.

He went down like a sack of cement. Gun still in its belt. She kicked him in the side of the head, and the hat rolled away. She kicked him again, a terrible regret filling her. What was she doing?

The cop was crawling away, toward Michael but clumsily, one

hand trying to protect his head, the other scrabbling for the gun. Michael still had the distant look in his eyes. But then something changed, and she saw what, until now, she had not known was in him.

The cop worked the gun out of his holster. Michael leaned down and plucked it gracefully, almost politely, from the man's fingers. Stepping back, he flicked off the safety and fired two shots from point-blank range.

Jana turned away, head throbbing, stomach roiling on the brink. But she had not eaten for twenty-four hours, so there would be nothing but bile to vomit.

Another shot, flat and undramatic.

A small echo.

PART FOUR

CHAPTER TWELVE

MARTIN LUTHER KING JR. AVE. SE, WASHINGTON, DC

Every morning, a courier from Nebraska Avenue delivered a zippered and locked portfolio, and every morning, the courier took away a signed receipt.

Every morning, Barry Innes, head of operations of the Washington Regional Threat and Analysis Center, opened the portfolio and divided the leads inside among the personnel in the conference room. Every morning—even today, Christmas Eve, although only six people had shown up to work—they split into teams and chased the leads down.

And every day, they came up blank.

Dalia could see them losing heart. Only the fact that the task force had the personal blessing of the chief of staff, who, in the wake of the Paris attacks, had given Homeland carte blanche, kept mutiny at bay. Cynically, she could not help realizing that the bloodshed, in allowing them to proceed without a lot of inconvenient scrutiny, had been a blessing in disguise.

Each day, teams deployed, grumbling, to investigate the latest batch of murders, missing persons, stolen cars, reported sightings of fugitives, suspicious purchases, packages left in public places.

When not chasing wild geese, they investigated dozens of

upcoming events around the Washington area that were deemed worthy of attention: the Cherry Blossom Festival, various White House holiday parties, the Strings of Joy concert, the State of the Union address, ZooLights, the Military Bowl, the Easter Egg Roll, the Saint Patrick's Day Parade, the Washington Auto Show, and more, always more. And always leading nowhere.

This morning, they interviewed an event planner who handled private FBI soirees, a tour guide who conducted an annual New Year's Eve cruise down the Potomac, the general manager of a meter-reading company whose employees regularly entered customers' homes, and the maître d' of a Farragut Square restaurant known to cater to members of Congress.

They stopped for a late lunch at a Foggy Bottom steakhouse. A wreath on the wall, tinseled and baubled, generated the sweet scent of pine. After ordering, Horowitz excused himself to call his family, leaving McConnell and Dalia momentarily alone. They could see him on the sidewalk, through the reverse-stenciled letters on the restaurant windows, smiling broadly as he listened to the phone.

"Feel bad, taking him away during the holidays," said McConnell. A basket of bread arrived, and he twisted off a piece and reached for a dish of oregano-laden olive oil. "Young kids. He should be home."

"But it's not his holiday. He's Jewish."

"Ah, it's cultural more than religious. Everybody celebrates. Even Jews, after a fashion. Chinese food." He dipped the bread and popped it into his mouth.

"Don't fill yourself up," she said.

"Really?"

"Just saying. You order a nice steak, then you—"

"Channeling my ex-wife, I swear to God."

"So it's official: we won't get married."

"No, we sure as hell won't."

"Probably tear each other's throats out."

"You can say that again. Wouldn't last two weeks. But you know, Dalia, there's nobody I'd rather have in my foxhole."

The steaks came. Horowitz was still on his phone outside the window, laughing. And for a moment, Dalia felt more homesick, more hopeless, more alone, than she had ever felt in her life.

CANNON HOUSE OFFICE BUILDING, WASHINGTON, DC

Christina Thompson was checking sight lines from the Cannon Rotunda when she got the call.

After hanging up, she put two fingers inside her wrist. Her pulse ran fast. She drew a breath and held it. If they knew anything, she told herself—if they even *suspected* anything—she would be answering questions through an attorney. This was ripples from the Paris attacks, nothing more.

She assembled her poker face carefully.

She released the breath.

She went to talk with Homeland.

It was starting to snow: light, tumbling flakes, just in time for a white Christmas. But after a few flurries, the slate-gray sky seemed to reconsider. And by the time Christina reached the East Plaza, the snow had stopped.

A blond male staffer spoke into a radio, made a pass with the wand, and told her the visitors were waiting in the Crypt. She found them there in the windowless room directly below Statuary Hall, standing between two neoclassical Doric columns. The day's last tour moved past, the guide chirping enthusiastically.

A chubby man a couple of decades older than Christina flashed his shield. Straight out of Central Casting: an Irish type, paunchy, with dark circles underscoring sharp green eyes. His partner was a handsome Semitic type with an aquiline nose and cleft chin. Bad cop and good cop respectively, unless they got creative and swapped roles. Tagging inexplicably along was a stout woman with silver roots, an inexpensive pantsuit, and a small stain on one lapel, which Christina at first took for a pin.

"Jim McConnell," said the Irish type. "Washington Regional Threat and Analysis Center, Homeland."

"That's a mouthful." Christina found a smile. "What can I do for you?"

"Just a moment of your time. You're in charge of the State this year?"

"I'm directing it, if that's what you mean."

"Quite a responsibility."

For a woman, he meant. Patronizing, but then, he was hardly the first. "This will be my fifth year, Mr. McConnell. I've been director of Capitol Media for seven."

"Same personnel at the State every year?"

"Few tweaks here and there, but I've got a team I depend on."

"OS-SAPs?" Operations and support special access programs.

"No. Yankee White, category two." Personnel working in direct support of POTUS: air crew, mess, communications and transportation, medical, Camp David, and contractors requiring regular unescorted access to presidential support areas.

"Vets?"

"Some. All cleared."

"So …" He consulted a pad. "We've got broadcast groups in gallery eleven. Ninety seats assigned to daily press, nine seats for periodical press, pool feed on the floor—"

"Seventeen print photographers in the gallery, fifteen rotating, one designated pool photojournalist. I hate to be rude, Mr. McConnell, but this is my crunch time. Might I direct you to Bob Sykes, who's handling presidential protection at the event?"

"We'll speak with him, too."

"That's a lovely ring," the stout older woman remarked. An accent—Italian, maybe?

"Thank you." Christina raised her left hand automatically. "It belonged to my husband's mother."

"Platinum?"

"White gold."

Michael Fletcher was passing by, lugging his kit. Shoulders and chest bulging, the definition visible even beneath his jacket. He put his eyes down and kept moving, but not before Christina noticed that his passing glance was touched with private contempt.

The stout older woman had also registered the man's scorn—perhaps only subconsciously, but her gaze followed as he moved past. "Who's that?"

"Pool feed, House floor."

McConnell cleared his throat, consulted his pad again. "Have you got children, Ms. Thompson?"

"What does that have to do with anything?"

"Indulge me."

"Two." As a matter of habit, she did not mention her husband's children, since it opened the un-Christian subject of the second marriage.

He made a note. "So during the address, the Supreme Court comes in the Senate side, yes? Meanwhile, the diplomatic corps, Joint Chiefs, Cabinet, and Senate come in through the House side, then proceed to the Chamber in groups. I'll need the names of every staffer they move past."

"Should I be scared?"

"Ma'am?"

"Did you get a tip? Should I be scared?"

"Just covering our bases."

"Because of Paris?"

He shrugged. "Every staffer, I was saying, that they move past …"

MANASSAS, VA

A green body bag lay on a porcelain embalming table.

Bottles of chemicals lined the floor. In one corner, pink rubber tubing wound like a frozen snake from a waist-high steel canister. Shelves held absorbent pads, moisturizing cream, hair gel, Kerlix gauze rolls, Johnson's baby oil, Revlon makeup, Vicks VapoRub. The scent of lavender, mingled with cool sharp menthol, hung in the air.

Dr. Emmett Thorpe switched on the vent fan, then unzipped a body bag. Seventy-two years old, he was a thirty-year veteran of the Northern District Office of Virginia's medical examiner system. The man on the embalming table was some years younger, redheaded, with freckles still visible on his parchment-like skin.

Thorpe leaned close over shadowed eye hollows, pursing his lips as if preparing to steal a kiss. The inlet where they had found John Doe was hypoxic, which made it inhospitable to larger scavengers. Often, crustaceans would take a submerged body down to bone in a matter of days, but in this case the shrimp and crabs had been out of luck. Cold temperatures had conspired with low oxygen levels to preserve the body astonishingly well.

He turned to a shelf, daubed VapoRub beneath his nostrils, pulled on surgical gloves, and took forceps from a black case. As he separated John Doe's ribs, a wave of rank air slapped him. His nostrils twitched. After a moment, the fan whisked it away.

Heart and liver were mostly intact, lungs mostly liquefied. Frowning, he withdrew the forceps and angled the harsh lamp hanging from the ceiling. The face was collapsing, so it was hard to be sure. But something … Very gently, following an intuition, he lifted the corpse's head from the shallow wooden block. Beneath the sloughing skin and carroty hair, he searched in vain for exit wounds. He returned the head to the table.

Using the forceps, he seized, after two tries, a flap of dangling white skin where the face had been. Usually, the brain was one of the first things to disintegrate—eager bacteria from the mouth chewed through the palate—but the icy water had retarded the process considerably. He poked through fibrous, spongy mass. After some fishing, he withdrew one, two, three .40-caliber pistol bullets. "Gotcha," he murmured aloud. "Little bastards."

He inspected the arms and hands. "Substantial presence of adipocere." He said it aloud—a habit from long-ago residency days. He bent closer. Again, hard to tell, but ... "Substantial maceration of hands. Fingertips missing." The technique was a favorite of Russian Mafia who wanted to conceal the identities of their victims.

He found no evidence of defensive injuries to the ulnar borders of the arms. No soft tissue or skeletal damage consistent with propeller injuries. Though it would likely yield no results, he searched anyway for indications of drowning. He found no admixture of proteinaceous material, no pulmonary surfactant in the airways. He might test surviving organs for diatoms, but in his learned opinion—unlike those of some younger coworkers—even a positive result here would be inconclusive.

The skin of the legs was the color and consistency of Japanese rice paper. Feet, a translucent blue. Toes, nearly intact.

He straightened. The Virginia State Police's missing-persons database contained three hundred twenty names. Two hundred eighty of those were children. Of the remaining forty, fully three-quarters were women. A middle-aged, redheaded, freckled man who had died within the past month ... Thorpe liked very much the odds of tracking him down.

A Christmas miracle, he thought. Good luck had conspired from every side. Had a parapet on the inlet's bridge not collapsed last week, engineers would never have found cracks in the bridge's support. The frogmen would never have gone down to inspect the foundations, and John Doe's weighted body would still be sleeping with the fishes. Instead, the man was on the table—and in relatively good condition, to boot.

Thorpe started cleaning up, whistling a soft but cheery tune. All part of His divine plan. The Good Lord worked in mysterious ways.

ELLICOTT STREET NW, WASHINGTON, DC

In eighteen days, Michael Fletcher would do his best to kill himself as near to the president of the United States as he could manage. But tonight, he sifted together flour and spices, then added the mixture to a bowl of sugar, egg, and vanilla.

Silas mixed without restraint, somehow avoiding slopping ingredients all over the floor. The woman watched with a smile. They dusted the countertop with flour, rolled dough into a wide flat leaf that reminded Michael of sheet explosive, and used cookie cutters to make gingerbread soldiers, which they transferred, all in a line, to a baking sheet.

In the back of his mind, Michael saw the baking rack they had put the rabbit on, and the pebbles of shit it had dropped on its brief journey from the cage. The spoon heating up and turning red. The drop of pea soup spitting and popping. And behind that, the image of the redheaded cop. SHERIFF: LOUDOUN COUNTY. Crawling klutzily, like Sandra Bullock trying to get onto her feet at the end of *Gravity* after finally falling back to earth; trying to protect his head and at the same time get his gun out of the holster. Then Michael's mind had shut off. *Not my fault, Judge; my mind shut off. Autopilot took over. Really, Judge, if you need to blame someone, blame Dr. Gross. Great name, huh? What's it called when something sounds like what it is? Dr. Gross, who told me it's not PTSD, it's "combat stress." He said combat stress is the prostate cancer of stress disorders—I swear, exact words. You watch and you wait and you see what develops. And while you're at it, blame Sergeant Laforna, who—you can't make this shit up—who had a good look at my record, my psych profile, my discharge orders, and decided there was no reason whatsoever to revoke Yankee White, category two. And while you're* still *at it, blame the camel-fucking raghead who strapped on a belt filled with RDX and broken nails and ball bearings and nuts and bolts and climbed onto that bus and, for no good goddamn reason except the fact that he was surrounded by Jews, killed my big brother.*

They slid the sheet of gingerbread cookies into the oven, and Michael opened a bottle of red. In the living room, the television was playing the end of *It's a Wonderful Life.*

"*A toast! To my big brother George: the richest man in town!*"

They settled onto the couch. Michael, the woman, Silas in the middle, Licorice jumping up to join them.

"*Every time a bell rings, an angel gets its wings.*"

As the credits rolled, Silas craned around. "Can I open a present now, Daddy?"

It was a family custom: one present on Christmas Eve. Michael nodded. He had grown up in a home where Christmas was not celebrated. Instead they'd had Hanukkah. The first night had been great: big present, candles, dreidels spinning, latkes and chocolate gelt. But by the eighth night, money and inspiration had run low, and little Jewish boys and girls might receive for a gift a battery, a pencil, a pack of gum. The pacing of Hanukkah was inherently flawed. Christmas, by contrast, had a perfect dramatic arc. Anticipation leading up, building, building, building; the night before, one present, whetting the appetite; the morning of, *pow*! Stockings to get it going, then an orgy of tearing open packages. The afterglow: gingerbread cookies, Christmas goose.

Silas scampered down, kneeling on the floor before the tree, relishing the moment, weighing his options. Michael sipped his wine and looked at the woman, who smiled in return.

Looking back at his son, he thought, *It's not too late. You can still change your mind. Take Silas, scoop him up, hold him close, and run, run, run.*

I know that voice. Poe had a name for that. Imp of the Perverse, innit?

Takes one to know one, thought Michael.

Silas made his selection and tore open the wrapping paper. A Nerf sword. His face fell. "Can I open another?"

"In the morning, champ. Go brush your teeth and change into

your pj's. I'll come read."

"Can Kristen tuck me in?"

Half an hour later, with Silas tucked in and the gingerbread men cooling on the rack (Michael saw the bunny again, eyes rolling, teeth gnashing), the living room dark except for the glowing tree, they poured more wine. *Eighteen days*, the voice editorialized. *In the morning, seventeen.*

They made a desultory effort at sex. Farther down the block, carolers sang off-key. On the couch, it was hard to find a position that worked. And Michael had drunk too much wine. But perhaps the problem was not entirely his. Usually, the woman smelled good. Like ripe fruit with an undertone of something slightly tart, cutting the syrupy sweetness. But tonight, the tartness seemed to have come to the forefront. It came through her skin, her pores, sour and bitter. After a few minutes, they gave up, the act incomplete.

They went upstairs. Soon she slept, breath flattening. Moonlight limned the faint scars on her cheek. Scents of gingerbread and wine lingered on the air. Michael lay awake, the wheels in his head grinding drunkenly.

He had almost fourteen thousand dollars in a 360 Capital One savings account. Enough to get out of town, at least. Enough even to start again somewhere new. Down south, maybe. A dollar went further down there. Of course, there would be complications. Without papers, how would Silas go to kindergarten? Maybe somehow they could get forged documents. But how, exactly? This wasn't the movies. In real life, how did you roll into a new town with your five-year-old and go about obtaining a fake Social Security number? He wouldn't know where to start.

And, of course, the Mossad would send its legendary assassins. Maybe even "Kristen" herself. Despite everything they had shared, she would show no mercy. Of that he had no doubt.

It was all fantasy anyway. He would not uproot Silas, who, considering the rocky past few months, had been doing exceptionally well. Few tantrums, no nightmares. The kid had wet himself a few times, but now even these accidents seemed to be tapering off. Stacy had been right: the split was for the best. Moving Silas south in the middle of the night, to a strange town, telling him to use a strange name, always looking over their shoulders … That would be no life for the boy.

On the other hand, having a father who committed suicide and, in the process, became the most notorious American traitor since Benedict Arnold—that would be no bed of roses, either.

Slowly, Michael became aware of a presence standing over the bed. When he thought back on it in the following days, he guessed it had been a dream. But it didn't feel like a dream. Or a drunken hallucination. He was lying awake, and the woman was breathing evenly beside him, and Silas was sleeping down the hall, and the carolers outside were calling it a night, and down in the living room the tree still glowed, fire hazard be damned, and on the air a trace of gingerbread still lingered, and in the upstairs bedroom a presence stood looming over the bed. A vision, a visitation, a revenant.

Seth.

Remember that time, Mikey, with Frank Wexler?

And Michael *did* remember.

He had forgotten but now it came back, not in a flood but as a taste, fleeting like honeysuckle on the tongue. They had been in high school. Michael was a freshman, Seth a junior. They were on a Young Judaea field trip. To a play, a museum—that part was lost. But the bus ride home, Michael remembered.

Dark, late. Little kids in bed by now. But in the back of the bus, young Jews, girls and boys, aged fourteen to seventeen, still awake. Both the chaperone and the driver, Michael remembered, had been immensely fat men. Up at the front, a world away. They could not move quickly enough to catch anyone back here. Here in the back of the bus, cloaked by shadows, kids were getting up to mischief. A girl and a boy were making out. The girl's face was dusted with glitter that sparkled in the headlights of passing cars on the highway. Glitter on her cheeks, her eyelids. Heavy breathing. In a nearby seat, a sharp sniff—not cocaine, Seth had told Michael later, but snuff. Seth had been sitting next to his little brother. And then Frank Wexler had craned around from the seat in front of them. Pressing something into Michael's hand. A cigarette. Yet not a cigarette. This had been before e-cigarettes, before vape pens, and Michael had not understood what it was, until Frank whispered, "It's a bat." And when Michael still looked at him blankly, "A one-hitter."

"It's for smoking pot," Seth had murmured.

The memory was giving itself to him now. The taste becoming a gulp, filling his mouth. He could smell Frank's breath, tinged with bacon cheeseburger. (Only two of the twelve members of the Young Judaea group conformed to the laws of kashruth.) He could see the strange smear of amber light behind passing factories on the highway, and feel the air stir as an eighteen-wheeler rumbled past. The bus had been rickety, practically open to the elements. He could hear Ariella Abramovitz moaning in a way she probably thought sexy, as Ben Schoenberg worked his hand under her panties. Frank Wexler was leaning over, flicking a butane lighter. In the sudden flare, Frank's face, all arched eyebrows and widow's peak and shadows, looked downright satanic. The flame went out. Michael put the one-hitter against his lips. The lighter flicked again, and he tried to inhale. He got a mouthful of nothing. Ariella moaned again. The lighter flared again. Glitter sparkled. Michael tried again to inhale. Then Seth was saying, "*Fuck, he's coming.*"

And suddenly, there in the aisle beside them stood their chaperone. Faster, lighter on his feet than anyone could have imagined. Frank Wexler was gone, mysteriously and completely. And Michael was busted, holding the one-hitter in his hand, his mouth full of smoke. The chaperone extended a flattened palm like someone offering bites of carrot to a horse. Rocking back and forth as the rickety bus moved swiftly down the highway. Michael froze. Busted. Finished. And then Seth turned up his face and said, loud and clear and firm, "It's mine. I double-dared him. It's my fault." He snatched the one-hitter from Michael's unresisting fingers.

And that did the trick, possession being nine-tenths of the law. The chaperone hauled Seth up—at least, in Michael's suddenly vivid memory—by the nape of his neck, like a mother cat lifting its kitten, and dragged him toward the front of the bus. Michael turned his head and let out the sweet-sour puff of smoke he'd been holding. The cracks in the bus whisked it away, dispersing it above the highway, into the obliging night.

The revenant standing over the bed smiled approvingly. *You* do *remember.*

Already the memory was drifting apart, like dandelion seeds on the wind. Had it meant suspension for Seth? Expulsion from Young Judaea? A conversation with their parents, with the rabbi? Must have. But Michael couldn't get it. That part was gone. But the memory of his older brother's sacrifice was there, bright and clean and hard. That was the part that mattered.

He closed his eyes, and the wheels stopped grinding. He felt peaceful, drifting into Christmas morning on the dark wings of a serene, dreamless slumber.

CHAPTER THIRTEEN

MARTIN LUTHER KING JR. AVE. SE, WASHINGTON, DC

New Year's Eve.

Only five people had shown up. Three of them were Dalia, McConnell, and Horowitz. Even Innes had opted out today. Dalia signed the courier's receipt herself.

They split into two teams of two, leaving McConnell, the most familiar with Washington, to navigate on his own. Or was it Jews sticking together, reflexively if not quite consciously?

Dalia and Horowitz took his rented Lexus to follow up a batch of leads from Northern Virginia. In a house on the banks of the Rappahannock, they spoke with an octogenarian who claimed to have seen the wanted girl in a supermarket. The old woman demonstrated a variety of facial tics and a practiced facility with racial slurs. Then they talked with a patrolman in Fauquier County who, the night before, had investigated a domestic disturbance involving a veteran from the New Way Forward—the official designation of the 2007 troop surge in Iraq. The man had given his wife two black eyes. The vet was chronically unemployed, persistently drunk, and notorious among the local cops for beating up his pretty wife. But no "failed marriage"—at least, not in the eyes of the law—and no young son to be used as leverage. Just another drunk, angry casualty of war.

By midafternoon, Horowitz was showing signs of battle fatigue. He wondered aloud whether he might make it home in time to spend the holiday with his family. Dalia felt fatigued herself. Sitting in the passenger seat of the Lexus, she turned her attention to their last tip of the day. A missing sheriff's deputy had been discovered a week ago, in an inlet near Manassas. The lead had come in three days ago. She bent over the GPS and programmed an address.

The Loudoun County Sheriff's Office occupied a boxy three-story building near a stoplight off Route 15. As they parked, a distant chainsaw buzzed, climbed, fell away. Inside, Horowitz flashed his HSAP ID. He and Dalia were shown through a long room of desks, mostly empty, to a room with frost-rimed windows and a buzzing space heater. They sat waiting before an aluminum desk that needed dusting. An air freshener shaped like a pine tree hung from a goosenecked lamp. On top of a filing cabinet, confiscated bongs of various shapes and sizes had been collected, apparently as trophies.

After ten minutes, the sheriff came in: a mustachioed and sideburned, gray-haired, pink-cheeked man of about forty-five who apologized for keeping them waiting, grumbling that New Year's Eve brought out the crazies even as it shrank his force by half. Sitting down behind the desk, he plucked a tennis ball from the dusty chaos on the blotter and squeezed it repeatedly.

"What brings you?"

Horowitz showed his shield again. "Watch the news?"

The sheriff, frowning, kept squeezing the ball. "Can't stomach too much of it these days, to be honest."

"You should have gotten an attempt-to-locate from NCIC. Pretty girl, early to mid-twenties, short dark hair …"

"Rings a bell." He sounded as though it didn't.

"We're sorry to hear about your deputy," Dalia said.

The hand stopped squeezing the tennis ball. "Goddamn right." He shook his head. "Willy Teller. Good man. Good friend. Left behind three kids. I don't know what to say. What kind of animal …"

He put it together. Blinked.

"We're just fishing," Horowitz said quickly.

The sheriff put down the tennis ball. "Fish away."

"When's the last time you saw him?"

"Week ago Saturday. Sitting right where you are. Wanted Sunday morning off. His kid had something. I said, 'You know, Willy, we can't change the schedule every time somebody's kid got something.' So he went out. Just doing the rounds around Snickers Gap. Didn't call nothing in. Must have taken him completely by surprise. Animals. Three times in the head. Point-blank range."

Natural-born killers, Dalia thought.

"Not two houses per square mile out there. I knocked on every door. Good people I've known my whole life. Only one possible lead. One of the houses was rented out. We tried to track the name down, hit a brick wall. But God only knows. People use false names. DFS had a look anyway. Didn't find shit." His eyes darkened. "Probably, 'tween you and me, some piece of drug-addict crap down from DC. Needs a fix, comes around looking for an easy B and E. Big, rich houses. Or so he thinks. He don't know white people got problems, too. For Willy it's just wrong place, wrong time. Three shots, point-blank. Forty caliber. Not like the old days, either, when MPDC would kick out all the stops until we catch the scumbag. These days, cop killers just vanish into the woodwork. Too much crime, too many drugs, too few boots on the ground. Just vanish into the woodwork, like any other lowlife."

* * *

When they came outside again, the air felt twenty degrees colder.

In cities and towns around the country, New Year's Eve countdowns were cranking up: lights, parties, balloons, champagne. Out here, driving into Snickers Gap, darkness overlay deeper darkness. The winter sky overhead seemed preternaturally clear. Pulsing satellites moved against powdered sugar on black velvet. Dalia could see the curve of the earth beyond the trees.

A dirt driveway branched off the dirt road. Beside it, the mailbox for 143 Saw Mill Hill Road was all but lost in overgrowth. At the driveway's end, a maroon Chevy Silverado was parked before a house of redwood and brick. Lights burned on both floors. In the silence, the crash of the Lexus doors closing made her flinch.

Horowitz was already moving toward the front porch. But Dalia paused, feeling the frisson in the cold air. Winter sky dazzlingly clear. Forest murmuring secretly. *The girl*, the trees whispered … The girl had been here.

Hurrying to catch up with Horowitz, she passed a woodshed, a toolshed, a long-disused outhouse. He was climbing the porch steps when the front door opened and a man came out. Armed, certainly, although Dalia could not see the gun—something in the bloodshot eyes, and the set of the shoulders beneath the stained, holey V-neck undershirt. He said, not unkindly, "I'll ask you to get the hell off my property."

"Sheriff sent us over." Horowitz held up his shield. "You're Ralph Korn?"

The man paused. From inside came voices through TV speakers: media personalities yukking it up in Times Square before the ball drop. "Let's see that ID again."

Horowitz handed over the shield. Ralph Korn examined it closely, made a pushing-air sound in his throat, handed it back.

Inside, a woman sat on a couch, holding a bowl of ice cream in her lap. She muted the TV as they came in. "Homeland," Ralph Korn said brusquely, by way of introduction. "M'wife, Hattie. Don't know what y'all are expecting to find. I already talked to Scotty. Boys from the lab already made a pass. Didn't see nothing."

"You rented out the place." Horowitz looking around, taking in the scene as he spoke. "The weekend the deputy went missing."

Dalia found herself standing near the wood-burning stove. She scuffed a grimy spot on the floor with her toe. The girl had been here.

"Yessir. And I already told Scotty everything. Ordinary-looking guy. Fit, brown hair. Mebbe brown eyes, too. Not sure on that one."

"White guy."

"Yessir."

"Height?"

"Average. And mebbe …" He paused. Horowitz's eyebrows rose slightly. Ralph shrugged. "Mebbe he served. I got that feeling. Served myself. Hotel two-five Weapons Platoon."

A flash between Horowitz's eyes and Dalia's. "A vet," Horowitz said.

"Just a feeling."

"Tell you why he wanted the place?"

"Nossir."

"Here alone?"

"Dunno. Cleaned up after himself real good. Didn't find so much as a hair on the pillowcase."

"Bleach," Dalia guessed.

He looked at her with minor-key surprise. "Yes ma'am. Bleach."

As they walked through the house, Dalia kept quiet, letting Horowitz question the man in a lazy, unhurried rhythm. They climbed creaky stairs. So the guest had given a name? Yessir, Stuart Williams. (But of course the sheriff had already tried to track down the name, and hit a dead end.) As they peered into a bedroom, Dalia caught the fugitive scent of bleach trapped in corners and crevices. What kind of car had he driven? Little blue Japanese thing. Did Ralph get a plate? No such luck. They retraced their steps, went down cobwebbed stairs to a basement, and poked around under a bare bulb beside a rattling dehumidifier. Dalia found a scattering of gray dust, thought for a moment she had discovered something, then realized that it was magnetic powder for picking up fingerprints. All the while, Horowitz continued his laconic interrogation. Paid in cash? Yessir. And made contact via email? Yessir. (But surely, Dalia thought, he had used a public terminal or an IP switcher. They covered their tracks, yes they did. Still, HSAP would follow up, just in case.)

They went upstairs again. Forensics went over the whole house? Horowitz asked casually. Whole house, yessir. Proverbial fine-tooth comb.

Standing in the kitchen, by the stove again. Dalia looked through her wavering reflection in the small window above the sink. Black woods, waiting patiently for the next thousand years to go by. Her eyes focused, through her own ghostly face, on the outbuildings. "Toolshed out there?" she asked.

"Toolshed, yes ma'am. Woodshed. And outhouse—now it's for storage."

"Forensics look out there, too?"

"No ma'am, don't think so."

"Got a flashlight?"

The woodshed was buttoned up tightly against the cold. And yet, the beam of the heavy-duty Pelican Kinglite picked out frosty wood, ice crystals glimmering like diamonds. The outhouse–cum–storage shed was not so soundly weatherproofed. Dalia had not brought gloves, and her hands were quickly turning numb. She searched anyway, taking the lead as Horowitz and Ralph Korn watched from the doorway behind her. Against these mounds of clutter, the beam seemed a thin and fragile spear. Rusty chainsaw, sagging net on a broken Ping-Pong table, coiled red and black jumper cables. The wind sliced through invisible cracks, cutting her exposed skin like a blade.

The toolshed was less cluttered and even more open to elements. Her teeth were starting to chatter now. The light played across a sooty lawnmower, hoe and spading fork, hatchet. And something else, registered immediately but subliminally. She had to run the light back and forth several times before it clicked. Glittering on the floor. Not sooty and rusted like everything else. She knelt. Here … and here.

Staples.

Her gaze crawled up the wall, into shadowed ceiling corners. She saw splintery old wood. Hoary grays and browns … with a faint but distinct rind of pink, thin as a razor's edge.

She stepped closer. Misty, aerated pink.

She found another staple, still clinging to the wood. Something had been stapled to the wall and then taken down. Stapled to cover an expanding mist of pink …

She turned. Horowitz was already on the phone.

ELLICOTT STREET NW, WASHINGTON, DC

Silas yawned, knuckling his eyes.

He lay facedown on the floor before the TV, working on a coloring book, feet idly kicking the air. A dusting of fallen needles from the Christmas tree surrounded him. On-screen, a tracking shot whooshed over the multitudes jammed into Times Square. Jana looked at those multitudes and saw a missed opportunity. Sitting beside her on the couch, Michael watched narrow-eyed. It was impossible to tell what he was seeing, and that disturbed her.

He felt her gaze and summoned a weak smile. "Champagne time?" he asked.

Ten o'clock. She shrugged. "Why not?"

"Can I have some?" Silas asked from the floor as Michael pushed off the couch.

"You." Jana nudged him with a stockinged foot. "You're a funny guy."

Giggling, he grabbed her foot. She pulled it away, but not before he got the sock off. "Gimme my sock."

Laughing, they wrestled. She got the sock back and said, "Go change into your pj's, kiddo."

He considered arguing. But he was already getting away with murder, being allowed to stay up so late, and he knew it. He vanished upstairs without complaint.

Michael came into the living room holding two flutes of champagne. They sat, toasted. Again she failed to read whatever was in his eyes. Something uneasy. Something clicking back and forth, like beads on an abacus. He looked as if he might say something, and instead drank silently.

Cheap champagne, but not the bottom shelf. Her brain immediately began to fizz. She snuggled close to him on the couch. All playacting, counterfeit fondness: teeth on edge, stomach churning.

Twelve days.

Outside, the wind rose to a howl. Windows set too loose in their frames rattled like castanets. Forced, lunatic merriment on the TV. A bleached blonde yelling into a microphone about the first Times Square celebration, over a century before: "*Two hundred thousand people gathered here that night. We've got five times as many here tonight! You can feel the energy in the air ...*"

* * *

Silas brushed his teeth, rinsed, and spat.

On his way out of the bathroom, he noticed the door to Daddy's bedroom hanging slightly ajar. Head tilting, he paused. The grown-ups were occupied downstairs.

Just a quick look around. Then he would slip back down lickety-split, before they noticed anything amiss.

He leaned against the door. The lock's tongue clicked the rest of the way from its hasp, and the door yawned open. Inside the bedroom, Silas paused again, savoring the thrill of illicit trespass. He rationed out a breath, nodded without realizing it, and moved again.

On the bookshelf, he found grown-up books: no pictures, lots of words, scary covers. He looked inside the dresser. Half-filled drawers, rumpled folded clothes. Inside the desk, he found a screwdriver, paper clips, loose batteries, a broken wristwatch. He tried on the watch, pretended to be Daddy. *Go brush your teeth, Silas. Hurry up, Silas, we're late.*

He slipped off the watch. His eyes moved to the closet door. Tightly shut, of course. Because the most important Grown-Up Things would be hidden in there. The most secret, mysterious things; the things kids were not supposed to find.

He eased the closet door open. Inside, he saw Daddy's clothes: shirts and pants, jackets and belts and ties. Shoes on the floor. A few unused hangers on the rack. Behind them deep, viscid blackness. On a high shelf, folded blankets. He frowned.

He took the chair from the desk and carefully, quietly, tongue protruding from the corner of his mouth, dragged it across the floor. Climbing up, he stood on tiptoes. The chair wobbled, but he could just reach the blankets. His fingertips quested. Everyone knew that high shelves were the place to keep the most secret, important things. That was where Daddy kept the leftover Halloween candy, after all: on a high shelf in the kitchen.

Fully extended on tiptoes now, trembling. Chair jiggling beneath him. But his fingers had touched something hard. A handle. He came very close to stumbling backward, falling off the chair, crashing to the floor. But he managed to check his balance and climbed cautiously down, holding the black case.

He cast a furtive glance toward the door, then set the case down on the fancy-patterned carpet. TV voices lilting from downstairs like distant music. He bent forward. The case had a latch, like on a door. And numbers a combination lock, like the kind he used on his bike when they rode to the library. Except that this lock was rusted and dirty and looked broken. He tried the latch. A number on the lock rolled, clicked.

The case opened. Outside, a thin winter whistle of wind rose, rattling windows, and then fell away.

* * *

Silas appeared, coming from the direction of the stairs.

He held something that Jana's conscious mind at first refused to identify. It could be a green toothbrush with a red tip. Or maybe a magic wand, the kind you found in those 1,001 magic-trick kits little kids sometimes had. Disappearing balls, weighted coins, fake dice. But it was neither of these things. On some level, she knew it, and was already standing, extending toward the boy a placating hand …

Michael saw it, too. His flute of champagne hit the rug with a soft, fizzing plop.

"Pow!" Silas brandished the ampoule like a toy gun. The cat, detecting that the frequency in the room had suddenly spiked, came out from beneath the couch and dashed for the kitchen. Silas followed her with the red tip of the glass tube. "Pow! Gotcha!"

"Silas." Pleasantly surprised by the steady authority in her own voice. Imperative but not threatening. "Careful with that. It's fragile."

"Silas," said Michael more sharply.

The boy paused, sensing from the tone some unforeseen power.

"Give it to me." Michael stepped forward, past Jana, extending one hand. "No games."

A fraught, loaded moment. Jana noticed the boy's red eyes and drooping lids. Well past his bedtime. Michael took another step forward. "*Silas*."

The boy stared trancelike at his father, tangled in the possibility of the moment. *Do it*, Jana told herself. *Don't think about it, just do it.* Like grabbing a snake. She glided forward, dropping to one knee, one hand reaching for the boy's shoulder, soothingly, as the other went for the ampoule.

"*That gets a slow clap*," said a woman on TV. "*Here's another tweet I got last night ...*"

Silas was dropping the ampoule. But Jana's hand was beneath it, plucking it out of the air easily, confidently. Her other hand landed on his shoulder, and she pulled him close, murmuring faint reassurances, handing the ampoule behind herself without looking. She felt Michael whisk it away, and she held the boy close. Not faking compassion, she realized, as she was with Michael. Life was strange. "Okay," she murmured. "'S okay, okay, okay, okay. Okay, okay, okay."

"*What color are your New Year's Eve underwear?*" the woman on TV asked brightly.

Silas had drawn in a breath, caught in the moment before tears.

Still stroking his back, Jana threw a look over her shoulder. Michael held the ampoule. He looked pale. Something had been dredged up inside him. His mouth hung open. It occurred to her that he might be every bit as dangerous, holding the ampoule, as his young son. She disengaged, felt the boy's entire body tensing just as she let it go. Gently she took the ampoule from Michael, and kept moving, gliding toward the stairs now, as Silas finished winding up and let his tears loose.

Upstairs. In the master bedroom, the black case sat open on the floor, the chair he had used beside it. She knelt, holding her breath. Apparently, the months buried underground had ruined the lock. She checked the ampoules. No broken glass. Checked again. And again. Now her own hysteria was bubbling up. What kind of a fucking joke was this operation, when a five-year-old kid could get his hands on …

Her eyelid was twitching again, worse than ever, pulling her face into a fun-house mask. She remembered suddenly a woman from her childhood: the crazy old cat lady of the neighborhood. All the kids had laughed at her. Always wearing soiled black, dirt on her face, dirt beneath her fingernails. Dead flowers on her balcony. No husband, no children, just the cats—a dozen at least. Nerves dead at one corner of her mouth, lips slack, face prone to erratic jerking and twitching. She had probably been about the age Jana was now.

Silas was still howling from downstairs, louder than the wind outside.

She counted down from five. And again. Her breathing turned to long, slow strokes. But the eyelid kept twitching.

At last, she stood again, joints creaking. The gristle of her knees popped hollowly. Tendons and skin, liver and spleen.

She had thought the case would be safe on the high shelf. But nothing was safe. She saw that now.

Twelve days.

She turned to the dresser. Michael's soon-to-be ex-wife's dresser. A few rejected perfume bottles still sitting on top. Drawers still half-filled with clothes. Jana had helped herself to the remnants of the woman's wardrobe. It gave her a feeling of secret power, a feeling that she was getting away with something.

She opened the top drawer, cleared space for the case, and tucked it back into the corner, covering it with a yellowing bra. She shut the drawer.

It was the best she could do for now. Tomorrow, if anything was open, she would have Michael buy a new case.

Twelve days.

Downstairs, the cries were abating. Disaster averted.

But her eye was still twitching, making her feel like the strange old lady, the laughingstock of the neighborhood.

BLUEMONT, VA

A K-9 van arrived at first light.

The men who climbed out moved gingerly and spoke quietly. The dogs sniffle-snuffled for a few seconds and then lunged toward the toolshed.

Someone handed Dalia a thermos of coffee and a foil-wrapped sandwich. Egg and cheese on a soggy, greasy roll. She took a bite, closed the foil, and left the sandwich on a nearby fender. Then she turned 360 degrees, drinking in the view. With dawn breaking, she could appreciate for the first time the beauty of the valley: snow-spotted glades, primeval forest rising in cathedral spires.

Horowitz stepped out onto the porch. Tired, shoulders sloping, safety goggles propped high on his forehead. Skinning off gloves, he came down and joined her. "Methylphosphonic acid in the basement."

And cyclotrimethylenetrinitramine in the shed. She nodded without surprise. They had also found a grand jumble of fingerprints throughout the house, left by the Korns and various tenants—but none belonging to Jana or, Dalia suspected, the mystery man. Bleach worked wonders on hard, nonporous surfaces carrying latents. It worked less well on aerated sarin and turpentine that penetrated invisible nooks and crannies on walls and ceilings.

A man standing near the edge of the search grid whistled. They went over, dodging the jury-rigged windbreaks and the scaffolding of big lights recently switched off, still warm. The man was young. He wore a nice shirt beneath his coat. He smelled of cologne. He had been planning, Dalia thought, to ring in the New Year in style. Instead, he was crouching here, pointing at a muddy spot below police tape that snapped despite the windbreak. "Tire track. Good one. Not the Silverado."

They bent to inspect a serrate tread with shallow ridges and grooves. To Dalia, it didn't look like a good track. It didn't look like much of anything. But the man was photographing it with an unmistakable air of satisfaction.

Inside the house, members of the forensics team were helping themselves to Hattie Korn's coffee. Many had been on the team that went over the house the first time, during the sheriff's investigation, and declared it clean. Their mistake had wasted valuable days. Dalia held on to the resentment for a moment. Then she let it go, took a place in line by the urn, and drew a mug of coffee both better and hotter than what was in the thermos.

Horowitz came banging through the front door again, looking energized. He drew a mug and joined her at the table. "Good news or bad?" he asked.

"Good."

"The tread belongs to a Kumho Solus KR-21. Original equipment on Hyundai Elantras and Sonatas since 2011. There's Ralph Korn's 'little blue Japanese thing.'"

She considered. "Bad?"

"Ten thousand, four hundred Elantras and Sonatas registered in the Washington metropolitan area alone. We can cut it down. Start with blue Hyundais registered in DC to military veterans with brown hair. Run plates; look for outstandings. But cars can get repainted, and registered to anyone with forty bucks and a signature. In the end, we'll have to go door-to-door … five-thousand-plus times."

Dalia closed her eyes. She felt a strange unmoored sensation, as if the earth had fallen out from beneath her chair and she were spinning dizzily through space, falling, falling.

ELLICOTT STREET NW, WASHINGTON, DC

"Here, kitty kitty. Here, Licky Licky. Here, girl." Michael made a puckering noise with his lips. "Kitty?"

The cat favored Michael with a flat, skeptical gaze, ears cocked forward. Leaning against the counter, the woman watched blankly.

"Come on, Licorice. Kitty kitty. Nice kitty." The kissy noise again.

Suddenly, Licorice came padding across the kitchen. She paused a few inches from his outstretched index finger, sensing something not quite right. Sat back on her haunches, tail switching, and gave him a look of great sagacity.

He moved his left leg closer to the cat. Near enough now that she could reach out and bat it with one playful paw, were she so inclined. He wagged the finger in her face. She leaned forward, sniffed, then bunted his fingertip aggressively with her forehead. Chancing a tentative lick, she laid back her ears and scrummed her face along the nail, leaving her scent. She gave no indication at all of sensing the Purina Whisker Lickin's tuna cat treats—her favorite—hidden inside the prosthetic leg mere inches from her face.

He looked at the woman. She nodded.

But now the acid test: the dogs.

He took off the leg: nine clicks. Then he shook the cat treats from the plastic casing onto the linoleum. Licorice pounced and gobbled them up. Michael felt something black and dangerous rising inside him. *Eleven days.* Would the woman really care for his cat as promised? He tried to picture it. The voice inside him started to offer an opinion. He shut it down, wet a paper towel, and cleaned inside the shaped cavities before refilling them with

Purina Moist and Meaty Burger with cheddar cheese flavor. *MMMMMMMMMMMM!* read the packaging. BEEFY, MOIST, MEATY, TENDER, YUMMY! QUICK, NO MESS.

Licorice, no snob, stood watching, tail switching again. He tossed her a dog treat. She sniffed, licked, then picked it up and carried it away like a dead mouse, to her treasure corner.

Michael closed the hidden compartments. He worked the vacuum seals, then washed his hands under near-boiling water. He filled a saucer with dishwashing detergent and hot water, dipped in another paper towel, and fastidiously cleaned the carbon fiber shell. Wiped it dry and cleaned it again. He wiped it dry once more, clicked it back into the liner's pin, and tugged down the cuff of his jeans.

New Year's Day. The dog run was crowded despite the cold: people desperate to get away from families they had been shut indoors with for a too-long vacation. Big dogs, small dogs, happy dogs, sad dogs, regal dogs, silly dogs, old dogs, puppies, and their owners. Michael had never been a dog person. Too slobbery, too eager to please. With cats, you had to earn it. Dogs had no standards. They loved indiscriminately. Which made their love worth very little indeed.

The woman had stayed home—they had agreed it was not worth the risk of showing her face outside. Michael stood alone by the edge of the run, leaning against the fence, the false leg with treats sealed inside pressing against wrought-iron bars. Plenty of space between those bars for the scent to waft invitingly into the run. *Here, doggy doggy doggy.*

The dogs ignored him.

It was the last hurdle, cleared and already receding into the past.

Eleven days, and he would be gone. He would be gone in eleven days. Say it enough and it might mean something. Eleven days, eleven days, eleven days. Gone, gone, gone. As a child, he had thought about death. He had lain awake at night thinking about it. Gone, gone, gone. Forever, forever, forever. No more Michael

Fletcher. *Forever.* Just words. They meant nothing. But with enough repetition, he had sometimes been able to get a flicker of meaning, a glimpse, a chill: *forever.* No more him. *Forever.* He had glimpsed just enough to scare the living shit out of him. *Forever. Gone forever. Forever, forever, forever.*

Like Seth, said the voice.

Like Seth.

Back home, he changed into sweats, bundled up, and went for a run. He ran until his heart pounded behind his eyes and his knee flared in pain with every footfall. He ran until his brain throbbed and his lungs twisted into a knot and he burned, shivered, trembled. Then he glanced over his shoulder and there was a rushing dark riptide, *forever, forever, forever*, threatening to grab him, entangle him, suck him under, drag him down. And he dug in, facing forward, narrowing his eyes, and ran harder.

CHAPTER FOURTEEN

ELLICOTT STREET NW, WASHINGTON, DC

"Dispatch, this is five-oh-five. I'm ten-twenty-three at one-thirty-two Ellicott Street Northwest."

"*Ten-four, five-oh-five.*"

They stepped out of the prowler into a cold, windless sixth day of January. Clouds hung motionless in the pale afternoon sky. Officer Jimmy McAlester caught the eye of his new partner and gave a small paternal nod. Beth returned it—good kid—and followed him up the walk, one pace behind.

Weapons holstered, faces parked in neutral, they stepped up onto the porch. The curtained windows revealed nothing. A pamphlet pushing life insurance stuck out of the mailbox. Jimmy reached forward and bent back the corner to check the addressee. Then he nodded at Beth again. *Play it cool*, his expression said. A knock and talk without a warrant was friendly and entirely legal. But anything the slightest bit overbearing, anything that could conceivably be deemed coercive, raised the specter of the Fourth Amendment, moving the encounter legally closer to a search and seizure and making the collective eyes of the ACLU pop with glee.

Beth rang the doorbell. They waited.

Footsteps. Creaking floorboards. When the door opened, Jimmy blinked. Then he grinned. "Well, I'll be dipped in shit. I saw the name, but I didn't ..."

He hugged the man in the doorway. Patrol Officer Beth Walsh watched with bemusement, her head tilting inquisitively beneath its peaked blue cap. Behind the man was strewn evidence of a child or children: Laser Pegs, Legos, a Tonka backhoe.

Jimmy laughed, leaving one hand fondly on the man's shoulder. "Should have put it together. I'll be goddamned." He turned to Beth. "Beth Walsh, Michael Fletcher. We fought Ali Baba together."

She smiled. "Thank you for your service."

"This guy. He could clear a Humvee like you've never seen. Talk about your WMDs."

"*This* guy," Michael Fletcher said, "he jerked off so much everybody *else*'s sheets turned stiff."

"Talk about stiff. This guy didn't *ever* change his underwear. End of the tour, they were walking around by themselves."

They grinned foolishly at each other. "Good to see you, soldier," Jimmy said finally.

"What you been up to, Jimmy?" A cat tried to dash outside, and Michael bent and scooped it up absently.

"DCFD replaced me, believe it or not, while I was out defending truth, justice, and the American Way. Waiting list to get back in. So ..." He flicked his forefinger against his badge. "Sergeant Jimmy McAlester, at your service."

"Ah, but that's a bonny lad," said Michael. "Stick with it, champ; you'll make your mama proud."

"This guy." Jimmy jerked a thumb. "Loves to bust balls. How about you, Mikey? Still sitting on the sidelines, watching other people's lives through a viewfinder?"

"You know it. But a better class of people. Up on the Hill."

"Good for you. How's Stace?"

Michael shook his head. "Heather?"

"Naw. I got a new one. Twenty-two years old. Tight as a drum.

How's the kid?"

"Good. Yours?"

"Pain in the ass. Listen, we oughta grab a beer."

"Definitely."

"I'll give you a call. I got your address." He gestured at the mailbox. "Speaking of which, guess you've got a car—came across the ticker."

"A 2013 Hyundai Elantra," said Beth. "Aqua."

Michael nodded toward the closed garage. "Gonna dust for coke?"

"Waste of time. I know a guilty man when I see him." Jimmy chucked Michael's shoulder. "Duty calls, buddy. I'll be in touch. Take her easy."

"Pinch the tip, Jimmy."

Back in the cruiser, Beth twisted her hat more firmly onto her head. "Gotta say …"

Jimmy McAlester looked at her. "What?"

"Nothing. Just, on paper, he hits all the marks. Brown hair, athletic build, vet, split from his wife, has a little kid—that's five for five."

Until this moment, during their four-month partnership, Beth had pleasantly surprised him by not saying anything stupid. But here was a doozy.

Only a kid, he reminded himself. And a good one at that. Just trying to do her job. "You couldn't tell, I guess, but that man gave a leg for this country."

She blinked. "I didn't mean to—"

"No, I guess you didn't. But show me a vet who *doesn't* split with his wife after he comes back. It just happens. Women, too. It's something that just happens."

"Sorry. I didn't mean anything."

"He's a goddamn war hero." Jimmy heard his own voice hot, shaking a little, and told himself to dial it back. "You gotta learn, girlie, that good police work's not about what's on paper. It's about reading between the lines. You got to develop a sense for people."

She nodded mutely.

"Salt of the earth, that motherfucking guy." He unclipped the radio from below the dash and clicked the button. "Dispatch, this is five-oh-five. We're ten-twenty-six. Moving on to Macomb."

"*Ten-four, five-oh-five.*"

* * *

From the high window, Jana watched the prowler pull away from the curb.

She heard Michael climbing the stairs: *clump, creak, clump, creak* ... He appeared in the doorway. Face crumbling. She nodded. He came to her. She embraced him, patting his broad shoulders, stroking them. "*Shh,*" she purred. "It's okay. They're gone."

* * *

By the eighth of January, four days before the State of the Union, a task force made up of MPD, FBI, INS, Secret Service, and the Washington Regional Threat and Analysis Center had investigated every Hyundai registered to a military veteran in the Washington, DC, metropolitan area.

So the net was cast again, wider.

State police, federal marshals, and ATF joined the effort. A new list was drawn up, including not just Hyundais manufactured since 2011 but also Kias, which could take Kumho Solus KR-21 tires in a pinch. ARGUS and StingRay and IMSI Catcher and packet interceptors and parabolic microphones and infrared cameras provided initial intelligence—Head of Operations Barry Innes being not nearly as concerned as Sergeant Jimmy McAlester about legally covering his ass—but ultimately, the owner of every car fitting the profile got a rap on their door, and a knock and talk, often followed by a request to be invited in for a look around. Most people were agreeable. Most people wanted to be good citizens and were eager to help out. Some refused and were looked at more closely. Several ran, were apprehended, and proved to have warrants out or drugs on the premises.

On Ellicott Street NW, Michael Fletcher, having slipped through the eye of the needle, sat down to Friday night dinner with his son and the woman who called herself Kristen.

Michael felt at peace now.

He coiled linguine on his fork, then kept coiling longer than necessary. He had accepted something. The struggle was done. Now came acquiescence.

The five stages of grief, the voice volunteered, impervious, it seemed, to his surface serenity. *Denial, anger, bargaining, depression, and blowing the holy fuck out of your fearless leader with a leg full of asphyxiating nerve agent! Beefy, Moist, Meaty, Tender, Yummy!*

Prattle on, voice. You can't get to me now.

Silas was telling a story. A scientist worked in a laboratory. Inside a test tube, a pink liquid bubbled. Turning around too quickly, the scientist knocked over the tube, which shattered. But instead of spilling across the floor, the bubbling pink liquid began acting out scenes from the scientist's past. All the mice in their cages lined up to watch the show …

"Did you make this up?" The woman sounded impressed. "It's really good."

In fact, Michael could picture it vividly: the mice lining up on their hind legs inside their little cages, tiny front paws clutching tiny jail bars. Pink liquid twisting, frothing, forming images like the tattoos on Bradbury's famous illustrated man. Here were two cops coming up a front walk. The dreaded knock on the door. "*Guess you've got a car—came across the ticker … A 2013 Hyundai Elantra. Aqua.*" How had they gotten onto the car? How had they gotten onto the goddamned car?

Calm. Accepting. Serenity now.

The linguine coiled like a tiny boa constrictor around his fork. The pink liquid bubbled, fizzed. Here a woman dropped a cop with a well-placed right hook. A man stepped forward, plucked a gun almost politely from the cop's fumbling fingers, and fired two bullets at point-blank range. Then one more for good measure. Here a rabbit drooled, teeth gnashing. Screaming, kicking, convulsing, vomiting and shitting blood. SLUDGE, they called it. Salivation, Lacrimation, Urination, Defecation, Gastrointestinal distress, and Emesis. Michael had read an article on Wikipedia. He found the acronym annoyingly twee: an incongruous ray of sunshine in a dark, damp place fuzzed with moss and crawling with dung beetles.

Here a man ate pizza with his guileless, innocent young son. "*Mommy's sleepover friend*," said the kid, with utter lack of malice. "*Can I go play?*" Here a young woman sat at the back of a bus. Cool gray eyes flecked with harlequin sparkles. Skillfully grafted burn scars running down her right cheek, continuing down onto the right side of her lissome body.

Another woman sat on a couch, stirring something in a Grumpy Cat mug, speaking with great care. "*I guess on some level this feels ... overdue.*" A man walked into an embassy and was escorted to a sterile Lucite cube of a room. The same man sat outside a Humvee in Hawija, concentrating hard on dials and joysticks as a motorcycle drove past and dropped something in the road. The same man rode past a ruined bridgehead in Kirkuk and saw a hand lying in a bed of smoldering rubble. Just the hand. A child's hand. And something slipped loose inside him: a cog breaking inside a watch, tumbling around free, gumming up the works.

So many stories in the bubbling pink liquid. Shifting, puddling, re-forming. In the back of a bus, a boy pressed something into another boy's hand. "*It's a bat.*" Ariella Abramovitz moaned as Ben Schoenberg worked his way beneath her damp Hanes cotton panties. In a bed built to look like a race car, a boy lay awake, crying. His older brother peeked into the room. "*What's wrong?*" They stayed up half the night learning about how the Lord, Blessed be He, King of the Universe, had delivered upon well-deserving Egyptian scum ten plagues, culminating with the slaying of the firstborn sons.

So many stories. Yet all the same story, really. The story of Michael. All leading inexorably to the here, the now. To peace, acceptance. And to determination. Most of all, to determination.

"Daddy. Daddy."

Silas had stopped telling his story, how long ago Michael had no idea. "Huh?"

"I said, 'Can I watch TV now?'"

He blinked. The woman was looking at him ungenerously.

Calm. Peace. Determination.

"Sure," he said easily. "Go watch TV."

* * *

Three days.

Earth kept rolling eastward, into the sun. Bright morning light. Rise and shine.

Showering. Dripping onto the bath mat. Patting lather onto cheeks. Taking safety razor from medicine cabinet. Downstairs, in the living room, Silas watched cacophonous Saturday morning cartoons with Kristen.

Michael shaved, did a hundred push-ups, dressed. Fixed the flag pin to his lapel, squared his shoulders.

Knowing that street traffic would be murder, he took the Metro. He emerged from the station to find Pennsylvania Avenue closed off: Capitol security running a drill. At the sight, horror flooded his veins. They knew. They knew everything. They had found the Hyundai. *How had they gotten onto the goddamned car?* They had come knocking on the door, and now they were giving him just enough rope, biding their time. And yes, *rope* was the right word—he would hang for this. That or a firing squad, or the electric chair, or a needle. Did it really matter which fucking—

God damn it, Michael, you know you're far gone when I'M THE MOTHERFUCKING VOICE OF REASON. Think about it. If they knew anything, you wouldn't be here!

The voice had a point. He drew a shaky breath, let it out. The next breath was more even. His eyes felt haunted, bulging. His face felt the color of chalk—and the same dusty, granular consistency. But he squared his shoulders again and walked forward like a goddamn man.

He moved through the first barricade just by showing ID. At the second, he was searched. Around him, a hive of activity buzzed. Cops and cops and more cops. After Paris, they were taking no chances. In sixty hours, the president of the United States would leave the White House, climb into the reinforced limousine nicknamed the Beast, and roll up Pennsylvania Avenue. The limo had been built on the frame of a Cadillac Kodiak, but about the only other thing it had in common with a regular Caddy was the crested wreath on the front grill. Eight-inch-thick armor-plated doors supported five-inch-thick bulletproof windows. The Kevlar-reinforced run-flat tires, big enough for a Greyhound bus, could shake off any puncturing agent. Sealed interior, foam-protected Duramax diesel fuel tank. And inside the trunk, fire-fighting equipment, oxygen tanks, a blood bank, tear gas, shotguns, even grenade launchers.

Overhead, a helicopter thrashed. On every side, sirens spun without sound, casting macabre multicolored light across the reflecting pool. Michael straightened his jacket and walked on.

At the next checkpoint, he saw an EMT station and, beside it, a circle of sandbags. In Iraq, you expected to see sandbags, HESCO bastions stacked two-high around the compound latrines. Not here. This was new. A grenade sump, he realized. If a live explosive was found and confiscated, they had to have somewhere to put it.

And everywhere, cops. Cops and cops and more cops, plain-clothes and blue suits, from every agency. This was not just Paris. It was more. They knew something was up. They were looking out.

But they don't know *know. Or I wouldn't be here.*

He was finding the sense of peace again: a fine bespoke suit, tailored specifically for his broad shoulders, into which he could slip comfortably. His bases were covered. The more they tried to prepare, the greater would be the impact when it happened.

Inside Statuary Hall, Christina Thompson gave orders. Their first dress rehearsal, she reminded everyone, but not their last. Pretend we're live. If something goes wrong, plow through it. She was nervous. The quaver in her voice reminded Michael of his own shaky breath. But he didn't think anyone else could detect it.

They ran through it six times, top to bottom. By the time they quit, it was almost dark and Michael was having trouble with the prosthesis. The modular given him by DC VA, although far from the electrographic ideal, had been custom fitted by Phil Eggleston. This one was theoretically a perfect copy, at least on the outside. But the fixture against his stump left tiny air pockets that, with continued use, led to chafing, soreness. After his last run, he had discovered a yellow-purple bruise. Now there was outright pain.

But tomorrow they would go all day again, because Monday and Tuesday they would have to work around Senate sessions. The final dry run would take place Tuesday afternoon, hours before the event. Every rite and ritual, every cue and placement, timing accurate down to the second. Everything just as it would be when the event was staged before television cameras and broadcast to a waiting world.

On the way home, he made two stops. At a beauty supply store, he paid cash for a straight black wig, spirit gum, and rouge. At a PetSmart, he bought a travel cage for Licorice, whom the woman had promised to take with her.

Back home, the vibes were mellow. The woman and Silas were watching TV again: the episode of *TMNT* where the turtles nurse back to health a mutant alligator rescued from the Kraang. Michael wondered whether they had moved from the couch all day. The boy curled against her, heartbreakingly trusting, the cat purring by his feet.

For dinner they ate leftovers. For TV time, they watched a few minutes of *Word World*—in Michael's mind an educational antidote to the Mutant Ninja Turtle overload. Once he was gone, who would steer Silas away from Cartoon Network, toward PBS? Stacy couldn't resist spoiling the boy. And despite this woman's promises, deep down he didn't believe a word. But he had made his choices. Now he had to live with them.

Or die with them. Right, Mikey? Wink-wink, nudge-nudge?

After fifteen minutes, he snapped off the set. Silas asked "Kristen" to put him to bed, but Michael insisted on doing it himself. "You know," he added, "I only get so many chances."

She shot him a warning look.

"Because you grow up so fast," he quickly added. But Silas wasn't paying attention anyway. The boy was sucking on a plastic squeeze tube of applesauce, trying to get out the last dregs, wearing a determined expression that reminded Michael of no one so much as himself.

They brushed their teeth together, side by side. After five seconds, Silas tried to rinse his brush. "Nuh-uh," Michael said, frothing like a rabid dog. "Top, bottom, front, back, inside, outside." Then he thought of the knock and talk, of Jimmy McAlester. "*This guy. Loves to bust balls.*"

They were continuing their Roald Dahl kick. Tonight was *Danny the Champion of the World.* "I will not pretend I wasn't petrified," Michael read. A strange silence from downstairs. He wondered whether she was eavesdropping. "I was. But mixed in with the awful fear was a glorious feeling of excitement. Most of the really exciting things we do in our lives scare us to death."

"What does that mean? 'Scare us to death'?"

"It means it's super scary. It doesn't mean you actually die."

"But *could* you?"

"Could you actually die?"

"Yeah, *could* you? From being scared?"

"I guess maybe you could have a heart attack. If something was really terrifying."

"What's a heart attack?"

"You know. The heart moves the blood around your body."

"It's a muscle." Silas touched his chest. "Right here."

"Right. So if your heart stops beating, you die."

The conversation had taken an unintended turn. Ruffling his brow, Michael lifted the book again. "They wouldn't be exciting if—"

"Why do you die if your heart stops beating?"

"Because you need your blood to carry oxygen all around your body."

"What happens when you die?"

For a few moments, the silence was pristine. No whisper of wind, no sound from the woman, wherever she was. The entire world waited on tiptoe for his answer.

"Nobody knows," he said gently.

"Julia said you go to heaven and be with God."

"Julia from school?"

"Yes."

"Maybe. Some people think that."

"Do you?"

"I don't … I'm not sure what I think."

Tell him about the seventy-two virgins, Mikey. Crowned with glory, spared the suffering of the grave. Guaranteed a place in paradise, sins forgiven, spared the horror of the Day of Judgment.

"I think," he said carefully, "that there's something called the circle of life. It means that everything that is born eventually dies. And then the things that die turn into vitamins to help other things be born. And it's beautiful, in a way, although it's also sad."

Silas was listening very closely. Wheels grinding inside that five-year-old skull.

"And nobody really knows what happens after you die. So people make guesses. And they come up with beliefs—that's things they choose to believe. But nobody knows for sure. So the important thing is to live well while we're here. To do things we're proud of. Even if …" A sudden clot in his throat. He squeezed his eyes and lips together. Willed the clot away, willed his voice steady and clear, and opened his eyes, praying the boy hadn't noticed. "Even if … just remember, Silas … after I'm gone … that sometimes things don't … sometimes things might seem one way but …"

She was in the doorway. From nowhere, silent as smoke. "Yay, Kristen's here! Kristen, read to me!"

She came forward. All gentle smiles. Nothing recriminating, although in her sidelong glance, Michael did pick up something that might be thought of as pitying.

She took the book from his hand. "Run along, Daddy. I've got it from here."

"Just remember, buddy," Michael said weakly, "I love you."

He just made it out of the room before the tears came. Licorice nudged his ankle, and he picked her up and buried his face in her fur. Inside Silas' bedroom, the woman picked up with a loathsomely steady voice: "I sat very stiff and upright in my seat, gripping the steering wheel tight with both hands. My eyes were about level with the top of the steering wheel. I could have done with a cushion to raise me up higher, but it was too late for that. The road seemed awfully narrow in the dark …"

MARTIN LUTHER KING JR. AVE. SE, WASHINGTON, DC

Sunday, January 10, 8:00 a.m. The conference room was empty.

No sign of Innes, Horowitz, McConnell. No courier, no zippered and locked portfolio, no leads, no assignments, no new ray of hope. The twelve monitors on the wall were dark. On Sunday, it seemed, even God rested in this Christian country.

Dalia fell heavily into a chair, sipped her latte, and stared at the blank, empty monitors.

They had nothing.

She sipped again, then pushed it away. All of a sudden, it seemed too sweet.

Start at the beginning, she thought. When in doubt, start back at the beginning.

In the beginning, a young girl named Jana Dahan had been the target of a checkpoint bombing in …

But no. The *real* beginning.

In 1947, the UN partition … No.

In the beginning, God created the heavens. Fourteen billion years ago, give or take. And eventually, the expanding universe cooled enough to allow the creation of subatomic particles. And He saw this and it was good.

And subatomic particles formed elements, and elements became stars and galaxies, and then, eventually, there was Earth. And then there was life on Earth. Single-celled life. Then multi-celled life. Then the first fish to drag itself onto land, gulping air through mutated gills. Then, seventy thousand years ago, *Homo sapiens* with its freakishly large brain. The cognitive revolution. The Agricultural Revolution, in which wheat domesticated man, training him to labor from sunrise to sunset, back bent, oversize brain baking under a sweltering sun, lugging water to spread the precious caryopsis to every corner of the globe. And then "civilization" and, with it, tribes. And with tribes, war.

And Jews. And not-Jews. And Moses, or at least stories of Moses. And Nebuchadnezzar and pogroms and the Dreyfus affair and Theodor Herzl and *Der Judenstaat*. And Zola and Esterhazy and the Turkish sultan and the German kaiser and the First Zionist Congress and *Altneuland* and then, finally, Zyklon-B. Zyklon-B, Zyklon-B, Zyklon-B. And *then* the UN partition resolution of 1947. And then modern Israel. *Never again.*

And then Sabras, the first generation born in modern Israel. And among them, Dalia Artzi. Once, there had been a young girl who thought she knew everything. Peace, peace, peace. *Never again*, yes, but also *peace*, and *two wrongs don't make a right*, and then she'd had children and that had made everything more complicated. She had taken conscientious objector military deferment, *sarvanim*. But her children had refused. Her children had wanted to do their part. By then Dalia had steeped herself in the history of tribal warfare, the better to defuse critics who might accuse her of naïveté as she fought for peace. But had it actually stopped anyone? "*Clearly you're nobody's fool,*" McConnell had said during their first meeting. "*A political naïf, perhaps—forgive me—but a tactical genius.*" She had tried to explain to her children that war led nowhere, that the vast majority of all battles were strategically inconclusive. Let others die for meaningless lines on meaningless maps. Not her, and not her children. But there was another truth that swept away her truth. *Never again.* And to their (admittedly callow) eyes, this was the bigger truth.

And then her son had been inside a tank. Shelling land that the world had decreed illegally occupied by Israel. And the "enemy" had taken him. And he was gone. And Dalia had spoken her mind to the microphones shoved in her face, and doomed him to remain gone. Until, that is, Meir and Feigenbaum—now sharing with their murderer an ignominious grave at the bottom of a New Jersey well—had given her a chance. In accepting their offer, Dalia had been selfish. But she had done it anyway. For Zvi.

And *then* had come Jana Dahan. Wounded by a checkpoint bombing. Undercover in America. A cellar in Oregon filled with explosive and nerve toxin. A mad plot and an effort to stop it. A traitor in the plotters' midst. And the hunt had begun. Dalia, McConnell, Horowitz. The veteran, the "woman in charge." Nissim Dayan. The red Ford, the rust-colored Grand Marquis, the blue Hyundai. Vermont, the dead deputy, the pink mist in the toolshed. The tire tread, the widening net. And always Jana Dahan, slipping through their fingers. Again and again and again.

And they had nothing.

She picked up her latte. It had gone cold.

There was a reason Dalia was alone here this morning. A reason she alone still pursued this fool's errand. She was stubborn. Like Jana Dahan. They were two sides of the same coin. They were the same.

Jana had not given up.

Dalia was not giving up, either.

She went to ransack the office Rolodexes for Nebraska Avenue's number. Sunday or not, she would request the day's leads.

PART FIVE

CHAPTER FIFTEEN

CAPITOL HILL, WASHINGTON, DC

The flag in front of the dome snapped hard in a cold winter wind.

But inside Statuary Hall, the temperature was climbing—well into the nineties, Michael Fletcher thought, but maybe that was only his imagination. He was sweating freely, and he was not the only one. One hundred thirty-three people stood jammed between the bronze and marble statues, gazing into lenses, jockeying with microphones and makeup and cameras, blathering, trumpeting, trying fiercely to seem important, knowledgeable, and authoritative, their voices bouncing stridently off the domed cast-steel ceiling, all beneath hot lights that blazed like bone-bleaching desert sunshine.

Michael's fight-or-flight reflex strained at the bit, champing, lurching, lunging. But no one could see that, he told himself. He was through the worst of it, he told himself. Through the security, the guards, the metal detectors, the dogs. Oh, the dogs. The dogs had been his biggest fear, Purina Moist and Meaty Burger with Cheddar Cheese Flavor notwithstanding. Some acid test—how fucking unscientific could you get, who the fuck do you think you're kidding, *acid test*, it had been a crazy chance he had taken, fucking Moist and Meaty Burgers, holy hot humping fuck me, but he had done it anyway and now here he was, he was through, he was past, the dogs were behind him, and soon now, soon, soon soon soon, soonsoonsoon …

Pouring sweat notwithstanding, he felt calm. Moist and Meaty Burgers notwithstanding, racing thoughts notwithstanding, let his mind race, crazy, mad, wild thoughts skittering like dog's claws on a polished hardwood floor, nobody could see his thoughts, nobody could tell what he was thinking, nobody knew, they could just see him sweating like everyone else, the lights, nobody could hear the voice, the voices, plural; nobody knew, he could think whatever he wanted, like *MMMMMMMMMMMM!* BEEFY, MOIST, MEATY, TENDER, YUMMY! QUICK, NO MESS, and nobody would be the wiser and soon, soon, soon, soon, very soon, very soon, very soonsoonsoonsoonsoon it would all be over.

The voice had no comment.

But other voices around him could not stop commenting:

"… inside this central legislative building more than two centuries old. Months of tireless preparation by press gallery staff, sergeants at arms, and Capitol Police come to a head here tonight as they stage what is beyond a doubt the most …"

"… hundreds upon hundreds of guests, dignitaries, and members of the press. Roads have been closed in preparation for the arrival of the contingent from the White House. Which should very soon, I'm being told, get started down Pennsylvania Avenue. Of course, we'll have live on-the-spot coverage …"

"… five hundred and thirty-five members of Congress on the House floor, along with the justices of the Supreme Court, and the Cabinet of the United States. The president will take a place on the rostrum, flanked by the Speaker of the House and the vice president, officially here tonight in his capacity as a legislative officer, president of the Senate …"

Matt Gutierrez, moving past on his way to work B-roll, tossed Michael a wink and a thumbs-up.

Michael smiled and gave back a double.

MARTIN LUTHER KING JR. AVE. SE, WASHINGTON, DC

On twelve monitors, ARGUS footage played: Capitol Hill during the preceding hour, with a live feed in the top left corner.

McConnell scowled at the wall of screens as if he had a chance of actually finding something significant in the seething mass of activity. At the far end of the conference table, Innes was drawing up a list of Hyundai owners he planned to follow up on in the morning. Across from him, another agent was making red check marks beside selected names on a printout. Horowitz huddled in a corner, taking a phone call from his family.

Dalia watched McConnell watching the screens. Here again he encountered the limits of his technology, his air superiority, his crushing advantage in manpower. In this cauldron of humanity, one woman did not register. And yet, one woman, in the right place at the right time, was all it would take. Anyone who had ever played chess knew the lesson. It didn't matter that your opponent kept all her other pieces, if one pawn sneaked through to capture the king. Capture the king, and the game was over.

In the live feed—speaking of the king—the presidential motorcade was leaving the White House. First came a phalanx of motorcycles with flashing lights and sidecars. Then limos with sirens. Then limos without sirens, glossy black and chitinous, like sluggish metal beetles. Then the Beast itself. Then more limos. A helicopter dipped briefly through the drone's sight line, and Dalia turned away.

In the corner, Horowitz said, "You've got to listen to your mother, honey … No, I don't … Yes. I know. But that doesn't … All right, I hear you. But sometimes we don't get exactly what we want in life. It's your bedtime and you've got to do what your mother tells you."

Dalia looked back to the live ARGUS feed: 8:09 p.m. In fifty-one minutes, if all went according to schedule, the president would step up onto the rostrum.

"She won't show," McConnell announced suddenly. Still

watching the screens, the sirens, the police, the helicopters, the cordons, the dogs, the motorcade.

Dalia didn't answer.

Horowitz was still murmuring on the phone. His tone, affectionate but disciplined, gave Dalia a sudden urge to talk to her grandkids. But her daughter had made it abundantly clear that a once-monthly conversation was quite sufficient, thank you very much. And, of course, Zvi was beyond Dalia's reach.

8:10. The presidential motorcade turned at a crawl onto Pennsylvania Avenue.

ELLICOTT STREET NW, WASHINGTON, DC

Jana wore the straight black wig from the beauty supply store.

She sat on the couch in the living room, holding the phone. She had used spirit gum to change the thrust of her brow, rouge to accentuate the slope of her jawline. She had photographed herself and laminated a new driver's license. Her next ticket would be bought in the name of Kari Anderson, from White Plains, New York. It would bring her to Montana, or maybe Wyoming. Big sky, wide open spaces. She wanted to see the horizon in every direction.

On TV, talking heads were nattering away, describing again and again the scene on Capitol Hill. Two thousand people had squeezed into the House Chamber "*anywhere they can fit them*," said a pretty woman with perfect golden hair, "*standing in back, along the walls* ..." The air buzzed with excited expectation. It reminded Jana of a New Year's Eve cocktail party. From time to time, she glimpsed Michael Fletcher, captured by an upstairs gallery shot, moving fluidly down the narrow central aisle. Kit balanced on his thick shoulder, somehow avoiding the tangle of people moving alongside him. Often, he was less than a meter away from the arriving dignitaries he filmed. Once, when a hiccup with a cable held up the procession momentarily, he was only centimeters from the chief justice of the United States. Jana felt the power in her hand, coursing up her arm, electric. Her thumb stroked the call button absently. The button held a deadly attraction. But patience. *Shvoye.* The main course would arrive soon enough.

The network cut regularly to footage coming directly from Michael's camera: the so-called pool feed, shared with dozens of credentialed outlets. Each network had its own team in the upper galleries, but downstairs, on the floor, all images originated from the pool feed. Michael Fletcher was the chosen one. Her finger trailed over the phone, lingering.

She felt calm. Her eyelid was still.

Her small suitcase waited by the front door, near the cat's travel cage, sitting there for Michael's benefit before he left the house. Glancing at it now, Jana made a moue of distaste. She would not be taking the cat.

8:17 p.m.

"The Senate gathers in the Senate Chamber," the perfectly assembled blonde was saying cheerily, "and convenes an official session with the gavel, which we should see any minute now. Sometimes, they'll take care of a little outstanding business, though more often not. Then they'll come in a procession to the House Chamber. Down the hallway, through the rotunda, through Statuary Hall …"

CAPITOL HILL, WASHINGTON, DC

Soon.

The chief justice was sitting on the aisle, one foot thoughtlessly sticking out. Michael almost tripped over it as he backed up before the diplomatic corps.

From the balcony came a ruffle: the First Family joining the vice president's spouse. For a few moments, all attention was focused up, beyond the rows of cameras mounted on balcony railings, beyond the lights, beyond the ranks of laptops balanced on journalists' laps. Michael took advantage of the distraction to push the chief justice's foot out of the aisle with his own. The man looked up, shocked at the effrontery of this peon with a camera. Michael smiled back down and winked. Then he headed back up the aisle to await the next arrival.

His smile was spreading: a fulsome grin, weird and suspicious. But he could not wipe it away. He could not stop grinning. And now his face was twitching, tugging. *Fuck's sake*, said the voice, *you might as well write it across your forehead: "I AM A SUICIDE BOMBER!" GET IT TOGETHER, YOU MAGGOT!*

He got it together.

An arctic wind seemed to blow through the chamber. Something wild on that wind. Something dead and rotting; and something resurrected, something returned; something ancient and hungry. No one else seemed to notice it. They chattered, awaiting the arrival of the guest of honor. Giddy as schoolgirls. They did not know about the ancient wind blowing through the chamber. They did not know about the wolf in their midst. They were sheep. They were pigs, Orwell's pigs. *Some animals are more equal than others.* They were sheep, pigs, fat cats, plummy in their tailored suits, passing legislation that doomed more Jews to more suffering and more death, throwing their piggy weight here and there as it suited them, now behind Arafat, the backstabbing cockteaser talking out of both sides of his mouth, and now behind BDS, Boycott Divest Sanction, just to get a few votes at election time, punish the victims, what the fuck kind of sense did that make, and fuck the right of Jews to defend themselves, sheep-pigs-cats raising silver spoons laden with caviar to their piggy mouths, talking more and more about a one-state solution, everybody knew what a one-state solution really meant: the end of the Jewish nation, the end of the dream, the end of Israel, the end of Jews, holding Jews to a crazy double standard, racist anti-Semitic pigs, piggy piggish pigs who deserved what they would soon get, who deserved the slaughterhouse, the blood running in rivers, let *their* blood spill for a change, see how long it took them to respond, to overrespond, to overreact in the tried and true American way, to send in soldiers and tanks and BFGs—big fucking guns—and drones and flying robot killing machines and bombers, angels of death, the Lord, Blessed be He, King of the Universe, with a strong hand and outstretched arm, and with great terribleness, and with signs and wonders, avenging themselves upon their enemies, delivering ten plagues, more than ten, Americans did everything oversized, it would be eleven, fifteen, fuck it, *twenty* plagues, big-box American plagues, not just locusts but more motherfucking locusts than the world had ever seen, the best locusts, the greatest top-of-the-line locusts, locusts turned up to eleven, culminating with the slaying of the firstborn sons, and not just the firstborn, with America, but first, last, and middle—*all* the sons dead, more tiny hands lying dismembered in more smoking ruins than the world had seen since Hitler …

He had wiped the smile from his face. Now his features felt dull, slack. Unresponsive. Someone was entering, moving down the aisle, shaking hands, and Michael was backing up before him, heavy kit balanced on his shoulders, flat faced, body moving of its own accord, practiced movements long since drilled into his limbic system.

Soon.

A cold sheath had enveloped him. But just beneath the surface was something hot, something burning, something like lust.

MARTIN LUTHER KING JR. AVE. SE, WASHINGTON, DC

8:23 p.m.

On the monitor, the Speaker of the House was calling a joint session to order. Closed captions scrolled across the bottom of the screen:

> The gentleman from Wisconsin, the gentlewoman from Arkansas …

A fine target, Dalia thought. Look at that target. Every dignitary in the nation, foolishly assembled at the same place, beneath the same roof. Ceremony, pomp. Hubris. Jews would know better. But America thought itself invincible.

A little *plastique*, a little sarin, and a great swath of death would be carved through that room. And the dogs of war would slip indeed. The wrath of America would be a frightful thing to behold. And Israel, even if she seemed in the short term to benefit, would in the long run lose. She would lose everything. For she would have sacrificed her ideals, her very reason for being. She would no longer be fighting *for* anything, but only against: dumb fighting reflex, like a mad dog.

The overkill security did not set Dalia at ease. American security was like American military policy, trying to smother every threat with manpower and equipment and technology, always and forever lacking the personal touch. Their TSA did not interview airline passengers, as did the Border Police for El Al. They only scanned mechanically, with metal detectors and X-rays, maybe sometimes with dogs. And so they missed things. Not just things—they missed everything that mattered.

She watched the coverage. All this technology, all this security overkill, and yet no focus on the *people.* It took only one, slipping through the gauntlet.

Horowitz was off the phone at last. He followed her eyes, seeming, as he often did, to read her thoughts.

On-screen, the closed captions, sprinkled with errors, scrolled on:

> … ritual of getting seats on the isle, where they can shake hands with the President on camera. People line up early, staking out spaces, or send staff or interns to hold seats. Then you'll see some cards chairs, some blocs held out—"Supreme Court"—and of course the aisle seed goes to chief Justice—and here, of course, we see the Joined Chiefs right up front …

> Another interesting status thing to look for is the official escort when the President moves down the aisle. It includes majority and minority leaders and wimps and some other strategic choices; a way of showing favor …

They cut to an overhead view, and Dalia could see the aisle down which the official escort would move. Cameraman backing up in front of arriving dignitaries. Close enough to reach out and touch them. Right smack-dab in the center of everything. What kind of security clearance had *this* man received? What kind of interviews had been conducted?

She recognized him. She had encountered him, briefly, when interviewing Christina Thompson. *Pool feed*, the woman had said. *House floor.* And Dalia had picked up something coming from the man—some almost subliminal scorn.

Yankee White, category two. That was his security clearance. But what did that mean, really? Just words.

She took a step nearer the monitor. The man looked fit. Had to be, to lug that camera for so long. Brown hair. Something shuffled in her mind. Thoughts trying to organize themselves into neat compartments. Brown hair, athletic build.

Horowitz came over, sensing something.

Again he read her mind. In the next instant, he had a phone to his ear. Murmuring, holding up one finger.

She watched the screen, suddenly nervous. Butterflies in her stomach.

The man in question moved as gracefully as a ballerina, threading his way backward in long, choreographed strides. But was something about him … off? Fixed, rusted into place, not swiveling loose? She frowned. Less than a feeling, less than an intuition. It was nothing at all, and as soon as she had felt it, it was gone.

Horowitz covered the mouthpiece of his phone with one hand. "Michael Fletcher. EOD vet. Five-year-old son." And suddenly it was back, so powerful that for an instant Dalia was transported out of herself; staring into space, as her mental compartments filled, one after another.

Still nothing, really. Not nearly enough to call a halt to the State of the Union as forty million people watched. But if this *was* the man who had rented the house in Snickers Gap, the man who had tested sarin and explosives …

Horowitz was still on the phone. Finding a pen on the conference table, scribbling down an address. Hanging up, checking his watch. "Thirty minutes by road," he said. "We might just make it ahead of POTUS."

And find what? Dalia wondered. *Jana herself?*

Nobody was paying them any attention. She hesitated for a last instant, then nodded and reached for her coat.

ELLICOTT STREET NW, WASHINGTON, DC

When the phone rang, Jana jumped.

For a crazy moment, she thought it was the phone in her hand. Then she realized it was Michael's phone, on its charger in the kitchen. She stood, keeping one eye on the television, and went to look at the display: STACY.

Another ring; the call went to voice mail. Jana walked back into the living room and took her place again on the couch. Her skin felt cold, her mouth hot and dry. Her thumb massaged the call button, gently and repetitively. The cat jumped up next to her and nosed against her elbow. She ignored it.

Outside, the wind blew. On the television, the House Floor was filling up. Coverage cut between Michael's feed and the cameras in the upstairs gallery. Commentators prattled. A clock in the screen's corner read 8:35 p.m. Beside it, the network had started a countdown:

SOTU ADDRESS BEGINS IN 24:59:04

The eyelid twitched.

Soon, she thought.

MARTIN LUTHER KING JR. AVE. SE, WASHINGTON, DC

They took the Lexus, Horowitz driving, following the GPS on Dalia's phone: north to Howard Road, then into a cloverleaf to merge onto I-295.

Across the Anacostia, the city sparkled. They crossed the water onto I-395—and ran into a roadblock. Capitol Hill closed, barricades sending them toward the Potomac. The dome a scintillating floodlit bauble in the distance. Dalia punched at her phone, cursing, and found a new route. They doubled back.

Horowitz drove fast, weaving around slower traffic. The internal combustion engine's revving, throaty drone sounded strange to Dalia's ears after so much time in the Prius. Heart leaping and bounding in her chest. The more she thought about it—the man on the floor, the camera—the more credible it seemed. Horribly, hauntingly credible. And the more she told herself to stop thinking and just see for herself. There was enough time—barely. The Colt still in her purse, nestled amid linty Kleenex and sugar-free gum. She remembered the look the man, Michael Fletcher, had given her. Brimming with private contempt. She had known it, had sensed it, but she had not had faith in her senses.

They drove on.

CAPITOL HILL, WASHINGTON, DC

Squee!

Michael could keep the lunatic grin off his face. He could wear that strange, inert mask. But he could not, he suspected, keep the mad glint from his eyes. Surely everyone could see it. Surely everybody knew.

The gavel was banging. The sergeant at arms was introducing the cabinet. People were standing. Michael had only minutes left on earth. Cabinet secretaries were being introduced: housing, state, defense. He was shooting them. He was shooting them all, moving on autopilot. Like when he killed the cop. Two shots and then a third to make sure. Point-blank. The attorney general moved down the aisle, shaking hands. Michael moved in front of him, keeping just out of the way. Back in the house, Jana would be watching, thumb hovering over the call button. He would not know when she pressed it. There would be no fade-out. Just a cut to black. A hard cut—end-of-*The Sopranos* hard. He was scared; he was jittery; he was nervous. He had never liked jack-in-the-boxes, even as a kid. The anticipation, the anxiety, wore him down. Wound him up. He could not enjoy being wound up that way. Worn down, wound up. *Don't think about it don't think don't think don't ...*

But what if wasn't a hard cut? What if it was just enough to take off the rest of his leg and leave him lying soaked in nerve agent, twitching and shitting and puking—SLUDGE they called it, Salivation, Lacrimation, Urination, Defecation, Gastrointestinal distress, and Emesis …

Lacrimation. That meant crying. And now he was starting to do just that. Thinking of Silas. Christ, but he loved that kid. Christ, but he was sorry. Christ, but he had not meant for it to work out this way. Christ, but … but why Christ, of all people? Why Jesus Christ? All bullshit anyway, what the fuck was religion anyway, what the fuck was *Jewish* anyway—an artificial idea, in-group out-group dynamics at work, weak minds at work, and what the fuck was he *doing* here? What the fuck was he *doing*?

He jammed his eye against the viewfinder. Hide the tears. Everybody standing, waiting, the president would be here soon, it would be over soon, soon, soon, soon.

Not too late, Mikey. Put down the fucking camera. Get away from the balcony gallery so that fucking witch can't see you on TV. And take off the fucking leg.

The Imp of the Perverse. That was what they called that.

The Imp of Fucking Reason, you mean. For Silas' sake, for the love of God, for that beautiful precious kid, TAKE OFF THE

FUCKING—

I can't hear you, voice. You can't reach me.

He sniffled. Tears drying up already. He had wavered. But now he was back on track.

Any minute now.

Here, piggy piggy piggy piggy. Soooo-ee!

He set his jaw, set his mouth, and kept shooting.

CHAPTER SIXTEEN

ELLICOTT STREET NW, WASHINGTON, DC

Dalia scowled through the windshield.

Addresses skimmed past. Bare-limbed trees, a Montessori school, an apartment complex, a soccer field. Nice, quiet block. But traffic was audible from Wisconsin Avenue, just a stone's throw away. Restaurants and bars, the Tenleytown Metro stop. "One twenty-eight," Horowitz read aloud. "One thirty …" He pointed. "Bingo."

He pulled to the curb and parked across from a Japanese maple. He killed the headlights, the engine. And then, despite the hurry, they sat for a moment, listening to the tick of cooling metal, feeling the presence of the house.

Curtains closed. Lights glowed on the first floor. One room occupied, at least. The second floor was dark. A garage door was closed. Dalia's instincts vibrated like a tuning fork. Horowitz felt it, too. They shared a look. Dalia took the revolver from her purse, and Horowitz drew his semiautomatic from the holster inside his waistband. They left the car silently, leaning the doors shut.

A last nod. He struck off around back, past the garage. Dalia went toward the front stoop. She could hear a television playing inside the house. There was no moisture in her mouth. She felt her lips working, her tongue. Like an old woman with no teeth. She was, in fact, an old woman. But she was an old woman with a gun, and her hands did not shake.

Closer. Listening beneath the window. She would not knock on the door. What was one more illegal trespass, all things considered? The television was playing—the State of the Union, she recognized without surprise. "*And any second now, Peter, they'll officially appoint the members of the escort committee. They'll exit the chamber through the lobby doors—I'm going to see if I can get a little closer ...*"

Licking her lips again. Rough as sandpaper. But the gun felt good in her hand. Solid. She remembered the Uzi, the liquid feeling of power. For a pacifist, she thought distantly, she sure did like guns. *Those who play with the devil's toys will be brought by degrees to wield his sword.*

She could feel her breath: quick, shallow, a flutter in her side. Yet at the same time, she seemed to be holding her breath. Maybe the fluttering was her heartbeat. She was rising on tiptoes, trying to see past the curtain. To see who was watching the television. Jana Dahan. She knew it. But she had to see.

She could not get high enough to see through the window. She was a sturdy old woman, strong but not tall. Good, flat-footed peasant stock. "*Built like a brick shithouse*," her ex-husband used to say with a salacious grin.

"*We're counting on you.*" That had been Meir. And: "*You have my word. My word is my bond.*" And: "*You must do your part.*"

The supreme goal of Judaism was not to crush their enemies but to practice *tikkun olam*, to repair the world.

She backed away, still holding her breath, if indeed she was holding her breath, side still fluttery, gun held away from her ribs, away from her body, in both hands. She went to the stoop, up the steps. Then she did breathe, gulping it down like a drowning woman, taking herself by surprise.

"*Members of Congress ...*" That was the sergeant at arms. "*I have the high privilege and distinct honor of presenting to you ...*"

CAPITOL HILL, WASHINGTON, DC

"… the president of the United States!"

Applause. Door opening. Official escort coming in. The crowd on its feet, straining to get a look at POTUS. Even the president's worst enemy was, at this moment, a groveling sycophant.

Michael Fletcher braced himself. Still shooting. Always shooting. The woman would wait until they were in the center of the chamber, halfway down the aisle. That would maximize the dispersion. Would the blast kill him outright, or just maim him worse than he was already maimed, leaving him for the SLUDGE? And did it really matter? Did anything really matter now?

Holding his breath. Jack, Jack, Jack-in-the-box. Playing your music, when will it stop? Jack, Jack, Jack-in-the-box. You're all wound up, time to pop!

Wound up, worn down. Breath held. Backing up. Official escort spreading before him like a puddle of blood. Smiling, waving, shaking hands. And then the president. Stepping in. An arm's length away.

A good shot. Centered in the screen. Going out to forty million. Perfect framing. Not so far gone that he could not take pride in his work. Once, he had been a photographer—not a cameraman, but a photographer. He'd used the vintage Pentax 67—not as heavy as this kit but still plenty fucking heavy, but worth it. He had loved that fucking camera. Durable motherfucking camera. Made you work for it. Like a cat. You had to earn it. Nothing easy about the Pentax. But when you treated her right, she put out nice as ice, smooth as silk. Some people said you needed a tripod with the Pentax but not if your hand was steady enough, if your muscles were strong enough. If you were strong and steady and had the talent and the drive, you could snap shots with that camera that would make your big brother proud. It had the wooden handle, it had the perfect shutter sound, that was what a *real* fucking camera sounded like, *kathunk*, a lost sound now, lost like typewriters and real phone rings, this younger generation …

The president was waving: the same tight-wristed Queen Elizabeth wave Michael remembered from a long-ago rehearsal. Head swiveling left and right in a way that reminded him of a robot mannequin at Disney World. He could almost see the hinge in the jaw. Thankyouthankyouthankyou. They were moving now, backing down the aisle. Pausing to shake hands. Each pause, each handshake, bought Michael another instant of life. Suddenly, every instant seemed precious: the burning lights, the heavy kit, even the anxiety, the bracing against the explosion. He turned to face these feelings, leaning into them, embracing them, savoring them. These were his life, this was his death.

Official photographers drifting just behind him. Sykes of the Secret Service. The president of the United States was a celestial object whose electromagnetic field pushed them all back down the aisle. Behind and around POTUS, senators and House members shook hands. Golden crumbs dribbled off their fearless leader, to be gobbled up hungrily by anyone who could reach them. Fat cats, pigs, dogs, sheep.

Michael blinked. Sweat trickled, stinging, into his eyes. Almost halfway down the aisle now. *Any second,* he thought. *Any second.* He expected some snark from the voice, but the voice was uncharacteristically silent.

So bring it!

He felt himself cracking. His mind was a tree branch coated with ice, and when enough ice built up, that branch would crack neatly in two.

Bring it!

But the woman was waiting, for the moment of maximum damage. Fucking ice queen.

Now! Please, for the love of God ...

The president took another step forward, shook another hand.

Do it now, Michael Fletcher thought, *or I'll scream, I swear to God I'll scream.*

ELLICOTT STREET NW, WASHINGTON, DC

After that, it happened very quickly, in the span of seconds.

But at the time, events seemed to move slowly, with syrupy grandeur. Dalia tested the front doorknob. Locked. At the same moment, there came a sound from around back. Horowitz, trying a door. The sound wasn't loud, but in Dalia's hyperaware state it was enough to register.

And then Dalia sensed something else. Someone inside the house had also caught the sound. She knew that in everyday perception, most cues picked up by the senses were shuffled aside as unimportant. But in this stop-time moment, Dalia registered everything: the barely perceptible creaking of floorboards, the changing glow of curtains as a figure passed before the television screen, the slight but distinct baffling of sound from speakers. The bizarre sharpness she had experienced in Hopewell was back, in spades. She knew that the figure was pausing, just on the other side of this door. Hesitating—probably facing away, toward the rear of the house, toward the sound on the rear stoop.

Those who play with the devil's toys will be brought by degrees to wield his sword.

Stepping back, she aimed a slow-motion kick at the door, just inside the knob. Her stout right leg pistoned out, her foot caught the wood—thank God she was wearing flats—and the door popped open with surprising ease. At that instant, a faint wall of sirens picked up far away down Wisconsin Avenue.

A woman standing in the foyer, turning around.

This was Jana Dahan.

She wore a straight black wig and had done something to change the shape of her face. But it was the same woman whose features Dalia had studied at such length in dossiers and on screens. Pretty, fox-like. Something of the hunter here, but also something of the hunted. Now the mouth formed a perfect surprised *O*. On TV they were cheering, on Wisconsin Avenue the sirens were moving away, and out back, Horowitz, having heard the thud of the door, was battering his own way in. But here, now, Dalia faced Jana.

Jana was holding something. Not a gun but a phone. And with sudden, sickening certainty, Dalia knew what it was. Oh, yes, she knew—knew how close they were to a scene all too familiar to any Israeli: screaming and crying and weeping and sobbing. And then the nightmare hiss, the dreaded sibilance, the last sound heard by countless victims in Auschwitz and Mauthausen and Dachau and Buchenwald, the reason bomb shelters in Tel Aviv were stocked with gas masks. And the wailing and weeping and screaming would become a partition, a barrier, a great divide between sanity and insanity, but too late. Too late.

The gun was up. Aiming at Jana's chest. Center body mass. Finger tight on the trigger. Another ounce of pressure and Dalia would shoot the girl dead.

Their eyes locked.

Dalia's throat felt oily. Jana held the phone in her right hand, thumb already on the button. Dalia's mind rolled, racing emptily without catching, then found sudden purchase on rocky soil and lurched forward, scattering tiny stones.

She shot Jana Dahan in the chest.

As the girl fell, Dalia shot again.

CAPITOL HILL, WASHINGTON, DC

Michael Fletcher backed up before the president.

Only with great effort did he keep his eyes open. It was the last moment before the jack-in-the-box popped, the last moment, and you wanted to look away, you wanted to squeeze your eyes shut; you wanted to protect yourself, avert your gaze, but you could not, you kept your eyes open, you backed up, nostrils flaring, jaw set hard, teeth gritted, braced, bracing, ready, ready, ready, *ready steady go*.

At the rostrum now. The entire chamber on its feet. Rolling, thunderous applause. Tiered platforms climbing away dizzyingly. Lenses staring blankly from balcony railings. Michael had lost the president. Through his viewfinder he saw only out-of-focus marble columns. He felt confused. He lowered the heavy camera. The official House photographer, standing just behind him, emitted an involuntary sound of surprise and disapproval.

The president was climbing to the platform. Applause booming from all sides. Bright lights. Stars and stripes. Dizzy. Michael reached out a hand to steady himself. He was dropping the camera. Someone was grabbing it. Someone else was taking him by the elbow. The inscribed words—UNION, JUSTICE, TOLERANCE, LIBERTY, PEACE: IN GOD WE TRUST—moved sideways, listing crookedly across his field of vision. Air hot and close, pungent with sweat and stress hormones.

Knees giving out. Sykes holding him up by his elbow. Dragging him from the chamber, into a hallway. Spinning, spinning. A mad exhilaration, a sense of freedom at last. Reaching for the leg. Trying to get it off. Get it off before the bitch could press her button. Anticipating the nine clicks as the pin left the housing mechanism. But Special Agent Bob Sykes must have misread the movement and thought he was going for a trigger and body-slammed him onto the floor. Pinning him down, knee sharp between shoulder blades, barking into a microphone, other agents running, polished black shoes trip-tripping against polished marble. And in the last instant before the door to the House Chamber closed completely, Michael heard the gavel rapping again. And then the president:

"Thank you, thank you. Thank you, thank you. Thank you. Thank you. Thank you. Mr. Speaker, Mr. Vice President, members of Congress, my fellow Americans, tonight I come here to report on the state of the union."

EPILOGUE

NORTH OF TEL AVIV, ISRAEL

Beneath twin shafts of moonlight, a man picked out aimless chords on an upright piano.

Dreamy major sevenths, tragic minor ninths. A diminished triad straining toward resolution ... but instead left hanging as a bell took the man's attention away.

He ran a bright glissando up the keyboard and got up from the bench, weaving slightly on his feet. As he reached the intercom, the bell rang again. The camera at the front gate presented two black cars with smoked windows. A dark-suited man with hooded eyes stared lifelessly back into the lens. Another stood behind him.

The ramsad started to reach for the button that would let the men through the gate. Then he paused and stood there for a moment, swaying. He turned almost indifferently as the bell rang again, and went out into the courtyard of Jerusalem stone and desert flowers. A warm night breeze caressed him. His glass of wine sat where he had left it. He forsook it in favor of the bottle. Weaving back inside to the piano, he slumped onto the bench and took a long swig of Cabernet Sauvignon.

Hunching again over the keyboard, he began to play. Despite his inebriation, he played well, swaying as he played, head bobbing, feet working the pedals, long fingers intuitively seeking out notes. His mouth twitched into a grimacing smile. The bell rang again. Now the two black Shin Bet cars would be pulling out of the driveway, making space for the armored assault vehicle with the tactical battering ram. Snipers would already be in position high on the hillside, taking aim through picture windows.

The ramsad played, pounding hard on the keys, lip curling, as they came through the gate, through front and back doors simultaneously, into the shafts of moonlight. Seizing him by the upper arms, they lifted him from the bench, turning him around, throwing him onto the floor, tying his wrists at the small of his back with strips of plastic, jerking him upright again, setting him on his feet like a plaything and then leading him toward the doorway, out of the room, out of the house, into his future.

ELLICOTT STREET NW, WASHINGTON, DC

A man wearing rubber gloves and a surgical mask wiped bloody Windex from framed pictures of snowmen, roller coasters, kids licking ice cream from sticky fingers.

As he worked, a cat came out from under the sofa: a tortoiseshell Maine coon. The cat meowed, butting his shin. The man frowned beneath his mask. One for the shelter, he thought. But when he packed up his gear a few minutes later, he changed his mind and brought the cat home as a gift for his five-year-old daughter.

Two miles away, another five-year-old, a boy, slept peacefully in the ambient light coming through a bedroom door left ajar. In a room down the hall, the boy's mother received a phone call. She listened closely. She asked if there had been some mistake. She hung up slowly, numbly, and then balled her fist to her mouth to hold in a rising scream.

PRINCETON, NJ

Outside the window, a black squirrel chittered on a branch.

Inside, the air was overheated and dry. Settling into a burgundy club chair, Dalia noted that McConnell had not stood to greet her, or even offered a hand. This was to be a negotiation.

He waited until the door had closed. "Next week," he said, "the Air-Land subcommittee of Senate Armed Services finalizes their budget proposal."

She waited.

"By now, I was supposed to have developed a program with your input. So I face a quandary, Dalia. Either I tell them that we lack results because you confessed to espionage—in which case you end up at Naval Consolidated Brig, Miramar—or I take the bullet."

She kept waiting.

"Of course, I'd hate for it to turn out either of those ways. But …" He plucked distractedly at a loose thread on the seam of his slacks. "Really, it's a question of doing the least harm to the fewest people. If I lose *my* job, how can I hire Horowitz? Kids gotta eat."

She waited again.

"Election year coming up." He plucked the thread free and dropped it carelessly to the floor. "We could use you in our corner. Consulting with Air-Land next week. Training and Defense Command the week after that. CENTCOM the week after *that.* And so on. People get nervous. No new ground combat vehicle this year. We could arrange something here at Princeton. A permanent position. There is the matter of those pesky international espionage charges. But I think the president would do you a solid, you ask nicely. Doesn't like to leave debts unpaid." He unfolded his legs and reversed direction. "So that's my pitch. What do you say?"

She hesitated.

"Oh, but there is one more thing. Off the record—and I make no promises." He closed his eyes for a moment, then opened them again. "A prisoner came into Jabalia. Two years ago, from Khan Yunis. We've got a friend there, shares information sometimes in exchange for petrol. I never told you any of this, by the way. But this prisoner fits the description of your son. Apparently high-value, kept personally under guard by a general of al-Qassam …"

The light in the room seemed to brighten, then dim. His voice came from some faraway misty vale.

"Give me the sign and we'll set wheels in motion. Quietly. See what we can do. Whatever happens, Dalia, it remains absolutely hush-hush. And again, I make no promises. And I would need your guarantee—"

"Anything."

"The Air-Land subcommittee …"

"Anything."

"We'll sit down with the provost, try to—"

"Anything." She could not stop saying it. "Anything."

"I'm glad to hear it."

"Oh, my God." The room was wobbling. She looked up at a glowing light in the ceiling. Brighter, ever brighter. "Oh, my God," she said again. "My God. My God, my God, my God. Thank you."

END